divine
INTERVENTION

IT'S A PLACE LIKE NO OTHER. AND THEY
PLAN TO KEEP IT THAT WAY...

"WONDERFUL...
A PAGE-
TURNING
ADVENTURE
STORY."
—ALLEN STEELE,
HUGO AWARD-
WINNING
AUTHOR OF
CHRONOSPACE

ken wharton

$6.99 U.S.
$9.99 CAN

ISBN 0-441-00886-0

9 780441 008865

50699

EAN

THEY'RE COMING . . .

"Don't you see, George," Prime Minister Channing argued. "Anyone who disagreed with the policy probably wasn't allowed on the ship in the first place. When you're picking a few thousand people out of a planet of seventeen billion . . ."

George nodded thoughtfully. "But not the frozen settlers. I'm sure they were selected by their bank accounts. And the fact that one of the crew members warned us with that message means that—"

"But he said they were in the minority," Channing interrupted. "And you know all of the settlers are going to look to this Simpson person for leadership. You have to see it from their perspective."

"I'm sorry, Alex, but any decent person . . ."

"Probably wouldn't be that rich in the first place," finished Channing. "This time around we're not getting the best and brightest that Earth has to offer. This is a completely different group of people than the Originals. And we need to do something about it."

"What can we do? Once they get here they'll have nearly three times as many people as we do!"

Channing cleared his throat. "Not if they never get here."

"*Divine Intervention* is a wonderful heresy, positive proof that a hard-SF novel can seriously deal with physics, religion, and interstellar colonization, and also be a page-turning adventure story. Reminiscent of Poul Anderson's best work, it signals the arrival of a fine new writer."

—Allen Steele,
Hugo Award–winning author of *Chronospace*

divine
INTERVENTION

ken wharton

ACE BOOKS, NEW YORK

DIVINE INTERVENTION

An Ace Book / published by arrangement with
the author

PRINTING HISTORY
Ace mass-market edition / December 2001

Visit our website at
www.penguinputnam.com
Check out the ACE Science Fiction & Fantasy newsletter!

ISBN: 0-441-00886-0

ACE®
Ace Books are published by The Berkley Publishing Group,
a division of Penguin Putnam Inc.,
375 Hudson Street, New York, New York 10014.
ACE and the "A" design
are trademarks belonging to Penguin Putnam Inc.

PRINTED IN THE UNITED STATES OF AMERICA

10 9 8 7 6 5 4 3 2 1

PROLOGUE

HAD ANYONE BEEN STANDING ON THE BAR-
ren surface of the planet, watching the small unmanned
probe descend out of the black sky, they would have
been thoroughly unimpressed.

This was not a picturesque world. The final remnants
of the atmosphere had boiled away into space over four
billion years ago when the nearby sun's tidal forces had
locked the planet's rotation. Now it was cleanly split in
half; frozen glaciers of dry ice would forever lie on the
dark side, and here on the sunlit side the landscape was
baked to more than 500°C by the enormous, immobile
sun. The incessant light and solar wind had seared the
surface, outgassing the lighter elements from the rock
and leaving behind a flat black wasteland of crystallized
silicon. The result was a surface with such a low albedo
that it was difficult to see; even with the impossibly
bright sun overhead, only the faintest red glow from the
hot surface showed where the horizon left off and the
blackness of space began.

The probe descended silently. With no air to transport

the sound, an observer would have heard nothing. Similarly, a descent plume that might have been spectacular in an atmosphere was here barely visible—the ejected plasma escaped off into the vacuum before the ions and electrons could recombine in a blaze of light. For much of the descent the only visible feature would have been the titanium alloy landing gear, reaching down toward the planet like awkward arthritic fingers. Not until the final seconds would it have been possible to see the other equipment: the usual folded solar panels, parabolic radio dishes, and arrays of diagnostic cameras.

At last the probe touched down, bringing the six legs into contact with six vastly different electrical potentials on the semiconducting surface. Twenty kiloamps of current instantly raced through the frame, easily penetrating the insulation that had protected the probe's electrical system. All of the emergency fuses blew instantly, isolating the redundant computer systems from both the batteries and the solar panels. The entire capacitor bank discharged, and many of the remaining electrical pathways melted within a fraction of a second. The resulting total power loss prevented the emergency routines from functioning, and any hope of remote repair was lost when the current spike jolted the main antenna out of alignment. The mission had been a complete failure.

No rescue would come. No further spacecraft would land. An observer might have assumed that only the enormous white sun, glaring downward from its fixed position in the otherwise black sky, would keep the probe company for a silent eternity.

An observer would have been wrong.

CHAPTER 1

There must be some fundamental psychological difference between a spaceship and a submarine.[74] Otherwise, why would this situation not be familiar to me? True, in the San Francisco[75] a safe environment was always a few thousand feet straight up. Here, between the stars, there is no such thing as an emergency landing.

But I don't think that is the main distinction. Under the ocean, we didn't think about the possibility of surfacing. We thought about death by water—being smothered and crushed by thousands of pounds of pressure. Perhaps it is the change in our nightmares that is important. Now we imagine ourselves not crushed to death, but rather sucked into the empty vacuum that surrounds us, our pressurized bodies exploding to fill the nothingness. Before we were able to band together, somehow using our collective spirit and exuberance to fend off the pressure. Now there is nothing out there, nothing to hold at bay. Instead

we have to consolidate a position within ourselves.
Each of us builds a fortress to protect against the
vacuum, and it only holds room for one.

Note 74. A self-contained underwater vessel, used
　　on Earth for military and research purposes.
Note 75. A spheromak-powered submarine con-
　　trolled by the W.U.S. Navy. Our Captain was
　　an officer stationed on board during 2089–90.

　　　　　　　　　　　The Journal
　　　　　　　　　　　Year 7, Day 330

"SO HOW OLD ARE YOU?"

Drew Randall glanced over at his best friend Sunit, who was clearly not enjoying being the center of attention. Sunit was playing with his hair, wrapping a blond curl around his left forefinger and then pulling it taut, a clear sign he was nervous. With his other hand he occasionally tapped a number onto his desk, and Drew watched the large blue digits reflect off of Sunit's polarized glasses. His friend was clearly not used to the new flatscreen consoles; the extra-large font mocked the resolution of the billion-pixel buckytube array, and working the calculator in polarized mode was simply ridiculous. Drew knew that Sunit was wearing the glasses not so much for the 3-D effect but rather to hide his uncertain, darting eyes. At last Sunit finished, scratching his head at the result.

"Nine hundred and ten?" It was more a question than an answer. Drew's transceiver emitted a quick burst of laughter, and he covered the speaker with his hands.

Miss Bradley smiled. "Almost the right idea. But 'percent' means that you have to—"

"Oh, yeah . . . yeah. I'm . . . nine. Nine Earth years."

He glanced at Drew and tried to scowl, but couldn't quite manage it with the embarrassed grin on his face.

"Very good, Sunit." She swept her good eye around the room. "That's right, most of you are already nine Earth years old." Many of the students began giggling about suddenly being two years older than they had thought. "Remember this when the Earthies arrive. Earth children will think they're older, but they really won't be. Drew, what will your Earth age be in three more years?"

Drew didn't bother to use the computer; he had gotten used to making the conversion at home. "Thirteen. But I'll be ten, really."

Across the room, Jon raised his hand. "So that's why the Originals didn't get real old on the Journey, right? Because the years are different here?"

Miss Bradley shook her head. "Clever idea, Jon, but the real reason is more complicated. A year is just how long it takes a planet to go around its sun, so here on Mandala we're not aging slower than Earthies, we're just counting differently. But Captain and all the other Originals really did age at a different speed while they were on their Journey. From everyone else's perspective the Journey took ninety-five years, but for the Originals it only took twenty. That's because most of the time they were traveling near the speed of light, and that made their local time slow down."

At this point everyone started asking questions about relativity, and Drew resignedly flipped off his transceiver. He usually liked Theology class, and he had really been looking forward to the third grade because he knew they'd be studying The Log this year. Now that they were seven, the teachers finally considered them smart enough to start learning the necessary science. In reality Drew had been ready for some time, but looking around at the silent scene of question-and-answer reminded him that he was probably the only kid here who learned about this religious stuff from his parents.

Of course, that was just because Daddy happened to be a full-time preacher and had done his best to see that Drew understood the concepts behind The Log as early as possible. Drew read from either The Log or The Journal every night, Daddy often sitting beside him, ready to explain the scientific jargon. He just had to keep reminding himself that not everyone's religious education extended as far back as they could remember.

HE PICTURED DADDY, NOT WITH HIS GRAY-ing hair, but instead the way he looked a few winters ago: standing in the light breeze, shouting helpful advice as Drew tried to navigate the ice for the first time. The notched aluminum on the front tips of his skates kept tripping him up, but Mommy had bundled him up so thickly that he barely felt the ice when he fell. Drew did have to be a little careful of the transceiver he wore like a pendant around his neck; already he had learned to instinctively cover it with his arms at the first sign of danger. He kept at it, and before long he was able to glide along in unsteady arcs, always curving slightly to the left.

"That's great, Drew!" Daddy skated over and helped him to avoid crashing into a snowbank. "Hey—here's a puzzle for you. Try to skate forward without lifting your skates. Or sliding them sideways."

Drew looked around, feeling confused. "You're silly, Daddy."

"No, see if you can figure it out. It's like being in outer space. There's nothing to push off from."

At the mention of outer space, Drew became very interested. He wanted to explore planets when he grew up, just like Captain had, so he figured that he should learn as much about space as he could. He tried bending his knees, but he just slid forward and back on the ice. Then he waved his arms around for a while, but that didn't really do anything either. Finally he dropped to the ice and started pulling himself along with his mittens.

Daddy laughed. "Clever! That's not what I meant, though. It's tricky, but I'll show you how to do it." He reached down to the bank and made a large snowball, packing it down before handing it over to Drew. "Here, maybe you can use this."

Drew stood up, took it in both hands, and thought about it for a little while. "Maybe . . ." He lifted the snowball over his head and threw it as hard as he could. It broke apart on the ice, and Drew slid backward a few centimeters before coming to a halt. He shrugged. "I went the wrong way."

"Nonsense!" Daddy shouted in his deep preacher voice. "You figured it out! You did great! And I can't believe how far you threw that. You must be the strongest four-year-old in the whole world!"

Drew's smile filled his face and he stepped forward to try to salvage what was left of the snowball. He knelt down, scooping some of the snow together, but he couldn't pack it with his big mittens.

"You know," Daddy began, "that's one of the reasons that no one thought space travel could ever happen."

Drew tried to turn around to pay better attention, but one of his knees slipped out from underneath him. Daddy helped him pull him to his feet, still talking.

"You see, Drew, people thought the only way you could get anywhere in space was to throw little snowballs out the back of the ship!" They laughed together at the idea. "And they wanted to go really fast, so they threw the snowballs out as fast as they could."

"Faster than me?"

He nodded. "They used some big snowball throwers. But which went farther? You or the snowball?"

"Me. I mean, I mean, the snowball."

"Right. So most of what they were doing was making the snowballs go fast, not the spaceship. You'd need so many snowballs there wouldn't be any room for you! And the more you carry, the slower you go."

Drew looked up into the sky, thinking about the *Walt Disney*, the ship that had brought their ancestors from Earth. He began to sing: *"Drilling wells from star to star, with light speed near and Earth so far!* . . . "Did Captain have to bring lots of snowballs?"

"No, Drew. There just wasn't room. But"—Daddy smiled his sneaky smile, like he always did when he told him about neat religious things—"but you can get away with a lot less snowball-throwing power if you can find something big to push off against. That's what a Tzengian Well does." He grinned at Drew's blank look. "Like this." He slammed his skatetip into the ice and pushed off toward the warming house.

DREW'S FLATSCREEN SUDDENLY LIT UP with a display of Miss Bradley's stern face. Drew jerked to attention and saw the real Miss Bradley staring at him from the front of the room. He quickly fumbled with the switch on his transceiver, but she wasn't talking, just glaring at him in stereo. Drew stammered an apology through his speaker.

"Andrew," she said, "just because you're the only one with that little switch doesn't mean you're allowed to turn me off. Now, are you going to pray with the rest of us or not?"

Drew flicked his gaze to the clock, not quite believing it was thirty-one already. "Yeah . . . of course I am, Miss Bradley." She was still obviously angry, so he blundered on. "I like to pray. The more you talk to God the better he understands you."

Her look softened a bit. "That's very wise, Drew. Did your father teach you that?"

Drew shrugged. "No. It's just something I've sort of noticed on my own."

She regarded him curiously for a second and then dimmed the lights to lead the afternoon prayer. Drew bowed his head with everyone else and waited patiently during the silence. He felt sorry for everyone, trying to talk to God but not really understanding how to do it. They were all looking downward, for goodness sakes. Didn't anyone know that God was *up*? All this talk about finding God within oneself was so misleading, but whenever Drew tried to tell adults, he inevitably got a boring lecture in return. He had learned long ago that it was better to go along with these ridiculous indoor prayers and keep his real prayers to himself.

Still, it had taken him a long time to realize that he had a special relationship with God. Everyone else thought they prayed to God, but recently he had discovered this just wasn't true. It was different for him somehow.

Drew toyed with the palm-sized transceiver that hung around his neck: a combined speaker, microphone, microwave transmitter, and receiver. He didn't really know how it allowed him to hear and speak. The necklace chain enclosed a fiber optic cable that ran up to the back of his neck, went under his straight black hair, and terminated at the tiny connector above his left temple. They told him that he had inherited his misshapen earbones and useless tongue from his mother, but Drew suspected that God might have had something to do with it as well. Maybe God wanted him to be deaf and dumb so he would get to have a transceiver to pray with. As for why his mother, with the exact same device, didn't even believe in God, well, that was one mystery he had never been able to explain.

Suddenly Miss Bradley's voice broke the silence. Drew smiled, knowing the school period was almost over.

"God, we thank you for your gift of this beautiful planet. We are always aware of you, and we remain open to your guidance. Guide us as you guided our Captain. We will follow."

"NINE HUNDRED YEARS OLD!" DREW NUDGED Sunit with his elbow as they made their way home along Main Street. Tall oaks lined the wide fused-dirt road as it wound its way out of town, roughly following the north bank of the American River. They had just passed downwind of both of the planet's breweries, and the pervasive, sweet smell of redhops told them that they would be home in another ten minutes.

Sunit was grinning. "Well, at least I wasn't off in Andromeda with Miss Bradley yelling at me for a whole minute."

The grimace on Drew's face was comical enough to make Sunit laugh. "No way. Was she really there for that long?"

"Yep! She called your name, maybe five times or something. I think she was about to go fractal, till you started honey-talking."

"Hmm." Drew shrugged, trying not to let his embarrassment show. Pondering some way to change the subject, he remembered what he had been meaning to tell Sunit all day. "Hey, guess what I found last evening. When you were at that stupid concert."

"Yeah?"

Drew smiled. "C'mon. I'll show you." He turned left between two electric beehives, led Sunit past a new condo development, and then entered the spruce forest that covered most of the valley floor. Thousands of tornado moths were instantly attracted to their movement, swarming out of the trees into a swirling white orbit around each of the boys. Drew's father had explained to him that the native insects weren't used to humans yet; in a mere 115 trips around the sun their hardwired instincts hadn't evolved to take into account the sudden presence of large animals on the planet. As a result their behavior went haywire when they were confronted with what looked like a small moving tree.

Drew and Sunit moved closer together and the two moth funnels merged into one, a shimmering Möbius strip of insects endlessly twisting around the two of them.

"Where are we going?" asked Sunit, trying to push through the feathery barrier. The moths just changed course around his hand, making a bulge in the living curtain.

"You'll see."

Sunit nodded. "You know, our rooster tried to kill himself yesterday."

"Ha."

"No, I'm serious. He jumped in the old well. My mom had to make this bucket thing to fetch him out."

Drew shot his friend a disbelieving look. "Didn't it drown?"

"Nah. The well's all dried up. But he's been depressed ever since we clipped his wings."

"Roosters don't get depressed, stupid. And I know they don't try to kill themselves."

"Yeah? Well, you should come over and watch him sulk. And animals do, sometimes. Kill themselves, I mean. I saw this Earth vid last week. About lemmers. They're like hairy fish, but with four legs. But they're not like fish, 'cause they can't swim, but just the same they go running off cliffs into the ocean and drown."

"That's pretty stupid. I bet they're just depressed because they have to live on Earth."

Sunit smiled. "Think they're bringing any on the spaceship? My dad said it'll be here in the fall."

Drew tried to imagine a four-legged hairy fish that couldn't swim. "I hope not. They sound pretty gross."

They emerged into a small clearing, and Sunit immediately ran over to the reddish bush on the far side, scattering the moth formation. "I don't believe it," he said. His fingers reached out toward the maroon leaves but stopped short of touching them. "It's fana. It's really fana."

Drew grinned, glad that Sunit was so interested in the discovery. "Yeah. I bet it's the only bush in the whole valley, besides the one they keep in the G.C."

Sunit shot a curious look over his shoulder. "Did you try some?"

"No! Of course not. I didn't even think about it."

Of course Drew *had* thought about it, and he knew Sunit was thinking about it, too. A kid couldn't help but be curious about Communion. They weren't allowed to participate until they were ten, but seeing what it did to their parents was enough to make them very interested indeed. You could only take fana once a year, which meant it must be dangerous. Or wonderful. People like the Burnouts in the Red Valley used it all the time, or so they said. And some people even left the City and turned into Burnouts just so they could use it all the time, too. Daddy had once told him that taking fana was the best way to open your mind up to God, but if you weren't ready it could be the worst thing in the world. He said it took him all year just to understand what had happened the time before and then get ready for the next Communion. Personally, Drew couldn't imagine opening up to God any more than he already did, so he figured that it must be pretty amazing stuff.

"So how do you think it got here?" Sunit asked.

Drew shrugged. "Maybe the wind blew some seeds over from the Red Valley," he said, gesturing up the hill to the north. "Or maybe they just missed it when they killed off the rest of them."

"I doubt it." Sunit narrowed his eyes. "Do you think someone in the City planted it so they could . . . you know."

"Maybe. Who do you think—"

In an instant, before the boys could even react, four men dashed into the clearing from different directions. Sunit managed to let out a quick yelp of surprise before a muddy hand clamped down over his mouth. Another man did the same to Drew, and Drew found himself so surprised that he kept quiet, even though the transceiver still dangled freely around his neck.

The two others circled slowly around their new prisoners, and Drew watched while his heart pumped double time. One of them was actually a woman, he realized, with short, dirty hair kept out of her painted face by a red bandanna. She was dressed entirely in close-fitting redweave, her exposed hands and feet painted like her face, with black and rust-colored stripes. A wooden quiver of steel-tipped arrows was strapped to her back, and a pair of knives hung at her side.

Drew had never seen Burnouts before, but he had always imagined that they would be nice to him, should he ever run into some. He was currently rethinking that assumption.

"So, what do we got here?" said a Burnout, this one definitely a man. He was dressed similarly, but armed with a large sheathed sword and a wooden staff.

"DCs," the woman said.

"Yeah, toss your DCs," said the Burnout holding Sunit.

Sunit pulled the little digital communicator from his pocket and handed it to the woman. Drew hesitated, but after a rough shake he grudgingly handed his over as well. It was brand-new, a replacement for one he had lost earlier that year, and he doubted his parents would get him another one.

Now the woman was paying closer attention to him, especially his transceiver. She held it in her hand, tracing the fiber optic to the back of his neck. Drew winced. Losing the DC was one thing; if they took the transceiver it would be weeks before he could hear or say anything. But maybe they just wanted the fiber. He had no idea why the Burnouts would be interested in such things, but this one seemed to be paying more attention to the fiber than the transceiver itself. Drew slowly reached into his pocket and pulled out his spare spool, which he used for repairs when his transceiver cable got broken. Sure enough, her eyes lit up and she grabbed it out of his hand.

"Thanks. Gimme your necklace, too."

Drew mentally sighed, taking care not to trigger a corresponding sigh noise in the transceiver. He realized that they didn't know what his "necklace" was, and he didn't want to give them any help in figuring it out.

"Hey, let me see that," said the Burnout who was holding Drew. He reached out with his free hand to take the spool from the woman, and Drew felt the grip on his face loosen.

Maybe this was his chance. "LOOK OUT!" he shouted through his transceiver. The woman jerked back, startled by the unexpected noise from the device. Drew elbowed the man behind him and twisted right out of his grasp.

He was so stunned to be free that for a moment he almost forgot to run, but his instincts took over just as the Burnout sprang toward him. Drew jumped between a pair of bushes, took a sharp turn around a dead trunk, and then ran flat out across the forest floor. He could practically feel the big man looming up behind him, about to grab his collar, but by the time he dared to glance over his shoulder there was no one there at all.

Quickly he came to a stop and crouched behind a silverbush. He had heard the stories about the Burnouts and what great warriors they were. He knew they could walk through a forest without making a sound and appear out of nowhere, just as they had done a few minutes before. His eyes darted from tree to tree, but he could see nothing.

He stayed put, trying not to breathe too loudly. Perhaps he had lost them. Perhaps they were stalking him. He wondered if he should go get some help for Sunit, or if moving would give away his position. Finally, unsure of what else he could do, he decided to pray.

As quietly as he could, Drew unfastened his collapsible antenna from his belt. At the touch of a button the frame opened and the thin, silvery mesh unfolded to form a parabolic dish about the width of his shoulders. He snapped his transceiver into the receptacle at the base of the dish and then started looking for the moon.

It wasn't easy, looking for the moon in the forest. He could see only small patches of the sky, and although it was obvious where the sun was, the moon was tough to find. Drew stopped to think, hoping it wasn't below the horizon, but after remembering a prayer yesterday morning he knew that it had to be in the sky. He tried pointing the antenna up in random places without success. Before giving up, though, he remembered that there was supposed to be a partial that afternoon. That would mean the moon's crescent might be too faint to see in broad daylight, but it was probably close to the sun. He repositioned the antenna in that direction and tried again. After a few seconds he made contact.

God! he said, checking to make sure the speaker volume was turned off. He wanted to pray, but he didn't want to broadcast his position to the Burnouts. *I've just been robbed! By Burnouts!*

ROBBED, ROBBED, ROBBED. DON'T KNOW A THING ABOUT IT. BURNOUTS, THOUGH. THEY'RE VERY SNEAKY. WAS DADDY ROBBED, TOO? THIS IS A BAD TIME TO TALK. THERE'S AN ECLIPSE COMING. I'M SCARED.

Drew smiled. Praying to God always made him feel better, even though Drew usually didn't learn very much. *Don't be scared. It's only a partial today. And I think my daddy's okay. But they got Sunit. And I don't know what to do.*

WHAT IS ROBBED?

They took things from us, from me and Sunit. They took my DC. And my spare fiber. And they almost got my transceiver, and then I wouldn't have been able to talk to you at all.

ROBBED, ROB, ROBS. IF SOMEONE ROBS YOU, ROB THEM. ROB WHAT THEY ROBBED. ROB, ROB, ROB, ROB, ROB, ROB, AND BE HAPPY. I'M SCARED OF THE DARK.

Drew nearly laughed. God had never told him to go steal things before. *Eclipses are nothing to be scared of. They happen all the time. But I still don't know what to do. Should I go for help or go look for Sunit?*

SUNIT, SUNIT, SUNIT. SUNIT'S YOUR BEST FRIEND. WHERE, OH, WHERE, OH, WHERE IS SUNIT? DOES SUNIT LIKE BURNOUTS?

No, I don't think he does. And you're right. I shouldn't have just left him like that. I'm going back to get him.

GET HIM, GET SUNIT. GET BURNOUTS. GET YOUR DC. GET ME. GET ME. CAN YOU GET GOD?

I don't know, God. He smiled. *I'm starting to think that nobody gets you at all. I'll talk to you soon.*

'BYE, DREW.

Drew collapsed the antenna and stood up. No one jumped out at him. He took a deep breath and started walking back in the direction he had come from, still trying to collect his thoughts. It must have been the Burnouts who planted the fana bush, he realized. His uncle Zeke had told him that the Burnouts couldn't go very long without fana. Zeke had told him a lot about the Burnouts, but Drew never really paid much attention.

But what had his uncle said that last time? Drew had been watching him work at the forge, molding the virtual metal using those black flexers that he wore like gloves. For some reason his uncle had been making a gun, and Zeke had said something about a defense force against the Burnouts. But Drew couldn't remember why Zeke thought they needed a defense force in the first place, other than all the recent thefts around the City that everyone blamed on the Burnouts.

Drew mulled it over as he approached the clearing where all this had started. Maybe the ambush was connected to what Zeke was talking about. Had they taken

Sunit somewhere to ask him how to attack the City? Was this the beginning of a Burnout uprising?

Sudden movement caught his attention, breaking his train of thought. It was Sunit, walking toward him through the trees.

"Sunit!" Drew called. "You okay?"

His friend shrugged, closing the distance between them. "I guess." Still, Sunit looked pretty shaken.

"What happened? Did they—"

"They let me go." Sunit tried to smile. "When you got away they started to chase you. But then they just gave up and started laughing. And then they just took our DCs and ran off. . . ." He pointed up the hillside to the north.

"Do you think . . ." Drew scratched his chin. "Do you think they'll be back? Do you think they'll bring more? My uncle thinks the Burnouts are going to start a war."

Sunit's eyes widened. "Really? I thought your daddy said they were nice people."

Drew felt the blood rush out of his face. Daddy. Just that morning Daddy had left on a missionary trip to the Outpost. If something was happening out there, he was going to get caught right in the middle. Without a word, Drew turned and started sprinting back toward town.

"Hey!" he heard his best friend call after him. "Drew?"

Drew didn't even slow down. He just hoped he could get a warning to Daddy in time.

CHAPTER 2

CAPTAIN: Report.

J. Hansen: *The planet was another Mars.[7] The ice caps are fairly extensive, but the bulk of the atmosphere has been gone for some time. However, the moon—*

CAPTAIN: *I thought you said it was a double-planet system.*

J. Hansen: *Yes, sir. As always, we refer to the larger one as the planet and the smaller one as the moon, even though they only differ by 5 percent in diameter and the moon actually has 10 percent more mass than the planet. And on the moon, as I was saying, we have initial indications of a nitrogen-based atmosphere. Secondary gases include oxygen and—*

CAPTAIN: *Was that . . . was that oxygen you just said?*

J. Hansen: *Yes, sir.*

CAPTAIN: *Breathable? It is breathable? What are the numbers?*

*J. Hansen: It looks good. Roughly 750 millibars
total, with 180 m-bars of O_2. CO_2 is 15 millibars, high but below danger levels. There will
be some natural physiological changes, and we
might feel short of breath, but we'll survive.*

CAPTAIN: (quietly) Landmasses?

J. Hansen: Excuse me, sir?

CAPTAIN: Are there any landmasses?

*J. Hansen: Well, it's hard to get a good reading
with all the cloud cover, but there are at least
two small continents. And at least one of them
seems to be covered by some sort of reddish
foliage, so apparently some form of eukaryotic
cell has evolved here.*

*A. Ryutov: Would you like to see a picture of it
onscreen, sir?*

*CAPTAIN: Yes, I—oh, God. It's a perfect, enor-
mous . . .*

A. Ryutov: Sir?

CAPTAIN: Mandala. We have arrived at last.

*Note 7. Slang term for a tectonically quiet planet
that eventually loses its atmosphere due to the
lack of a CO_2 cycle.*

*The Log
Year 27, Day 125.40*

THE ACCELERATION HAD DROPPED TO 1.5
g's, and Samuel felt like he might go airborne with every
step. He strolled down the rubbery corridor of the *Mayflower* with a smile on his face; the worst was over. The
spaceship's engines would continue to ease up over the
next two weeks, passing through his native 1.0 g and
finally leveling off near the 0.78 g at which he would
spend the rest of his life. It was going to be wonderful.

But first, he reminded himself, he would get to enjoy the pleasures of zero gravity for a few days when they went into orbit around Mandala. Over the last five years he had taken advantage of every engine failure to rejoice in the sudden freedom, flying down corridors and up stairways, bouncing between the walls via well-placed kicks from his short, muscular legs. Every time, though, the warning siren had come too soon; he had grudgingly returned to the floor and let the rapidly building acceleration drag him back down to the standard 1.9 g's required by this interminable interstellar journey.

He had handled the pressure better than most. Being only a meter tall came with a few advantages, and dealing with high accelerations was one of them. True, he had spent his share of time in the salt baths and the pressurefoams, but his nineteen crewmates had had it worse; he was the only one to avoid a sprain, broken bone, or other high-g injury over the past five years. But despite his fortunate size, spending years at high g had still been simply miserable. He had often found himself wishing he was rich enough to be one of the thirty-three thousand colonists sleeping blissfully in the cryotanks. Those people didn't know what they were missing.

As he walked, Samuel pored over the script that Captain Simpson had wired to him a few hours ago. They were finally going to radio ahead to the Mandalans, announcing the *Mayflower*'s successful trip across seventy-five light-years of interstellar space. He chuckled silently as he read it, painfully aware that any input he might have as an expert of twenty-first-century culture was already way out of date.

Simpson had written the whole speech in modern English, which would have sounded ridiculous when the *Walt Disney* had left Earth centuries ago. Perhaps Mandalan English had evolved in the same way, but that was rather unlikely. The best guess he had for local linguistic conventions was the Standard English of 2099, so Samuel had immersed himself in that particular dialect for the past five years. He had gotten to the point where even his thought processes took on a twenty-first-century word order, but as he looked down at the speech in his hand he knew it was pointless to try to edit it in that fashion. It was pointless to predict anything about the society they were about to encounter. They had flown across 150 years of history in a mere 5, and the best they could do now was go down and witness the result.

It was an amazingly unfortunate situation, and the laws of general relativity were entirely to blame. The *Walt Disney* had been Earth's first and last blind-shot colony ship. Four hundred people sent out into space to find an extrasolar planet with a breathable atmosphere. The technology had been so new that unmanned probes weren't yet an option, and although deep-space interferometric devices had been able to image planets in nearby star systems, they couldn't tell which planets were habitable. The *Walt Disney* visited six systems, its crew aging only about four years per system thanks to their relativistic velocities. But Earth aged much faster, and the light-speed communications slowed things down even more; every thirty years or so Earth would get a message from the *Walt Disney* that detailed their discoveries, the lack of any habitable planets, and their next destination. Each time, Earth had broadcast an immediate reply, but it was a wasted gesture: by the time the messages arrived, the *Walt Disney* had long since moved on.

Finally, after a full two centuries had passed on Earth, the big news arrived. Long chalked off as a failure, the *Walt Disney* had finally succeeded. They had found Mandala. Construction of the *Mayflower* had begun at once, cannibalizing abandoned spaceship projects still in Earth orbit. After a mere eighteen months they blasted off on their seventy-five-light-year trek to rejoin that lost island of humanity.

But there was a huge information gap. The *Walt Disney* had actually arrived at Mandala seventy-five years previously; it had taken that long for the message to reach Earth. And although this current trip seemed like only five years from Samuel's relativistic frame, it really lasted nearly seventy-six more. It all added up to humans living on Mandala for more than 150 years before the *Mayflower* would even arrive, most of that time without any communication from Earth at all. As a result, absolutely no one knew what awaited them.

Theories abounded, and Samuel had gone through a few of his own. At one time, he remembered, he was very worried about a strong anti-Earth movement developing on Mandala. He had pressed to get the *Mayflower* outfitted with basic defenses, just in case, but no one seemed to take the threat seriously. No weapons were authorized, although they did increase the ship's acceleration from 1.4 to 1.9 g's, thinking that by speeding up their arrival no such movement would have time to get off the ground. As it was, the ship would be arriving less than a year after the messages that announced their departure from Earth.

With this precaution in place, his paranoia had ebbed over the course of the five-year journey. After all, why would anyone want to harm them? They came only with the best of intentions, and they were bringing technology that would make life easier for everyone. The idea that they would meet armed resistance was nothing but a foolish notion, dreamed up after watching too many science-fiction vids.

Samuel cleared the text, folded it up, and slipped the

blank page into his pocket. There was no point in second-guessing what might happen, no point in changing a single word. He felt that only one thing was certain about this impending meeting of cultures: Nobody had the faintest idea what to expect.

CHAPTER 3

This evening I had a religious experience.

Already the sensation is fading away, but my understanding is not; my epiphany is surviving the transition. I feel I could explain it to anyone with the necessary scientific and philosophical background. And I will. For this may be the ultimate knowledge, the one true connection between the laws of physics and the innate spirituality of humankind, and it is now my duty to teach others.

The truth is so simple, and yet I tremble as I put it into words. On a cosmological scale, the universe is symmetric in time. What we know as God is simply the collective consciousness traveling opposite to our temporal orientation. God's realm is our unknowable future; everything that is real to Him remains only possibility to us. Ironically, the reverse is also true: The reality of our past remains unknown to God.

Our biased temporal perspective has obscured the truth for so long, but it is now so clear. Our

connection with God can occur only where bound-
ary conditions from both ends of the universe can
interact. A God traveling in an opposite time di-
rection can only influence us in the one place
where neither time direction has determined re-
ality. From God's perspective the future is fixed;
from our perspective the past is fixed. The only
room for interaction is where physics demands
complete time-symmetrical ignorance; the realm
of quantum mechanics.

This is why we only sense God through our
minds and not the macroscopic world! Only
through the quantum action of our human brains
can God truly speak to us, guiding us to bring our
future—His past—into existence.

And I see now what the future holds for hu-
manity. As our technology continues to advance
we will eventually become godlike ourselves.
Sooner or later, our descendants will find a way
to transfer themselves into immortal beings, per-
haps in the form of pure energy, and they will
survive the transition into the recollapse of the
universe. And then—the beautiful symmetry!—hu-
manity will be the God, and today's God will be
some alternate version of humanity, evolving back-
ward in our temporal frame. I have no doubt that
when we are God, we will guide them just as He
is guiding us now.

The Journal
Year 5, Day 19

PAUL RANDALL CLUNG TO THE HANDHOLDS
on the side of the tradervan as it bounced up the old
mining road. The ride was rough; automated vehicles

made jerky steering corrections due to the finite number
of radio beacons in the road, and this particular route
hadn't been designed for passengers. For Paul, hanging
on was simply the easiest way to climb out of the American Valley, and he tried not to begrudge the fact that
there were probably some discarded couches inside the
tradervan. Only the security measures kept him from
resting comfortably among the old clothes, sacks of
flour, and bottles of nitrous oxide.

The view made up for it, he told himself, as he peered
down to see the sparkling American as it cut westward
through the green earthwood forests of the valley floor.
Farther downstream lay Captain's Lake, surrounded by
an array of circular farm plots, the red and green crops
resembling an enormous color-blindness exam that extended past the hydroelectric dam, all the way to the
outskirts of Mandala City. Of the City itself, he could
only make out a few large features: the russet grass of
the playing fields, the bright blue buildings on Industrial
Row, the silver hull of Government Cone towering over
the center of town. He tried to spot his house on the
south bank, but the trees were too thick. On the far side
of the City the only distinguishable feature was the sun
glinting off of the Biodome where his wife, Katrina, was
probably working at that very moment. Beyond that lay
only the tidelakes and moonmarshes of the west coast
where the American met the raging, moon-driven ocean.

His view of the valley disappeared as the tradervan
took a hairpin turn, and he tensed up his arms to keep
from being thrown off. The scenery up here was far less
impressive; few Earth species could survive well on
these windy, soil-poor slopes, and Mandalan scrub brush
was not exactly the prettiest of the native ecosystems.
But Paul perked up when he saw some blue sky peeking
through the brush. They were almost at the crest.

He went to work unlashing his pack from the higher handholds and prepared for the jump. The trick was to leap off before the van picked up too much speed down the opposite side, but to wait long enough so that he would land on the grassy north-facing slopes, rather than the rocky terrain that characterized this side of the ridge. This time he hit it perfectly, tossing his pack first, and then landing and rolling down the steep but soft hillside.

After sliding to a halt in a small patch of unmelted snow he got to his feet and stretched, watching the trad-ervan speed down into the Red Valley on its way to the Burnout Kingdoms. He sometimes thought about staying on the van and riding all the way down, but he knew he would not be welcome there. And besides, he had few illusions about being able to help; those Burnouts had been gone from the City for several generations at least. It was the Outpost that needed him, and that was where he was headed. He climbed back up to the ridge, paused briefly to shoulder his pack, and began hiking west, back in the direction of Mandala City.

The wind wasn't too strong today, and he kept a good pace as he made his way along the narrowing ridge. Unlike the American, the Red Valley was a mostly na-tive ecosystem, and the differences were dramatic when seen from this height. Maroon chaparral and dark green sapvines sprawled over the top of the roottower forests, pink mushrub patches graced the hillsides like miniature alien settlements, and iridescent patterns of water ants decorated ponds along the valley floor with their quickly shifting shades of blue and green.

The Red Valley had richer soil than the American, probably because it was closer to the highly volcanic range to the north. Still, the American had been settled first, and so the Red Valley was largely undisturbed. The agricultural plots of the Burnouts were both fewer and

smaller, arranged in tiny hand-harvested squares and often obscured by the surrounding flora. There were few
obvious population centers due to both the small number
of Burnouts and their tendency to be decentralized.
Some of the bigger kingdoms, though, had had a recent
spurt of construction projects, no doubt taking advantage
of this relatively peaceful period amid several decades
of sporadic small-scale warfare. Paul looked northward
in an attempt to see some of the new buildings, but it
was hard to see much from so far away, and it seemed
the light was starting to fade already.

He stopped and glanced at his watch, momentarily
wondering how it had gotten so late, but seeing that it
was only a quarter past thirty-two, he remembered that
there was supposed to be a partial today. He peered upward through a crack in his fingers, and sure enough,
the eclipse was already well under way. The edge of the
moon looked nearly straight as it cut across the center
of the sun, but there was just enough of a curve that his
eye was fooled into thinking it could see the rest of the
moon as well, stretching three sun diameters away from
the interface of light and shadow.

Paul pulled his gaze away after a moment, quietly
cursing himself for looking at it for so long. Even without an eclipse, human reflexes didn't always kick in
quickly enough to avoid retinal damage from Mandala's
sun. His Earth-evolved eyes didn't react properly to the
high ratio of UV to visible light, and even here at 38
degrees latitude the noon sun was a real danger for a
sizable part of the year. Having a large moon and frequent eclipses merely exacerbated the problem, and he
knew that peeking through his fingers didn't help very
much. He blinked a few times, trying to clear the after-
image, and after a moment he began his descent into the
Red Valley.

Before long he came upon one of the higher-altitude mushrub fields. After that, he didn't have to worry about shielding his eyes from the partial; the constant task of avoiding the plants was keeping his attention fixed on the ground ahead of him. The hard clay here could support only a few lone roottowers; the rest of the landscape was dotted with mushrubs—smooth, half-domed plants covering the surface exactly like a hazardous minefield.

And with the mushrubs came the memories, as always. Seven years, now. He reached down and clenched his electronic Journal, forcing back the most painful thoughts and concentrating on the pleasant ones. The four of them picnicking in the hills, his daughters crawling around the house like they were worms. . . . Paul suddenly jolted to a halt as he realized he was about to step on a mushrub. It turned out to be a pink one, but he had stopped paying attention; it could easily have been otherwise.

The real surprises were all waiting under the dead, translucent domes. Inside, sealed off from the outside atmosphere, bacteria lived off the minerals in the clay, mutating and evolving for hundreds, even thousands of years. These were the worst kinds of diseases: less advanced than the sophisticated versions that lived off the native plants and insects but able to synthesize all of their amino acids from the simple organics in the ground. This gave them the rare ability to thrive in the alien biology of a human host, and many of them were extremely toxic. He knew the dangers all too well: His daughters had been killed during the last outbreak, which was eventually traced back to one of their classmates, who had spent an afternoon popping mushrubs in the foothills.

Paul still had to consciously stop himself from projecting his loss and anger on the plants. To that end he made an effort to avoid the live ones, although they were almost completely safe, and even sidestepped the seed-lings that hadn't yet fully sealed against the firm ground. Paul had to admit they were beautiful, sprouting up like miniparasols and extending their light red fabric in all directions to catch the sun. Eventually gravity won the battle, pulling the edges of the sticky web to the ground, where it often formed a perfect seal and began to reg-ulate its internal gases.

Mandalan biologists, his wife included, still argued over exactly what benefit the mushrubs received from this, but it was generally accepted that the higher gas pressure allowed a complex nitrogen fixation process that would have been impossible at Mandala's ambient pressure. If the reports were to be believed, some of the larger species in the Eastern Canyonlands contained measured pressures of more than 3 atmospheres. Those giant species, which often sealed up entire canyons with miniecosystems, were much more visually impressive than the smaller versions here in the valley. But Paul had never been there, never traveled much farther than the Outpost, and even this was farther than most City residents ever ventured.

Paul came to a quick stop and pulled his recorder out of his wallet. One of the mushrubs had a beautiful image of the partially eclipsed sun glowing brightly on its pink dome. A series of holes in an overhanging roottower frond were acting as natural pinhole cameras, and the resulting projections of the quarter sun on the curved surface were truly remarkable. The mushrub even hap-pened to be blooming; the mauve flower topped the scene beautifully, sprouting from the precise peak of the plant. Paul walked around it and shot a couple of gigs, capturing the eclipse as best he could for Drew. He was sure that his son would appreciate it; Drew loved watching eclipses, although he never really liked the fact that he wasn't allowed to look directly at the partials. This view certainly beat squinting through those awkward filters.

THE PARTIAL WAS LONG OVER BY THE TIME he arrived at the Outpost. As he passed underneath the outer watchtower he waved and called up to the wooden platform hidden among the roottower fronds. "Hello up there! It's just the Mish, here for another visit!" Strangely enough, there was no response. He tried to get a better view of the platform, but he couldn't see much. It was usually manned forty-four hours a day, but perhaps the break in the fighting kept them from worrying about the once-common raids from the various Burnout kingdoms.

He shrugged and continued walking along the dirt path into the center of the Outpost. Even before he entered the main clearing he knew something strange was afoot; the ever-bustling commune was nearly deserted. He looked around at the ring of log cabins, extremely puzzled. A few of the older residents sat outside, some knitting, some resting in hammocks. Old Man Curtis glanced up at him disinterestedly for a moment and returned to his writing.

Paul's first thought was that most of the Outpost had suddenly left to find a new kingdom; such large-scale emigrations had sometimes occurred in the past. But the more he looked around, the less that idea made sense. The usual amounts of drying laundry still hung between the cabins, the chicken coops were bustling with activity, and wooden beer barrels remained stacked under a roottower grove; there was no sign of an organized departure. And the bored expressions belied the possibility that something horrible had happened.

Paul heard some shouts from behind the central cabin, and when he walked over to investigate, he found many of the Outpost kids playing a game of soccer. They would tell him what was going on. He spotted Jave, one of the children he knew from his other visits. "Hey, Jave!" He succeeded in getting everyone's attention, and the game slowed to a halt. "Where is everybody today?"

Jave started walking over to him, displaying a concerned smile.

"Nobody's nowhere!" shouted one of the older girls. "Ain't that right, Jave?" Jave turned to look at him and nodded slowly. "And even if they are somewhere, they'll be back soon enough." The other kids murmured in agreement.

Paul smiled at her logic. "Ah, it's a secret, is it?" He caught a flash of confirmation in Jave's eyes and looked around at the other children, trying to decide what to do. He was curious as to where everyone could be, but he always made a great effort not to be too inquisitive up here. It wouldn't be too hard to trick the truth out of one of them, he knew, but this was probably something pretty sensitive if they had left instructions with the kids. Paul decided he was better off being patient; he was sure everything would become clear sooner or later. "So when do you expect everyone back?" He caught the gaze of the girl who had spoken earlier. "Assuming, of course, that they're somewhere to begin with."

"Before sundown," said Jave. "Slackers are over there, by the middle cooking fire."

Slackers? Paul hadn't heard that word up here before, although that was often how the City residents referred to the Burnouts as a whole. He strained to look and spotted a thin wisp of smoke. "Thanks, Jave." He turned

to leave, then paused after a few steps. "By the way, I'll
be telling some stories tonight, so be sure to come by."
The children were always his best audience, when their
parents would let them listen. He waved a good-bye and
headed over to the fire.

A DOZEN PEOPLE LAY AROUND THE SMALL
fire pit, most of them eating baked potatoes with gravy.
Shari was there, sitting cross-legged some distance from
the blaze, roasting her potato on a ridiculously long
branch that she supported across her pregnant belly. Several children were present as well, but he had to keep
himself from wincing when he noticed that one of them
had stuffed his dinner with crimson fana leaves. For all
the adjustments he had to make at the Outpost, that was
still something he didn't think he'd ever get used to.

As he continued to walk around the fire he spotted
Foz under a tree on the far side. First, though, he made
a point of greeting everyone else. As usual, he got only
a few gravy-tainted grunts in response, but he still main-
tained his smile as he made it around the ring to where
Foz was sitting on the soft, mossy ground.

"So where is everybody today?" he asked as he settled
himself under the tree. "I don't suppose everyone decided to rejoin society this morning?"

Foz didn't look up. "Hold on, man," he managed.
"I'm finishing."

Paul shrugged and leaned back against the trunk to
survey the Outpost. The log cabins on this side were all
arranged very haphazardly, as followed from the lack of
central planning. Paul had helped to build two of the
newer ones, and he felt pretty proud that they still looked
good even after a few winters. What impressed him the
most, though, was that the Outpost could continue to

function without a clear leader. The fire was built, the food was grown and harvested, and yet nobody had any assigned roles in this makeshift society. He knew that this somewhat smooth-running system had not always been the norm, however, and was glad that even the Burnouts had discovered some rudimentary lessons of civilization.

He turned back to Foz, who was suffering through the usual postfana symptoms. His eyes were fluttering, and his limbs twitched with small muscle spasms. The braid that had been keeping his long hair in check started unraveling as a result of the shaking, and the clumpy brown tendrils began to obscure his face. At length the tremors passed, and Foz took a couple of long, deep breaths. His glassy blue eyes remained focused somewhere beyond the horizon, but it seemed to Paul that somehow his *presence* had returned.

"What's that you said?"

Paul cleared his throat. "I was just wondering where everyone was."

"Oh, you know . . ." Foz waved his hand vaguely as he spoke with a slow, gliding voice. "Everyone dreaming, dreaming. Not gonna come to nothing. Just thinking it will. I don't care. I'm not going nowhere."

Paul suppressed a smile. Apparently, Foz wasn't quite . . . *finished.* "Where? Where aren't you going?" Paul pressed.

Foz opened his mouth to speak but then seemed to think better of it. He turned to look at Paul for the first time. "Hey, what're ya trying to do? It's none of your damn . . ." A spasm of coughing suddenly racked Foz's body, and he doubled over with the effort.

"It's okay, really," Paul said. "I was just asking." He watched Foz cough dramatically. "You want me to get you a drink?"

Foz shook his head, and after a while the fit subsided. He leaned back against the tree, smiling weakly. "I know this bothers you, Mish," Foz said. "Me tripping all the time."

Paul shrugged. "Not too much. When used properly, fana can be truly wonderful."

"You should do it more than once a year, then."

"I suppose it could be more often. Or less often. Our Capt——I'm sorry. The Captain held Communion once a year, and so we follow his example. Personally I think that's about right; any more and the experiences would be less meaningful, any less and you'd forget what you learned. But the most important thing is to be in the right frame of mind, no matter how often you take it."

"I see. So when I trip, my frame of mind *isn't* right." Foz seemed to have more of his wits about him.

"I don't know. Do you do anything to prepare yourself beforehand? Do you try to focus your mind in any way?"

Foz turned away again and chuckled silently. "Man . . . you think you're so bloody open-minded. . . ."

Paul raised his eyebrows. "What do you mean?"

"You never just let the fana *take* you. You think you're opening your mind up to God, but all you're doing with your little prayers and rituals is seeing what you *want* to see. You just close yourself off from anything you're not prepared for."

"Actually, in my twenty-seven Communions, I've never once been prepared for what I've seen. But tell me, with all your experiences, have you really never sensed anything that you thought might be God?"

This time Foz laughed out loud. "Man, one time I thought my left arm was God. I was running all over the cabin, waving it at everybody and screaming, 'Behold! Behold!' Finally I tried to throw myself into the fire, and Neppy had to drag me away." He shook his head at the memory. "That's when he broke my finger."

Paul shook his head, smiling. "That's almost being as literal as my son."

"Your son?"

"Yeah. Drew. He's just starting to figure religion out for himself, and he's tending to take everything far too literally. He has quite an imagination, too. For a while he was pretending that when he prayed to God they were actually having a literal conversation. He even said that God wasn't using very good English! So I had to be the one to inject some mysticism, try to get him to take God less literally."

"But that's what I was talking about. Your kid's just starting to put things together, and then you come along and ram your ideas down his throat. Why, he might be more right than you are. The way I see it, people who start from scratch get a whole lot closer to the truth than anyone else. I mean, maybe your Captain had a lot of good ideas, and maybe he actually hit on something there. But now you make your kids learn this stuff in school, turn his ideas into a formal *religion,* and then you have to start compromising all over the place. You're turning it into a big community thing and just getting farther away from whatever truth might have been there in the first place. For all you know, your kid could be stumbling onto some hidden secrets of the universe, and there you are, trying to convince him that he's going about it all wrong."

Paul took a deep breath. "I don't think leaving religion up to the individual is always a good thing. Captain was an extraordinary man. He was able to discover amazing truths about God and connect humanity's basic spirituality with what we know about the natural world. But not everyone is going to figure that out for themselves, so we should pass on his teachings. Just as I'm up here, trying to pass on his message to you."

Foz shook his head. "I don't know why you bother, Mish. You're never going to get through to any of us. I mean, I don't understand quantum mechanics or backward causation or any of that religious science stuff. How do you expect me to believe in this God of yours?"

"You don't need to understand quantum to appreciate God. I mean, for a century after it was first developed, no one really understood it. Did you know they used to interpret quantum completely differently than we do now? They used to think that objects could be both particles and waves at the same time. And acting like a wave, they thought a single particle could spread out and be in two or three places at once! Supposedly particles kept up this mysterious behavior until a measurement was made, and then it would collapse into a particular spot, just as you looked at it."

A low chuckle emerged from Foz's throat. "Why did anyone believe in anything so ridiculous?"

"It was the only theory around that fit all the experiments. Lots of people disliked that way of thinking about things, and they tried to disprove it or come up with a better explanation."

"Well, why did it take them so long? I mean, a century is a long time."

"That's a good question. The evidence was all there. Everyone knew the Dirac equation had two solutions, one traveling forward in time and one backward in time. But for decades physicists just tossed out the backward-time solution because they couldn't make sense out of it. Even though the laws of physics are symmetric, they still insisted in using a time-asymmetric theory of the microscopic world. They knew that the direction of time we see is just statistical, based on the low-entropy con-

ditions at the beginning of the universe. But our particular temporal orientation is so fundamental to our
worldview that for a long time physicists had trouble
thinking of a quantum world that was truly time-
symmetric."

"But there is a direction of time. You can see it all
around you."

Paul smiled. "Only on the macroscopic level, where
temporal paradoxes come into play. And even then,
we're only seeing the half of the universe whose boundary conditions lie in our past. The other half of the material in the universe has future boundary conditions, and
if we could observe it, it would look just like a vid
played backward. Causes would happen after the effects."

Foz shrugged. "Time travel. I don't buy it."

"No, our past is fixed, because that's the direction our
boundary conditions are in. Every particle in your body
is an effect of the Big Bang's cause, and there's only
one way for them to get there from here. The future,
though, is limitless. We choose our future. God is in the
reverse situation; there are no special conditions he has
to meet at the Big Bang. All of his boundary conditions
are determined at the Big Crunch—the end of the universe for us. From our perspective, his future is fixed
and his past is open. Of course, since we're so close to
the Big Bang, he has much less future left than we do.
But he's had much more past than us; that's why he's
God and we're still mortal."

Foz was shaking his head. "Wait. I've never liked this
part. If God's future is fixed, then shouldn't that fix our
future as well? I mean, the future's either fixed or not
fixed, right?"

"Well, think about it. Suppose God told us about our
future. That would mean we would be forced to fulfill

it, and that would mean we would have no free will. But we do have free will, right?"

Foz looked down at himself and flexed his hand. "Well, it sure *feels* like I do. But hey, maybe it's just an illusion."

Paul shook his head. "No, Foz. You *do* have free will. And the way physics allows it is by preventing God from communicating with us in a way that connects our future to his past. God's constrained by paradox prevention and all the other laws of physics. He's not omnipotent. It turns out all he can do for us is affect things on a quantum scale. But as it turns out, the most important thing in the universe happens on a quantum scale."

"And what's that?"

Paul pointed to Foz's head. "Human consciousness. God is able to influence us through the quantum effects in our brains. And because God is looking out for us, we should all do our best to listen to what he has to say."

Foz nodded while he slowly stood up and stretched. "Well, right now he's telling me to get some food." He turned and called over to a teenage boy by the fire. "Hey, Scrap! Any 'taters left for me and the Mish?"

A thin, muscular man glanced over their way. "Come get 'em if you want, but Neppy said he had dibs."

Foz beckoned for Paul to join him. "S'okay. Neppy owes me."

Paul stood as well, dusting himself off. "Wasn't Neppy the one who kept you from burning off your arm?"

"My point exactly." He held up his crooked index finger. "Let's eat."

CHAPTER 4

The planetologists are ecstatic, and I feel re-deemed. All those planetary mysteries they wanted to stay and study, a full five systems worth. And always I allowed them only cursory explorations and ordered that we move on. "Just another week!" Raoul always begged. "What difference could another week possibly make?"

Well, he doesn't have to beg now. This is turn-ing out to be the most interesting planetary system we've found yet, and Raoul has the rest of his life to study it. The Mandala-Asgard system itself is fascinating. Who would have guessed that two similar-size bodies in the same orbit could have turned out so differently? Farther away we have Odin, the most massive solid planet on record and the only one with a ring. We'll be sending the SPEED probe there just as soon as we check out the true anomaly of this system: Hades.

We didn't even notice Hades for a full week after we arrived. It's the closet planet to the sun,

*so it's gravitationally locked. But unlike Asgard's
3:1 spin-orbit ratio, or Mercury's 3:2, it's the only
known non-moon to be locked 1:1. And since the
same side always points to the nearby sun, the
atmosphere has either boiled off into space or frozen onto the night-side surface. It also has the expected solid tides, general relativistic effects, and
heat conduction through the mantle. But what is
unexpected, and what currently defies explanation,
is why the sunlit side of the planet is so utterly,
terribly black.*

*The Journal
Year 27, Day 290*

PRIME MINISTER ALEXANDER CHANNING
hurried up the circular stairway that wound through his
three-level apartment, loosely gripping the center post as
he spiraled upward. Leaving his office level behind, he
climbed through his living areas and finally emerged into
the tall, conical sunroom.

The sunroom lay at the very top of the Government
Cone; it was the highest room in the entire City. The
top of the cone towered above and around him, one-way
plastic that converged at a point thirty meters overhead,
directly over the room's enormous diamond centerpiece.
Around both the diamond and the top of the stairway
stretched the only piece of furniture: a white, C-shaped,
chicken-feather couch. The gap in the C pointed due
west.

Channing didn't feel like taking the long way around.
Instead he skirted around the giant diamond and vaulted
over the eastern side of the couch. Landing on the far
side, his aging legs ached with the impact. *Got to stop
doing that,* he thought, pressing his forehead against the

angled window. He spotted the Interferometeric Station in an instant, the row of parabolic dishes clearly visible at the edge of town, but Zhang was nowhere to be seen.

Five minutes ago Zhang had interrupted Channing's routine with the news that an important message had arrived. But that was it. Zhang would tell him no more over the DC.

"Curse him," Channing muttered aloud. He scanned the paths below, but saw only farmers biking down tree-lined streets, children walking home from school, little people going about their business. No sign of the Minister of Information hurrying over to give the message in person, as he promised.

Channing felt himself growing anxious, and even a bit angry that there was "important" news that wasn't immediately passed on to him, the Prime Minister of Mandala. Still, Zhang's passion for secrecy had to be commended. Channing had been Zhang's mentor ever since the man's first foray into Mandalan politics, and Channing had always stressed secrecy above all else. Information is power, Channing had taught him. And for Zhang, the Minister of Information for the past eight years, that had proved to be excellent advice: Contact had made Zhang the second most powerful man on the planet.

With a sigh, Channing turned from the window to face the room's centerpiece, the two-meter-high cone of perfect diamond. The gigantic crystal, perhaps the most expensive decoration in the universe, refracted the sunlight into a broad rainbow that stretched across the surrounding couch. Channing admired the diamond not for its beauty, but for the fact that it had endured the largest long-term concentration of power in all of recorded history. And it had not cracked under the strain.

The diamond was one of the original six from the

Walt Disney and the only one that had been brought
down from orbit. The cone weighed more than twenty-
two tons, even without the original buckysteel driveshaft
attached. From the side the conical crystal looked like a
perfect equilateral triangle—minus the very top corner.
Channing had always thought it would look much better
as a complete cone, but of course without the flat top
his ancestors never would have made it out of Sol System. That little circular platform was one of six surfaces
that had pushed the fifty-thousand-ton *Walt Disney* at
1.4 g's of constant acceleration, propelling the Originals
on their epic Journey.

But while staring into the perfect diamond was mildly
calming, it didn't help Channing to answer the puzzle
that Zhang's quick call had left behind. Why, out of all
the messages Mandala had received from Earth over the
past seven years, was this one so special?

SEVEN YEARS AGO, BEFORE CONTACT, MOST
Mandalans thought that the messages from Earth would
change everything. Channing had been no different. All
his life he had known that two Earth centuries of scientific advances were quietly making their way across
twenty-three parsecs of interstellar space, and he had
been determined to have them for himself.

Everyone had assumed that there would be a lot to
learn. After all, their ancestors had left the planet in the
midst of the Tzengian Revolution, when the stagnation
of the mid-twenty-first century seemed to have finally
been overcome. Einsteinian physics had been supplanted
by Tzeng's Vacuum Inertia, and it became clear that
interstellar travel was suddenly within reach. The resulting wave of growth and invention promised to put a
permanent end to human misery. A practical spheromak

fusion device could transform the ocean's deuterium into cheap, clean energy, and new biomech facilities had the potential to stabilize the Earth's ecosystem once and for all. After all, if they could create an indefinitely recyclable biosphere inside of a spaceship, than surely transferring that technology to the Earth as a whole was only a matter of scale. It seemed obvious that Earth was headed for the long-promised Golden Age, and Channing wanted to be the one to reap the benefits of Earth's new technology.

But the scientific furor of the Tzengian Revolution had not lasted. Indeed, looking back at it now, it had ended almost before the *Walt Disney* had left Earth orbit. The Golden Age had fallen victim to the short-term profits of capitalism run amok. The most powerful businesses had surpassed the most powerful governments, and as a result politics was no longer the domain of the nation-state. Governments had become little more than large public-service organizations, caring for the populous underclasses while the multinats dealt with everything else. Government-sponsored scientific research was a forgotten memory, and the underinvestment of the business community in basic science had slowed the once-exponential pace of scientific discovery.

No one had been able to stabilize Tzengian wells in a planet's gravitational field, and the problem was now considered insoluble by Earth scientists. The promised Tzengian Fountain, once touted as the final solution to all humanity's energy needs, had been relegated to the pipe dreams of history. A feasible space elevator, self-replicating nanomachinery, a miniature fusion reactor—all were costly long-term goals, and the expensive R&D had been pushed aside in deference to the altar of short-term profits.

Of course, scientific advances had been made where

the market forces were favorable. Medicine, in particular, had made remarkable strides. Cryogenic technology had been perfected, and genetic manipulation was commonplace. This knowledge had spilled over into an enormous biotech industry, which had gone on to create amazing new resources and materials. Computers also had continued their advances, fullerene quantum computers having finally surpassed their silicon predecessors as the dominant machines on Earth. Artificial consciousness, as always, was supposedly just a few decades away.

But for Channing, the news had been devastating. All that waiting, all that planning, and for what? How would faster computers and better metadrugs give him the godlike power he had envisioned? Biotech didn't help him much at all; specific bioinventions could only be re-created here if they had the same genetic base to start with. As it was, a very small number of Earth organisms had survived the radiation-ladened Journey; only the plants, some insects, and chickens. And while Earth had been able to recover from the few disastrous genetic engineering accidents, a situation like the Nebraska Aphid Outbreak would totally wipe out the food supply for their small colony.

But maybe, Channing considered as he stared at the diamond, the one advance he really wanted from Earth had finally come through after all. Maybe that was why Zhang was hurrying over here with a secret so big he couldn't speak it over the encrypted digital communicators. Immortality.

Contact had seemed to put an end to that dream. Earth's biogerontologists had discovered several fundamental limits to biological systems, and longevity was one of them. The basic mechanism of aging, the telomere DNA sequences that governed the human body's built-in clock, had been unraveled long ago. But stopping their countdown to death, although possible, had raised an old specter from the past: cancer.

As it turned out, longevity treatments not only caused cancer but also kept the successful cancer drugs from working in the first place. Aging was not only inevitable from an evolutionary standpoint, it was also necessary to keep the body's cells in check. In social humans, where it was genetically advantageous to live past one's reproductive years, natural selection had already found a near-ideal balance between death and uncontrolled life. So after raising the average life expectancy to an Earth century, there was little extra room for improvement. The connection between aging and cancer was a fundamental obstacle; a few had been kept alive by the new longevity enzymes, but the vast majority of those who had risked it were dead in ten years.

But maybe now Earth's scientists had found a loophole.

By the time Zhang arrived, forcing his large bulk into the apartment, Channing had convinced himself that this was the big news. The biological secret of eternal life. What else could be so important? Earth must have finally come through for him after all.

One look at Zhang's face told him he was completely wrong.

"What is it?" Channing asked, suddenly anxious all over again. "Bad news from Earth?"

Zhang frowned. "Not exactly from Earth."

Not from Earth? Channing thought. *But that could only mean . . .*

"Maybe we'd better sit down," Zhang suggested. "This isn't going to be easy."

* * *

TWO HOURS LATER, CHANNING BURST INTO
the conference room, allowing everyone to scramble to
their feet before motioning for them to remain seated.
He slowly walked around to the head of the table,
sweeping his gaze over the hastily assembled group.

Zhang and Riko occupied neighboring seats on one
side of the table—the Ministers of Information and
Technology, respectively. Riko was much smaller and
quieter than Zhang, and usually stayed out of the spotlight unless some scientific issue was explicitly discussed. But despite their differences, they were the two
Ministers whom Channing could trust. The three others—
the female Ministers of Agriculture, Religion, and Society—had not been informed of this emergency gathering. Channing was glad to see they hadn't found out
about it through other channels.

On the other side of the table sat a dozen men, lined
up in two rows of evenly spaced chairs. Croll sat front
and center as their unstated leader, practically a Minister
in his own right. There was no official position for Minister of Defense, but Croll filled the post anyway, in his
usual intimidating manner. His stout, muscular frame
wasn't nearly as striking as his completely bald head;
the man had been born without a single follicle. Most
of the planet knew Croll as Channing's quirky personal
trainer and bodyguard, but even those who guessed at
his political influence would have been surprised to learn
how far his duties actually extended.

Croll's younger brothers sat to either side, Rick and
One-Arm George. They were no more talented than the
other members of Croll's elite force, but held positions
of command by virtue of their relationship to Croll.
Apart from the three brothers, Channing only knew a

few of the men by name, but he knew *who* they were. All of them had fought in the inter-Burnout wars together, mercenaries for the sheer excitement of it, and their influence and high-tech weaponry had shifted the balance of power enough to spark the all-kingdom truce a few years back. Now Croll and his men had no more battles to fight, but they trained together every weekend, just in case. They considered themselves the first line of defense against a surprise Burnout invasion of the City, something Channing thought a ludicrous possibility. Still, their military-type training would certainly be useful in what was to come.

"This information is not to leave this group," Channing began. "The Earthies will arrive in seven days."

"Seven days?" Rick called out. "That's impossible! They're not due for another half year!"

Channing remained impassive. "We received the first transmission just two hours ago. Zhang?"

Zhang tapped a few commands on his console, then settled back to watch as the main display turned on. A handsome black man in a colorful uniform appeared, seated at a table, fidgeting impatiently, as if he didn't realize that his image was already being transmitted. His muscled frame was impressive, and of course necessary for withstanding the long periods of high acceleration associated with interstellar travel.

After a few seconds of awkward silence, the man began to speak in the lilting, accented English of Earth. Everyone present had been listening to this evolved dialect since Contact, but very few of the linguistic oddities had been picked up by Mandalans. Channing himself had quite a bit of exposure to Earthspeak, but somehow it still managed to sound completely alien.

"People Mandalan. Allow me as the first to send

greetings. I am Captain Peter Simpson of the starship *Mayflower,* and—"

Zhang stopped the recording in midsentence as some of Croll's men stiffened noticeably. He hurried to explain. "The word 'Captain,' of course, originally referred to a military rank. It is simply his title, just as it was our Captain's title."

"But still—" One-Arm George objected.

Zhang cut in. "If you think about it, you'd realize there was no way they could possibly know what the word 'Captain' would mean to us. There are going to be a lot of cultural adjustments to make."

Channing made a mental note that many of Croll's men had strong religious feelings. It was always good to know how people could be reached.

Zhang unfroze Peter Simpson from his awkward between-word pause, and the recording continued: ". . . we are to report happily that we have completed successfully—or completed nearly at that, a journey seventy-five light-years that brought us nearer to light-speed than any other spaceship in history. We should be in orbit around your planet after two weeks, at the point we hope that your leaders will accept our invite for a meal truly exotic in our dining hall onship. I can't promise that you haven't heard of the food that you'll be eating, but you can be sure that you've not ever tasted athing of this like.

"We have, of course, brought many gifts, and well as thirty-three thousand people frozen currently in cryogenics. We realize that this is not an increase insignificant to your population, but we know that Mandala can use all this humanpower. We also have brought stocks wide and varied of animals domestic, which should prove useful enormously."

He paused, sipping a drink that had been resting on

the table. Channing noticed a drop zip down the side of
the glass with remarkable speed, a reminder of the constant high-g deceleration the *Mayflower* was experienc-
ing as it approached Mandala. "There is more much I
have to say, but there will be time later. For now, we
are but eager to arrive and meet you, our neighbors and
companions new. We await anxiously your reply. Simpson out."

After a few moments of silence, Croll was the first to
speak. "Thirty-three thousand people." His voice was
nearly emotionless.

"So they're frozen?" asked one of his men. "And they
don't need food or anything?"

The Minister of Technology spoke up. "Not exactly.
The problem with cryogenics is that no matter how cold
you make someone, their body won't come to a complete stop. Even at absolute zero, quantum tunneling allows chemical reactions to take place at a rate
comparable to a temperature of about 12 Kelvins.
Earth's cryotechnology can only get around this problem
by, in effect, teaching humans how to hibernate. But that
means—"

"Hibernate?" interrupted Rick. "You're going to have
to be a little less technical, I'm afraid."

Croll scoffed at his brother. "C'mon, didn't you take
any Earth bio?"

"What, it's one of those land vertebrate things? Well,
if chickens don't do it, I'm going to have to plead ignorance."

"Think of it as a return to the womb," Riko offered.
"The point is that even though the bodies are stored in
liquid nitrogen, they still haven't come to a complete
halt. That means they have to be given nutrients and
oxygen, through a sort of mechanical umbilical cord.
And that means they can't stay frozen indefinitely. Ac-

tually, their journey has already lasted four years in their reference frame, and that's over half of the safe limit. After that they'd be risking permanent damage."

"What's our population supposed to be by now?" One-Arm George asked. "Based on the original projections, I mean."

Channing nodded gravely. "Over eighty thousand. And that's probably the number they're expecting. I'm not sure they know that they're going to be nearly tripling our population." *And making us the minority,* he added silently.

"And there's not nearly enough food in storage," Zhang pointed out. "We weren't expecting them until after the harvest."

"If they can stay frozen for a while longer, we wouldn't need to thaw everyone at once," added Croll.

Channing tried to suppress a smile at the gross understatement. Croll's men nodded in agreement.

"They're here in one week? Or two?" someone asked. "Didn't he say it was two?"

"Fourteen Earth days," Zhang explained. "Seven and a half of ours."

One-Arm pounded his prosthetic on the table. "This is going to mess up everything!" Channing relaxed and leaned backward, willing to let the debate proceed without his input. Apparently George shared his feelings on the matter, and he was sure they would all come to the correct conclusions about what needed to be done.

"I mean," George continued, "when are we going to deal with the Burnouts now? They might even use the arrival as an excuse to attack!"

Channing's confidence in the group suddenly disappeared. What was George talking about? What did the Burnouts have to do with this?

"That's true," added Rick. "We won't be ready for

Restoration in time. The North Mine Project isn't even finished."

Channing covered his eyes with his hand as Croll's men began discussing the Burnouts, their planned attack, and their renovation of the North Mine as a military base. Was that all these men could think about? He recalled Croll's description of Operation Restoration: a quick raid into the Burnout Kingdoms to knock out the technological base they had been developing over the past few years, forcing them back in their traditional role as a primitive society. It had all seemed rather harmless when the arrival was well in the future, but as of today he couldn't spare any resources for a pointless armed assault.

"Look," interrupted Channing at last, "the Burnouts aren't the ones we need to worry about—"

"Don't be so sure about that, sir." George looked deadly serious. "Ever since the Johnson-Rasta pact they've been making some pretty amazing advances. Giving them access to the Oracle database was obviously a big mistake. From the looks of it they have developed electrical power, mining capabilities, metal processing, and huge food stockpiles. There's even one enormous building, probably half the height of the G.C. Sophisticated weapons are probably well within their capabilities right now. And we know that Burnouts are prone to fighting; it's just a matter of time before they attack us."

Channing had heard these reports a hundred times. He had tried to explain that they were inventing imaginary dangers because no real ones threatened. He had tried to assure them that the Burnouts were simply content to be apart from the City, living their lives in drug-induced bliss. And even the fana wasn't enough for them; lately the Burnouts had been trading food and metals for other drugs. Just a few weeks ago the Rastas had once again increased their order for the nitrous oxide canisters that were sent up in the tradervans. Any society that inhaled that much nitrous simply could not be a threat. And the Oracle Satellite hadn't made a difference for generations; what would be their motivation to build a technological infrastructure now? Apparently Croll's men were so locked into this anti-Burnout mindset that they couldn't grasp any other dangers. Well, it was time to give them a new enemy. A real enemy.

Channing stood up, quickly silencing the conversation with his stare. "Listen to me. The critical issue here is not the Burnouts. It's the impending arrival from Earth. Here we are, about to be invaded—yes, invaded—by thirty-three thousand people we know little to nothing about, and you are worried about a few thousand Burnouts? And it's much worse than it appears. You see, the reason I was late to this meeting was that we just got another message from the *Mayflower*." He produced a datacard, which he fed into his terminal. Zhang looked on quizzically.

George shook his head in confusion. "You mean this Simpson person called back?"

"No. It was someone else."

THE MAN IN THE SECOND TRANSMISSION was seated at the same table that Peter Simpson had broadcast from, but he was not wearing a uniform. His graying hair and lined forehead contrasted with Simpson's, as did his furtive expression.

"This is a transmission unauthorized," he said in a quiet voice. "But you need to know"—he paused, shaking his head—"not all of us agree with the MDC's policy, and some of us thought you should be aware of it.

Hopefully it will all come to nothing, but . . ." His right hand clenched above the tabletop. "Well, there's some concern about the levels of radiation that the *Walt Disney*'s crew members received en route to Mandala. No one expected them to be out so long, and we're still not clear if the meteor collision spread spheromak debris throughout the ship."

He paused for a moment, taking a sip of water from a glass, apparently the same one that Simpson had used in the earlier broadcast. "I'm sure that by now your numbers of mutations serious have dropped to levels normal, but I'm afraid that the Mandala Development Council has mandated that all of the original descendants undergo a genetic exam extensive to ensure that the gene pool is free of any variants potentially dangerous. Unfortunately, the details involving the implementation of this mandate are not pleasant, and several of us question the morality of a sterilization program compulsive."

He cleared his throat and seemed to make eye contact with someone standing off-screen. Nodding briefly to the unseen observer, he hastily concluded, "Hopefully, all of this will only be a nuisance minor, and there won't be any need to carry out these procedures mentioned. But if matters are worse than we have predicted, we thought you should be aware of the MDC's intentions before we arrive. Out."

THE SCREEN WENT BLANK, AND A FULL SEC-ond passed before the conference room exploded into complete pandemonium.

CHAPTER 5

Every time we approach a new star system, my mind fills with possibilities. Possibilities of an end to this endless journey, of course, but it goes beyond that. It's amusing to think of these systems in the framework of the archaic observational quantum mechanics,[9] with every new planet existing in an uncollapsed wave function. Trillions of possible worlds superimposed together, all existing simultaneously until we show up to collapse the wave function by our human observation, choosing just one possibility out of the quantum soup.

A foolish idea, long dismissed by the Madrid Interpretation, I know; yet compelling all the same. And for all practical purposes, the idea has some merit—as far as we're concerned there really are trillions of possibilities, each persisting until we take our first measurements and discover what surprises the universe has in store for us this time.

Some of the crew have expressed the concern that some of these possible planets might harbor intelligent life. Some think it will be more advanced than us, some think less advanced, but always the concern is that it will be hostile. I try to tell them not to worry. God has told me that of all the possible worlds out there, only Earth has intelligent life. Indeed, if there were more than one sufficiently intelligent species on each time-half of the universe, we would have to compete to see which species would become God in the other half. And our God would only care about the winner; the others it would neglect. This is such a horrible possibility I can hardly bear to think of it. No, we are the only one. I am certain.

Note 9. The original interpretation of quantum theory, contending that individual particles could be in more than one quantum state at one time, unless an observation "collapsed" them into a particular reality. Rendered obsolete by the Madrid Time-Symmetric Interpretation of 2017.

The Journal
Year 16, Day 209

KATRINA RANDALL KNELT IN THE MINERAL-poor soil that made up the northeast corner of the Biodome, pulling out the dead remnants of the flamingo plants. *Why wouldn't they grow?* she asked herself. The obvious explanation was useless. After all, no Earth plants could survive in this Mandalan soil either; there wasn't nearly enough potassium. It was a beautifully simple theory, and the only thing that ruined it was the hard fact that flamingos *did* grow in this soil. Up the valley, in the mountains, all over the damn planet. Just not in the lab.

Katrina stood up, feeling the space suit material peel away from the back of her sweaty knees. She understood the contamination issue, but she still hated these bulky outfits. The suit was centuries old, and the weary cooling system had trouble radiating away her own body heat. She mentally sighed before reporting her findings. *The flamingos are all dead again, Trevor. I'm telling you, we're missing something.*

After a few seconds she received a reply. *And I've told you, we can't be missing anything. It's either already in the soil, or the plants don't get it. I bet we're watering them too much again.*

She thought for a moment. *Maybe that's it. Maybe we're not simulating the rain properly. What if the water's a lot richer in minerals than we think?*

Then it would show up in the soil. It's not in the soil, so they just have to make do with what they have.

But . . . She adjusted the suit's defogger, trying to get the condensation off the inside of her faceplate while she pondered the problem. She knew the details of Mandalan biology extremely well, probably better than anyone else on the planet. And she knew these plants couldn't grow without potassium. So where were they getting it? *What about insects? Nightants. Or even chemoflies. It could be some sort of symbiotic relationship that we haven't documented yet.*

Same problem. It would show up in the soil.

Katrina closed her eyes, mentally brainstorming the problem. There must be some unwarranted assumption she was making. She tried tossing out well-known fact after well-known fact, hoping the changes in perspective would give her an idea. And then suddenly something clicked.

But Trevor, if it was insects, it wouldn't have to get into the ground. She started to get excited as the idea made more sense to her. *You're assuming that they can only get the minerals through their roots.*

There was a pause in the conversation, and Katrina started making her way over to the healthy flamingos in the southern plot. She felt like running, but the suit prevented anything but a slow, ambling walk. Finally Trevor responded from his post in the Control Room. *So what are you saying? They soak up bugshit from their stalk?*

Katrina laughed. *Maybe, maybe. I'm going over to look at one of the live ones. I'll let you know if I get any ideas for an experiment.*

Okay, Randall. But I still say we're watering them too much.

She arrived at a small plot of flamingos, named after the Earth bird that she had once seen in a vid. They did look remarkably similar; the dominant photosynthesizing pigment on Mandala was red, and she could see why the Originals had thought that the thick, curved stalk looked like the bird's neck. But right now she was examining the tiny hairlike extensions that grew around the plant in fuzzy rings. She recalled that as a little girl she had never liked them in the wild; they smelled terrible. And that bad smell might be something that insects would come to feed on; most of the mirror-image Mandalan sugars seemed nasty to her Earth senses, so they might be perceived as a tasty treat to native life. But where did the odor come from? That was one disadvantage to being in these suits. Fancy scientific instruments could never make up for the amazing human abilities of touch and smell. She rubbed her gloved hand against the stalk, and the hairs seemed sticky. She could easily find out if it gave off a sugary solution; such details had been well documented over the past two centuries. But if those hairs could act as miniature roots, and if the insects somehow traded minerals for sugar . . .

Trevor. I bet it's the chemoflies. They probably make all sorts of waste products. I'm sure potassium is one of them. Chemoflies were one of the nastier insects on the planet, using the principle of binary chemical weapons to hunt and defend themselves. Their bodies made two different chemicals and stored them in separate sacs, each harmless by itself. But mixed together they became an explosive and toxic substance that could go shooting out the proboscis at targets nearly a half meter away. They were too dangerous to keep in the Biodome, but she knew that they did research on them over in farm science. Maybe they could deliver a hive over here and then set up an experiment in a separate chamber. *Trevor, why don't you see if you can get Mrs. Dodds to send over a chemofly hive. We'll set something up to see if they can keep the flamingos alive.*

Ma . . . the . . . Daddy!

Katrina froze instantly when she heard the faint voice. That had sounded just like . . . She listened for a few moments, but there was nothing else. She slowly backed out of the flamingo plot, careful not to step on any of the seedlings, all the while swiveling her head around to try to pick up the signal. Still nothing.

She tried to look out of the glass window across the main garden, but it was too fogged up from the temperature differential to see anything. It was hard for her to imagine that she was on the cool side of the glass; this month the biosecure area was being kept at a constant 12°C, but the temperature inside her suit felt more like she was exploring the bright side of Hades.

Trevor? she called. *Was that you just now? Or is my son out there with you?*

There was a short pause before she received the response. *Uhh, negative on that, Randall. Nobody out here but us. And we've been off the radio since . . .*

The rest of the transmission was drowned out by the sudden familiar presence of her son. Drew's frantic calls were loud enough to easily overwhelm the control room's message, so she knew Drew had his microwave antenna fully opened. She didn't need an antenna herself; she was already connected to the space suit's outer transceiver, allowing her to communicate with the researchers in the control room.

What's wrong, honey? she asked, not caring what her eavesdropping coworkers would think.

Drew's thoughts were still too wild to express themselves as words, but the overall impression of his feelings was loud and clear: He was afraid that something was going to hurt his father.

Calm down, calm down, darling. Where are you? What's going on? Everything's going to be fine, just calm down, okay? She spun around, trying to get a directional fix.

But . . . Burnouts . . . Daddy . . . he said . . . Drew's torrent of signals began to slow, and individual words started to form out of the mentalese soup. *The Burnouts! They're out in the forest, and they're—*

The signal abruptly cut off. Katrina hesitated for a moment and then ran forward through the flamingo plot, trying to pick up the transmission again.

What's going on, Randall? For an instant she thought the voice was her son, but she recognized Trevor easily enough. She chose to ignore him. Where was Drew? The continued silence brought a horrible tightness to her throat. He must be moving, she realized. Maybe he's trying to run here and went behind a hill or something. She made it to the fogged-up glass and rubbed it with her suited hands, trying to see out. It didn't work; most of the condensation was on the outside.

. . . out there all by himself!!

She leaned against the glass, sighing. *Drew! Is that you? I lost you for a minute there. What are you doing?*

There was a brief pause before he responded. *I'm coming to see you. On Daddy's bike.*

Drew! She smiled despite herself. *You're going to hurt yourself on that enormous thing. Why don't you just wait for me, I'll be home in . . .* She glanced over at the airlock, and then to her unfinished soil samples on the far side of the dome. If she left now, the sterilization requirements and reentry procedures would add another two hours to her workday.

I'm almost there, Mommy. I just crossed the river, and I can see the top of the dome already. Katrina knew he was telling the truth; the foul stench of the nearby soil factory was being broadcast along with Drew's mentalese, and it smelled like they had just set the dung beetles on a new load of chicken manure.

Okay, but be careful on that bike. I just have to finish up in here and then I'll meet you outside, in the main control room. But keep talking to me. Tell me what happened.

There was a brief pause before Drew responded. *Well, Sunit and I got robbed.*

Robbed? Katrina leaned against the glass, trying to calm herself down so she would stop transmitting her worry to her son. *By who? Are you okay?*

Yeah. It was some Burnouts. They took my DC. And Sunit's, too. And my spare cable. And then we got away, but then I was thinking about something Uncle Zeke said—

Zeke? She shook her head, wondering if this was somehow all her brother's fault. Zeke was one of the bigger gossips on the planet, and she could only imagine the scary Burnout stories he might have passed on to her son. *Okay,* she said, sighing, *what did your uncle tell you this time?*

HALF AN HOUR LATER THEY LEFT THE BIO-dome together, Katrina having skipped her usual shower. It was much easier to leave the area than it was to enter; one only had to prevent Earth-based bacteria from getting into the pure Mandalan ecosystem, not the other way around. Now, walking out to the bike racks, she held his small, perfect hand in her own misshapen fingers, marveling at how beautiful it was. Drew had turned out amazingly well, considering the genes she had passed on to him, except, of course, for being deaf and dumb like herself. And given the interesting side effects of the neuroelectrics, that hadn't turned out to be a bad thing at all.

Can I have your bike, Mom? It looks a little smaller. Katrina nodded, and they began the ride home. His thoughts were so peaceful it was hard to imagine that the recent scene had even happened. Before Drew had arrived they had talked at length about the Burnouts; Katrina had managed to convince him that the Burnouts hadn't meant him any harm and wouldn't hurt his father either. She wasn't so sure herself; the story of the encounter scared her more than she'd like to admit. But she had kept a firm lock on her fear, kept it from being transmitted to Drew, so by the time he had arrived at the Biodome his panic had mostly subsided. And now that he was really there beside her, not just a voice in her head, it almost seemed as if the whole incident had just been a figment of her imagination.

So Zeke was making a gun at the forge? she asked

him as they pedaled along. As soon as Drew had arrived at the lab he had been able to retract his antenna, using the regular low-power transmitter to communicate. Of course they could have turned their speakers on instead, but it always felt awkward having her thoughts interpreted electrically, changed into words, broadcast as speech to his transceiver, and then having his computer interpret the sounds as thoughts once again. Talking via microwaves and bypassing the awkward sound system just seemed to make more sense.

Yeah. It was right there on the holosphere. He asked me how I knew what a gun was—

Katrina glanced at him. *It's those Earth vids, isn't it?* She shook her head. *You know, I didn't find out about guns until my last year of school. But why was Zeke making one?*

Drew broadcast some mentalese babble before answering. *For the Prime Minister, I think. Or maybe someone named Crow. He said there was some sort of defense force—*

Croll, corrected Katrina. It had to be Croll. She wondered what Channing's trainer was up to. She should let Paul know that Croll's little militia might be planning an attack on the Burnouts.

No, Mommy, Drew said suddenly. *They're just going to stop a Burnout attack. Zeke said the Burnouts are going to attack and that's why they've stopped fighting each other and started stealing everything instead.*

Katrina winced; her thoughts had been unconsciously broadcast to Drew again. That was one of the few drawbacks of the transceiver system: Drew sometimes heard more than she meant to say. Amusingly enough, that was the one side effect that her husband had foreseen before he designed Drew's transceiver. All the other benefits had come as a big surprise.

Mentalese had actually started out as something they were trying to avoid. When Drew was born with similar mutations to his mother, it was clear that he should be given the same neuroelectric equipment that had worked so well for her. The only question was how the two of them would communicate directly. Paul finally decided to electronically convert their thoughts into microwaves *after* the speech processor had already translated the neural signals into English phonemes. That way Paul could program the system using the standard voice-encryption algorithms, and Katrina and Drew would be able to understand any existing microwave transmissions. This had been convenient, allowing Katrina's co-workers to communicate with her when she was suited-up at work. But the main reason for the decision was so Drew could grow up learning English, not some new mental language that could only be communicated to his mother.

But as it turned out, Drew became bilingual.

They had neglected to take into account one simple fact: The speaker around his neck was limited to audible frequencies, while the language processor was not. As soon as the microwave transmission module was added to their speech systems, a new feedback process began on a high-frequency bandwidth. And the frequency cut-off in the speaker meant that no one else could listen in; it was a completely private communication between Drew and his mother.

The nature of this new communication was a direct result of the neuroelectric technology. Obviously no natural brain module had evolved to control implanted silicon wafers, but portions of the brain were under generic "voluntary" control. Connections to these frontal lobe regions, with the proper feedback loops, could "teach" someone how to mentally control an external device. By the mid-twenty-first century this was already being done with artificial limbs; using an artificial voice was only a logical extension. But no section of the brain was truly unused; fractal connections sprouted everywhere, and Drew's speech control was meshed in with other mental modules. The modules that had the strongest connections to the wafers in Drew's inferior parietal cortex included his sense of smell, spatial perception, and certain emotional states. These connections formed the foundation of a new "mentalese" feedback with his mother. He was able to understand his mother's emotions at a very early age, and even before he had learned to talk he was responding to her on the high-frequency bandwidth of the microwave transmissions.

At first Katrina hadn't even noticed the new level of communication between them. Drew's emotions at that stage in life were fairly straightforward, and there are few things more transparent than an infant's facial expressions. So when Katrina felt fear when her baby was scared, it seemed perfectly natural. It took a long time for her to realize that some of her feelings weren't her own, but were instead being transmitted from her son.

When it finally became obvious what was happening, they made a brief effort to filter out this new level of communication. But the resulting feeling of disconnectedness—both for Katrina and for Drew—was enough to keep them using the new mentalese. Amazingly, it didn't seem to adversely affect how Drew related to other people. Of course he had the usual enunciation difficulties; not having to actually speak meant that he had to learn the large number of phonetic rules that natural speakers were physically constrained to obey. But apart from these normal problems and a slight difficulty reading facial expressions, he interacted with others as if he didn't know that there was any other way to communicate.

There's not going to be a Burnout attack, Katrina said at last. *And don't go around repeating what Uncle Zeke tells you. He's always talking about things like this, but it has never come to anything.*

Drew didn't respond, even on the emotional level, and they finished the ride home in silence. Sunit Bernstein was waiting on the porch as they coasted to a halt.

"Well?" Sunit asked Drew. "Where did you run off to? My parents won't believe me about today. They think I lost my DC."

Drew flipped on his speaker. "Sorry. I was just worried about my dad, after those Burnouts. He left for the Red Valley this morning."

Sunit's eyes widened. "Really? Is he okay?"

"I guess . . ." Drew shrugged and looked at his mother, broadcasting new signs of worry. "I mean, we don't know for sure, but . . ."

Katrina rolled her eyes. "You boys come on inside. We'll talk about it over a snack."

She followed them into the house and warmed up some corn muffins while Drew gulped down two glasses of apple juice.

"So." Katrina looked them over as they started in on the muffins. "Who do you think the Burnouts are, anyway?"

Drew could talk fine with his mouth full, but he kept quiet until Sunit finally answered the question. "They're crazy people. People who left the City 'cause they're crazy and just want to eat fana and fight all the time."

"Yeah, they're all crazy atheists." Drew nodded in agreement.

Katrina smiled. "Even the children?" She could tell by their faces that they hadn't considered the possibility that there might be Burnouts who were their own age. "Some Burnouts have been out there since long before I was born, if you can imagine that. There are lots of kids and grandkids out there now. Even some great-grandkids. And they all have to pitch in to help grow the food, fix the meals, build the cabins. . . . If they were all crazy, then none of that would get done."

Sunit looked puzzled. "I thought they just ate plants and stuff."

Katrina was about to respond, but Drew beat her to it. "No, they have to eat Earth food, just like we do. All the other stuff is . . . backward or something."

Katrina nodded. "That's right. There are a lot of differences between the proteins and sugars on this planet compared to Earth. And even the ones that are similar are all mirror images of the molecules our bodies need. So most of them don't give us any nutrition, and that's why we have to grow the food we brought with us from Earth."

"But Mommy, what about the creamplants?" asked Drew. "I'd never thought about that. And honey and flatfish."

"Bees are from Earth, darling, so honey's fine. But you're right, anyone who tried to live off of flatfish and creamplant would probably starve to death. They're not bad for you, they just don't have much nutrition that we can use. But the point is that the Burnouts need to do a lot to take care of themselves. They don't have electricity, or DCs, or any of the things that make our lives easier."

"My dad thinks they have electricity up there," said Sunit. "And they just pretend like they don't."

"I bet they're tired of working," added Drew. "And so they come down here to steal things. That's why they were in the forest today. Uncle Zeke says—"

Katrina cut him off. "Drew, people are more suspicious than they should be. Especially Zeke. Sure, the Burnouts are different from us. And people tend to think that because they're different it means that they're bad people. But they're both good and bad, just like the rest of us. It sounds like you ran into some of the bad ones, but most of them aren't like that."

"But Mommy, no one from the City ever would have robbed me. Everybody's nice here."

"Not everyone. We have problems just like the Burnouts, and people from the City have done a lot worse things to the Burnouts than they've done to you. A bunch of men even used to go up to the Red Valley and help the Burnouts kill each other, and they'd probably do it again if they could ever find an excuse. So for goodness sake don't tell your uncle Zeke about this. The gossip circles here don't need any more anti-Burnout stories." She looked them over. "All right?"

Drew and Sunit nodded, getting to their feet as they sensed that the lecture had come to an end.

"Now go on outside and have some fun." Katrina gave Drew's hand a quick squeeze. "Dinner's at thirty-four. Sharp." They nodded again and hurried toward the door. Katrina watched them leave, a smile on her face. "And Drew!" she called after them. "Don't worry about your father, please. He'll be back home in a week." And then they were off, running out of the house and into the slowly lengthening shadows of evening.

CHAPTER 6

R. Morales: Bright side of Hades, coming into view now, sir.

CAPTAIN: How many times do I have to tell you? The mission's over, so you can stop calling me "sir"!

R. Morales: Sorry, sir.

CAPTAIN: Funny, Raoul. And what do you mean by "bright side of Hades," anyway? There's actually some light down there?

R. Morales: Well, I just meant the sunlit side. But look—there is a little bit of red. Yeah, it's faint, but you can see it on the screen here. And it's starting to get brighter.

CAPTAIN: Guess it's not as dark a place as we thought.

F. Lumpkin: No, it's as dark as we thought. Darker. Take a look at the spectrum.

R. Morales: Any lines?

F. Lumpkin: Maybe some silicon emission. But it's almost a perfect blackbody. Temperature, 590

K. And it's getting hotter as we get farther from the terminator. We can get a perfect map of the temperature distribution on the surface if we want.

CAPTAIN: Where are all the impact craters?

R. Morales: That's the other strange thing. Sort of reminds me of Jupiter's moon Callisto.

CAPTAIN: In what way?

R. Morales: Well, Callisto does have big impact craters, but very few little ones. And the surface is blacker than it should be, too. Maybe it's the same mechanism here, but more extreme. I mean I see a few possible impact regions, but—

CAPTAIN: Let's land the probe.

F. Lumpkin: What?

CAPTAIN: Let's land it. I want to see what's down there. I thought you said we can do it, Raoul. The gravity well's small enough that we could take off again afterward.

R. Morales: If we want to risk it. This is the last probe we have. And if something goes wrong—

CAPTAIN: What could go wrong? This is an interesting place, Raoul. And I have a feeling we should explore it.

R. Morales: Sir, if you have another one of your feelings, nobody's going to stand in your way.

The Log
Year 27, Day 308.59

IT WAS DUSK BY THE TIME EVERYONE RE-turned. Paul wasn't sure what direction the Burnouts arrived from; one moment only eight of them were sitting around the fire, and the next nearly a hundred people were there, laughing, tapping a beer barrel, crowding around to get warm. A few dozen hovered around a smaller fire in a neighboring pit, but most stayed at the original fire, scrambling to cook their dinner.

Paul kept quiet, listening intently to their conversation, hoping to pick up a clue as to where they had been. A few of them had soot marks on their clothes, which was surprising, and most of them looked pretty tired. Some of the Burnouts simply lay down on the ground and stopped moving, as if they had skipped daysleep altogether. But the conversation offered no clues to what had happened; he only picked up local gossip, food talk, and arrangements for tonight's poker match. A few teenage girls pulled the giant grill over the fire with the clever pulley system, and after a moment it was filled with potatoes, bowls of stew, and even a chicken. Besides humans, chickens were the only land vertebrates on the planet, but that distinction hadn't helped this particular bird; it had been ripped apart and basted with some type of black sauce that made the flames leap up when it dripped into the fire.

"Looks good!" Paul called over to Big Red, who had thrown it on the grill. "What did you put on it?"

At the sound of his voice the background chatter lessened noticeably, and suddenly far too many eyes were focused on him.

"Well, if it isn't the Mish," said Big Red. "Up from the City to do a little spying on us?"

Paul held up his open palms as innocently as he could, but Foz cut in before he could speak. "He's been here with me since he got here, so hold your fana."

Another voice boomed out from the far side of the fire. "Oh, if Foz was keeping an eye on him then I'm sure he don't know a thing!"

Laughter erupted from around the grill. "Yeah," a thin

woman piped up. "No way could he have wandered off with Foz looking after him!"

Most of the hostile looks had disappeared by now, and Paul breathed a sigh of relief that no one was taking the sarcasm seriously. "Well," he began, hoping he wouldn't spoil the good mood, "guess I won't be asking anyone where they went today. Anybody have an extra mug?"

There was a brief hesitation that Paul didn't like at all, but then Big Red starting walking over with his cup, and everything seemed to revert to normal.

"Thanks, Red," Paul said after a sip. "I'm starting to like this stuff better than the City's."

"And a good thing, too." Big Red grinned through his namesake beard. "Or we might not have any respect for you at all!"

Paul laughed, and Big Red turned to leave. "And stop being so paranoid!" he called out after him. "I couldn't care less where everybody was this afternoon." He regretted the lie as soon as he had made it, but Big Red didn't respond. Maybe he hadn't even heard.

He felt someone nudge his shoulder and turned to see Foz holding a mug in one hand and a pair of fana leaves in the other. "Just do what you do, Mish," he said, "and no one will get upset."

Paul smiled, looking down at the fana. "And you just do what *you* do, Foz, and I'll help straighten you out in another hour." Paul sat down again and lay back, watching the Burnouts as they chatted around the crackling fire. He had no idea what was going on around here, but it really wasn't his business.

He had almost managed to convince himself of this when he saw a woman emerge from a cabin. A woman he had never seen before in his entire life.

Quickly he raised his beer mug to hide his face, still

keeping one eye fixed on this mystery person. New people joined the Outpost every year, but they were exclusively City residents who had given up on that life and decided to spend their time dropping fana in the wilderness of the Red Valley. No one from a kingdom would want to join the Outpost if it was the last place on Mandala. But this woman had to be from a kingdom. She was dressed like one of the warriors he had seen in old footage, and as she started to walk in his direction Paul noticed that she had the long, graceful strides of a lifetime Burnout.

Paul had to drop his gaze as somebody intercepted the mystery woman, stopping her with a gesture in the direction of the fire. Paul felt sure that she was being warned about his presence, and indeed when he glanced back up again the woman was quickly walking off in the other direction. Paul watched her go from behind a long sip of beer, and was again startled to see the mystery woman bring a DC up to the side of her face as she disappeared behind another cabin.

He glanced down at his own digital communicator, for a moment sure that someone had stolen it from him, but it was clipped to his belt as always. What could a Kingdom Burnout possibly be doing at the Outpost with a DC? They didn't even work up here. Just to make sure, Paul reached down and casually turned it on, and was floored to see the READY indicator light up. Had the City built a transmitter here in the Red Valley? He quickly keyed Katrina's code, thinking how surprised his wife would be to hear from him, but READY was quickly replaced by ERROR, so he shrugged and flipped the device off. He tried not to be disappointed, telling himself that he knew they didn't work from this valley in the first place. He drained his mug, shooting one more glance across the clearing where the mystery woman had disappeared. Already he was half-wondering if his mind had just invented the whole thing. He shook his head vigorously, got to his feet, and wandered off in search of a refill.

IT WAS ALMOST DARK BY THE TIME HE started the first story, and Paul was feeling rather drunk. He tried to set aside part of his mind to evaluate his performance, but he couldn't concentrate enough to tell if he was slurring his words or not. Not a good sign, he knew.

The crowd was as thin as always, with most of the Burnouts off playing cards or betting on the war beetle fights. But many of the children were there, as well as some regulars and others who were simply too drunk or too lazy to get up and move away from the light of the fire. At the moment, Paul could identify with them completely.

"Let's see," he began. "Has everyone here heard the story of the Accident?"

Groans erupted from most of the audience. "You told us that one the last time you were here," reminded Jave.

"Let's hear a better one," someone else called out.

"A better one?" He slowly surveyed the crowd. "I don't think you all understand the Accident's importance. Noneofyou . . ." He tried again, keeping his words more distinct. "*None* of you would be here right now if it weren't for the Accident. None of you would be alive at all."

"But we all know that one," complained an old woman in the back. "Let's hear something new."

Paul nodded, pulling out his electronic version of Captain's Journal. It had Log capabilities as well, but those literal transcripts from the *Walt Disney*'s recording system were usually overly technical and difficult to read out of context. Even the Journal could be technical, though, and he scanned through his bookmarks, looking for passages with relatively few footnotes. The footnotes were a hotly debated addition to both Journal and Log, but Paul thought that on balance they were a good thing; most people didn't get all the technical details, and the footnotes helped to explain Captain's highly scientific theology.

Finally he found something he thought might work. "Okay. What about the Prevented Accident? That's the third of the Seven Miracles." Nobody seemed to put up an argument, so Paul dove straight into it. "Well, as you should all know by now, the halfway point in any interstellar journey is by far the most dangerous. To start slowing down you have to detach the meteor shield, spin the ship around, and then reattach it, all while zooming along near light-speed. And for those minutes you're at the mercy of whatever happens to be in your path."

"Why didn't they just use radar to see what was there?"

Paul was completely taken aback. He looked up to see the speaker, a middle-aged woman off to the side. Paul knew she wasn't the brightest in the bunch—just three years ago he had explained to her how the seasons worked. And now she was asking about radar? "How do you know anything about that?" he asked.

She just smiled. "I've read a few things."

Paul took another sip of beer. "Well, radar, for those of you who *don't* know, is when you bounce certain kinds of light waves off of whatever happens to be in front of you. In this case it's interstellar dust grains, which Captain called 'meteors.' But when you're traveling at near the speed of light, the radar signal is reflected backward at almost the same speed as the meteor itself! So by the time you see anything way ahead of you, it's already smashing into your ship."

He looked around and was surprised at the number of understanding nods among the adults. Had everyone started downloading physics lectures from Oracle? Maybe there was hope for the Burnouts after all.

"Okay," he continued. "Since you can't use any kind of radar, the only information Captain had about what was in front of him was direct from God himself. So it was all up to him to clear his mind and listen to what God was saying. If he chose wrong . . . Well, you all know about the Accident. And it could have been much worse."

"But the Accident was a good thing," pointed out Jave.

Paul nodded. "Yes, God, in his wisdom, showed our Captain how he could turn disaster into salvation. But that was a very special circumstance. If there had been a meteor impact this time, all of the Originals would have died. And it was up to Captain to keep that from happening. So, as the time approached, Captain went down to his cabin, turned off the lights, and prayed. He asked God when he should turn the ship around and cleared his mind to listen for God's response."

He surveyed the children around him. "And this is something all of you can do," he said, interjecting a little lesson into the story. "God is talking to us all the time, in the only way he can. Through our minds. God's not able to write words on the ground or force you to act in certain ways. He can only put suggestions in human minds, and if you don't listen for it, you might go your whole life without ever finding out what God wants you to do."

A small girl sitting in front, a few years younger than

Drew, raised her hand politely. "Does God talk to chickens, too?"

Paul smiled. He always got the best questions from the kids. "Why, I suppose he could, if he wanted to. They have basically the same brain structure, only smaller. But chickens aren't very smart, and they probably wouldn't listen. God's interested in people because we're the only species who is intelligent enough to survive until the end of the universe."

"What about aliens?" asked a smirking teenager. "They'd have different brains."

Paul shook his head. "There are no intelligent aliens," he said. "God told Captain many times that we are the only intelligent beings in the universe. It's up to us. No aliens are going to step in and do the job for us if we fail."

He lifted the mug to his lips, then thought better of it and lowered it again. "So, Captain was in his cabin, and he couldn't concentrate. It's hard work to talk to God, and for some reason he couldn't seem to do it. Days went by, and still he couldn't understand what God was saying. And the deadline was approaching. If they waited too much longer they wouldn't be able to slow down enough by the time they got to the next star system. And in all this time, there hadn't been a single dangerous meteor impact. So finally Captain decided to just turn the ship around anyway.

"Of course, there were a lot of safety procedures. Everyone had to get into their space suits and gather in the middle of the ship, where it would be the safest. But finally they were all ready, and Captain was about to give the order to begin. Everyone was waiting for him to start, but he didn't say anything. You see, he was trying to give himself one more chance to hear God. And this time he did. God spoke loudly, and Captain suddenly *knew* that it was a bad time to do it. And our Captain listened. They had spent a lot of time getting ready, and someone else might have ignored the feeling that God sent. But Captain understood. He called off the whole procedure. And you know what? Six minutes later they had a class two meteor impact. Not very dangerous with the shield on, but if they had been spinning the ship around, the damage would have been very serious indeed."

"So when did they spin the ship?" asked Jave.

Paul nodded but stayed silent for a moment. In fact, Captain had been unable to get any further divine feelings and had ended up guessing blindly. They spun the ship the next day and got lucky; there were no impacts. Actually, the odds were rather against having a meteor strike in midspin, regardless of when they did it. But that wasn't a very good ending to the story, so Paul only gave a partial answer. "Well, they spun the ship the next day, and everything went smoothly. And everyone thanked God for saving them from an accident."

"Sounds like he just got lucky."

Paul looked up and was surprised to see Foz sitting quietly in the back. Apparently he had recovered from his latest fana trip and had been listening to the whole thing. "Well, Foz," he said, "if you look at it that way, I'd say that Captain had to be the luckiest person in all of recorded history."

Paul made eye contact with his friend, and for a moment he thought he saw a glimmer of understanding, a hint of acceptance. Could Foz finally be coming around? he wondered. Had he finally gotten through to him? But the moment of connection was over before it had really begun; Foz just shrugged, turned away, and wandered off into the darkness.

CHAPTER 7

CAPTAIN: Look at it this way. Say the universe is
a footrace.

J. Hansen: What?

CAPTAIN: The beginning of the race is the Big
Bang, and the end is the Big Crunch. We find
ourselves racing along somewhere not too far
from the start, not too far from the Big Bang.

J. Hansen: Okay, but—

CAPTAIN: Hear me out. We look around at the
other people in the race, and they're all running at their own speed. But we can calculate
backward and discover that at the beginning,
everyone started in the same place.

J. Hansen: But what does that mean? At the Big
Bang the entire universe was all in one place.
That's a—

CAPTAIN: It's just an analogy. I'm just making
an analogy to the low-entropy conditions at the
start of the universe. The important thing is that
a race has initial boundary conditions. Every-

one started at the same time. That doesn't seem too strange, from our perspective. But what would it mean if I told you that the laws of physics meant the race had to be symmetric in time? Not the details, just the overall race structure.

J. Hansen: *I know where you're headed. If it was symmetric in time, there would have to be final boundary conditions, too. All of the racers would have to finish at the same time. But that's ridiculous. That would mean that the runners don't have free will. They're forced to finish together.*

CAPTAIN: *Right. If a runner has two boundary conditions, he's constrained. He can't have free will, at least not all the time. But is there any way to have a race that's symmetric in time without having two boundary conditions on a single runner?*

J. Hansen: *I don't think so. If the runners start together, they have to all finish together. There's no way around it if you want time symmetry.*

CAPTAIN: *But there is! What if the runners who all finish together are entirely different people? What if half of the runners have an initial boundary condition and the other half have a final one? We can end the race however we want, and they can begin the race however they want. Each of us has only one boundary condition, but it's still a symmetric race.*

J. Hansen: *Well . . . maybe. But why wouldn't we see the backward runners from our point in the race?*

CAPTAIN: *We can. But the future-boundary com-*

ponent of the universe can only interact with our past-boundary component on a quantum level, and it turns out that our brains are the perfect detector. The evidence of the other half of the universe is our perception of God.

The Log
Year 11, Day 101.37

"YOU BLOODY SHITHEAD!"

The door had only just closed behind Channing, but the unexpected onslaught made him inadvertently back against it as Zhang came storming across his apartment.

"Goddamn go behind my back?" Suddenly Zhang was there in the foyer, jabbing his finger into Channing's chest. "The comms are *my* baby. Who doctored it? Riko? That meteor-ridden . . ."

Channing hated being on the defensive. Had he thought about it, compared his tall, slim body to Zhang's massive bulk, he would have been more cautious, but his instincts took over and he returned Zhang's fury. "Calm down, dammit!" He shoved Zhang's chest with both hands, and sheer surprise made the big man back up a single step. Channing used the opportunity to slip around him and into the living room. By the time Zhang caught up with him, Channing was settled in Zhang's black foamchair, trying to portray a level of comfort that he didn't feel.

He searched Zhang's angry eyes, trying to decide if he should bluff this one out. Something told him it wouldn't be a good idea. "Okay." He gave Zhang a conciliatory shrug. "How could you tell the second transmission was a fake?"

"How could I tell? It'll be a miracle if nobody else figures it out!" Zhang paced nervously. "Bloody unprofessional, that's what it was. What, you never watch the vids?"

Channing nodded again. "Linguistic errors?"

"Putting it mildly. You misused idioms, your use of possessives was atrocious, and if Earth *did* create a Mandala Development Council, it'd be the CDM, not the MDC!"

Channing shrugged. "That's why we made him an older man. So that you could rationalize any verbal mistakes as being remnants from his youth."

Zhang shook his head in disbelief. "Well, I certainly didn't do any rationalizing, and I don't think—"

"That's because you were sensitized to it. You know I've done things like this before. Croll's men, on the other hand, they won't even think twice. Just because the morph was simple to do doesn't mean that they'd be looking for it. They can't imagine us lying to them like that."

"Don't get too cocky there, Alex. And simple? Maybe that morph should have been simple, but you guys blew it. Who was the model? You?"

"No." Channing frowned.

"Well, you should have done a real body shot and only half-morphed the face and hands. There was a shirt stain that kept disappearing, and when your morphman took that drink of water I saw Simpson's gold cuff link through the glass! And Captain knows I didn't catch everything."

Channing shrugged. "I guess Riko didn't have enough time to make it perfect."

"Riko!" Zhang suddenly seemed infused with a new dose of anger. "It was him! Why the hell are you two going behind my back on this one?"

Channing tried to keep his voice level. "I just thought it would be simpler this way. And it's good to have some feedback like this, even if you are taking it a bit personally."

Zhang's red, sweaty face shook violently. "Don't give me this trash, Alex. You didn't tell me about it because you thought I'd be more likely to go along with your little plan. Well, forget it. I'm seriously considering backing out of the whole thing."

"What?" Channing couldn't quite mask his look of concern. "You can't. Things have gone too far."

"For you, you mean." Zhang took a deep breath and slumped down onto a couch. "But you haven't even figured the whole thing out. I mean, what are you going to tell the public when an entire spaceship fails to show up? And what happens afterward? You just going to leave it in orbit?"

Channing shook his head. "No, that wouldn't work. Someone would eventually notice that we had an extra satellite. I'm working on some other ideas."

"Such as?"

"Well, we could crash it into the moon."

Zhang stared back at him for a few seconds, then suddenly got up and walked across the room to stare out of a window. "You know, of course, that you're completely mad," he said in an unusually quiet voice.

Channing sighed. "Look, Zhang, you know as well as I do that—"

"Thirty-three thousand people, Alex," Zhang interrupted. "Human *beings.*"

"I don't like it any more than you do."

Zhang spun around. "Then dock the damn thing to the *Disney,* for Captain's sake! Or let them fly off to find their own damn planet. But if you're planning to kill *everyone* . . ." He gave a sinister chuckle and turned away again.

They played the silence game for a few minutes, and

Channing finally gave in. Or claimed to, anyway. He managed an apology and promised to keep the *Mayflower* docked to the *Disney* for the foreseeable future. But even as Channing walked out the door he knew that it wasn't a long-term solution, and the lack of a cover story was bothering both of them. At the very least, though, Zhang seemed to still be on board. Hopefully it would last through the week.

And that was supposed to have been the easy encounter. Next he had to go see Croll's men, make sure they all understood what was at stake, and Channing had no idea how they would respond. But they had to know that these weren't just harmless colonists up there. They were people who would ruin this planet with their destructive, Earth-formed ideas. People who would forever alter their peaceful Mandalan society. And, of course, people who were *their* leaders. A few who, if they got their way, would undoubtedly rule them all. Channing, for one, was determined to make sure that did not happen.

CHANNING DECIDED TO VISIT ONE-ARM first, after remembering his reaction to the faked transmission. "Forced sterilization!" George had raved in the conference room, waving his prosthetic in the air. "What right do *they* have to decide?"

But George was much calmer this time around. In some ways Channing was glad; decisions made in the heat of passion never lasted long, and Channing needed this one to last for at least a week.

"It won't hold up," George had calmly explained. "Most of them can't possibly agree with this crazy . . . MDC policy."

Channing inwardly winced at hearing the acronym he

had invented that very morning. Did One-Arm George really not notice the linguistic error that Zhang had pointed out? He moved the conversation along quickly, hoping it would just slip on by. "Don't you see, George," he argued, "Anyone who disagreed with the policy probably wasn't allowed on the ship in the first place. When you're picking a few thousand people out of a planet of seventeen billion. . . ."

George nodded thoughtfully. "But not the frozen settlers. I'm sure they were selected by their bank accounts. And the fact that one of the crew members warned us with that message means that—"

"But he said they were in the minority," Channing interrupted. "And you know all of the settlers are going to look to this Simpson person for leadership. You have to see it from their perspective. And from their perspective the policy could be seen to make some sense."

"I'm sorry, Alex, but any decent person . . ."

"Probably wouldn't be that rich in the first place," finished Channing. "This time around we're not getting the best and brightest that Earth has to offer. This is a completely different group of people than the Originals. And we need to do something about it."

"What can we do? Once they get here they'll have nearly three times as many people as we do!"

Channing cleared his throat. "Not if they never get here."

George looked him straight in the eye, seemed about to speak, then stopped himself for a long, thoughtful moment. Channing stayed silent, too, holding his mental breath. He shouldn't have brought it up so soon. George was about to make his final decision on the matter and they hadn't talked about it for five minutes. But it had slipped out and now anything further that he said would seem like he was applying pressure. He'd have to wait this one out.

Minutes slipped by, and George no longer looked at Channing, but gazed out of his window at the thin crescent moon shining over the blue horizon. Channing's body started to tense up. He had been sitting perfectly still and now he felt the overpowering urge to change his position in the chair. But he did not want to risk the distraction. He sat still and suffered through it.

At long last, George looked down to his prosthetic arm and seemed to slump down into his chair. Channing knew he had won but was careful to keep his mental grin off his face. Another minute passed, and finally George spun around to face him. "I'm listening," he said.

CHANNING HAD BEEN DETERMINED NOT TO make the same mistake with Rick, but looking back at it now, he had definitely overdone it. After a heated hour-long discussion about universal religious beliefs, the atheistic morals of Earth, and the possibility of a Mandalan civil war, his mind was exhausted. Finally, feeling that Rick was leaning in his direction, he detailed his plan for the impending arrival.

"Of course!" Rick had responded. "Why didn't you just say that in the first place?"

Channing allowed himself a long sigh. "You agree?" Apparently Rick took after Croll much more than George did.

"Of course I agree. That's been my inclination right from the start. I'll even pilot the spaceplane for you. I bet we can rig up a quick torpedo system, just in case things turn ugly. Do you think they'll have any weapons of their own?"

Channing was still digesting the fact that he had wasted his best arguments on the wrong brother. "Weapons? On the *Mayflower?* I doubt it. We're not going to need a torpedo. All the action's going to be inside the ship."

Rick shrugged. "Don't be so sure. In case your plan doesn't work out as expected, it's always good to have a backup. I mean, what if one of the crew members escapes the ship?"

"Good point. I hadn't thought of that. But you can't pilot the spaceplane. We're making this look like a regular maintenance mission to the *Walt Disney;* that way no one gets suspicious."

Rick shook his head. "But that's no good. Can we trust the regular pilots? I can fly the thing better than they can, anyway. I still got my license and everything."

"Maybe," Channing said, getting to his feet. Now that his work was done he only wanted to leave. "We could put you in as a last-minute substitution. But there will still be two other astronauts. If we change too many things around, people might take notice."

Rick frowned. "Two regulars? That's a shame. But I'll take care of them. Don't worry."

Channing nodded as he walked to the door, no longer caring what Rick was talking about. "Great. I'll be in touch. Thanks for your support. And you understand—"

"Complete secrecy. You got it."

Channing tipped his hat and hurried to his car. Next stop was the Big Man himself.

CROLL WAS IN HIS PRIVATE TRAINING area in the Cone, using some complicated exercise equipment that he had personally designed. Channing walked across the mat, noticing the dummies hanging on the wall; throwing stars projected from them in high-precision clusters. From the looks of it, Croll hadn't missed once.

"One more," Croll managed in a strained voice. He was benching some obscene amount of weight, the electrodes on his arms helping his muscles with the load that no mere human could have lifted. One time Channing had asked him why he didn't just shock his muscles and leave out the physical weights altogether, but Croll had told him that huge muscles were useless if the body didn't know how to use them; this mixed technique apparently gave him the bulk without losing the coordination.

Channing paced nervously while Croll finished. "So your brothers are both on board. Rick's more excited about it than One-Arm. You're sure the others will listen to the three of you?"

With a loud clang the weight machine released Croll from his workout; he emerged from the device, toweling the sweat off his bald head. "If you got George to sign off, we're all set. Who's dealing with the beer?"

Channing couldn't help from looking around to make sure no one was eavesdropping. "Riko's on it. And Rick wants to pilot the spaceplane."

"Good idea. It'll keep him busy."

"I guess." Channing stretched his neck. "Zhang knew the second transmission was a fake. He thinks some of your men will figure it out."

Croll shrugged. "So what if they do?"

Channing nodded but didn't say anything. Nobody on this planet truly wanted the colonists to arrive, but everyone seemed to have trouble rationalizing a reason to stop them. Well, he was fulfilling that function. He was doing everyone a favor by taking the matter into his own hands, fabricating excuses for the weak of heart. Channing just couldn't figure out why no one wanted to face up to the real danger. Did no one care what happened to this planet? Did no one care that they were about to become a minority among people who had never done a day's worth of hard labor in their lives? He hadn't worked his way from a farmer to Prime Minister only to let these colonists show up and ruin this planet as they had Earth. He just wished everyone would realize this was in their best interests and be a little more supportive.

"Croll," he said at last, "once it's done, people will understand. We won't have to keep it a secret."

Croll smirked. "If you say so." And with that he walked off toward the shower.

"You'll see," Channing called after him. "The City will thank me!" Croll didn't respond, and in a few moments he was gone. "They will thank me," he repeated to himself. Or would they? After all, what people really wanted was to not know about the tough decisions that help shape their lives. Humans had a tough time with guilt, and if saving their planet meant harming others, Channing supposed they'd be happier not knowing the details. Well, if someone had to bear the guilt for what was going to happen, he was the man. Although the majority of Mandala might never find out, Alexander Channing was going to be their savior.

BACK IN HIS SUNROOM, CHANNING LAY ON his couch with an empty beer mug on his chest. The sunset had been beautiful, but now, even before the remaining blue light was fully banished from the horizon, the stars had already filled the sky with their shimmering designs. The moon had set hours ago, and Odin shone brightly through the diamond cone. Channing made a fleeting effort to find Hades, the closest planet to the sun, but he knew that even on the darkest night he would barely be able to see it with his naked eye.

He managed to remember that Hades had been a scientific curiosity, as the planet should have been much brighter than it actually was. However, there hadn't been much speculation on it for many years, so he assumed that Mandala's physicists and chemists had come up with some sort of explanation for its black surface. Suddenly he felt infused with energy, and he sat up straight, thinking furiously. Maybe *that* was the solution. He picked up his DC and keyed Riko.

"Technology here." Riko's voice was formal and steady.

"Riko," began Channing, "I have an idea." He paused to formulate his thoughts. "Now, during the Journey, sometimes Captain swung the ship around a star to slow them down, right?"

"No, sir," came the impassioned voice. "In the star's frame of reference you can't change your energy, just your direction."

Channing frowned. "But I remember . . . they still swung around anyway. Why?"

He heard Riko clear his throat before the response came. "Well, at Tau Ceti, for example, we came in almost normal to the plane of the ecliptic, and there were a couple of planets we wanted to explore. And because Tzengian wells are unstable in a gravitational field, we had to use conventional propulsion in the inner star system, and we wanted to be as efficient as possible. So we came in fairly fast and made a hyperbolic orbit around the star that brought us into the ecliptic."

"The ecliptic . . . that's the plane the planets are in?" Channing made sweeping motions with his hands, trying to envision how that would work. "I think I get it. So if you swing it just right you can just coast away from the sun, right past all the planets that you'd want to explore." He took Riko's silence as an assent, and he nodded to himself. "So is there any conceivable reason why the *Mayflower* would do the same thing?"

Riko spoke after a few moments. "Well, the Earth does lie only thirty-six degrees from this system's normal, but they know exactly where they're going. They don't really need to execute that particular maneuver."

"Okay. But does it make any sense that they might do it anyway?"

"I suppose. If they happened to come in too close to the sun and on the opposite side from Mandala. It might be easier for them to use the sun's gravity rather than change course. But what are you getting at?"

"Well, Hades is a very dark planet, and close to the sun, too. If they came around the sun and found Hades right in their path, they might not be able to change course in time, without the main engines working and all."

"Hmmm. Well, they might be able to swerve around it with their conventional thrusters. It depends on how fast they come in and how soon they notice the planet. But the odds against it are astronomical—literally—and they'd almost certainly see it before they even entered the system."

Channing was getting excited. "But it's possible, right? It's hard to see, and it might be behind the sun from their perspective."

"No. It would never be all the way behind it. But if Hades was on the opposite side, lined up with Mandala, they might not spot it, and a gentle hyperbola around the sun could conceivably set them on a collision course."

"Then that's it! That'll be our cover story! We'll crash it into Hades when we're done, and feed that story to the public!" He was feeling all the awkward parts of his plan click together. "We'll even send out a rescue mission, just to make it look really good and all."

Riko laughed. "No need for that, sir. We lost a probe on the planet shortly after we arrived in this system. It's a very interesting phenomenon; apparently the surface—"

"Riko! I'm not in the mood for another lecture."

There was an uncomfortable silence. "Sure. I was just saying there wouldn't be any survivors."

"Okay, whatever. Just work through the numbers, and figure out the most plausible time that this . . . uh, scenario, could happen."

"That might not be easy. In theory, it would work only if the Sun, Hades, Mandala, and Earth all lay in the same plane. And the trajectory would have to take into account—"

Channing cut him off. "Sure. Don't sweat the details too much. No one will notice if the calculations happen to be a little bit off. And we can probably claim it happened anytime in the next year."

"All right. I'll get to work. Anything else, sir?"

Channing smiled. "No, Riko. That's quite enough for now. Out." He tossed aside the DC and lay back on the couch, somehow discovering a more comfortable position than the one he had been in before. He sighed, closed his eyes, and drifted off into a dreamless sleep.

CHAPTER 8

R. Morales: Touchdown in one minute.

F. Lumpkin: Still not much structure in the spectrum. It's definitely a silicon surface, though. Probably used to be silicon oxide, but maybe the oxygen's been blasted away by the solar wind.

CAPTAIN: But then wouldn't it be more . . . silvery? I've seen pure silicon, and—

R. Morales: Depends on the impurities. And the molecular structure.

F. Lumpkin: Yeah, maybe it's black, just like a giant solar panel.

R. Morales: Thirty seconds.

CAPTAIN: A planet-sized solar panel. Sounds plausible enough. Hey, you think we could run a big extension cord out to Hades? We could stop working on that dam.

F. Lumpkin: Sir! The distances . . . they're so big and they're constantly changing and—

CAPTAIN: I'm kidding, Forrest.

F. Lumpkin: Oh, right. Right. I mean—

R. Morales: Ten seconds.

F. Lumkpin: Hey, look at this!

CAPTAIN: What? I can't see anything.

R. Morales: Five, four . . .

F. Lumpkin: There's some structure in the radiation. I can't quite make it out, but—

R. Morales: Touchdown. Shit!

CAPTAIN: What happened? Where did everything go? My screens are all dark.

R. Morales: Mine, too. Forrest? You got anything? What the hell happened?

F. Lumpkin: I don't know. The probe just stopped transmitting.

CAPTAIN: Why? Did it crash?

F. Lumpkin: I don't think so. Wait a second . . . there, that's the history of the signal level. This is all normal, and then there's this huge noise spike, and then . . .

R. Morales: And then what?

F. Lumpkin: Then nothing.

> *The Log*
> *Year 27, Day 309.87*

PAUL HURRIED DOWN THE OLD MINING trail that led into Mandala City, anxious to be home. The sun wouldn't rise for another hour or two, but the full moon gave off enough light to color the western sky a beautiful deep blue, and he had no trouble seeing the branches and rocks strewn along the trail. Navigating around them, however, was a different matter. Even though his ancestors had evolved on a planet with 28 percent stronger gravity than Mandala, the long downhill trek had hurt his knees, and the effort required to dodge obstacles on the trail was making it worse. He forced his legs onward, despite the pain, until he finally had crossed the eastern drawbridge and was within sight of his small white house.

They lived in a third-generation structure, nearly a century old now, but still modern enough to have an Earthwood frame. The house had its share of problems, most notably the ancient plumbing, but he was happy to live with a few leaks rather than move to one of the new complexes and give up their relative privacy. As it was, being the Eastside preacher already led to enough people dropping by for spontaneous counseling. If he lived in a complex he and Katrina would never have a moment to themselves.

Walking around to the front, he noticed that the bedroom light was on. Apparently Katrina was having trouble sleeping again. After dumping his muddy pack and synboots in the grass, he entered the house to find her reading in bed.

She reached down to enable her speaker as he closed the bedroom door behind him. "Hey, you," she said softly. "What are you doing up at this time of night?"

He shrugged, moving over to her. "Oh, you know. Couldn't sleep so I thought I'd get some reading in."

She nodded. "Yeah, and I just thought that the middle of the night would be a good time to hike over the mountains."

"Hey, watch it." He grinned as he kneeled on the carpet beside the bed. "It's a full moon, you know. And I have a sermon to give."

"I know." She leaned over to give him a hug. "I was expecting you home this . . ." Suddenly she paused, making a face. "Ugggh!" her speaker blared. "Is that you?"

Paul looked startled. "What?"

"That smell!" She rolled away, burying her face in a pillow.

"Sorry!" he said, laughing. "I'll take care of it right away!" She waved him away without coming up to breathe, and he retreated into the bathroom. He had only managed to brush his teeth, though, when he heard some commotion through the door.

"Yes, he's in there," Katrina was saying, and then Drew burst through the bathroom door in his Earth-animal pajamas.

Paul stooped down to give him a hug. Surprisingly, Drew didn't say anything, and after a moment Paul realized that his speaker was turned off. He reached down to flip it on, and Drew's distinctive voice started up in midsentence: ". . . miss you too bad. And I knew you'd be okay, but I'm happy you're home!"

"Well, I knew I'd be okay, too!" Paul gave Katrina a quizzical look through the door, but she just gave him the standard "we'll talk about it later" signal. After a moment Drew relaxed his embrace and led Paul back out to the bedroom. "You didn't smell too bad to me," he was saying.

"Probably because I brushed my teeth."

"Even before that."

"Huh?" It took Paul a moment to figure out what he was talking about. "Oh, that . . . Hey, were you sleeping with your transceiver turned on?"

Katrina gave Drew a stern look, and he responded with an embarrassed grin. "Yeah. I thought you might be home tonight."

Paul smiled. "Well, good." He shot a playful glance at Katrina. "For a moment I thought you could smell me from the other room!"

"I wouldn't have been surprised," Katrina observed.

"Okay, okay." Paul made a show of sniffing his

jacket, although he honestly couldn't tell anything was out of the ordinary. "Hey, are either of you up for a midnight snack? I'm starving."

"Midnight?" Katrina glanced at her watch. "It'll be time to get up in another hour."

"Great. We can have an early breakfast."

Katrina frowned. "Paul, dear. Drew really should . . ."

He looked down at Drew. "Are you going to be able to get back to sleep?"

Drew shook his head vigorously. "I'm wide awake! Honest!"

Katrina sighed. "Okay, okay. But we have absolutely nothing in the fridge." She got out of bed and tightened her bathrobe as she came over to give her husband a kiss on his lips. "Better," she said. "But please, shower first, then food."

THE THREE OF THEM SAT ON THE PATIO, looking out over the south bank of the American. It was a surprisingly warm night for this time of year; Mandala's forty-four-hour day meant that the temperature extremes could be rather severe, but the nearby heat reservoir of the ocean had kept it bearable tonight. The reeds by the shore swayed gently in the fast-moving water, their long moon-shadows playing along the surface as if they were conducting a complex symphony of babbling water and insect beeps. The shiny ripples on the surface flowed out of sight to the west horizon, creating the illusion that the entire river was bound for Asgard, the enormous orange moon that hovered on the edge of the sky.

The moonset was a rare sight. Usually the western cloud cover was fairly heavy, but tonight was perfectly clear. Asgard looked even larger than usual but less bright; only the ice caps still hurt to stare at for too long. The jagged scar of the Valhalla Mountains jutted out directly at them, the peaks seeming to come within a stone's throw of the reddening horizon, Meanwhile, the eastern sky was brightening with light of its own as the sunrise approached. Already some of the eastern clouds were turning a dull red underneath, and shortly the entire sky would be filled with color, lit up by the sun and moon's light mingling together across the edge of the planet.

"So, has Shari had her baby yet?" Katrina asked between sips of her hot cider.

"Any day now, it looks like. Although . . ." He made a face. "Did you know that Burnouts take it during childbirth?"

"Huh?"

"Fana." He poured some soy milk on his cereal, shaking his head.

Katrina shrugged, glancing over at Drew. He followed her gaze; their son was watching the moon through half-closed eyes, leaning his elbows on the table to support his head. Apparently he wasn't that awake after all. "Fana?" she replied. "Well, it actually doesn't sound like that bad of an idea."

"Trina! For Captain's sake . . ."

She grinned. "Calm down, dear. If you were the one who had to go through with it you might not be so disapproving."

Paul rolled his eyes. "Still . . ." A brief movement from Drew distracted him, and he noticed that his son had turned his speaker off. Only his speaker, though, and not his transceiver. He sighed as he realized what that meant. Of course he *had* been gone for a whole week, and the two of them would be used to talking to each other in mentalese, but he still didn't like them having these private conversations. It was bad enough, knowing the speech that he heard was only part of their many-leveled communication. But right now he was being deliberately shut out. Paul focused on eating his cereal, trying to not get upset so soon after arriving home.

Katrina was looking at him seriously. "I hope you're going to talk about your week with the Burnouts in your sermon tomorrow."

"Why? What about?"

Katrina paused for a moment, looking out at her son. "Well, Drew . . ." She broke off with a concerned look on her face.

Paul lowered his gaze to his cereal. "Drew's saying something?"

"What?"

"I was just wondering what Drew was saying to you right now. His speaker's off, if you can't tell."

Katrina exhaled sharply. "Honestly, Paul. Haven't we gone over this enough?"

"What—you're not . . . ?"

"No! I *always* turn off my transmitter when you're around. We really don't need to hash this out anymore, okay?" She stood up and started to clear off the table. "Sometimes you can be so . . ." She stepped into the kitchen without completing her sentence.

"So . . . what?" He grabbed his cider and followed her inside. "I'm sorry, Trina, I'm just a little tired and . . . and all week long I've been thinking about that argument from before I left. I guess I was just a little bit . . ."

"Paranoid," she finished for him. Paul sighed and sat down at the kitchen table as she quietly put everything away. The silence grew uncomfortable, and Paul looked back outside at Drew. His son had unfurled his antenna dish and was pointing it toward the setting moon. "Don't tell me he's still doing *that*," Paul said to his wife. "I thought he quit praying to the moon after I had that talk with him."

Katrina shrugged. "I catch him doing it every now and then. I think he just doesn't want us to know about it." Paul sighed loudly, and Katrina turned toward him with a smile. "What's the matter, dear? Didn't you used to think it was kind of cute?"

"Well, at first. Both us of did. But he's seven years old now! I hope I've taught him well enough that he knows God doesn't sit on the moon with a microwave transmitter waiting to chat with him at his convenience!"

"He's just trying to be like his father."

A quick laugh escaped his lips. "Oh, you see me out there, hooking up electronic equipment so I can talk to God?"

"Come on, Paul. He doesn't see it like that. You're always saying that God has a direct line of communication with you, how he *tells* you things. He's just taking you a little too literally."

"Well, why didn't he take me literally when I told him he doesn't need his antenna to pray?"

Katrina shook her head and sat down across from her husband. "It's not that big of a deal. I don't know why this makes you so upset. You designed that thing for him in the first place, and now you have a fit any time he actually uses it!"

He covered his eyes with his hand. "Look . . . I don't know why we're arguing about this. I just can't imagine that you approve of this . . . behavior."

"There's nothing wrong with our son having a healthy imagination. But I don't want you lecturing him about it without even understanding where he's coming from."

Paul looked out the window at Drew. His son seemed more awake now; Drew's eyes were open and he was sitting straight up. "Well," he said, "I'm really glad

you're able to *understand* him so much better than me."
After a silent moment he shook his head. "I'm sorry. I
didn't need to say that."

She shrugged. "No, you didn't need to."

They were silent for a long while, looking at each
other across the table. Paul was the first to speak. "Have
I mentioned how nice it is to be back home?"

His wife shook her head slowly, her eyes sad. She
reached out to touch his arm.

"Well, it is." He took her awkward hand into his own,
keeping his gaze fixed on her beautiful brown eyes.
"And I love you, too." He smiled as she nodded in response, and he suddenly remembered what she had said
earlier. "So why did you say I should give my sermon
on the Burnouts?"

It took her a moment to respond. "Last week, the day
you left, Drew got robbed by a group of Burnouts."

"Robbed?"

She nodded. "They took his DC and spare cable. I got
him some more cable, but the DC will be a while."

Paul looked at his son through the kitchen window.
"He's okay, though. Isn't he?"

"Yeah, but that wasn't all." She closed the fridge and
came over to join him at the table. "He thought you were
in danger out there. That they might try to hurt you. He
got really upset, rode your bike over to the Biodome and
everything."

Paul widened his eyes. "What in the galaxy gave him
that idea?"

"Well . . ." Katrina leaned back into her chair, adjusting her transceiver. "Let me tell you, Paul, there's a lot
of hostility building up around here. Toward the Burnouts, I mean. Apparently lots of DCs are turning up
missing. There've been reports of all sorts of thefts
around Eastside, and people say they've seen Burnouts

sneaking around at night. And Drew was talking to Zeke and heard some of the really bad rumors. He just got worried about you up at the Outpost. Anyway, I just thought it would be a good idea if you talked about them in your sermon tonight. It might calm a lot of people down."

"I'm not so sure." He thought about the strange activity he had witnessed over the past week. Every morning most of the Burnouts would disappear, not returning until just before sundown, skipping even daysleep. He never did find out what they were doing, but he did know they weren't coming over here to the City; they went in the other direction, toward the kingdoms. If he didn't know any better he would have thought that they were helping out with some of the new construction projects down there. But Outpost members would never trade their labor for anything; as far as he knew those Burnouts didn't want anything except to be left alone. Although there was that woman with the DC the night he arrived . . . "I don't know, dear. Things are a little strange up there these days."

"What do you mean? Is there something—"

"Mommy! Daddy! They're here!" Drew came rushing in through the door, carrying his fully extended antenna.

Paul looked out the window, expecting to see somebody. "Who? Who's here?"

"Them . . . the . . . the Earthies!" However sleepy he had been before, he was wide awake now.

Katrina moved to get up. "What!? You saw them land?"

"No, no . . . they just got here, up, up there." He pointed out the window at the sky. "They're stopped next to the *Walt Disney!* But they're here!"

Paul beckoned his son over. "Drew. How do you know they're here?"

Drew paused, apparently not certain what to say. Finally he lowered his eyes to the floor. "God told me."

With a sigh, Paul reached down and hit the button to collapse his son's antenna. Then he lifted Drew onto his lap and put his arms around him. Katrina looked on with a concerned smile.

"Drew," he began, "do you remember that talk we had? When we talked about your . . . praying?"

Drew nodded enthusiastically. "But Daddy, you don't understand. . . ."

Paul exchanged a brief glance with Katrina. "Listen, Drew. I know you've been hiding this from me, doing this praying when I'm not around. And you don't need to hide that. I don't mind it at all, okay? All I mind is that you think you're talking to God. The real God doesn't talk to you in words. He works with ideas and instincts, guiding you toward the right decisions without telling you what to do. And you have to do your listening, and praying, on the inside. To talk to God properly you have to close your eyes, shut off your speaker, and yes, turn off your transceiver, too. Now, you can keep talking to the moon, or whatever you were doing out there, but you need to come up with a new name for whoever it is you're talking to. Because it's not God up there. Okay?"

Drew seemed about to respond, but his speaker remained silent. After glancing at his mother's impassive face, he looked at the ground and emitted a few nonsense syllables.

"Don't mutter, Drew," said Katrina. "Tell Daddy what you think."

He looked up at Paul with a weak smile. "I'm sorry. I know you're right. I won't do it anymore."

The reply was a little too conciliatory, and he searched his son's eyes, trying to tell if he was holding anything back. One problem with his microwave system is that it had made Drew an excellent liar; many of his usual facial clues were instead transmitted over his high-frequency mentalese. And because Katrina wasn't listening in on that bandwidth at the moment, she couldn't help decipher it. But there wasn't a trace of sadness or regret in those large brown eyes of his, and Paul wanted to believe that this really would be the end of it.

"Okay, Drew," he said. "You know you don't have to stop altogether, right? Just keep in mind what's real and what's not."

"All right." Drew hopped down from his lap, and had almost left the room when he turned around. "Daddy?"

"Yes?"

Drew looked down at his shoes. "If the Earthies *do* get here tomorrow . . . then will you believe me?"

"Drew! I thought . . ." Paul trailed off at the sight of Katrina's glare. Rubbing his forehead in frustration, he watched Drew, still standing bashfully in the doorway. "Okay, Drew. If they get here tomorrow I'll believe you. But if they don't, will you please stop this?"

"Good!" Drew seemed to perk up; he smiled and turned to leave again.

"Do we have a deal?" Paul called out after him. He didn't turn around, but Paul saw him nodding his head as he walked down the hallway. "I guess that's a yes," he remarked to Katrina. She didn't respond, and he looked over to see her cryptic smile. "What? Was that what you had in mind?"

She shook her head. "A little better. But . . ." Her smile broadened into a big, mischievous grin. "But what are you going to do if they *do* show up tomorrow?"

Paul shrugged. "They're not due until fall, right? I think I'm pretty safe." He paused for a second, considering. "Well, maybe he does know something we don't . . ." Suddenly his face lit up with amused alarm. "Wait—did something happen while I was gone? Are they really coming tomorrow?"

There was a brief moment of silence, and then suddenly Katrina was laughing so hard that tears came to her eyes. "You . . . you should see the look on your face."

Paul started to laugh himself. "Am I being ridiculous?"

"And you're giving us far too much credit," Katrina said, wiping her eyes. "I wish we had come up with something like that . . . but I haven't heard anything. Who knows, though? Maybe he is talking to someone with that contraption. Do you think he can listen in on Zhang and the communication gang over at Interferometry? They'd probably be the first to know."

Paul considered it for a moment, then shook his head. "No, most of the Earth transmissions are on totally different wavelengths. The radio messages are lower frequencies, and the laser pulses are much higher."

Katrina nodded. "Well, I figured he couldn't hear any of that. But I meant that maybe he's picking up on some DC talk or something."

"No, DC transmissions are coded for particular people. Maybe there are some things he could be listening to, like the comms you use at work, but I'm not going to worry about it too much unless that ship shows up. Then I'd have to figure out the explanation."

"That's just like you, Paul," Katrina said playfully. "Always leaving yourself an out. What's Drew going to think if you have to renege on your half of the deal?"

"Hey, you're the one who got me thinking about it."

Katrina smiled. "No, I was just thinking. I mean, if by some stretch of the imagination he really was talking to God, he'd still probably never be able to convince his poor, obstinate father."

Paul shook his head, the smile disappearing from his face. "Trust me on this one, Trina. If he was talking directly to God, we'd know."

CHAPTER 9

Sometimes I still find myself wondering why any
of us ever consented to set foot on this spaceship.
Here we are, trying to spread the human race to
another star system before we've even put a permanent base on Mars! Now we are traveling an
Earth-Mars distance every subjective second, and
if the past eighteen years have taught me anything,
they have taught me that humankind was not yet
ready for this great leap.

But I bought the story as readily as everyone
else. As soon as we heard the news from the Ven-
ture expedition[98] everyone thought that the standard exobiology theories had been proven correct.
If life could exist on those suboptimal planets, it
would be everywhere, right? All we had to do was
get to a sunlike star and we'd find a habitable
planet, a completely new world where we could
start over. That was the hook, and I was as eager
to believe it as the greedy multinationals. But I

wasn't looking to send waves of ultrarich citizens to a new planet. I wanted to go.

But was there honestly no time for a probe mission before they sent this colony ship? Did we have to fulfill both duties? True, the private investment was already very long-term, much more long-term than they were used to, but didn't our lives count for something? I know they considered the probability of failure. Otherwise why would we have enough fuel on board to take us to twice as many systems as we've already explored? And if they did know, why didn't they supply us with thicker shielding from the galaxy's radiation? Even though we're careful to avoid a Doppler upshift by not traveling in the galactic plane, I have the feeling that the years of Lorentz-boosted cosmic rays have already taken a serious toll. I suppose the answers to these questions are obvious when we look at our corporate sponsors in a more cynical light, but did I truly never entertain these thoughts while I was still on Earth?

Note 98. The first extrasolar mission that discovered life on two planets orbiting Alpha Centauri A. Several species on Eureka have begun the oxygenation of the atmosphere via an analog to photosynthesis. If current trends continue unaided, Eureka could be habitable in roughly 250 million years.

> *The Journal*
> *Year 19, Day 2*

THE *MAYFLOWER* WAS AWESOME. CHANNING gazed at it through a window in the spaceplane, remembering how large the *Walt Disney* had seemed during his off-planet field trip as a teenager; now it was a mere afternote, resting humbly beside the newer ship, as if in frozen orbit about it.

Of course, the comparison was somewhat unfair. The *Walt Disney* had been cannibalized extensively, refined metal being an extremely precious commodity for those first few years. Now, with three of the six original hextants completely removed, the ship looked like a long, trapezoidal greenhouse, the flat underneath section sprouting awkward girders where the other half of the ship had been gradually severed. The cone-shaped meteor shield also was gone; in a remarkable maneuver, Captain had managed to send it down from orbit in one piece, and now it formed the outer frame of the Government Cone itself. Support beams for mounting the shield stuck out from both ends of the old ship, adding to its unfinished look. Channing had never actually seen it with its shield attached, but after a lifetime of reenactment vids and paintings it seemed like the *Walt Disney* had lost an essential part of its character.

On one of these ends—the end Channing knew to be the "bottom" of the ship—scars from the Accident were plainly visible. The outer shielding bulged around the exit puncture, the metal frame bent as if an enormous pressure still lurked within the ship. Channing almost imagined that he could see the tiny black hole where the meteor had punched its way out of the hull. Behind that hole, he knew, lay the remnants of Spheromak B, a twisted wreck of a fusion reactor destroyed by a tiny speck of interstellar dust. After the intervening years, the radiation levels would be down to tolerable levels, but there was no point in a salvage operation now. Spheromak B, along with Spheromak F on the opposite side, would remain up here in orbit, a silent memorial of the

Accident that had guided Captain to the beautiful blue planet that stretched beneath them.

The *Mayflower* was in much better shape. It was actually two different ships bound side by side, both of them relics from the Tzengian Revolution. Each one of them was a scaled-up version of the *Walt Disney,* nearly twice the diameter and more than three times as long. Both had remained in Earth orbit for decades, not fully completed until Earth had received word of their arrival. Then, in a sudden burst of activity, many modifications had been made, including construction of additional decks that filled the empty space between the two ships. What made it look so much larger than the *Disney,* however, was the fact that it had two meteor shields, pointing in opposite directions. Because the *Mayflower* was so much wider than the *Disney,* the buckysteel cones had to be proportionally longer as well. As a result, the combined length of the shields was longer than the rest of the body, making the ship look like some sort of enormous throwing weapon, a weapon aimed at the heart of the planet below. As if to add to the effect, the sun glinted menacingly off of the metallic structure, lighting it up like a hot poker.

The shuttle drew closer to the *Mayflower,* and soon the *Disney* had passed out of Channing's field of view. The original plan had been for them to board the new ship via the *Disney,* but someone had realized that the *Disney*'s only functioning airlock would be taken up by their shuttle, and the *Mayflower* would be unable to join the proposed three-ship union. Instead, in a move that made Channing very uneasy, they were docking with the Earthies directly.

"Is that torpedo operational?" he asked Croll.

"Yeah, we got one shot loaded up. But we won't have

to use it. This is going to go a whole lot smoother than you think."

Right, he told himself. *Just relax. The plan will work. It has to.* He took a deep breath and leaned back into his seat, feeling the flexible material stiffen with the increased pressure, just as it had during takeoff.

THE SPACEPLANE SHUTTLE HAD LEFT MAN-dala in broad daylight, from the airfield south of the City. Channing had decided that although few people would see or hear a nighttime launch, those who did would undoubtedly be suspicious. Instead, in an attempt to be as inconspicuous as possible, he made the expedition as obvious as he could. Preventive maintenance—based on "newfound fears" that the *Walt Disney* was slowly falling apart—was the stated reason for this mission, announced on the weekly government report days beforehand. And the plan seemed to be working; as far as Channing could tell, few were paying it any attention at all.

But some precautions still needed to be taken. Had anyone suspected that Channing was on board, or that even a single minister was involved, the speculation would have quickly spiraled out of control. As it was, all four of them—Channing, Riko, Zhang, and Croll—had secretly boarded the shuttle the night before. They had managed to catch a couple of hours of nightsleep before being joined by Rick and the other crew members at dawn. George had decided not to come; he was afraid of flying, and they'd need him on the ground when the mission was over to smuggle them off the plane. Channing wasn't going to spend another night in here if he could help it.

The two regular astronauts were surprised, to say the

least, but Riko filled them in on the situation: The Earthies had arrived early, and it was to remain a secret for now. Channing eyed the pilots warily, wondering if he could trust them, but they soon disappeared into the cabin with Rick. A few more minutes and they were ready to go. After a final cursory equipment check, they found themselves speeding down the runway toward the rising sun.

Spaceplanes were an inherently safer way of getting into orbit, at least compared to the ancient multi- and single-stage rockets. It boggled Channing's mind that any of the first astronauts had ever been willing to board those primitive towers of liquid explosives. True, that was on Earth, where the greater mass and size of the planet made rockets more of a necessity. Mandala was more suited for spaceplanes; here a low-orbital velocity was less than Mach 17, only slightly above the capability of the plane's scramjet engines. The final acceleration was still done with rockets, but the total energy needed was relatively small, and the plane was kept under much tighter control.

After liftoff Channing pressed his nose against the glass and looked down at his City, stretched out like a checkered quilt along the glittering America. Then they burst through a layer of low-altitude clouds and he turned his attention to the sky, watching the blue deepen to violet as they reached that perfect altitude where the scramjets had just enough air pressure to ignite. They continued to climb higher as they picked up speed, the on-board computers now handling the exact trajectory, compensating for the local pressure instabilities that occurred where the atmosphere encountered the interface of space. Soon stars began to appear, pinpoints of untwinkling light against the ultimate black backdrop. Then, in a surprising instant, the stars all went out. A full three seconds went by until he realized the autopaquer had darkened his window when his side of the shuttle rolled over to face the sun. With a sigh he pulled his head back into his seat's molded depression and turned his thoughts to the *Mayflower*.

The question all boiled down to whether they suspected. Channing had gone over it many times in his own mind, but it always came down to not having enough information, not enough understanding of the Earthies. And how could he? Earth was totally alien to him, and a few years of vids didn't make up for centuries of isolation.

Warning alarms went off, and ten seconds later the rockets fired, pushing him forcibly back into his seat. He tried to turn to look out of the window again, but his neck muscles were too weak to fight the acceleration. After a brief effort he simply closed his eyes. The final boost into orbit always seemed longer than the actual twenty seconds of burn time, but at last the force stopped, the vibrations ended, and the sudden sensation of falling caused Channing's stomach to leap up into his throat. The transition to zero g hadn't bothered him in the past, but this time he felt like he was about to throw up. He quickly opened his eyes and focused on a small spot on the seat in front of him until the sensation passed.

"You okay over there?" It was Zhang, from across the aisle. "Want some beer?"

"Shut up." He almost lost it again when a small booster engine fired, pushing him to one side. He tightened his lips and rode it out.

"Hey, Riko, I think the mightiest man on the planet is about to float his food!"

Riko was his usual deadpan. "You mean he's going to vomit?"

"Yeah, the no-g blow! The Technicolor satellite. He's gonna launch his lunch into—"

"Zhang!" Channing finally found his voice, though he kept his gaze fixed straight ahead. "I'm in *no* mood."

BY THE TIME THEY BEGAN THE DOCKING procedure with the *Mayflower,* Channing was feeling better but still not ready to take Riko's special Communion Juice.

"If I can't keep it down, do we have any extra?"

Riko shook his head, offering the small vial one more time. "You'd better keep it down."

Croll and Zhang had already finished theirs, but Riko was waiting to drink it with him. Channing nodded and grabbed the vial. "Okay. Let's do this." He popped open the valve with his thumb and made a toasting gesture. "To Mandala." Riko nodded, and they both downed the drink in one gulp. Channing took a moment to make sure his stomach was accepting the liquid, and turned to find Zhang looking at him. "Not a word, Zhang. Not a word."

Zhang shrugged and propelled himself toward the front hatch. "I think we're ready to go. Shall we go face the Earthies?"

Croll rolled his neck around in slow circles. "I'm ready." He reached down to unfasten the case of beer.

Channing nodded. "Then I guess we're ready, too. Shall we—"

The cabin door opened, and one of the pilots stepped out. It wasn't Rick; Channing saw him through the door, still seated at the controls. He tried to remember this man's name but failed completely. "Uhh," the pilot stammered. "Mr. Minister . . . Ministers . . . we're, ah, we're docked."

"Well?" Channing motioned toward the door.

The pilot wordlessly showed them through to the airlock. Croll, Zhang, and Riko floated in behind Channing, pulling themselves along by the numerous
handholds. The pilot then retreated to the cockpit, sealing the hatch behind them. Rick had been given strict
instructions, but Channing suddenly felt very uneasy
leaving them behind. If things went bad, would they
leave to save their own skins?

A rush of air interrupted his thoughts, and he looked
down to see Riko opening the hatch. Almost immediately a strange stale smell filled the air, and Channing
involuntarily began coughing. *They're gassing us!* was
his first thought. But after a few breaths he realized that
it was just their air; sealed and recycled for four years,
it was bound to smell poorly.

"Hello down there!" a voice echoed. They looked
around at each other, not sure whether to respond. After
a moment Channing pulled himself over to the hatch.
"I'm going first," he whispered. He made the attempt to
lower himself into the hole, but after a few futile moments of trying to pull himself down the ladder with his
feet a laugh erupted from below.

"You indeed haven't done this before, have you?
Climb up! Up!"

Up? Finally Channing realized what they were saying,
and tried to perform a midair somersault to change his
orientation. He only pushed himself away from the
hatch, however, and Croll had to stop him from flying
across the airlock. Finally he got into position and
looked through. Peter Simpson, the man who called himself Captain, looked back at him with a broad, white
smile. Channing forced a grin in return, and began
climbing toward him, ready to face his greatest enemy.

*   *   *

"DON'T BE EMBARRASSED!" SIMPSON CLAP-
ped him on the back, a mighty blow that would have
sent him spinning across the room had he not been shaking hands with some of the others. "Why, after this journey here, I've forgotten my training oh-g as well!"

"Yes, well . . ." Channing tried to compose himself as
the other ministers joined him in the spacious airlock.
"We don't get up here much. Few come up more than
once."

"No program space?" He arched his bushy eyebrows.
"Interesting."

Channing looked questioningly at Zhang, who had
just begun the round of introductions. "He said that
there's no space program," Zhang explained. "It's not
that hard to understand."

"Ahh, perhaps I should introduce myself," said a
voice, and Channing looked up to see a boy floating
directly above him. No, not a boy, he corrected himself.
A midget.

"Yes," said Simpson, moving away from the entrance
hatch. "This is Samuel Zagala, one of our doctors and
also a sociolinguist. Expert twenty-first century, actually."

Channing smiled and shook hands for the dozenth
time, this time stretching upward to do so. "Very nice
to meet you."

"And it's amazing to meet you." He used Channing's
handshake to pull himself down into the group. "Over
one hundred and fifty years of isolation and no percep-
tible vowel change? Really, quite remarkable." He
lacked the usual Earthy accent; clearly he was making
an effort to make them feel comfortable, and Channing
immediately became suspicious. There was no getting a
word in edgewise, however, as the little man continued
to chatter, floating at eye level to avoid any height dis-

crepancy. "As you must know, there have been many inflection shifts popularized in your absence, and most of our models predicted larger changes up here. But perhaps punctuated equilibrium doesn't apply—evolution has often turned out to be a difficult analog to linguistics, after all. Are there old tapes or vids that children are regularly exposed to? Really, it's all just quite amazing."

Channing took a breath and tried to shift mental gears. Whatever scenarios he had imagined, being questioned by midgets about his planet's linguistic history was not one of them. The noise level in the *Mayflower*'s airlock was building, and the acoustics were terrible. Several men were questioning Zhang about his redweave shirt, and Riko was already in deep conversation with a young woman about technical specifications of the big colony ship. Channing's ears started to buzz, and he was starting to feel nauseous again when Simpson raised his hands.

"People, people! Please!" He gave Channing an apologetic smile. "It's been a long time since we've talked to others, so we don't want to overwhelm you right off. And it's cramped a bit in here. Why don't we start the tour? Samuel?"

Channing's forced smile slipped a little bit. *A tour? What did they have planned for us, anyway? How long is this going to take?* He cleared his throat. "Uh, Mr. Simpson, I thought . . . I thought we were invited up here for a meal. . . . Maybe we'd all get better acquainted sitting around a table."

Simpson slapped him on the back again, and this time Channing *did* start floating away. "And we will, we will! And it may be nearly eve for us, but it's morning for you, no? And we are not the hosts ungracious who would force on you a meal large so early! Samuel, let's begin in control main."

"All right. Follow me, gentlemen." The little man pushed on a pair of shoulders, sending him out of the mass of floating bodies, and after a quick course correction off of a wall he disappeared through an open doorway.

Everyone else began to follow at a slower pace. As Channing awkwardly pulled himself along, he found himself envying the small man, with his compact form and small inertial mass. As it was, he had to continually push off others to keep himself from soaring to the far end of the room. Suddenly Simpson himself was at his side, walking along normally and offering a hand. Surprised, Channing looked down to notice his black magnetic boots.

"Hey, where can I get a pair of those?"

"Ah, yes, indeed they would be useful." He smiled broadly, and Channing resisted the sudden urge to punch his white teeth out. "Perhaps we can find you some in control. Before me?"

It took him a moment to understand. "No, no. After *you*." He motioned toward the exit. "I'll catch up."

IT WASN'T UNTIL HE STRAPPED ON HIS boots that he really started taking a look around. The main control room was mostly done in green, except for the white flatscreens on the walls. Fixed-position chairs sat in front of multiple computer consoles, and several large glass spheres decorated the center, presumably some sort of holodisplay. The floor gave slightly under his feet, and he would have thought it was some sort of plastic cushioning were it not for the fact that his magnetic boots were attracted to it.

". . . only twenty people to run the whole thing," Samuel was saying. "Which turned out to be an overestimate—only two of the twelve spheromaks needed minor repairs, and most of the time we were bored out of our skullbones."

Channing smirked at the midget's mistaken idiom, but his smile quickly disappeared after catching sight of the flatscreen over the door he had just entered. It was not white, like the others; instead an overhead shot of Mandala City filled the screen. The Government Cone sat in the exact center of the picture, and were it not for the one-way glass windows, he would have been able to see directly into his apartment at the apex. It was a live picture, and the magnification was able to resolve small groups of people biking and walking around the city—a view much like the one he enjoyed from his apartment.

Channing's blood began to boil. He couldn't explain his reaction, but that screen, the knowledge that they were watching *his* City, nearly caused him to fly into a rage. Trying to maintain control, he spied Croll standing quietly against a wall and started to make his way over to him. Walking in the boots, however, was not nearly as easy as Simpson had made it look, and by the time he reached Croll, his shins were already sore.

"I can't handle this, Croll. We have to get this over with. Soon. How long is our Communion Juice good for, anyway? I'm the only one who's used it before, and I'm worried I may have built up some sort of resistance or something."

Croll barely shrugged. "Relax. In through the nose, out through the mouth. Calm yourself down." Croll looked very relaxed himself, except for his blue eyes, which where alertly scanning the room.

"Yes, you're right. I know you're right. I just . . ." Channing turned around again to look at the image of his City, and saw the midget floating over in their direction. "Not this guy again," Channing muttered.

"Tell me," Samuel began, even before he made it all the way across the control room. "Your forty-four-hour day. We tried adjusting to it after we left Earth, but it made us tired all the time, and some of us got really depressed. I know you've dealt with it all of your life, but is that still a problem here?"

Channing inhaled sharply through his nose. "You tried two shifts of twenty-two, I bet."

Samuel nodded. "It wasn't so bad at first, but when we added the light cues and made it hot every other morning—"

"That's not the way to do it. We sleep much longer at night than we do during the day. Daysleep is only a few hours, and most people do okay that way. Some people do still get synched out—depressed, like you said—and we have Earthrooms where you can go recover, spend a week at twenty-four."

"Wow." Samuel shook his head. "I can't believe that works. Conventional wisdom says that alternating short-long sleep cycles is really bad for you."

Channing shrugged. "So, is this the whole tour? I'm getting a little hungry." Actually, food was the last thing he wanted, but they had to get to that table soon or he was going to lose it. He decided a little lie wouldn't hurt. "One of our biggest meals is morning breakfast, and we skipped it to come up here. So anything you could do to move us along . . ."

"Sure, but . . ." Samuel pointed back at Riko, deep in conversation with Peter Simpson. "I just heard the Technology Minister ask to see life support. Think you can make it through that?"

*   *   *

NINETY MINUTES AND FOUR STOPS LATER, it was all Channing could do to keep his anxiety off his face. Each time that he had tried to pull Riko away he was calmly reminded that this tour would be the only information they would get about the ship. After dinner, things would be changed forever. Channing tried to explain that the technical information didn't matter, that this tour didn't matter, the only thing that mattered was ending it now before something went wrong. But with Riko hanging on every word, the Earthies couldn't seem to resist showing off their home for the past four years. Both Zhang and Croll seemed strangely subdued, and they quietly followed Riko and Simpson around the ship, visiting the spheromaks, the cryotanks, and now one of the twelve engine rooms.

Channing had to admit that this last stop was interesting, but still, he wondered, why did Riko want to know all these details? Perhaps crashing the ship into Hades was more complicated than he realized, or perhaps he was just being scientifically curious. Whatever the reason, they seemed to be giving Riko very long answers to all of his questions.

Thinking that it might make the time go by faster, Channing tried to focus on the conversation. "You're still using adaptive plasma optics?" Riko was asking.

"Yes, but look. No final parabola. We use a grating parabolic to recompress, focus, and sweep the pulse. It must sweep, of course, to launch the wells upward with some velocity initial."

Riko looked stunned. "Does that work? How many orders of control do you need on the plasma grating?"

Channing looked through the glass into the laser room; pulses of white light scattered from a table full of mirrors and lenses. White light? Weren't all lasers one particular color? He frowned, trying to remember an old lecture on high-power, short-pulse lasers. Like computers, he knew, peak laser power had improved at an exponential rate for a long time. But one of the tricks involved having many different laser frequencies that were all amplified separately and then merged together with giant gratings. Maybe this laser had so many frequencies that it looked white.

"These are some of the amplifiers," Simpson was saying. "Liquid quantum dot lasing medium. And we form the final plasma compression grating by interfering these two beams, here."

As they continued to prattle on about details of the laser, Channing walked over to an observation window. The only windows in these interstellar spacecraft were on the inside, looking into the engine tubes that ran up into the center of the ship. Channing peered into the vacuum and saw the outline of the diamond cone in the center. It looked to be the same size as the one in his apartment, but it was hard to be sure without a reference. He pressed his forehead against the glass, trying to see some stars down below; all he saw was blackness. After a moment he remembered that this ship had *double* meteor shields, and one of them would be covering up the engine tubes underneath. He frowned. That meant that as the ship accelerated upward, the laser-produced Tzengian Wells would smash into the shield.

"Mr. Simpson," he said, interrupting some talk about the attosecond oscillators, "how can this work with a meteor shield on the back of the ship? Don't the wells need somewhere to go?"

The big man smiled. "Indeed, you are interested in these things. But it was the same on your *Walt Disney*. The wells need to be stripped and dissolved as they pass, down there by the superconductors." He pointed down through the window, but Channing stubbornly shook his head.

Channing snorted. "No, it's not the same. The *Walt Disney* had only one meteor shield, so the wells could just go flying out the back of the ship."

"Only when the ship's accelerating," said Riko. "When it's slowing down you have to spin the ship around, and then the meteor shield is covering up the bottom, just like this one. They figured out the well stripping way back in—"

"Thank you, Riko," Channing snapped. He turned away, shouting mental curses as he headed for the entrance.

Simpson called after him, his voice soothing and annoying all at once. "Mr. Minister . . . perhaps you would like to eat now? We can continue this at a time later."

Finally. Channing tried not to look too relieved, but he was sure he didn't succeed. "That would be good," he carefully responded. "I am very hungry."

ZERO GRAVITY, THOUGHT CHANNING, MADE for an interesting mix of what was necessary and what was habit. There they were, sitting around the banquet table with Velcro strips to keep them in their chairs. And why? There were no weary legs to rest up here; floating in front of the table would be just as comfortable, if not more so. Even the concept of a dinner table suddenly seemed ridiculous. The plates and cups all had to be secured from floating away, and most of the food was encased in plastic, making the silverware completely useless. He imagined that if humans weren't so stubborn in their ways they might be floating around a transparent dinner sphere, all partaking from a common central food source via tubes and other bizarre eating devices. Instead they were locked into traditions that were painfully inadequate for the current situation.

The original plan had been to wait until after dinner, but Channing couldn't take this stress for another minute. As soon as everyone was at the table he unfastened himself from his seat and produced the beer.

"I know that you probably have your own drinks, but we wanted to bring up a Mandalan specialty to welcome you. Individual bottles of our finest local beer."

"Beer?" Samuel shook his head. "You brought hops from Earth?"

Channing allowed himself a smile. "Not hops. Redhops. And local grains. They're all native."

Simpson nodded. "With sugars Mandalan, you must have yeast native as well? But then we humans do not get drunk on the alcohol-inverse, no?"

"Fortunately for us," Riko said, "alcohol is nonchiral, so it doesn't matter which planet's chemistry it comes from. And yes, we do have native yeasts that are very different from Earth's but still produce the same important result."

"Well, you must let us try," Simpson said. "Though this is indeed a way long to come for a drink novel!"

Indeed, thought Channing as he took a small bottle and began passing around the basket, *it was a very long journey for merely a drink.* He counted eighteen Earthies at the table and figured the other two must be in the kitchen. That fact was just starting to make him nervous when another one got up to leave. He glanced over at Croll, but he didn't look concerned at all. Channing nearly said something, but just then all three of the missing crew reappeared and helped themselves to a bottle of beer each. He breathed a quick sigh of relief that Croll had been right; as predicted, none of them had wanted to miss the first toast.

At last the basket had made it around the large table, and Simpson raised his still-sealed bottle. "A chink," he said.

"A toast," corrected Samuel.

"A toast, then. A toast to friends new, to lands new, to possibilities and dreams."

"To dreams," echoed Channing, and then popped open the cap with his teeth, feeling the beer squirt into his mouth with the sudden drop in pressure. He grimaced at the bitter taste, watching the others do the same. It was a shame they couldn't try the real beer; the fana that had been laced in these bottles had destroyed the complex textures, leaving only the harsh taste of Communion.

Compliments began to be uttered, no doubt completely out of politeness. Channing looked around, trying to tell if everyone had drunk, but without gravity it was impossible to tell if the bottles were full. Very soon he would find out. And he would find out if the Communion Juice was still working inside of him, ready to counteract the effects of the fana. The existence of such an antidote was not widely known on Mandala, and Channing meant to keep it that way. Riko had developed it for him years ago as a way to keep his wits about him during the annual Communion service. He had been too nervous about what he might say under the influence of fana, and the thought of pretending to talk to God in such a state seemed very dangerous indeed. But with the juice, he was able to put on a great show every year, ranting and raving, yelling and screaming, working the hallucinogenic crowd like little children, all without losing control himself.

"Very interesting," Simpson was saying. He took another sip. "You know, I think I can feel it already—"

He looked up suddenly, staring directly at Channing.

Did he suspect? Did he know? Channing felt fear well up inside of him. Channing couldn't tell if he was starting to hallucinate, or if Simpson's eyes were actually *talking* to him, saying that he understood, that he knew why it had to happen, saying he was sorry it had to be this way. Then the gaze wavered, and Simpson hesitantly pushed himself away from the table, turning toward the exit.

"What the—" someone said, and at that moment chaos broke out.

THE NEXT FEW MINUTES SEEMED LIKE HE was trapped inside of a twenty-first-century neosurreal theater. Crimson color splashed on Simpson's forehead, splashing musical notes across his white suit, his Cheshire smile disappearing behind the table like a slowly setting moon. Croll was asleep in his chair, perfectly still except for his dozens of fingers, busy firing weapons that sounded like cellos and making the far side of the table fold in on itself like a Klein bottle. Zhang was shouting, his red face floating several feet above his body, shooting forth a sour smell while he said *Stop!* but Croll didn't, and the music got louder and louder until the room was so bright that Channing had to hold his breath. Multiple midgets flew across the floor and into a gaping mouth on the far side of the room. *Escape!* sang Riko, and the mouth turned into a wall of clouds and then Croll was gone and the room grew quiet except for the grainy textures seeping out of Zhang's eyes and the dozen miniature volcanoes spewing their zero-gravity lava up into the thickening air.

It's over, he thought to himself. *We did it.*

CHAPTER 10

[class 5 meteor impact]

W. Baxter: Dammit!

A. Ryutov: Plasma dumped. Will! Grab your—

W. Baxter: Whoa. Shit. Hey, slide me a vac, some-body. I got a floater here.

A. Samuel: Will! How many times do I have to tell you? It doesn't matter how long it's been since we've lost thrust, you still have to keep your drinks—

A. Ryutov: Quiet! The Autos aren't working. We're off a—no, two degrees already! Will, don't just float there!

W. Baxter: Throw me something, then! I'm stuck center!

A. Samuel: I'm coming. . . .

W. Baxter: Oof. Hey, watch the . . . [crash]

CAPTAIN: You two doing a reenactment of the collision? How're the cones?

A. Ryutov: Captain on the bridge. Sir, looks like a class five. Don't know about the cones, no *hazards lit anyway, but the stabilizers still haven't fired, and—*

CAPTAIN: *Lieutenant, who's at your post? If this is another cluster—*

W. Baxter: *On my way, sir. Sorry, I was—*

CAPTAIN: *Just get us straightened out. Anything exposed?*

A. Ryutov: *F and a piece of A, stern. We just passed five degrees.*

CAPTAIN: *Why didn't the alarm sound, then?*

A. Ryutov: *Uh . . . I don't—*

CAPTAIN: *Manually, then! Just hit the whole ship, close the airlocks. And get us straight! Full page. Attention, crew. Hextants F and A are outside the shield, I repeat, outside the meteor shield's shadow. Evacuate or suit up immediately. We could be in another cluster. Captain out.*

W. Baxter: *Thrusters firing, sir. Approaching safety zone.*

CAPTAIN: *Just don't panic and overcompensate. Alice, get me a visual on the cones. Which ones were on-well during the collision?*

A. Ryutov: *C, E, and F. Primarily C.*

CAPTAIN: *C . . . damn. Same side as the meteor. Oh, there. It looks okay, huh? Good. . . . How about a rest mass check?*

A. Ryutov: *Not until after—*

CAPTAIN: *Right. How are we, Will?*

W. Baxter. *Down to two degrees, sir. Shall I cancel the alarm?*

CAPTAIN: *No! Not until we're at normal for a full minute.*

W. Baxter: *Okay. No need to yell, sir.*

CAPTAIN: *Lieutenant, I spent the first two—no,*

don't look at me. Get this thing normal! I spent
the first two years of this leg agonizing about
the nine hundred and seventy-five seconds it
takes to flip this ship around. I can handle
that—only because I know we have no choice.
But if you think I'm going to accept one addi-
tional moment outside our shield's shadow,
you're quite mistaken. Don't shrug this off,
Will. And it won't happen again. And what is
this? Somebody get a vac and clean up this
juice before it floats into a vent! Honestly!

A. Samuel: Right on it, sir.

CAPTAIN: Okay, Alice. After we're stable, cancel
the alarms and then scan the diamonds. And
find out what's wrong with the computer!

A. Ryutov: It's strange, sir. It used to be able to
handle that sort of jolt.

CAPTAIN: Before eighteen years of radiation, you
mean. It's killing us, Alice. This space is killing
us.

The Log
Year 18, Day 171.72

SAMUEL DIDN'T DRINK THE BEER FOR REA-
sons that he didn't fully understand. He enjoyed a drink
as much as anyone; no scary drunk experiences or alcoholic parents marred his past. And like all of the other
crew members, he had put up with the dry policy of the
Mayflower for the past five years, looking forward to the
day where he could get thoroughly flitzed on the new
world of Mandala. He had wanted a drink very badly
indeed. He was also curious; a fundamentally new kind
of alcoholic beverage was being offered to him, something that hadn't come along on Earth for hundreds of

years, and he couldn't wait to find out what it tasted like.

But still, he didn't drink.

At one time he had been very suspicious of what sort of society they would encounter here on Mandala. The science of closed-group interactions had come a long way in the past two hundred years, and it was widely accepted that the original planners of the *Walt Disney* mission had made some very serious errors. At the top of the list was the near-exclusive selection of secular humanists for the crew. Human beings were naturally spiritual, the Evopsych argument now went, so it was impossible to have a stable society without some organized religion. Most of Earth's sociologists believed that a mystical religion would have emerged on Mandala, giving them an Eastern-like philosophy that didn't conflict with their technical background.

Samuel disagreed. To him, the lack of religion could be counterbalanced by another, stabilizing factor. After all, this group was not some broad segment of society; they were scientists and descendants of scientists. What use had they for a God when they had already performed a feat like star travel? Instead, Samuel theorized, their society would stabilize around the knowledge that they were a special group; out of the billions of people in the universe, they were the only ones who had left Earth for good.

Independence would be an important theme, thought Samuel. They had accomplished everything on their own, without help, advice, or even casual contact with their home planet. Modern enlightenment aside, human nature tended to look at societies in an "Us" vs. "Them" framework, and there was no doubt that anyone from Earth would be squarely in the "Them" category. Samuel foresaw a potential for some serious conflict, and as a result he had been one of the major proponents for a more cautious Contact.

But over the course of the five-year journey, filled with boring drills and endless card games, his opinions had changed. Indeed, why would any group of humans *not* welcome them? There they were, traveling seventy-five light-years at fantastic expense, bringing free labor, new resources, and advanced technology, all of which would improve their lives. He not only convinced himself that there was nothing to worry about, he also forgot that he had had so many reservations in the first place. It had been a very gradual shift in his thinking, and he had not recognized the large net effect until the moment Peter Simpson had raised the bottle to his lips.

His desire to drink along with everyone else was so powerful, so automatic, that his old suspicions surfaced instantly, almost as if they had never left. And suddenly he *noticed*. He noticed the way that the bald man's eyes were on fire, darting from person to person to watch everyone drink while not partaking himself. He noticed the nervousness in the Prime Minister's voice, the way his fingers trembled with excitement or trepidation. He noticed the collective breath held by all four Mandalans when everyone raised their bottles and drank. And he noticed the open kitchen doorway, only five feet from the end of the makeshift banquet table.

After faking a long sip of the beer, he pretended to lower himself back into his seat, but continued his slow motion downward, and by the time the shooting began he was fully underneath the table. Even after hearing the first shots, he still couldn't bring himself to believe it was really happening. That they would come up to *kill* them! Not to give warnings, not to state demands, but to take them by surprise and kill them! Even his worst fears had not included this scenario.

But when blood started to float underneath the table, he sprang into action. He was not wearing magnetic boots, so he grabbed a leg of the table and launched himself, mere inches above the floor, toward the kitchen. The gunfire got louder as he passed in front of the bald man's seat, but he only pushed off of another leg to increase his speed, and then another. By the time he emerged from underneath the end of the table he was traveling fast, but not fast enough.

Quick shouts informed him that he had been spotted, but his momentum left him little choice but to continue. He torpedoed through the door and into the kitchen, expecting to be shot from behind at any moment. He spun himself by swatting at the floor and pushed off the row of cabinets with his legs. His lower body overrotated, but the maneuver managed to send him behind the zero-g oven and toward the main exit.

Facing backward now, he saw the bald man emerge through the doorway just before the oven blocked his view. He was wearing magnetic boots, Samuel noticed, which would slow him down. He had seen people try to run in them, and it aiways failed miserably. But still, in a few moments the bald man would round the corner, and then it'd be all over.

He pushed off of the frame of the exit as he passed into the central hallway, all the while thinking furiously. There were no weapons on board that he knew of, and that meant that he had to hide. But where? The cryotanks seemed to offer the best chance; the huge, cramped area would be ideal to lay low in, depending on how persistent they would be in tracking him down.

Then he mentally smacked his forehead. *Of course* they would be persistent. After what had just happened in there, they couldn't afford to leave anyone alive. It didn't matter where he hid; they would find him even-

tually. If he barricaded himself somewhere they would
either force their way in or post a guard until he starved
to death. So he had to escape. He had to get into one of
the shuttle planes that would be capable of landing on
Mandala. The fact that he had no idea how to pilot one
of them didn't bother him at the moment; he knew that
was his only chance.

Approaching the end of the hallway, he swiveled his
legs in front of him and braced for the impact. There
were three ways to go: A closed hatch lay directly in
his path, and two open doors to the right and left led to
different stairways. He wanted to go straight, but he decided he didn't have time to open the hatch and would
have to settle for a roundabout route. But the collision
surprised him; the hatch gave way and he tumbled
through, smacking the top of his head on the frame in
the process. His momentum carried him forward, and
the hatch rebounded off of the wall, slamming shut
in the nick of time. A sudden burst of noise told him
that the bald man had rounded the corner and was firing
at him. Samuel wanted to go back and lock the hatch
shut, but he was already too far away to change direction
now. *The bullets aren't coming through the metal,* Samuel thought, and was momentarily glad that they hadn't
been so shortsighted as to bring up weapons that could
pierce the hull of the ship. *That's the last thing you have
to worry about,* he thought, trying to grab one of the
overhead handholds to correct his course. He was still
moving a little too fast, but on the third try he caught
one and propelled himself to the right.

I'm going to make it, he thought. *I really am.* The
airlock to the main shuttle lay just ahead, and he kicked
off of a final wall. He caught himself on the hatch and
immediately pushed it open, revealing a pitch-black
room. *Damn.* He frantically searched for the light

switch, pressed it on, and then threw himself inside the airlock. But just as he passed through the threshold he remembered the safety mechanisms; the opposite hatch wouldn't open unless this one was closed.

No! He tried to rotate in midair, grabbing backward, but it was too late; he found himself soaring across the center of the airlock. He would have to go back and shut it. After what seemed like forever he hit the far wall and pushed off again, listening to the sound of the approaching magnetic boots echoing outside. Finally he reached the hatch and pushed it closed, again just in time; the bald man pulled into view with a pair of long strides, and started in his direction just as the door slammed shut. Samuel quickly set the locking levers, hoping that the bald man wouldn't discover how to unlock the hatch from the outside.

Shots were fired on the far side, but Samuel knew he was safe behind the door. In fact, the bullets didn't even sound like they were hitting the hatch. One more time he pushed himself across the room, faster than before, but he had just left the wall when he noticed the hissing noise.

What? Stopping himself on the far hatch, he jabbed the release button, but nothing happened. He tugged on the door for a moment, but it was still locked shut. Suddenly he noticed the change of pressure in his ears and started to panic. *He's pumping out the air!* He knew that the safety mechanisms wouldn't release the locks unless the pressure was the same on both sides of the hatch. Frantically he searched the controls, and when he saw the emergency release lever he didn't hesitate. He smashed open the plastic cover with his elbow and yanked the lever down so hard that his body rose up in the opposite direction. Finally he heard a click, and the light on the release button turned on. *It's open!* He pulled on the hatch, but for some reason it still wouldn't move. Shifting his short legs to get better leverage, he straddled the hatch, pulling one more time. It didn't budge.

He cleared his ears to compensate for the changing pressure. His heart was beating overtime and he felt short of breath; he had no idea how long it would be until he lost consciousness or exploded. *Anything but death by vacuum,* he thought desperately. He double-checked that the hatch was unlocked. Assuming the shuttle was up to air, the drop in pressure in the airlock should be pushing on the hatch from the other side, popping it open even without any assistance on his part. *Unless . . .*

He glanced around the room, his gaze finally freezing on the digital pressure gauge on the side wall; it read 1.42 SAs. *1.4 Ship Atmospheres? And rising? The bald man was filling the airlock, not emptying it!* He returned his attention to the hatch, pulling with all his might. With every second, more pressure was pushing against the door, sealing it shut. He cleared his ears two more times, straining even though he knew it was already too late. A quick glance told him it was up to an Earth atmosphere, nearly two times usual ship pressure. He quickly did a mental calculation; even taking into account the pressure on the opposite side, there still was more than half a kilogram pushing on each square centimeter of the large hatch. The total force was now more than he could possibly lift. Nodding pointlessly to himself, he pushed back across the airlock, toward the pressure control station.

It didn't take him long to discover that the electronics weren't operating correctly at all. He pushed the touch-screen in the correct location a dozen times, but the pressure menu never came up. Instead the screen flickered on and off, as if power surges were plaguing the computer.

"How are you feeling in there?" The voice sounded dull and lifeless through the steel hatch. "That was quite a chase you led me on."

Samuel took a deep breath. "Why? Why did you have to do this?"

Hollow laughter echoed through the airlock. "Good. You are in there. For a moment I thought you might have escaped." The voice fell silent, replaced by the harsh sound of metal scraping on metal.

Samuel thought furiously, knowing that convincing this man to spare him was his only chance. "You've killed everyone else, right? I'm the only one left. I'm the only one who knows how to run this ship. You can let me out. I'm small and I wouldn't be dangerous. You can keep me under armed guard, and I won't try anything, honest. If you kill me you'll never be able to use this ship on your own. Please."

Laughter again. "Save it. And besides, this door is never opening again, ever. I just jammed the gears, and you won't be getting out of there without a blowtorch."

"Then get a blowtorch! You can't afford to lose me!"

"Hey, sounds like the pressure's really getting to you!" Hollow laughter. "Actually, I just blasted the controls and it started filling up the airlock all by itself. Pretty funny, huh? Says here you're at three ship atmospheres already. I wonder how you'll die. Probably your lungs just won't be strong enough to breathe after a while. Or the pressure might start pinching shut your arteries. Or maybe your skull will implode. Wish I could watch."

Samuel cleared his ears again, not responding. Clearly this man was not one to reason with. He glanced up at the large vents in the ceiling, wondering how high the pressure could rise. The air might be coming from a low-volume tank, which would mean that it should empty out before too long. But if it was connected to the atmosphere generators in life support, the only limiting factor would be the pressure that the air was stored at down there. He didn't know what that pressure was, but he guessed that he wouldn't live long enough to find out. He glanced at the still-rising pressure gauge: 3.8, 3.9, 4.0. Had it slowed? He thought so, but he couldn't be sure.

The bald man spoke again. "Well, while you're having fun in there, I think I'm going to head back and help mop up. I'll be back to check on you, so don't go anywhere."

For the first time Samuel carefully looked around the airlock, trying to find something that might give him an idea. A pair of space suits hung in the corner, useless without their helmets, but two cabinets sat behind them and he pushed his way over in that direction. Pulling one open, his heart leaped when he saw a set of tools, and he started rooting through them furiously. Screwdrivers, a tap and die set, Allen wrenches, pliers, files, and tape measures all went flying up behind him until his fingers finally closed around a set of drill bits. He had to release this pressure and quickly. But where was the drill itself? Apparently it had been taken elsewhere.

After a final check in the first cabinet, he opened the other one. No drill. He was about to slam the cabinet door when he spotted a battery-operated screwdriver sitting on the bottom shelf.

Feeling a burst of hope, he pulled it out and spun the Phillips head a few times to verify that the batteries weren't dead. It didn't turn very fast, but it worked. He briefly experimented with the drill bits, seeing if they would fit in the device, but they were made by different companies and looked totally incompatible. If he wanted to drill a hole, he'd have to use the screwdriver head and that would take hours or even days. He held it up to read the markings; at least it was diamond-coated and wouldn't wear away before he could finish. Moving back to the entrance hatch, he looped his arm through the handle to give himself some leverage. *Here goes nothing,* he thought, flipping on the driver and pushing the tip against the neighboring stainless steel wall.

CHAPTER 11

Raoul is convinced we lost the probe to a huge electrical pulse. That's the only thing that could have explained all the noise spikes, he thinks. It almost makes sense. After all, weren't we talking about the surface of Hades being a giant solar panel? The photoelectric effect from the sunlight could certainly have supplied the necessary energy. But what could have held the voltage difference?

As Forrest pointed out, even though the legs of the probe were metallic, for there to have been any current there must have been a voltage across them. He doesn't think that was possible. I suggested that maybe one of the legs landed on something that wasn't silicon, but he assures me that the spectral data don't allow that possibility. Raoul is now looking into more complicated voltage mechanisms, like surface auroras.

The way he explained it to me, surface auroras are like the regular auroras we have here on Man-

*dala, except that Hades doesn't have an iono-
sphere, so the current has to be drawn through the
surface of the planet. I suppose the magnetic field
lines need to be linked somewhere, so in theory
that would create voltages across the semiconducting surface. Except, no matter what the planetary field, it doesn't seem possible that we could
get the necessary voltages over just a few meters.
I still don't understand what happened.*

*Maybe the only way we'll ever figure it out is
to rescue the probe. We're not even considering it
for the time being; we could build another for a
fraction of the cost. But maybe one day, just to
satisfy our curiosity, we'll go back to see what
happened. With no atmosphere to corrode it, I
suppose it'll still be there thousands of years from
now. I hope it won't take that long to unravel this
mystery, but who knows? Perhaps there are some
mysteries that just aren't meant to be unraveled.*

The Journal
Year 27, Day 310

DREW FIDGETED WITH THE PRAYER BOOK,
wishing that he hadn't come to church at all. He felt like
several hundred eyes were watching the back of his
head, making sure he didn't misbehave in his front-row
seat. The front row was reserved for the family of the
preacher as well as for the leaders of the planet, but
although some days it was fun to sit next to those very
important people, today he was all by himself. Even
Mommy had stayed at home. He didn't dare turn around
to see who was watching him; instead he forced himself
to focus on Daddy, standing before the model *Walt Disney* that hung in the front of the church. He was

dressed in the usual uniform, one of the actual work outfits of the Originals, and he looked extremely serious.

The ceremony began with a minute of silence for the two astronauts who had died earlier that day. Drew bowed his head along with everyone else, again wondering why he had come to church. After his behavior that afternoon, he had nearly been forced to stay home with Mommy. Daddy had finally relented at the last minute, mostly because Drew hadn't missed church in years.

ALL DAY LONG DREW HAD BEEN UNABLE TO concentrate on anything, waiting breathlessly for the announcement that he knew was coming, the announcement that the Earthies had arrived. Finally he would be able to prove to Daddy that he *was* talking to God, that he wasn't just making it up. With no school today he had spent all morning watching the news station, even though most of the time they showed only incomprehensible Earth programs. After what seemed like forever he went to bed for daysleep, but was far too excited to get any rest. He kept expecting someone to come bursting through the door with the big news, saying that the Earthies had finally arrived. And when he finally heard the sonic boom, he leaped out of bed, only to find out that it was merely the spaceplane returning from a scheduled maintenance mission.

That had nearly drove him crazy. He *knew* the Earthies were here. Why were they waiting to announce it? His mother had eventually calmed him down, and then he spent a good part of the afternoon watching the news again, sure that one of the astronauts would have seen the ship when they were up there working on the *Walt Disney.* Even if the Earthies had a broken transmitter, he knew the new ship could be *seen,* and last night the two ships had been right next to each other. God himself had shown him a picture of the spaceships, and the fact that no one else seemed to know about it was driving him crazy.

Finally the real news had come on, talking about the astronauts who had just landed. Apparently there had been an explosion in the middle of some routine welding, and two of the three pilots had been killed. The only survivor, a person named Rick who had only been added to the mission at the last minute, told his story with watery eyes, describing how he had been unable to retrieve the bodies. He had been forced to bring the spaceplane down all by himself, and had nearly crashed into the ocean. He didn't say anything about the Earthies, other spaceships, or anything out of the ordinary at all.

Drew nearly started yelling at the image on the flatscreen, but the real threat of being sent to his room for the rest of the day made him try to keep his head. He mentally reviewed what he knew: The Earthies had arrived in their big spaceship sometime last night, no one seemed to know about them, and now two people were dead, two astronauts who had just been up in orbit. There was only one way that he could make sense of everything, and he didn't like that explanation at all. Neither did his parents, and he nearly got sent to his room anyway for just voicing his ideas.

"This is a real tragedy!" Daddy had yelled at him. "You should have a little sympathy for their families instead of trying to think of horrible things like that!"

"But what if they *were* murdered by the Earthies?" Drew asked. "Shouldn't we try to find out?"

Daddy only glared at him after that, and Mommy didn't respond either. Finally he ran into his room, slammed the door, and shoved his face into his pillow to try to stop the tears.

* * *

THE MINUTE OF SILENCE HAD ENDED, AND
Daddy began reading a passage from the Journal, the
old story about Captain breaking up the fight in the control room. Drew had heard it a dozen times, and he
pulled his doodle page out of his back pocket, keeping
it down low so no one else would see it. He unfolded
the clear fabric on top of the prayer book, smearing out
the wrinkles and then pinching the corner to erase some
random color blotches from the surface. Then, presented
with a clear page, he pulled out a toothpick that he kept
for such occasions and started drawing. He didn't even
know what he was making at first, but after he noticed
that he had unconsciously set the background to black,
he knew exactly what he was doing. He poked the color
table, selected silver as his primary, and began drawing
the spaceship that God had showed to him that morning.

"History," Daddy was saying, "has seen thousands of
religions, millions of cults, billions of individual belief
systems. All of them have been a search for truth, however misguided. Everyone felt the same innate spiritual
feelings, but rationalized them in very different ways.
And how indeed was prescientific humanity supposed to
find the truth? It would have been easier to deduce the
inner workings of the sun by staring at it. There was no
framework, no alternate source of truth from which they
could determine why our spirituality existed.

"But with science came that framework. A framework
that blatantly contradicted the false truths that most religions had already locked into their belief system. The
literalist religions contended with the heliocentric solar
system and biological evolution, both in disagreement
with supposed "truths" that had been locked in by people
who simply could not have known better. Even mystical

religions, with fewer scientific premises to contradict, had their own difficulties. They had to contend with the realization that there was no unphysical soul, no sharp division between mind and body, no action at a distance. Humans had an instinct to seek out the truth, but instinct without a framework only drove them in the wrong direction.

"So what was science's advantage over primitive religions? The advantage of being wrong. To a believer, a religion cannot be wrong, and its evolution is fundamentally limited by this supposed fact. Beliefs that are locked in cannot change, because to change one part requires a questioning of the whole system. But a scientist is always wrong, always in doubt. Constantly framing hypotheses and disproving them, science is always narrowing down the field of what is not true, instead of finding what is true in a single step.

"Science can never be true in the way that a religion can; there are always uncertainties, always the possibility that some new revolution can overthrow the old ways of thinking. And the scientists themselves welcome the revolution! Those who turn their science into a religion, those who instinctively believe in the old theories as absolute truth, they are left behind in the next revolution. Again, instinct without science leads . . ." Drew looked up after the midsentence pause and then followed Daddy's gaze to the back of the church. With everyone getting to their feet, Drew couldn't see who was coming down the aisle, but he figured it had to be someone pretty important.

"Welcome, Mr. Prime Minister. We have only just begun." Drew thought Daddy's voice was remarkably calm for someone who was addressing the most important person on the planet. The Prime Minister was usually too busy to come to regular services, but not always.

Drew's heart jumped in excitement, knowing that they would be sitting next to each other in the front row. Sure enough, there he was, quickly shaking a few hands as he made his way up to the front.

"Please, Paul, continue. Don't stop on my account." Drew looked up admirably at the man addressing his father. Every time he saw the Prime Minister he was struck by what a genuinely nice person he was, never conceited or letting his high station change how he treated ordinary people. Drew smiled broadly when he took a seat next to him, and after a moment Daddy went ahead with the rest of his sermon.

"Over most of human history science did a vastly better job of locating the truth—by burning down the alternatives—than did religion's wild stabs in the dark. And eventually, thanks to science, there wasn't much darkness left. And—to no great surprise—in the small patch of darkness where science had cornered truth, there wasn't a single traditional religion left.

"Yes, most religions claimed they fit in with modern science, but it was usually science that they were warping to fit their religion. In some cases new religions sprouted up, modeling themselves after modern science, Quantum Buddhism being the most notable example. But it was still a case of forcing known science onto an existing religion rather than simply looking into the darkness and finding the God that had been hiding there all along. So when the new interpretation of quantum theory was framed, the Quantum Buddhists were again left with an outdated religion that could not evolve.

"So why didn't scientists, once postmodern physics was complete, announce that they had found God? Why didn't they come up with the theological concepts of Symmology on the spot? Because science has never been a way to find *the* truth, only a way to narrow down the alternatives. Science was incapable of finding God because science is, by definition, always in doubt. It was left for a man like our Captain, a leader familiar with science but not a scientist, to discover God's now obvious hiding place. It was our Captain who stabbed the remaining patch of darkness and discovered that postmodern science actually required the existence of God—a God no one had ever considered. It was our Captain who let his spiritual instincts be guided by science's discoveries but not eclipsed by science's theology of doubt.

"But this is all ancient history, you're all thinking. Everyone here knows how important science is to our religion. No one here would think of following their instincts without heed to what science had to say. Or would you?"

Daddy paused for a moment, looking around the church. "Here's an example. Our instincts tell us that we are more important, more *human* than everyone else, but science tells us that this is just an evolutionary survival strategy. Our families come next on the humanity scale, but science tells us this is just our genes wanting to spread copies of themselves. And what about our friends, our acquaintances, our fellow residents of Mandala City? Our instincts humanize them because of cooperation and trade benefits. But all this is just our genes talking; science tells us that we're all equivalently human.

"But do we really take this lesson to heart? In our minds, do we extend humanity beyond our borders? How many of us, consciously or not, dehumanize the Burnouts? How many of us agree with our instinctive feeling that they are somehow *less* than we are, their lives somehow not as important as our neighbors'?"

Drew smiled. He had known that he was going to talk about the Burnouts, but for the first part of the sermon he hadn't mentioned them, and he had started to wonder if Daddy was giving the wrong speech. But now he got into the heart of the matter, reciting lines that he had heard over and over again at home, and his attention faded back to the doodle page on his lap. Looking down at the nearly completed picture of the spaceship, he suddenly got an idea. After all, if anyone should know about this, it should be the Prime Minister. He picked up his toothpick, and in bright green wrote beside his picture: I THINK MAYBE THOSE ASTRONOTS WERE MURDERED. Then, ever so slowly, he started to scoot sideways toward the Prime Minister.

Before he got too close, the Prime Minister seemed to notice him out of the corner of his eye and made a quick glance in his direction. Quickly, and as unobtrusively as he could, he slid the doodle page across the wooden seat. The Prime Minister looked at it briefly and then did a double take. He picked it up and examined it closely, although what he was looking at Drew had no idea. How long did it take to read a single sentence, anyway? He thought that maybe he was admiring his artwork, but he had a too-realistic view of his abilities to take that train of thought very seriously.

After a few moments, the Prime Minister looked him in the eye for the first time, and Drew got the feeling that he was being studied. The Prime Minister's usual relaxed smile was nowhere to be seen, and Drew hoped he hadn't upset the man too much. Then he made a writing motion over the page, and Drew figured that he wanted to write something himself. He slid over the toothpick, and after the Prime Minister scrawled something on the page, he passed both items back to him.

He had written two things: WHAT IS THIS?, with an arrow pointing to his drawing, and WHAT DO YOU MEAN?, with an arrow pointing to his sentence. Drew quickly saved the page in memory, and then cleared it so he could write a full response. THAT WAS THE EARTHY SHIP, he wrote. THEY GOT HERE LAST NIGHT AND I THINK MAYBE THEY DON'T WANT US TO KNOW. MAYBE THE EARTHIES MURDERED THE ASTRONOTS SO WE WONT KNOW THEY'RE HERE.

He passed it back, but after reading it, the Prime Minister didn't do anything for a long time. Drew looked at his expression, but it didn't reveal anything; he looked like he was just listening to the sermon. Finally, he picked up the page, cleared it, wrote a single word in big red letters, and then passed it back. NONSENSE, Drew read, and he figured that was the end of that. *But at least he'll know, when he finds out the Earthies really are here, he'll know that there's something special about me.*

"And if someone feels that way about the Burnouts," Daddy was saying, "if someone can dehumanize these people who live ten kilometers away, then what will happen in the fall when the Earthies arrive? If the Burnouts, who are our distant cousins and relatives and live on our same planet, if they are so far removed from what we consider humanity, then I shudder to think what will happen when we are forced to deal with *true* strangers. For dehumanization not only leads to fear, but it also is the path to war. And unless all of us can come together, embracing all of humanity as one glorious group of conscious beings who all have a direct line to God, unless that can happen, all of these unfounded fears we have been harboring just might become a terrible reality."

AFTER THE SERMON, DADDY WAS SURrounded by people: shaking hands, asking questions, congratulating him on another great speech. It was always the same; they kept him busy for nearly an hour, while Drew slipped out the back door and played outside. Sometimes he prayed to God, but tonight he found that the moon hadn't quite risen yet, so he walked over to a tree that he liked to climb on the edge of the forest. The service had gone late tonight, and it was getting pretty dark, but there was enough light from the church to let him see the lower branches. Still, he hesitated at the bottom of the tree, peering into the dark woods. Ever since the incident last week he had been worried about the Burnouts getting him, and neither his mother's lecture nor Daddy's sermon had totally eased his fears. It was just too realistic a scenario: the savages leaping out of the darkness again, grabbing him, and carrying him back to their kingdom, where he would be forced into a lifetime of slavery. It was too horrible not to think about.

"Hello there!"

At the sound of the voice behind him, he nearly leaped into the tree. He spun around, backing against the trunk, but was very relieved when he made out the shadowy form of the Prime Minister.

"Scared you, did I? Sorry about that. Your name is Andrew, isn't it?"

Drew nodded, his heart still beating double time. "Drew," he muttered, wishing his computer-generated voice didn't sound so squeaky and uncertain.

"Well, it's nice to meet you, Drew!" The Prime Minister extended his hand and he shook it, trying to use a firm grip. "I remember you when you were just a baby, but I don't think I've spoken to you before, have I?"

Drew just shook his head, not trusting himself to say something intelligent.

"Anyway, I just wanted you to know that I was interested in what you had to say in there, and I thought maybe we could talk about it sometime."

Drew felt his heart rate picking up again, this time with excitement. "I thought you said it was nonsense?"

The Prime Minister nodded. "Well, I did." He rubbed his chin for a moment. "But that was just my initial reaction, and I'm very interested to hear more about your ideas." He paused as a car pulled up next to them, shining its headlights into the forest. It was *his* car, Drew knew; only the ministers of Mandala had personal automobiles. "Well, my ride is here, and I must get going. We'll talk again soon, I hope." Before Drew could respond, he walked over and opened the car door.

Drew stood under the tree, trying to figure out what had just happened. Was the Prime Minister taking him seriously, or just being nice? Regardless, Drew knew he had to convince him that the Earthies were here. If anyone had to know, it was the Prime Minister. But now he was leaving, and he'd probably be too busy to talk to him anytime soon.

"Oh, Drew?" The Prime Minister leaned out of the half-closed door. "It just occurred to me that you've probably never seen the inside of a car before. Would you like to take a look?"

Drew nodded furiously, and hurried to the car before the Prime Minister could change his mind. Clambering in, he noticed the bald driver up front and tried to remember where he had seen him before. It was a small city, and everyone usually looked familiar to him, but he really felt he should know who this person was. Had he been on the news today? Before he could remember, the Prime Minister began showing him around. There wasn't much to see, actually; just a pair of flatscreens and a built-in DC system, as well as a small fridge down in the corner. But when the Prime Minister asked him if he'd like to go for a ride, Drew knew he'd never get a better chance to talk to him about the Earthies.

"Sure! I'd love to. My dad won't be done in there for a long time."

The Prime Minister grinned. It wasn't his usual grin, Drew noticed, because it showed some of his teeth. "Great. Driver? Let's take this baby for a spin."

CHAPTER 12

One of the things that makes Symmology so appealing to me is the potential for it to be proved false. Consider the difficulty humanity has had in constructing an artificial consciousness. All of scientific conventional wisdom says that such a thing is possible, and yet no one has been able to succeed. Why? Symmology has an answer: There can be only two consciousnesses in the universe, humanity and God. Constructing a third would knock the whole symmetry out of balance.

Of course, this leaves Symmology open to future disproof if someone was able to construct such an artificial mind. To some this makes my religion weak, but to me it only makes it stronger. My religion, unlike most, is capable of being disproved.

Forrest once asked me how I would respond to news that Earth had created an artificial consciousness in our absence. I told him that I would have to modify my religion but that the question was ill-posed. For I know, beyond a shadow of a doubt, that such a thing is impossible. I will never have to respond to such news; the laws of universal symmetry simply will not allow it to happen.

The Journal
Year 17, Day 305

KATRINA PICKED UP HER DC ON THE THIRD buzz, clipping it to the transceiver around her neck.

"Trina!" It was Paul. "Is Drew there?"

"No. Did he leave church early?" She glanced over at the clock. "It's late. What's taking you so long?"

"You really haven't seen him? You don't know where he is?" If she didn't know her husband any better, she would have thought he sounded a little frantic.

"Not yet. Maybe he just left. He might not be here for another—"

"I've been looking for fifteen minutes already. He's never gone home alone before, either."

"Huh." Katrina walked over to Drew's room, just in case she hadn't heard him come in. "Where do you two normally meet? You checked that tree he likes to climb?"

"Of course. And the ditch with the vines that he swings on. And the balcony in the church. Do you think he might have gone home with one of his friends?"

She felt a twinge of nervousness. "I'll make some calls, but I doubt it. I told you we should have gotten him another DC."

"I know, I know. It's just that he hardly ever—"

"Okay. We'll talk about it once we find him. I'll call around, and you dial emergency."

"Emergency? Do you really think—"

"Paul! It's dark out there. Call them."

"Okay. Buzz me as soon as you hear anything."

"Same to you." She hung up, but didn't key anyone else for a few moments. She stood there, thinking. She thought about the moment when Freddie Shooshani died, the boy who had brought that bacterial infection into her daughters' classroom seven years ago. At that moment, although she kept up hope for her own children, a part of her knew that they, too, would soon die. She never had felt so helpless in her entire life. And now again, that same helplessness was coming back, a feeling that something was horribly wrong and there was nothing she could do. She fought it away, telling herself that this was nothing like last time, but the feeling persisted. Finally, in an effort to quell her fears, she started calling the neighbors.

Two hours later, from Katrina's view on the rooftop of her house, it looked like every light in the entire city was turned on. Everywhere she could see, people were brandishing flashlights and lanterns, combing not just the church grounds, but the entire City. A group of men on rafts slowly made their way up the river, scraping the bottom with their long wooden poles. It was past bedtime for most of the children, but they were out as well, holding on to their parents' hands as they searched the tall grasses. Katrina watched behind moist eyes, wondering if the kids had asked to help, or if it was mostly the parents' idea. With Drew's disappearance she was sure they were keeping a close eye on their children so the same thing wouldn't happen to them. And she'd be doing the same if her daughters were still alive . . .

Katrina pushed the thought from her mind and steadied her hands to raise the antenna one more time. Although Drew carried his antenna with him everywhere

he went, she hadn't unfolded hers in many years. Tonight, though, she had taken it out of the closet and gone
up to the roof, trying to locate her son by amplifying
his microwave signal. One more time she slowly turned
in a circle, calling out to her last remaining child. She
paused often, listening as carefully as she could, but despite the busy activity all around her, the microwave
spectrum was dead silent.

Finally, after nearly completing her circle, she set her
eyes on the half moon rising above the horizon. It was
bright, but not nearly as bright as the full moon had been
that morning, seemingly ages ago when Paul had returned from his missionary trip. She smiled, thinking of
Drew, and how he sometimes prayed to the moon.
Maybe he was lost somewhere, praying to the moon
right now. She pointed her antenna directly at the orange
half circle of Asgard, wondering what she was doing.
Drew! she called for the millionth time. *Are you up
there, hiding out on the moon?*

WHAT'S THAT?

Upon hearing a response, she stumbled backward,
nearly losing her balance. Quickly, she repositioned the
antenna. *Drew, is that you?* A mixture of emotions tightened her throat. Maybe he was praying to the moon right
now and the signal was bouncing off of it, coming
straight to her. Was that possible? She wasn't sure.

*I'M NOT DREW. YOU'RE NOT DREW. WHERE,
OH, WHERE, IS DREW?*

Her heart beat faster and faster. What was going on
here? The individual words sounded a little like Drew,
but the overall effect was completely alien. *This is his
mother. Who are you? Do you know where he is?*

*I DON'T KNOW A THING ABOUT MOTHER. BUT
I KNOW YOU'RE NOT DREW.*

Katrina momentarily closed her eyes in confusion.

What do you mean? I'm his mom! Who are you?

IS MOM MOMMY? ARE YOU MOMMY?

Yes! she yelled, trying to steady her shaking hands so the antenna wouldn't go out of alignment. *I am Drew's mommy!*

IT'S NICE TO PRAY WITH MOMMY.

She felt tired all of a sudden, tired and weak. She started to wonder if she was dreaming, or perhaps if she was going mad. Quietly, she tried once more. *Who are you?* It seemed like a long time before she received an answer.

I'M GOD. YOU DON'T BELIEVE IN ME, BUT THAT'S OKAY.

Slowly, ever so slowly, she sank to her knees on the rooftop, weeping.

IT WAS NEARLY MIDNIGHT WHEN PAUL RE-turned to the house, shuffling in with a small group of their friends. She sat in a chair with her hand over her eyes, only glancing up at them for a brief moment. "Any news?" she asked.

A couple of them cleared their throats, and Paul hurried over to kneel beside her. "Not yet, dear. I'm glad you came down from the roof, though. They're pretty sure he didn't fall in the river, and—"

"Send them home," she said, not making eye contact. "We need to talk."

Paul hesitated for a moment and then stood up. She overheard a hushed conversation by the doorway, and when she glanced up, she saw they were all looking over in her direction.

Mr. Yang spoke first. "If there's anything we can do, Mrs. Randall . . ." And then they were all voicing their regrets and their optimistic forecasts, promising to bring her boy home safely.

"Thank you, thank you all," she interrupted. "You've all been more than kind."

"All right, then," said Mr. Yang to Paul. "We're getting back to work. Let us know if you need anything." He put his large hand on Paul's shoulder, and her husband nodded silently in response. Finally they all filed out, and Paul walked over and sat down on the couch, holding his head in his hands.

"I should have offered them a hot drink," he said. "It's getting cold out there, and—"

"I found something," she said.

Paul's head jerked up, his eyes suddenly wide. "What?"

She shook her head slowly, brandishing a pained smile. "You know . . . I never went out to pray with him. All these years. I thought it was just a silly game he was playing, but I guess I was too proud to ever go out and pretend to talk to God with him."

"What are you talking—"

She held up a hand to shut him up. "When I had my antenna out, up on the roof, I talked to the moon, just like Drew used . . . like Drew does."

"And?"

"And it talked back."

Paul shook his head quickly, like he was trying to dry his hair. "I don't understand."

She shrugged. "Neither do I. But all this time, all this time . . . this hasn't been his imagination. He's really talking to someone."

Paul stood up, an incredulous expression on his face. "What are you saying, Trina? That . . . That . . ." He gestured silently, pointing up at the ceiling. "God?" he finally managed.

She laughed softly, tears starting to stream out again. "That's what he said, anyway." She rocked back and forth in the chair, wiping her nose. "But he didn't know anything. Said he hadn't talked to Drew since last night. Right after you came home, I suppose."

Paul still looked stunned. "But . . . God actually . . ."

She shook her head. "He's not God, dear. He just called himself God. If there is a God, he's definitely not as clueless as . . . as . . . whoever it was I talked to."

"Is . . . is this 'God' still listening?"

"Probably. I couldn't take it anymore, so I came inside."

"What do you mean, you couldn't take it?" Paul was starting to pace excitedly. "Don't you think whatever it is might have something to do with what's happened to him?"

She shrugged. "I told you. He doesn't know where Drew is."

"Or so he said. C'mon outside. Let's figure this thing out."

Katrina remained in her chair. "The whole thing was very unnerving. I don't really want to do it anymore."

"Trina, if there's any chance this could help us find Drew . . ."

She made a sighing noise with her speaker. After a few moments she got up and let Paul lead her out onto the deck. A few people waved up in their direction, shouting encouraging comments. Katrina didn't want to hear them. She massaged her temples, not at all sure what she was doing. The first time she had done this it had been very upsetting for her, although she didn't quite know why. Finally she took a deep breath and pointed the antenna up at the moon, turning down her speaker volume, but leaving it on low so Paul would be able to hear her half of the conversation. She took a deep breath. "Hello? God? You still there?"

I'M NOT THERE.

She nodded at Paul, lowering the antenna for a moment to talk to him. "I guess he's still there. What should I say?"

"Well, we have to find out who you're talking to. Maybe you've tapped in on some other communication channel or something, although I can't imagine there are any other communications you'd be picking up on this thing. Ask him where he's located."

She shrugged, returning her attention to the moon. "Where are you?"

I AM IN TIME.

She nearly laughed. Paul looked at her curiously, but she didn't bother repeating the answer. "And where, exactly, is time?"

"Time?" asked Paul. She shushed him with a stern look.

HERE, ON TOP OF THE WORLD.

"Where? Where is that? The North Pole?"

I AM UP HERE, AS HIGH AS HIGH CAN GO THIS WAY. ON TOP.

She related the responses to her husband. "This isn't getting us anywhere. He's making about as much sense as someone on fana."

"Hmmm." Paul frowned. "I'm trying to think. If you're hearing a transmission bouncing off the moon to somewhere else on Mandala, then there should be a light-speed delay between the time you send the message and the time it's received—a little over a second, I think. And then it will take at least another second to respond. So are you noticing a two-second break between your questions and the answers?"

"Maybe. I wasn't paying attention. I don't think so, though."

"Here." Paul pulled off his watch and started the timer. "Watch this, and ask a short question. See how long it takes to get an answer."

She waited until the 0.0 second mark rolled around before asking "God" if he was still there. She heard a *YES* in response about a second later. "No, that must not be it. It was definitely less than two seconds. More like one."

"Hmmm." Paul scratched his head. "Then it has to be bouncing off of the ionosphere. But I didn't think that the plasma density was high enough to reflect this frequency."

"But if it was a reflection, why do I have to point it at the moon? Drew always prays to the moon."

Paul shrugged. "Coincidence? Maybe it doesn't matter where you point it."

She moved the antenna to the other side of the sky. "Hello? Are you over here, too?" There was no response. She tried a few other places, but there was still nothing. Finally she decided to try just above the horizon, where the moon had been when she first talked to God, more than an hour ago. Again, nothing. "No, it definitely has something to do with the moon."

"That doesn't make any sense."

"Well, you think maybe I'm talking to somebody on the moon?"

Paul gave her a funny look. "Like who?"

"It could be a transmitter or something. Something left up there from a long time ago, when Captain first got here. Didn't they do a lot of exploring in this star system, even after they found Mandala?"

Paul smiled. "But if it's a transmitter operated by someone on Mandala, you'd still need that two-second delay. If you're talking to someone on the moon, they'd have to *be* on the moon. Right now. And as far as I know, no one has set foot on it for a century."

"So there's no way anyone could be up there."

"Well, *something's* going on, unless you're making all of this up to drive me crazy."

"Paul!"

"Sorry. But I have to admit, from my point of view, that's the most plausible explanation for everything you're telling me." He gazed upward for a minute before he spoke again. "C'mon inside. Let's look something up."

OVER THE NEXT HALF HOUR, PORING OVER the Encyc program on the dining room table, Katrina learned more about Asgard than she had in her entire life. The Mandala-Asgard system had been produced three and a half billion years ago, when two good-sized planets had made a glancing collision. Unlike Earth's moon, which had been formed by a relatively direct impact, the glancing collision had left both planets with close to their original masses and densities, but in a widely elliptical orbit around each other. Over time, the tidal forces had made the orbit much more circular, but also had the effect of slowing down the rotation of both planets, which was why Mandala now had such a long day.

The moon's early surface had looked a lot like Earth's; lots of water from an early bombardment of comets, and a primarily carbon dioxide atmosphere. However, Katrina learned that CO_2 was unstable in the presence of water, and over millions of years it settled down into sediment on the ocean floors. Here the histories of the two planets diverged; Mandala's continental drift system pushed the sediment deep underground, where active volcanoes were able to recycle some of the CO_2 into the atmosphere, thereby maintaining the greenhouse effect that kept the planet warm enough for liquid water. But Asgard was tectonically quiet for reasons that were not fully understood, and the lack of CO_2 led to a runaway glaciation effect. As soon as some of the water on the moon turned to ice, the white surface reflected more of the planet's sunlight, cooling it down even further. As the ice age continued, without any volcanism the situation got worse and worse, until eventually even the remaining carbon dioxide began freezing in the wintertime. Finally the remnants of Asgard's thin atmosphere could no longer prevent the sun's ultraviolet light from disassociating the ice into hydrogen and oxygen. All of the hydrogen and much of the oxygen was lost into space over a billion years ago, the rest of it oxidizing the surface.

The reason why this hadn't happened on Mandala was still an open question. The most popular theory pointed to the fact that most of Mandala's volcanism occurred directly under the moon's orbit. It was postulated that the solid tides of the moon physically moved the crust of the planet enough to keep the convection process going, driving Mandala's continental drift. Opponents of this theory suggested that if this were true, the even larger solid tides caused by Mandala on the moon should also have driven plate tectonics there. The arguments from that point on became too obscure for her to follow; they consisted of complicated geometrical considerations taking into account Asgard's large axial tilt and whether the moon's ancient oceans covered the proper regions to have lubricated the convection process.

The important thing to Katrina, though, was that indications of primitive life had been found on the moon.

"It's not living there now, of course," Paul had argued with her. "It just existed a billion years ago when there was still liquid water."

"Well, maybe it is still there. I mean, what if intelligent life had evolved?" She was talking faster now, as she always did when she brainstormed. "As the water froze up, maybe they moved underground. And now there aren't any surface traces left of them at all . . . but they're still up there! And lately they've started communicating with Drew."

Paul looked uncertain. "But we didn't find evidence of complicated life on the moon. Just bacterial traces and some weird kind of diatom. If intelligence evolved, there would be a huge fossil record."

She saw his point, but liked her idea enough that she didn't want to give up on it quite yet. "You're assuming that things went the same way that they did on Earth. Maybe it was sea life that became intelligent. Sea life without bones, like Earth squid or something. And then, when the water started to dry up—"

"Okay. So say there are intelligent aliens still on the moon, buried down in some underground refuge. Do you really think that they could have learned English? Just by receiving some patterns of microwaves from Drew's childhood prayers? I mean, that's quite a stretch, especially assuming that we wouldn't have anything in common with them. They'd have to start from scratch, and wouldn't even know about the *concepts* Drew was talking about, let alone the actual meaning."

Katrina smiled. "You just don't like this train of thought, because you think human consciousness is the only one in the universe, don't you?"

"That's completely irrelevant. There's just no way that we'd ever be able to communicate with an alien without some large-scale effort. It's a really difficult problem, you know, sending a message that can be decoded without any common assumptions. Some people even think it can't be done, except maybe if all you talk about is math and science."

"But Paul, the more I think about it, the more it makes sense. Whatever I talked to up there didn't use any words Drew wouldn't know, and the words themselves sounded just like Drew's speech. It strung the sentences together differently, and didn't make any sense half of the time, but it didn't seem to know anything that Drew wouldn't be able to teach it! Okay . . . suppose one day Drew was praying up to the moon, with his antenna open, and whoever it is up there received his prayer. They wouldn't understand it, of course, but they might send the same message back to Drew. Then he'd know that there was really something to talk to up there, and he'd do it all the time. You remember how much time he spent praying as a little boy, right? And once it learned a few words, it would start to be an interactive communication. Maybe they have whole teams of scientists up there, all working on decoding Drew's prayers full time! And maybe they're much more intelligent than we are. I'm telling you, Paul, whoever it is up there isn't necessarily human!"

Paul was shaking his head. "But learning those first few words is the hard part. I'm telling you, an alien would have no common assumptions at all!"

Katrina thought for a moment. "It called itself God, right? If Drew kept opening every prayer with the word 'God,' it might figure out that the word referred to it. Then it might start calling itself God. And the fact that it said it was praying with me, that's another word that Drew might have taught it!"

"I still don't buy it. And regardless, we still have to

figure out how this . . . God . . . is related to Drew's disappearance."

"You think it's related?"

Paul quoted from the Journal: "Coincidence is the skeptic's word for the Divine."

She smiled. "Let's go back out and talk to God some more. Maybe he does have something interesting to say after all."

CHAPTER 13

I'm rather surprised that cosmologists never followed up on their "Advanced Antimatter" theory. If all matter is constrained by the boundary conditions of the Big Bang, given CPT[19] symmetry and a closed universe one would expect that an equal amount of antimatter is constrained by the boundary conditions of the Big Crunch.[20] But what would it mean to be constrained by future boundary conditions? It means that the entropy of most of the antimatter in the universe is increasing in the opposite time direction as matter! So from our perspective we would see "impossible," entropy-decreasing behavior; antimatter behaving more and more improbably to "match up" with the future, low-entropy boundary conditions. Or alternately, viewed backward in time, it would look exactly like the matter-dominated universe we know.

So where is the other half of the universe? Heat death. Just as the black holes and baryons in our half of the universe will eventually decay into maximum-entropy radiation in the near-infinite future when the universe begins to recollapse. But we are unable to see the time-reversed radiation; we're always looking into our own shadow.

All this has been debated for years. But why did no one realize that perhaps not all of the antimatter would meet such a high-entropy fate? Why didn't anyone see that if consciousness could evolve in our matter-dominated universe, it might have done so in the antimatter one as well? Our backward-evolving counterparts have been around so long they must have found a way to escape their entropy death as they became God. But although He is as real as we are, we cannot observe Him. Observing God in any macroscopic way would create an impossible causal paradox. Instead we must communicate with our God in the only way we can: through our quantum minds.

Note 19. CPT=Charge, Parity, and Time Symmetry. All of the known laws of physics are symmetric under a reversal of all three at once; therefore a backward-in-time, mirror-image, antimatter system must behave exactly like the original.

Note 20. The opposite of the Big Bang; the end of the universe.

The Journal
Year 5, Day 42

CHANNING PACED AROUND THE DIAMOND cone in the center of his apartment, massaging his temples. It was so late—or so early?—that nothing was making sense to him anymore. Unreasonable anxieties itched at the edge of his mind, his fears mixing with reality and leaving him unsure what to believe.

Everything had gone so perfectly, too. The crew from Earth had been killed, more easily than he had expected, and even the midget who escaped was trapped in an airlock and done in when Croll overfilled the pressure. When Channing's fana spell was over they had left in the spaceplane, landing safely in midday while most people were asleep. Croll and Rick had killed the two astronauts then, something that Channing hadn't expected or even considered. Still, he quickly realized that it was for the best. The fewer people who knew, the happier everyone would be.

The ministers and the dead astronauts had been carried off of the shuttle in supply boxes while Rick had given his heart-wrenching account of the explosion on the *Walt Disney*. When George had carried Channing safely out of view and let him out of the container, one look at Channing's smile told One-Arm what had happened.

"You killed the whole crew." George didn't look quite as pleased as he should have.

Channing nodded slowly. "Things went as planned." He noticed that he felt a little lighter, as if the gravity of the planet had changed while he was away. Perhaps it was just that the worry of the past year had been lifted off of his chest. Whatever it was, he felt good.

But George and some of the others didn't look quite as pleased. They hadn't been informed about the next phase, so they were only now facing the question of what to do with the frozen settlers. A brief debate followed, and Channing listened patiently. Best to keep them in orbit for now, was the consensus; they would be released when the time was right.

Of course, Channing had other plans.

So for a few hours, everything had been perfect. He
was in such a grand mood that he even decided he would
go to church. And that was when, from the most unlikely
of places, he found out that his supposedly perfect secrecy had already been breached.

He glanced over at the boy sleeping on his white
couch. *How did he know?* Channing asked himself for
the thousandth time. He had asked the kid in so many
different ways, but even when he got answers none of
them made any sense. He fought back the impulse to
wake up the boy and shake him until he found out what
he wanted to know. The kid was exhausted, and Croll's
strong-arm tactics had only made him clam up. He'd
have to try more of the nice-guy approach, but he wasn't
sure how well that would work, keeping him here
against his will.

The kid hadn't started to get worried until they arrived
at the Government Cone and Channing had invited him
up to see his apartment. Before then the boy had been
talking nonstop, and Channing now cursed himself for
not getting more answers at the time. Instead, he had
focused on getting the boy into somewhere more se-
cluded, and he only nodded and smiled politely while
Andrew tried to convince him that the Earthies had arrived early. He found the boy really difficult to talk to;
he was one of those mutant kids, and having his voice
come from a speaker around his neck was awkward. He
didn't know whether to look at the speaker, or the kid's
unmoving lips. Very disturbing indeed.

But as it turned out, that had been the kid's only talk-
ative spell. After getting to the G.C. he became a little
nervous and asked to be taken back. He complained that
he had to get to the church, that his daddy would be
looking for him and worried. Finally, after promising to

let him call home once they went inside, he allowed Channing to take him up to the suite in his personal elevator.

There the inquisition began.

Some inquisition. All the kid did was ask to use the phone. Over and over again. *Could I please use the DC, Mr. Prime Minister? I really have to call my parents.* Finally Channing couldn't take it anymore and snapped at him, telling him no, he couldn't use the phone until he answered some of his fucking questions. That had been a big mistake. The boy broke down, weeping eyes hid behind his hands while his useless mouth silently wailed, and it had taken forever to calm him down again.

After that, the boy no longer looked at him in the same way. The earlier admiration and excitement of talking to the Prime Minister had given way to fear and uncertainty, and even when the boy started answering some questions, Channing certainly didn't get the feeling that he was telling the truth.

"ONE MORE TIME," CHANNING HAD ASKED. "What makes you so certain that the *Mayflower* arrived here last night?"

Drew blew his nose while he responded, a combination that Channing found rather unsettling. "I just know. It doesn't matter. You wouldn't believe me, anyway."

"Try me. I'm a very understanding person."

"Then why don't you let me use your DC?"

Channing valiantly tried not to lose his temper. "Who told you the ship came last night?"

He lowered his eyes to the carpet. "God did."

"God. Who's God?"

"You know. God."

"Are you trying to protect someone? Is that a code name?"

"Okay, now I told you. Now will you let me use the DC?" He started crying again, already knowing the answer would be no.

THINGS HAD GONE ON LIKE THAT FOR hours. Nonsense answers and half-truths. The kid was good, he had to admit. Even when he had left the room and let Croll take over, the kid still didn't change his story. He had listened from downstairs, and it sounded like Croll had gotten pretty rough with him, but after a little while the kid simply stopped speaking altogether. Finally Channing burst into the room, screaming at Croll to leave the poor boy alone, and chased him out. But even after letting him cry in his arms for a while, and then nursing the bruises that were forming on his upper arms, he still didn't open up with any new information.

After a bit he tried a new set of questions, aimed at finding out who else the boy had told. At last he finally seemed to be getting somewhere. Supposedly he had told only his parents, and neither one had believed him. For the briefest moment Channing relaxed, congratulating himself on his quick action after the church service.

But his comfort was short-lived. He had to understand how the boy had discovered the truth in the first place. He knew that despite his justifiable actions today, if they ever became common knowledge his reign as Prime Minister might come to an abrupt end. And if that happened, only Captain knew what would happen to this beautiful society he had spent his life shaping. He couldn't let the public destroy itself. He had to find and stop the leak.

He reviewed the facts in his mind one more time. The

boy knew not only that the Earthies had arrived last
night, but also he had drawn a picture of the ship! True,
the first part could be a wild guess, or maybe he had
seen it up in the sky, a gradually slowing star, its orbit
merging with that of the *Walt Disney*. But explaining
the doodle was much more difficult. Until he had gone
up into orbit this morning, Channing himself didn't have
a clue what it was going to look like. And the picture,
although crude, had clearly indicated that the boy had
seen it before. There had even been an unfinished shape
next to it that looked like it could be the *Walt Disney,*
although the scale didn't seem right. It seemed impossible that he could draw such a thing.

But now that he thought about it, he realized there
may have been some pictures of the *Mayflower* on the
Earth vids a year ago, from just before it left Earth orbit.
He had never seen any, but it was conceivable that the
kid had. So could that explain it? Some astute stargazing
and a good memory of a year-old vid? He shook his
head. It didn't make sense to him. If that was the case,
why didn't the kid simply admit it? What was all this
talk about God?

Eventually, after getting nowhere for too long, he had
decided to leave the boy alone for a while. He descended
down the circular stairway and went to get some work
done in his office. Fortunately he couldn't concentrate,
and after a few minutes had come back up to see what
the kid was doing. Drew was no longer on the couch,
and after a frantic moment Channing located him over
by the eastern window. Relieved, he was about to turn
away again when he did a double take on the metallic
structure opening in the kid's hands. It looked to be
some type of miniature antenna dish.

Channing sprinted over to him and nearly caught his

collar, but the kid twisted away and clambered over the back of the couch. Channing followed without hesitation, leaping after him and tackling the kid on the carpet, their heads nearly colliding with the diamond centerpiece. Even before they hit the ground the kid was flailing and kicking at him, but Channing was able to grab the antenna dish and roll to one side before he got his face scratched. The kid made a brief, futile effort to recover the dish, but Channing made it to his feet, and the kid collapsed into a ball by the diamond and started crying again.

"What the hell is this?" asked Channing, breathing heavily from his exertion. "Why do you have an antenna? Who were you trying to talk to?" There was no response. He examined the object closely, stretching the reflective fabric a little and then watching it snap back into its parabolic shape. It had a connection on the back that presumably went into the boy's speaker-thing. Finally he found the button that collapsed the microframe structure, and was amazed at the tiny package it folded itself into.

"No wonder I didn't notice this thing. I thought it was just a toy."

The kid looked up at him with red eyes. "Why were all those lights on near my house?" He motioned to the window with his head. "Are they looking for me?"

Channing shrugged. "I would imagine so. You've been missing for a long time."

He stared back at the Prime Minister, expressionless and unresponsive.

"So, what is this for?" Channing held up the folded antenna, trying to keep his voice as friendly as he could. The boy didn't respond right away, but Channing waited patiently.

"My dad made it so I could talk to my mom, even

from far away." He kept his eyes on the carpet as he spoke.

"Your dad, the preacher? Made this?"

"He used to be a 'lectrical engineer. Before my sisters died."

Channing made a mental note to look into his family's history. He had a feeling that he should already know what had happened to his sisters, but he couldn't seem to remember. "That's right. Let's see, how old were you then?"

Finally he looked up at him. "I was born a little while later."

Channing nodded. "So you were. So you were. I think I remember—".

"What happened to those astronauts?"

"What?" Channing blinked at the sudden subject change.

"You know the Earthies are here. You knew the whole time. You're keeping it a secret. That's why I'm here."

Channing smiled despite himself. The boy wasn't asking questions. He acted like he was simply stating facts. "Yes, you're right," he said. "You're a smart kid. I just hope that . . ." He trailed off and walked back over to the stairway.

The kid was starting to look nervous again. "You hope that what?"

He started to descend the stairs. "I hope you're smart enough not to wind up like those astronauts." He paused and glared at him just before his head sank out of view. "You know, they wouldn't answer my questions either." And then he was gone, leaving the kid alone on the floor.

* * *

IT HADN'T TAKEN LONG FOR THE EX-
hausted boy to fall asleep, but Channing couldn't do the
same and eventually found himself back up in the living
room, pacing around the diamond. Assuming he
wouldn't get any answers in the morning, he'd have to
figure out what to do with the kid. He couldn't leave
him here; the cleaning staff knew better than to come in
when he was present, but as soon as he left, someone
would find the boy. He'd have to be taken somewhere
more permanent, but his options were limited, especially
because only he and Croll knew the boy was here. After
thinking about it for a while, he went downstairs and
keyed Croll on his DC.

"Did I wake you?"

"No." Croll's voice sounded tired. "I've been out
searching for the kid with the rest of the town."

"You have? Why?"

"People need me for this. They need a Minister of
Defense, even though there still isn't one. People are
really nervous, Alex. I hadn't realized the effect this
would have. It's been real interesting listening to the
reactions."

"What do you mean?"

There was a brief pause before Croll continued. "I
think it's almost time, Alex. I hadn't realized how strong
the anti-Burnout sentiment was already. And this event,
this missing kid, it's sparked a lot of anger in a lot of
people. I think it's time to take on the Burnouts."

Channing shook his head. "Wait a minute. What does
this have to do with the Burnouts?"

Croll chuckled deeply. "This kid's father, the
preacher, he just got back from a week-long trip up to
the Outpost. People are starting to put things together.
It's obvious the kid didn't just get lost, and they think
the Burnouts got him. The most popular theory right

now is that they're blackmailing his father, keeping him from talking about something he saw when he was up there."

"But I just heard him give that sermon. He was saying how people needed to be more tolerant and—"

"The people out here are rationalizing that, too. They think maybe he was *instructed* to give that sermon, maybe with threats to his family. And now they took his kid so the threats would be more credible. I'm telling you, Alex, getting that kid was a stroke of genius."

"Fine, Croll. But I really don't think we need to deal with this right now. We just took care of the Earthies, for Captain's sake, and we still have the *Mayflower* up there! And this kid, too. That's what I was calling you about in the first place. We need to do something with him. He can't stay here."

"Did you find out how he knows?"

"Not yet. But we need to focus on this. We can deal with the Burnout problem later. They're not going to be a threat for years."

"That's exactly why we should deal with them now! You don't understand what an opportunity we have here. People are begging me to do something about it, and that's just what I'm doing. I've already gotten a few dozen men to volunteer, and we're going to start training in a few days."

"Training? What are you talking about?"

"The army. You know that base we're setting up in the North Mine? Well, it's ready. I'm going to start using it as a training camp."

"Croll, I'm telling you, this isn't a good time to start this."

"You don't understand. It's starting whether we want to or not. People are scared, and they're going to do something. We can either lead or watch it happen on its own. And I'm going to make sure it's done right."

Channing scratched his head. "Okay. Fine. But we need to move the boy. . . . Hey, let's move him to this camp of yours. In the North Mine."

"No chance. As soon as one of my men saw him, I'd lose my army. I don't think you understand what a flash point this kid is."

"Dammit, Croll, he can't stay here! If you want funding and support for this little war of yours, you're going to take the boy up there. Keep him closed in somewhere safe. I know some of your men will keep a secret. They can bring him food. If you don't trust them, you can feed him yourself. But I want the boy moved out of here before sunrise. Got it?"

After a long silence, Croll finally spoke. "I understand, sir. I'll be by in an hour or so."

"Fine. I'll see you then." He clicked the DC shut, swore under his breath, and walked back upstairs to check on the boy.

CHAPTER 14

Engineer Wong came to see me today; she is pregnant. I suppose it was only a matter of time. Even if our next destination finishes this endless voyage, it will be a minimum of three years before we could possibly be off-ship, and for M. Wong and the other older crew members, that may well be too late. And, of course, if the next system turns out to be uninhabitable like the others, then soon everyone will be clamoring to have children on board.

My feelings about this are absolutely certain. Apart from Shiprules, every moral fiber of my body demands that she have an abortion immediately. For in this case, allowing one child will certainly bring many more. And have we learned nothing from our species' legacy of overpopulation and depleted resources? This spaceship is a small, fragile ecosystem, and what right have we to endanger the whole for the sake of the few? Indeed, we are also endangering the babies, no child has *ever been born in the radiation levels of interstellar space.*

I told her my views. I pleaded with her. But why, when I confronted her not three hours ago, was I unable to order the necessary procedure?

Perhaps it is because I am a minority captain; a male commanding a 60 percent female crew. Perhaps I was thinking about the possibility of this journey lasting for generations. But I think the real reason is that I did not feel comfortable forcing others to bend to my own moral standards. Regardless of circumstances, can I reach into someone's life and make a crucial decision that would normally be theirs alone? Perhaps. But then what kind of captain would I be?

The Journal
Year 17, Day 258

PAUL SOLDERED ONE FINAL CONNECTION TO his makeshift contraption and then woke Katrina to test it out. She had fallen asleep on the couch while he had worked, and after staying up for most of the night, she did not wake easily.

"What time is it?" she asked weakly.

"Just after ten. The sun'll be up before too long. But I need you to turn on your transceiver and talk into this." He gestured to the antenna he had just repaired. It was one of Drew's old ones, and he had hooked it up to an extra speech module, a microphone, and a small speaker, all mounted on a small breadboard.

"What do you want me to say?"

"Doesn't matter. Just make sure your transceiver is pointed at the antenna."

She flipped a switch on the device around her neck.

"Testing," she said, but the speaker was silent.

"Huh," said Paul, frowning. He reached down to check a few connections, and Katrina flopped back onto the couch.

"You know," she said, "it'd probably just be easier to change my transceiver to . . ." She stopped talking when the speaker started echoing her voice back at her.

"Volume," explained Paul. He looked up at her. "You ready to go talk to God some more?"

EARLIER THAT NIGHT THEY HAD RULED OUT the possibility that God was actually some ancient Asgardian intelligence, speaking from a shelter beneath the surface of the moon. Out on the deck, Katrina was the first to point out that because Asgard rotated with respect to Mandala, any alien transmitter would spend half of its time on the far side, unable to communicate. Paul checked the Encyc and calculated that the moon had undergone almost half a revolution since Drew had talked to God the night before.

"That would mean they would have to have multiple transmitters if they're always going to be in contact," Katrina said. "And I have to confess, I think that's a little unlikely. I sort of pictured a very few of them, huddled together in some isolated cave. If they were all over the planet, I suppose we would have noticed them by now."

"Unless they have a moving transmitter," said Paul, nodding. "Which is pretty unlikely, too."

"What about a satellite?" asked Katrina. "Around Asgard."

Paul smiled. When his wife started brainstorming, there was no stopping her. "Sure, you could keep a satellite on this side of the moon all the time, with the right orbit. But we definitely would have noticed that."

"How? Anyone doing Asgard astronomy anymore?"

Paul shrugged. "Maybe not now. But when Captain first arrived, they would have noticed an ancient alien satellite. No doubt about it."

"Okay. So maybe it's not an ancient satellite. Maybe it's a new one. Aliens could have arrived here from somewhere else, in a spaceship. They could have gone into orbit around Asgard, watching us from up there. And then one of them decided to start up a relationship with Drew."

"I just can't tell you how unlikely I think that is! I'm telling you, the only spaceship in this system is the *Walt Disney*."

Katrina's eyes widened. "What about the Earthy spaceship?"

"Trina. Drew's supposedly been talking to this thing for *years*."

"I know, I'm not saying the Earthies are God. I'm just thinking that maybe their ship really is here. Drew said it got here last night. We didn't believe him, but when we found out he was telling the truth about praying to God, we didn't stop to think that he might be telling the truth about that, too. I bet they are here after all!"

"But they're not here. They never showed up. Drew was looking for it all day."

Katrina shrugged. "Maybe it's here anyway." She pointed her antenna upward again and flipped on her transceiver. "God, what did you tell Drew last night? Was there anything about a spaceship?"

After a moment his wife nodded in his direction, and he felt his heart leap. The Earthies *had* arrived. But why did no one seem to know? No, he told himself, they can't be here. It didn't make any sense.

"Did it arrive last night?" Katrina asked. "A big

spaceship? From Earth?" She paused, then flipped a switch and turned to talk to her husband. "He says yes. It arrived last night, and went into orbit around our planet . . . around *your* planet, was what he said . . . right next to the *Disney.* He called the *Disney* by name."

"Our planet," Paul muttered to himself. "But wait, if it was right by the *Disney,* then that repair mission today should definitely have seen it. So it can't be up there . . . it must be talking about something else. I bet it saw the repair mission, the spaceplane. That went right to the *Disney.* Drew must have misunderstood it and thought it was talking about the Earthies."

"But the shuttle didn't leave until this morning. Drew knew about it just before sunrise."

Paul frowned. "So what are you saying? That it *is* here, and no one seems to know about it? That those astronauts didn't see it up there? Or that the Earthies murdered them, like Drew was talking about today."

She shrugged. "Maybe. Drew seemed awfully sure of himself, like he *knew* they were here, beyond a shadow of a doubt. You can see why he got so frustrated. I mean, if they are up there, it's hard to imagine those deaths were completely accidental."

"But . . . that whole scenario of Drew's. It didn't make any sense. You agreed with me. I mean, what about the third astronaut, the one with the big breakdown on the news tonight? He should know the Earthies are up there. And if he's not talking . . ."

Katrina nodded. "Then he's hiding something. Maybe there's some sort of conspiracy. Who would be the first person to know the Earthies were here?"

Paul smiled weakly. "You mean besides our son?" He thought for a moment. "The Minister of Communications, I would imagine. Zhang."

"Well, maybe Zhang and this astronaut—what was his

name again? Rick? Maybe they're keeping it a secret. And they killed the other two because they wouldn't stay quiet."

"No, no, no," Paul said, shaking his head. "Occam's razor. This is getting far too complicated. The simplest explanation is that"—he waved his hand up at the moon—"that God doesn't know what he's talking about. The simplest explanation is that the Earthies *aren't* here. Otherwise, you have to invent all these other things to explain the situation. Conspiracies, murders, cover-ups . . ."

"I'm just saying it's a possibility. Just because it's complicated doesn't mean it's not true. And I think there is something to it. God said he saw something, a really big spaceship, bigger than the *Disney*. That has to be the Earthies. Drew believed him. And so do I."

"*Who* do you believe? You don't even know who you're talking to up there. How can you know whether to believe it or not?"

"I don't know. I just do."

Paul sighed. "Okay. Maybe *you* do, but I'm not going to know what to believe until we figure out who it is. We need to get some answers. Ask him . . . what did he say a little while ago? Oh, yeah, ask him what he means by Mandala being *our* planet. Ask him where *his* planet is."

She sent up the question, and seemed to wait a long time for the answer. Finally she turned back to him. "He says he's from a lower planet. The lowest planet."

"See, he's talking complete nonsense. Nothing he says makes any sense at all. I don't even know why we're bothering."

She shrugged. "Maybe he is making sense. Maybe we're just not trying hard enough to understand."

"Okay. Think. Maybe we're just not asking the right

questions. What have we asked? Who he is, where he is, where he's from . . . Ask him how big he is."

"Sure." She turned to the moon once again. "Are you big, God?"

"Deep question," Paul commented.

"Smaller than what spaceship? The Earthy space-ship?" She nodded at Paul to indicate the answer. "Are you in a spaceship?" She suddenly lit up with an amazed smile. "I was right! He said he was in a spaceship! A small spaceship! It's some alien spaceship up by the moon!" Without hesitating, she turned her attention back to God. "Are you in orbit around the moon?" Her smile softened a little bit. "He says . . . he says the moon is going around him."

Paul shrugged. "Well, it's all a matter of perspective, I suppose. But I still don't buy this alien business."

Katrina rolled her eyes. "I'm sorry, dear, if it messes up your theology and all that, but I'm telling you, we're communicating with an alien intelligence here."

Paul was shaking his head, trying to concentrate. "Okay. Why does he keep talking about high and low if he's in space? He says he's from a low planet, and that . . . what did he say before . . . that he's on top of the world? There's no up or down in space! It doesn't make any sense."

She mulled that one over for a while. "Well . . . suppose it is an alien. That would mean that Drew taught him what the words meant. Up and down, high and low. So from Drew's perspective, God was high and he was low. Hmmm. I don't know what a 'lower planet' could mean, but—"

"Maybe . . ." Paul started to get an idea, and all of a sudden he saw a different way to look at it. "That's it! Gravitational potential! He's at the . . . the . . . Lagrange point!"

"What?" Katrina looked confused.

For a moment Paul couldn't speak; he had so much to say that none of his words would come out. "Up there," he finally managed, "God has a higher gravitational potential than we do down here. Maybe that's what being 'high' means to him. And along that axis he's the highest that he can go!"

"Which is . . ."

"The Mandala-Asgard Lagrange point! The point between here and the moon where the gravitational fields cancel out. If he moved toward us or away from us, he'd be going *down,* either into the moon's gravitational field or our own. So he's at the top, the top of . . . well, the top of this local system, anyway. And from here, it always looks like he's right in the center of the moon! And that also explains why he just said the moon was in orbit around *him.* He's not far from the center of mass of the two-planet system. The moon and Mandala *do* orbit around him!"

Katrina frowned. "So where is he from? What does that make the lowest planet?"

"I dunno. The one closest to the sun, I suppose. Although that would be Hades, and there's certainly nothing living from *there.* Maybe he means the planet with the highest surface gravitational field. Or maybe he's not even from this star system."

"That's what I've been saying."

Paul nodded. "Okay. Let's figure out what we can do with this. He's about . . . halfway to the moon. Eighty thousand kilometers."

Katrina looked down at her antenna with admiration. "This thing can go that far?"

"Well, the microwaves barely interact with the atmosphere, and I think the frequency is too high for the ionosphere to bother it, either. So the only thing that limits it is the beam spreading out as it gets farther away."

"Wow. You didn't need to give these things that much power."

"It's not your power." He pointed to the antenna in her hands. "If you were eighty thousand kilometers from Drew, you wouldn't hear a thing through that. Whatever it is up there has a much bigger antenna dish. And a more powerful transmitter, too."

"But if Drew can't use his antenna . . . then there's no way God could find out where he is."

"No. Not unless . . ." He paused, doing a quick calculation. "Wait a second. Even with the small antenna on the transceiver . . . that's a twenty times wider beam angle . . . so if God comes twenty times closer . . . that's four thousand kilometers! That could work!"

"What? What are you talking about?"

Paul's hands started to shake, and he gripped the railing tightly as he voiced his idea. "Tell . . . Tell God to come down to a low orbit. Actually, tell him to go to the *Walt Disney*. It's about two thousand kilometers up, I think. Anyway, at closest approach he'll be forty times closer, and since Drew's signal will spread out only twenty times as fast, God might still be able to hear him."

"But would Drew know where to pray? He won't be in front of the moon anymore, right?"

Paul rubbed his chin. "Well, he could come down to a mandosynchronous orbit, but . . . no, that'd still be too far away." He shrugged. "You're right. He wouldn't stay in front of the moon. But I think the *Disney*'s orbit passes pretty close to the moon most of the time."

"And then Drew might happen to pray to God one of those times, even without his antenna."

"Exactly. I think the *Disney* orbits once in a little over

two hours, and it's visible for half an hour at a time. So he'd have a one-in-four chance at any given moment that God would be in the sky. What do you think?"

She smiled broadly and stepped into his arms, kissing him forcefully on the lips. "I think it's worth a shot," her speaker announced in midkiss.

NOW, HOURS LATER, BOTH OF THEM SAT ON the roof scanning the heavens in different directions with their respective antennas. The moon was off to the southwest, and had shrunk to a thick crescent during the night. As a result, the sky was dark enough to see the half-moon auroras off to the north, faint curtains of shimmering turquoise that twisted into fantastic structures while they watched. Paul looked at them curiously, reminded of the strange space plasma conditions at the Lagrange point and wondering why any spaceship would choose to go there.

In a unique configuration, the magnetic field lines of Mandala connected with the magnetic field of the moon, creating an enormous magnetocylinder that enclosed both planets. When Asgard's phase was near a half moon, that cylinder was edge-on to the solar wind, and the magnetic field lines filled to capacity with charged particles, streaming from Mandala to Asgard and back again. The field lines focused down in the middle, and so did the particles, which made the Lagrange point an area with particularly turbulent plasma flow. It was still low-density plasma, but the resulting magnification of the solar wind created conditions that were as harsh as anywhere in the solar system, unless one got too close to the sun itself. Like Hades, he thought, briefly wondering if God could really be from that dark planet. Then he brushed the idea away. There was no life on Hades. It didn't even have an atmosphere.

Below and around them, the ground search for their son was still going on, although not with the previous large crowd. A lot of their friends had promised to come back after dawn, though, expressing hope that he'd be easier to find in the light. They all said not to worry, that even if he had fallen into a hole or something that he'd be sure to make it through the night. But for Paul, wearing his warmest clothing in the freezing night air, it sounded like pretty tenuous optimism. Instead he focused on the sky, trying to locate the mysterious spacecraft that might be the only way to locate Drew.

Neither of them knew exactly where God would be, of course, but at least he wasn't answering from his spaceship's position in front of the moon anymore. It had taken forever for Katrina to convince him to come down to a low orbit, and pleading with him didn't seem to help. God's main complaint seemed to be that there would be "lots of eclipses," apparently a reference to spending much of its time in Mandala's shadow. Paul presumed that it ran primarily on solar power, but Katrina was still under the impression that it had traveled here from another star system, so it should have an independent energy source. Katrina had finally convinced God to come down after stressing that it would only be for a short time and that Drew was in trouble. The concept of "helping" seemed to be a difficult one to get across, but eventually Katrina had gotten God to understand.

"HELLO," crackled the voice from the speaker. "I'M FALLING. I'M FALLING DOWN."

"Got 'em," said Paul. "You're right. It does sound like Drew. But he's still pretty close to the moon. Must not be very fast."

She nodded. "It actually sounds a lot more like Drew on that thing than it does on mine."

"God," Paul said into the microphone, "how much longer until you're in orbit?"

"WHO ARE YOU? SO MANY THINGS ARE PRAYING. COMPLICATED, COMPLICATED."

"It's Paul. Drew's father."

Katrina shook her head. "Say you're his daddy," she whispered.

He shrugged. "I am Drew's daddy."

"HELLO DADDY. WHERE'S MOMMY? WHERE'S DREW? WHERE'S DREW?"

Paul smirked at his wife. "Mommy?"

"Names, Paul. Just names."

Paul sighed. "You're coming closer to us?" he asked.

"YES. I'M FALLING DOWN."

"Good. Have you heard from Drew?"

"I TALKED TO DREW."

Paul blinked his eyes in astonishment. "You have? When?"

"I TALKED TO DREW YESTERDAY."

It took a moment for the response to sink in, and then Paul rolled his eyes. "Was he being this literal with you?" he asked Katrina.

She nodded. "Sometimes. Just phrase everything very carefully."

"Well, he hasn't heard anything. Do you want to wait inside? I'll let you know if there's any news."

She shook her head. "Not a chance. I'm staying up here."

He paused, thinking of something to ask God. Was he really an alien? How could they tell? "God, are you human?" he finally asked.

"I AM GOD" was the only response.

Paul smiled. That wouldn't work. If he was an alien,

he would have to use words learned from Drew. "Do you have a daddy? A mommy?"

"DO I HAVE YOU? DO YOU HAVE ME? DO YOU HAVE MOMMY?"

"Frustrating, isn't it," said Katrina.

Paul nodded, thinking furiously. "Do you have eyes?"

"I DON'T KNOW A THING ABOUT EYES."

"Eyes are . . . eyes are what you see with. . . ." He got a sudden inspiration. "When you saw the spaceship last night. You saw it with your eyes."

"OKAY."

Katrina smiled. "He says 'okay' sometimes. I think it means, 'I understand.' Maybe."

Paul grinned and asked another question. "How many eyes do you have?"

There was a long pause, and Paul raised his eyebrows at his wife. "This could be interesting. Does he know numbers?" Katrina only shrugged, and they continued to wait.

Finally the answer came, a single word amid a burst of static: "SEVEN."

After a second of silence, Katrina burst out laughing. "See? What did I tell you?"

Paul squinted upward. "I still have no idea what's going on. And I'm too tired to think about it anymore." He looked up at God's position in the sky. "It's going to be at least half a day before he's down to a low orbit. I think it's a good time to get some sleep. Care to join me?"

She shook her head, still smiling. "I'm staying up."

"You're going to collapse. And freeze."

"I'll be okay."

He shrugged. "Always the stubborn one. Okay. Good night, I guess." He climbed down the ladder and walked around the house, where he found a group of five men sitting on his doorstep. They smiled when they saw him, rising up to give him a big group hug.

"We're glad you finally came down from there." Paul recognized the speaker as Zeke Wellington, Trina's sister. "You two should get some rest. Isn't she coming down, too?"

Paul shook his head. "She's going to be up there for a while, I think. But if you can convince her to get some sleep, please do. She needs it." He laughed. "Hell, I need it."

Zeke nodded. "So, no luck reaching him on that radio gizmo? Rolph here says he thought he heard you talking to someone."

Paul hesitated, not sure what to say. For a moment he considered telling them everything, but after realizing how silly it all sounded, he decided to keep quiet for now. "No, no luck. We were just talking out loud to Drew, in case he could hear us but couldn't respond."

They nodded, standing around in an awkward circle. "So," began Zeke, "we've been sitting around, talking about what might have happened. Wondered if you might like to hear some of our ideas."

"Sure." Paul sat down on the doorstep, and Zeke sat next to him.

"Well, you see," he said, his big hands gesturing broadly, "things like this just don't happen every day. I mean, there's got to be some reason why it's happened now. Something's going on here. I don't think any of us think that little Drew just wandered off."

"I don't understand. What are you saying?"

Zeke looked around at the others. "That someone else is involved in this thing."

Paul immediately thought of Katrina's conspiracy theory, with the Minister of Information and that astronaut. Would they have kidnapped Drew? Why?

"I mean, now of all times," Zeke was saying. "It's really gotta make you wonder. Kind of makes you re-think what you said in church, I bet."

Paul looked him in the eye, perplexed. "What are you talking about?"

"About the Burnouts. About them being harmless and all."

He stared at Zeke for a few seconds, and the black-smith seemed to grow embarrassed and lowered his eyes to the ground. Paul shook his head. "The Burnouts . . ." He trailed off, unable to complete the sentence.

"We don't mean to offend you, preach," said one of the others. "But Zeke's right. Things have been building up to this for a while now, no matter what you said in there tonight. They took your kid, sure as I'm standing here."

"The Burnouts kidnapped Drew?" Paul's tired mind tried to comprehend what they were saying. "But . . . why?"

Zeke looked at him again. "That's what we were just trying to figure out. We know he was robbed last week. Maybe they thought he knew something. Thought maybe you might have some ideas."

Paul shook his head. "No, I . . . I guess I don't." The Burnouts? Kidnap Drew? Unbelievable. But there *was* something funny going on during his last visit to the Outpost, and he never did find out what it was. Suddenly he rose to his feet. "Gentlemen," he said, "we'll talk about this more tomorrow. I'm so tired I can't even think straight. I don't think the Burnouts did anything, but . . ." He turned and opened his front door. "We'll talk tomorrow," he repeated.

"We're not going anywhere, Mr. Randall," Zeke said. "And if it *is* the Burnouts . . . why, we'll do something about it, you can count on that. We'll get Drew back for

you, Mr. Randall. Even if it means going all the way
into the Red Valley."

He smiled at them from inside the doorway. "Thanks,
guys. Good night."

They gave him a chorus of good nights, and Paul
stumbled to the bathroom. Looking at himself in the mirror, he thought about it some more. What possible reason could the Burnouts have to take his son? Blackmail?
Did they want him to do something for them? Would he
get a note with a set of demands in the morning? Or did
they think he discovered something during his week at
the Outpost, and wanted to make sure he'd stay quiet
about it? He shook his head after he washed his face,
trying to clear his mind. It was too late to think about
these things. He had to get some sleep for tomorrow.

But he couldn't sleep. He couldn't get the idea out of
his head. He tossed in his bed, picturing Drew as a prisoner of one of the Burnout kingdoms. Back when they
had always been at war with each other, horrible stories
had surfaced of atrocities performed on Burnout prisoners. No one knew if they were true, but now all he
could think of were those same atrocities performed on
his son. He shut his eyes tight, trying to make the images
go away, but the scenes only became more vivid. Then
he saw himself there, tied to a stake with his hands behind him, surrounded by crowds of leering Burnouts.
Hundreds, thousands of them, all painted up, ready for
battle, and circling around and around, always looking
him in the eye. He cried out, and they moved closer,
closer, pressing in on him, and he cried out again and
suddenly an aisle opened up in the crush of bodies, and
he saw his son on the far side. "Drew!" he called out,
and the aisle moved wider, the Burnouts backing away
so his son could advance. Drew had a smile on his face,
a broad, wicked smile, and he walked toward him

slowly, his hands behind his back, walking and walking but never getting any closer, and then he brought his hands out to reveal a fistful of sourhoney and a jar of war beetles, and then he knew he was in for the worst torture of all.

Paul bolted awake, gasping. Two minutes later he was back on the roof.

"WHAT DO YOU MEAN, YOU'RE LEAVING?" Katrina managed to look indignant and confused at the same time.

"God's trying to tell me something."

"You mean about having seven eyes?"

"No!" he yelled at her, and she blinked, leaning backward. "Not *that* God. God. The real God. He spoke to me just now, just as I was falling asleep. That halfway place between dreams and reality. That's where God can best influence me. And he told me. I have to go."

She kept her voice quiet. "But the Burnouts? What do they have to do with this?"

"I don't know. Maybe they have Drew . . . I don't know. But I need to go there. To one of the kingdoms."

She arched an eyebrow. "Not the Outpost? You're going to a kingdom? By yourself?"

He nodded. "I'll probably start at the Outpost. But that's where I have to go."

She didn't say anything, but she didn't look at him either. He knew she didn't believe in God. She had lost her faith when her daughters had died; ironically, the same event had driven Paul to become a preacher. But he also knew she understood. Somehow, despite everything, religion was something that had never come between them. And he hoped it wouldn't start tonight.

"I need you," she finally said. "I need you here to

help me get through this." She shut her eyes tightly.

"And I need you," he said. "But we both need Drew. If it weren't for Drew . . ." He didn't say what he was thinking, that if it hadn't been for Drew they would no longer be a couple. That if Drew hadn't already been conceived when their daughters had died, they almost certainly would have gone their separate ways. But he didn't have to say it. He knew that she understood. "Anyway, God's telling me I need to go. Or we may never see him again. I know you don't believe it, but I do. And that's why I have to go."

"Okay," she said after a while. She wiped a corner of her eye with her index finger and then wiped his eye as well. He was surprised to feel the wetness smear across his cheek. She gave him a smile: nice, although obviously forced. "I'll help you pack."

CHAPTER 15

J. Hansen: I still don't understand how this Symmology of yours can accommodate free will.

CAPTAIN: What don't you understand? The future's not fixed from our temporal reference. We determine what happens to us. There's no big mystery here.

J. Hansen: Our temporal reference. But you say it's not the only possible one. You think there are Gods out there—

CAPTAIN: One God. It's a collective consciousness.

J. Hansen: Whatever. It's coming backward in time, so it knows what our future is. It's already determined! There's no room for free will anymore.

CAPTAIN: But don't you see? Our future may be determined in some other reference, but it's determined by us, by our free decisions in this reference frame. At the end of your life if you were able to fly back in time, would you tell your younger self that he no longer has free will because your decisions have already been determined?

J. Hansen: If I could fly back in time there would be all sorts of paradoxes.

CAPTAIN: Only if you could tell yourself what your future held. But if you were restrained from saying anything about the future, then there are no contradictions. Your younger self still has free will.

J. Hansen: So what keeps God from telling us our future and setting up a paradox?

CAPTAIN: According to the Madrid Interpretation, that's one of the foundations of quantum mechanics. You can derive the whole theory from symmetry considerations and the impossibility of paradoxes. God is constrained by the fundamental laws of nature.

J. Hansen: But God talks to you, right? How is that possible?

CAPTAIN: He doesn't tell me the future. He doesn't tell me any facts at all. But our minds, our consciousness, it's all based on quantum effects in our brains. And quantum mechanics allows Him to affect our quantum minds in subtle ways, regardless of his temporal orientation. He can add constructively to some waves and destructively with others, probabilistically guiding us in the right directions if we listen.

J. Hansen: I don't know. Still sounds too deterministic for me.

CAPTAIN: [sighs] I hope you're wrong. But I think I'd sooner give up free will than my God.

The Log
Year 15, Day 59

SAMUEL ZAGALA POUNDED THE CONTROLS IN frustration. He had worked so hard to escape, come so close to death, and for what? So he could now die in a slightly bigger prison? It just wasn't *right.*

THE DIAMOND-COATED PHILLIPS HEAD screwdriver had worked remarkably well. Or rather, it hadn't worked at all well until he hit upon using the cutting solvents in the tap and die set. It was amazing what that stuff could do. Just one drop occasionally smeared on the wall and his makeshift drill worked ten times as well as before. But still the job took forever. After half an hour or so his hole was still only a centimeter deep, and his mind had started to wander, dredging up facts learned and forgotten back in his medical school days, trying to figure out how the pressure would kill him.

The digital pressure gauge had long ago maxed out at 9.99 ship atmospheres, and although he was pretty sure the air inflow had leveled off, his entire body seemed to feel more and more crushed as time went on. The bald man had been wrong, of course. His head was not going to implode. But there were other dangers.

The first one he had worried about was nitrogen narcosis. That wouldn't kill him directly, but it would probably render him helpless, unable to finish drilling an exhaust vent. Everyone had a different level at which high pressures of nitrogen would make them feel drunk, and Samuel had no idea at what pressure it would happen to him. "Rapture of the deep" they called it in the scuba portion of his astronaut training, and he knew it generally happened to divers below 30 meters. Mentally, he converted that to about 4 bars of pressure, or roughly 8 SAs. And he was at least 2 ship atmospheres over that already. He tried to monitor his brain, tried to tell if he was becoming illogical, but quickly realized the folly of trying to diagnose himself in that fashion. Instead, he simply became more and more panicked, pressing down on the screwdriver with all the force he could muster. Then he remembered that ship air contained a much lower nitrogen percentage than Earth air. So perhaps nitrogen wasn't a worry after all. Perhaps.

But now, having remembered that the air had a higher percentage of oxygen, he was reminded of a new danger: oxygen toxicity. Oxygen was actually a very nasty substance, and back when it began polluting Earth, it had caused endless havoc. Countless organisms died, unable to cope with the free radicals O_2 helped produce. Some species managed to adapt, learned to harness its energy. But still it was dangerous at high pressures, even to humans. It probably wouldn't kill him right away, but if the pressure was too high for too long . . . Samuel tried to remember some numbers but failed completely. One bar of pure oxygen was mostly safe, he knew that. But right now he was breathing air that was at least twice that level. He tried not to think about how exactly the oxygen would kill him, but grisly possibilities presented themselves as he drilled.

And then, over the course of an agonizing minute, the screwdriver died.

The battery pack had run out. All he could do was stare at it in disbelief. Recharging in here was out of the question. He tossed it aside and released his death grip on the hatch. He let himself float into the middle of the room, once again completely at a loss, and after a few seconds he heard footsteps.

It was the bald man, come back to finish him off.

But would he be able to get inside? Even if he hadn't

jammed the hatch, the pressure would make it impossible to open. Maybe if all was quiet, the bald man would think he was already dead. He held his breath, for a moment glad the battery had run out.

"You still in there?" Samuel balled his fists upon hearing that voice again. "Everything going okay?" And then the voice was much softer; he could barely make out the words. Was he talking to somebody else? He listened carefully. ". . . pressure's still . . . should be . . . right . . . safe . . ." Were there two different voices? He couldn't tell. Finally the footsteps moved away, but Samuel didn't budge. It might be a trick. He could just be waiting outside to see what happens. But minute after minute ticked by, and the only noise was his quiet breathing. Eventually he realized he was stuck in the middle of the airlock with no easy way to get anywhere. He swam the breaststroke in place for a few minutes, pushing off of the thick air until he gained enough speed to make it back to the hatch. Then, just in case, he pressed his ear against the wall. Nothing.

Frowning, he glared over at the screwdriver, floating amid some other tools in the far corner. The batteries were dead, and now he had to find something else. He returned to the tool cabinet and started rooting through it again. Maybe he could manually turn a drill bit. No— that would take forever. Maybe the files. Or this chisel. He started completely emptying the cabinet, tossing aside electrical tape, insulated wiring, rubber bands, nuts, washers, batteries, pliers, miniature alignment lasers. . . . He stopped suddenly, turning to look at the floating box of batteries he had just thrown behind him. More batteries. He took a deep breath. For a moment he wished the situation would finally become hopeless so he could give up and die peacefully. But once again there was a thread of hope tugging on him, keeping him from spending any of his last moments in peace. Okay, he thought, taking out another battery pack. One more time.

Half an hour later even the residual hissing from the vents had stopped, and he knew the pressure in the airlock had peaked. But how high was it? Was he going to die in a few hours regardless of what he did? The irritation in his lungs had gotten worse, and breathing was starting to hurt. Probably pulmonary oxygen poisoning, he realized. He also noticed that his peripheral vision was constricting, and tried not to think about what it might mean. Instead he focused on his hole in the wall, making it deeper and deeper, stopping occasionally to blow out the metal shavings and apply more solvent. It was nearly three centimeters deep now, and at any moment he expected to break through. But the hole only grew deeper and his lungs became more and more tired.

Now he started to worry that his efforts would spark a fire in the superoxygenated chamber and he'd roast to death. Of all the ways to go, he thought, burning was the worst conceivable way. No, make that the second worst way. The worst way was death by vacuum, the death he had worried about for the past six years of his life. Vacuum! Samuel almost laughed at the realization that he was finally going to be done in by the exact opposite.

Finally, with an explosive pop, the airlock was breached. The screwdriver was suddenly lodged in the hole, air violently hissing around the handle. After a brief struggle Samuel pulled it back out, letting more of the air escape. It made a shrill whistle, but it was a sound he was very happy to hear. He turned to watch the digital display with a smile on his face, watched it drop below 9.99 SAs for the first time. Because he had made the hole on the inner wall, it would drop all the way to ambient ship pressure; then he'd be able to open the far hatch and enter the shuttle. He would have been in there more than an hour ago if it hadn't been for . . .

More than an hour ago! He had been under high pressure for more than an hour. And now he was venting it. All at once.

"Shit!" he yelled, and frantically started looking around for something to plug the hole. He needed some O-rings. There had been some rubber bands in the cabinet. He launched himself across the room, grabbing a small red loop that was floating in midair. And now something to seal it. He searched around, looking for something, anything that would be flat enough. The tap and die set was still in the cabinet and he took it, hoping the flat plastic case would hold the pressure. Then, with one more powerful kick, he sent himself back over to the hole he had drilled.

When he got to the hole, he told himself to relax. The last thing he wanted was to get a finger caught in there. He held the rubber band gingerly with both hands and placed it around the hole. Fortunately he was in zero gravity, and it stayed in place. Carefully he pulled his hands away, grabbed the plastic case, and brought it down over the hole. It snapped into place, held there by the strong pressure, and the noise suddenly stopped. Samuel held his ear close and thought he heard a soft hissing, but he couldn't be sure. He took a deep breath, feeling the change in air density already. Hopefully the change hadn't been too abrupt on his system.

Samuel cursed himself for not thinking about decompression sooner. He knew all about the dangers of decompression sickness; he just had been so keen on venting the chamber that he hadn't stopped to think. Under high pressure, large amounts of nitrogen could be absorbed by the blood. That alone wasn't dangerous: as long as the nitrogen was dissolved, it couldn't hurt you. But once the pressure dropped, the nitrogen started to come out of the solution, and that *was* something to worry about. Small nitrogen bubbles would start forming in your bloodstream, carried along by the flow. The bubbles would get lodged in narrow capillaries and cause all sorts of mischief, depending on where the blockage was. It often happened in the joints, leading to painful contractions that had come to be known as the "bends." But that was the best you could hope for. Bubbles could lodge anywhere; they could cause paralysis if they were next to your spinal column, or even cause a stroke in the brain. The massive decompression he had just attempted would almost certainly have led to a quick death.

But now he had to decide how to decompress himself. How long should he take to get back to ship atmosphere? He didn't know, and decided that he should probably play it safe, taking as long as he possibly could. Without food or water in here he might last two days, he decided. Would that be long enough? The deep-sea researchers and commercial divers on Earth—who lived down under the water for months at a time—could take a week to decompress. And they weren't even all that deep. Decompressing for only two days might kill him. But any longer than that . . . He took a deep breath and started looking around for something he could use as a better seal.

TWENTY-SIX HOURS LATER HE COULDN'T take it anymore. Ship air always made him thirsty; it was produced dry down in life support, and the small amount of added moisture never seemed to do the job. And this air, Samuel had decided, had no water vapor in it at all. It must have come from a large compressed-air tank, he thought, and simply bypassed the moisture-adding stage. Whether this was true or not, he was absolutely parched. Hunger had come and gone, but he couldn't survive another hour without a drink. He had urinated once, after the first hour, and had had the foresight to save most of it in a plastic bag. Not that he would ever consider drinking it, he had told himself. But just in case.

He had finished the last of it twelve hours ago.

Recently he had accelerated the venting process, knowing that he wasn't going to make it at this slow rate. For a while he had been a human valve, inhaling the oxygen-rich air and exhaling his carbon dioxide through a tube that he ran through the hole in the airlock. He hadn't wanted to choose between CO_2 poisoning and a poor decompression. But even after letting more of the air out, the gauge was still at 2.2 SAs, and he knew this final stage could be the most dangerous of all. He hadn't felt any symptoms of decompression sickness yet, but he knew these things could take a while. Even after it was completely vented, he wouldn't know for hours if he was safe. But it was either that or die of thirst. He ran his dry tongue over his parched lips and removed his bruised thumb from the end of the plastic tube. The air rushed out with a sharp whistle.

2.0 SAs, he read; 1.8, 1.6 . . . It was slowing down now, and he could hear the whistle change to a lower frequency. He hurried over to the shuttle hatch and started pulling on it; 1.2, 1.1 . . . There! The hatch popped open, a rush of air blew past him, and then suddenly it was freezing.

He stopped breathing, shocked and terrified at the same time. Of course! This air has been outside in the shuttle for five years! By now it's probably equilibrated itself with outer space and . . . His panic started to subside as he realized that the air was merely freezing, not frozen. If the temperature had dropped *that* much, liquid nitrogen would be streaming out of the hatch right now. Apparently someone was intelligent enough to have left low-level heaters on for the journey.

Samuel hurried into the shuttle's dark airlock and then on into the main ship, pushing himself around through the cold interior. It didn't take him long to find the lights, but finding some water was a different matter altogether. The small bathrooms were empty except for the zero-g chemical toilets, and for a while he had feared that there was nothing to be found on the entire shuttle. But finally, after a harrowing five-minute search, he stumbled upon some emergency rations in a small closet. Grabbing a bottle, he filled his mouth with water, and with a great effort managed to swallow some of it. He was going to make it after all.

ONCE HE HAD MOSTLY RECOVERED FROM HIS ordeal in the airlock, he began preparations to fly the shuttle around the *Mayflower*. Landing on the planet was out of the question. Not only was he completely unqualified for that sort of thing, but he also had no doubt that he'd be killed as soon as he reached the ground. Perhaps by the bald man himself. No, he had to make it around to a different airlock and then start to unfreeze the backup crew. Then they'd all figure out what to do together.

He knew that there were two unused airlocks the shuttle could dock to, and even if the Mandalans were still here, he knew at least one of the airlocks would be free. That wasn't the hard part. The hard part was learning how to fly the thing in the first place. The controls looked a little tricky, but after going through the electronic manual he thought he could pull it off. All that remained was to try it.

He returned to the airlock that had been his home for far too long and slammed the hatch shut. Then he returned to the controls and prepared to release the shuttle from the dock. He took a deep breath, typed in the proper command, pushed a button, and the entire shuttle jolted slightly. And then all the lights went out.

"Dammit!" he yelled into the darkness. All this time he had been running on power from the main ship. He had never connected the local batteries. A sudden thought chilled him. He had never checked the batteries, either. For all he knew, they were completely dry. The only light left on was the glow coming from the electronic manual that he had activated earlier. Conveniently, though, that was the only thing he needed to see right now. He clicked his way to the proper section, read how to activate the power, and then managed to flip the proper switches using the light of the manual itself. As the overhead lights came on, he breathed one more sigh of relief. *Okay,* he thought. *That's the last mistake I make.*

He checked his position relative to the main ship, and reached down to push the throttle. Nothing happened. *Okay, no problem.* He checked the manual one more time. That should have been the right one. Another try. Still no response. *Maybe it has something to do with the power failure,* Samuel thought. *Maybe the engines need time to charge up or something.* He clicked his way to the troubleshooting section, and the moment he saw it at the top of the list he knew exactly what was wrong.

The shuttle had no fuel, and there was nothing he could do.

He knew the probable reason. Regulations. Explosion

concerns. The fuel tanks probably couldn't be filled until the *Mayflower* had slowed to a certain speed. And this hadn't been the priority in the past few days; this was the larger shuttle, to be used for the thousands still frozen in the cryotanks. Perhaps they had filled the tanks of the smaller crew shuttle, but that was on the other side of the ship. He had chosen the wrong airlock.

So now he was adrift, with only two options. The first was to stay there until he was dead: either by starvation, thirst, running out of oxygen, reaching lethal carbon dioxide levels, freezing to death after the power died, or having the bald man come back into orbit and pump bullets into his body.

And the second option was really scary.

There was no way in hell he was going to try it now. He had been making too many mistakes. He was too tired. His mind was exhausted and wasn't functioning properly; his present situation was proof enough of that. During the decompression he had tried to get a little sleep, but obviously it hadn't been enough. He'd get some rest, and then think about it some more.

First, though, he checked the stability of the shuttle's position with respect to the *Mayflower* and decided it looked pretty good. From what he could tell, the ship was only a few meters away and holding. He hoped they wouldn't drift too far apart.

Still making incoherent resolutions, Samuel strapped himself into one of the reentry seats and was asleep within a minute. He slept for a long time.

CHAPTER 16

God does not want me to turn back. He has con-
veyed that message to me so many different times
that it has become something I no longer question.
But so far, he has not guided us to a habitable
planet.

What does this mean? What does God want
from me? Technically, we could go on doing this
forever. Eventually we will run out of fuel, but it
should take only a year or two to harvest the necessary materials. But what then? Continue to fly
from star to star, investigating five or six systems
per generation, and beaming our findings back to
Earth? Assuming that there is still someone listening to our transmissions . . .

So what else are we out here to accomplish?
According to protocol, if I find "reason to believe
that habitable planets are extremely rare," then
our usefulness has come to an end and we are
supposed to return to Earth. But it has been so
long since we have heard from them, I no longer

consider myself to be following their ancient or-
ders. I work for my crew, and I work for my God.
And if my God tells me to press on, there is a plan,
and although I don't understand it, I will obey. I
will obey, even if that plan is simply to exist in
this spaceship for generations, while perhaps some
horrible event destroys all human life on Earth, so
that our unique human gift of consciousness will
not be lost forever. Perhaps one day a future cap-
tain of this ship will be guided to return to Earth
and attempt to start over.

But how I hope that instead a planet is out there
waiting for us. And how I hope that God will
choose to guide me there. It may take forty years
of wandering in this airless desert, but when the
right moment comes, I will be ready.

The Journal
Year 23, Day 190

DREW HAD NEVER FELT THIS COMPLETELY
alone. At least they had let him keep his speaker, after
he promised not to shout for help. But it didn't matter.
There was simply no one to talk to.

He slowly paced around his cramped cylindrical
prison, feeling the rough rock walls. He thought he was
in some kind of mine, but there was no way to be sure.
The scrapes on the walls had a pattern to them, he noticed, and might have been made by machines. Or
maybe some ancient monster had burrowed these tunnels
millions of years ago, using razor-sharp claws to dig
through the stone. The floor was smoother, but it, too,
was solid rock. He ran his fingers over a small gash in
the wall, feeling the sharp edges. Veins of some shiny
black substance branched in lightning-like patterns across

the brownish-red rock, reflecting light if you looked at it from just the right angle.

The only light source was the single bulb on the ceiling, directly over the metal-frame bed in the corner. Next to the light was a small vent—just a pipe that quietly blew cool air into the room. Apart from those fixtures, the only nonrock feature was the wall of wood at one end of the room. The door set in the middle of the wall was firmly locked, and had opened only once since he was thrown in here. A man had brought him some food and water, and Drew had recognized him. It was the astronaut who had survived, from the news yesterday. Drew screamed, calling him an Earthy in disguise, promising that he would never, ever eat or drink anything he gave him.

But that had been a while ago, and now the empty plate and cup sat beside his bed. And he was starting to wish someone would bring some more.

At first he thought he might be able to escape. Everyone always seemed to be able to escape from these situations in the Earth vids, either using some clever trick or getting rescued by friends on the outside. He couldn't think of any clever tricks, so he held out hope that a rescue attempt was on the way. He tried not to think about the fact that no one knew where he was.

His night at the top of the Cone had been horrible. For the longest time, he couldn't believe that it was really happening, that the Prime Minister was really a bad person. First he had thought it was just a big misunderstanding. But then he started to think that maybe this person wasn't the Prime Minister at all, but someone just *pretending* to be him. During the endless, repetitive questioning he had come up with a complicated scenario where the Earthies had come down and taken over the planet, replacing all of the leaders with exact duplicates.

They had kidnapped Drew, of course, because he was the only one who knew what was going on. And Earthies didn't believe in God, so they didn't believe him when he told them the truth.

That was the worst part. He had told the truth, and they still didn't believe him. He had tried to think of a good lie, but he couldn't come up with one. Talking to God was the only way he could possibly have known about the Earthy spaceship. But the Prime Minster, or whoever he was, didn't want to hear about God. That was why Drew knew that he was a fake; the real Prime Minister talked to God all the time. He was a very religious man, and watching him at Communion was a super experience, even if Drew was too young to take the fana with the adults.

But the fake Prime Minister hadn't been nearly as bad as the other guy, Croll. Drew couldn't decide if the Earthies had replaced him, too, or if he had just always been that way. The few things he had heard people say about him were not nice at all. Zeke said that he even fought for the Burnouts once, a long time ago. He massaged the bruises on his arms. One thing was certain: Whoever he was, he was an evil, evil man.

AS THE HOURS DRAGGED BY IN THE CAVE, Drew grew more and more discouraged that he would ever be rescued. He started to imagine his parents being worried about him, looking for him everywhere. Maybe God would talk to Daddy, tell him where he was so he could be rescued. But did God even know? Daddy always said that God knew everything, but Drew knew that wasn't true. God hardly knew anything unless you told him. Then again, lately he had been thinking his God must somehow be different from Daddy's God.

He could really use Daddy's God right now, he realized. A God that you could talk to anywhere, even if you were deep underground without your powerful antenna dish. He sat down on the bed and turned his speaker off, closing his eyes and concentrating. *God? Are you there?*

He waited awhile, but there was no response. He frowned, trying to think about what Daddy always said. That you can't talk to God the way he usually did. That God doesn't speak in words. But then why did Daddy sometimes say that God had "told" him to do something? He tried to think, tried to remember the lectures he had never really listened to because they didn't make sense. He did remember something Miss Bradley had said in school one day. That God puts ideas in your head, but they seem just like your own ideas. That you have to figure out which ideas are coming from you and which ideas are coming from God. And then you should listen to the ones from God, even though those are the quieter ideas, the ones you really have to clear your mind to hear. That's why people took fana, he suddenly realized. He had never made that connection before. People took fana to clear their minds, so they could listen to God.

Okay. He could do this. He lay down on the bed and closed his eyes one more time. He had to clear his mind, and then God would give him a good idea. He just had to make sure he didn't clutter up his head with his own thoughts. *Just stop thinking,* he told himself. But it wasn't that easy. In fact, it was downright hard to stop thinking. The moment he stopped thinking about one thing, he'd think about the fact that he had stopped thinking about it. And then something else would pop into his mind. But he kept trying, kept listening for the quiet voice of God to tell him what to do.

Finally he opened his eyes again, biting his lip in frustration. This was impossible! How did people do it? He thought about Daddy again, when he prayed in his room. Sometimes he prayed with his eyes closed, but sometimes he sat cross-legged on the floor and stared into a candle. Maybe that helped clear his mind.

Drew looked around the room for something to stare at. He briefly tried to stare at the bulb on the ceiling, but it was too bright. He glanced around at the walls and the bed, looking for something to focus on, but the only things that stood out were the plate and cup from his earlier meal, and they didn't look like they would be good objects to meditate on. At last he dug through his pockets, hoping he would find something useful. He pulled out some empty candy wrappers, the new spool of spare fiber optic cable, and a yellow rock that had caught his fancy yesterday. He looked at everything for a moment and suddenly got an idea. Finding both ends of the fiber optic, he wedged one end between the cup and the plate and then positioned it so it pointed at the lightbulb. Then he looked into the other end, and sure enough, it shone with a dim white light.

Preparing himself now, he sat cross-legged on the floor, just like he'd seen Daddy do, and he gazed at his makeshift candle. But still his mind wouldn't clear. He thought about how clever he had just been to make something like this. He thought about the last time he had done something clever with this cable, making a really long connection to his transceiver, and then dragging it around during a game of blindman's buff. The transceiver had nearly gotten trampled, but he never got tagged. Not once.

And suddenly he realized that God had come through for him, after all. The idea he was looking for was staring him right in the face.

* * *

BY THE TIME THE NEXT MEAL CAME, HE WAS ready. The bed had been made up to look like he was in it, using the sheet to cover the pillow and the blanket. He even put his shoes at the bottom, hoping to add to the illusion. He had worked on it for a long time, trying to make it look just right. He knew he'd get only one shot at this, and he didn't want to mess up.

The key question was where to place the transceiver. Putting it right on the bed would have been the most realistic, but then he probably would have to leave it behind. He didn't want to escape without it; not only would he be unable to speak, but he'd be deaf as well. He settled on a compromise location under the bed, telling himself he would leave it behind if he had to, but unwilling to give it up without an effort.

Laying the fiber optic down was tricky, but it was clear plastic and was hard to see except where it crossed the black veins in the rock. He managed to find a path where it didn't cross too many of them, and by the time he was done, you could barely see it at all.

Then he started to wait. He thought about calling someone in, but he decided it would only make them more suspicious. Besides, no one had answered his calls when he was first thrown in here. Finally, though, he heard the bolt being drawn back, and the astronaut walked through the door with his food. Already he had started crying loudly, and just as he hoped, the man started walking to the bed.

"What's the matter, kid?" he said. "Hey, calm down now."

Meanwhile, Drew began tiptoeing out from his hiding place from behind the door, still wailing as loud as he could. In hindsight, he was glad he had taken his shoes off. "It HURTS!" he yelled, hoping the astronaut would come even closer. Drew positioned himself right in the middle of the doorway.

"What hurts? What . . . ?" He rested his hand on the mound in the bed, and at that moment Drew yanked on the fiber-optic cable as hard as he could. The transceiver clanged on the bedpost, bounced off of the astronaut's boot, and Drew started reeling in the transceiver with both hands.

"Hey!" the man yelled, looking down at his feet. Then he spun around, but the transceiver was already most of the way across the room. Drew pulled it through the doorway with one final yank, and with wide eyes the astronaut started sprinting across the room. Drew quickly grabbed the door and backed up, pulling it closed. The bolt was high up, but he could just reach it. For a horrible moment it got stuck and wouldn't latch, but finally it snapped into place just as the astronaut reached the door, rattling it savagely.

"Let me out, you little bastard!"

Drew spun around and picked up his transceiver, wrapping the long cable around his hand so he wouldn't trip. He looked around and realized he was in a room almost identical to his cell. That made him a little nervous, but this one had another door on the far end, and it was open. He raced for it, thinking that this was a strange way to make a prison, where you had to go through one cell to get to the next.

Running through the door, he entered yet another identical room, and then another. The third one, though, had a small duffel bag thrown in the corner, and the bed was messed up. Were there other prisoners here? Or maybe this was like a secret hotel, and it wasn't supposed to be a prison at all. He reached the last door, but it was closed, and he stopped to listen before opening it. He could still hear the astronaut yelling from three rooms behind him, and wished he had closed the doors in between. The yelling echoed down the tunnel, and if anyone was outside, they would almost certainly hear him.

Sure enough, a patter of footsteps sounded from outside, and Drew backed away from the door. He was trapped. Quickly he scurried under the bed and managed to pull his legs in just before the door opened. One person stepped in, calling down the hallway. "Rick! Is that you?" He walked through the room, muttering swear words under his breath, and then disappeared into the inner room.

As quietly as he could, Drew crawled out from underneath the bed. He peered at the inner door, wondering if he could lock this guy inside, but he didn't see a latch. Drew knew he probably had only a few seconds before the astronaut told him what happened. His only chance was to run for it.

He peered out the other door and saw that it opened up into a much bigger tunnel. A pair of old rails ran down the center, and overhead fluorescent lights ran in both directions. There was no one in sight, but he knew his luck couldn't last. The astronaut would be freed any second.

Drew picked the direction that seemed a little brighter and began to sprint. The rock was cold on his bare feet, but like the smaller tunnel, it was mostly even. More wooden doors led to other side tunnels, some open and some closed, but he was pretty sure he had found the main one. But then the main tunnel itself branched off, and he hesitated, not sure which way to go. One of the two tunnels had sets of rails, one coming from behind him and one coming from the other fork. He picked the tunnel with two sets of tracks, and it turned out to be the right choice. Moments later he rounded a corner and saw a bright circle of daylight framing the silhouette of a single man standing with his hands on his hips.

Drew instantly knew who it was. There were other bald men on the planet, of course, but he knew without a doubt that it was Croll who was blocking his only escape.

Instantly he darted to the edge of the tunnel where there were some dark shadows, but he knew that he had been spotted. There was no way around it. The man was looking right at him. Or could he have been looking in the opposite direction? He'd know soon enough.

In the shadows, he noticed a small tunnel going off to the side. Quickly he darted into it, but he hit his head on a rock after only two steps. It was a dead end. He sank to the ground, holding his forehead, trying to make himself into as small a ball as possible. He was still in direct view of the main tunnel, but it was dark in here, so he had some hope of not getting caught.

Dozens of footsteps started echoing through the cave. *What's going on?* he asked himself. *Are the Earthies here?* It sounded like an entire army was coming this way.

As it turned out, that was exactly right. Croll walked by first, followed by a bunch of men with guns resting on their shoulders. None of them spoke. Their expressions were grim and determined, but silent. And there were dozens and dozens of them . . . maybe a hundred. And the horrible thing was that he recognized them.

It was all he could do not to cry out when he saw Sunit's dad walk by. And Pedro. And Mr. Bradley and Rolph. And by the time he saw his uncle march by with the rest of them, good ol' Zeke, Drew was weeping silent tears.

Did the Earthies really come down and replace the

entire city? Or was something else going on? Either way, these people were obviously friends of Croll, and that meant he couldn't trust them. None of them. Not even Uncle Zeke.

He waited until the footsteps sounded very far away before he peeked out. Through his tears he saw that there was no one else between him and the exit. But all the adrenaline was gone—he was no longer so excited about escaping. Glumly, he stepped out of his hiding place and walked outside.

HE EMERGED ON A MODERATE SLOPE, OVER-looking the City. Drew quickly moved to the side so no one could see him from inside the tunnel. Almost by habit he started scouring the sky for the moon, but it had gotten pretty cloudy and he couldn't find it. Besides, he realized, he didn't have his antenna. Still, maybe it was worth a try. He turned off the speaker volume, held the transceiver over his head, and began praying. He tried pointing it all over the sky, mainly at the big clouds and at the area around the sun, but after a minute or so he gave up. He had lost all track of time, but he still had the feeling that the moon wasn't out at the moment. And praying without his antenna was one of the stupider things he had ever thought of.

But maybe Mommy could hear him. If she was pointing her antenna up here, looking for him, she might be able to hear his signal. He tried pointing his transceiver out at the city, calling for help over and over again. But again, he got nothing in response.

He was about to tuck in his transceiver and start hiking down the hill when he heard a faint voice. *drew . . . hello drew . . .*

It was God! But where was it coming from? He

pointed his transceiver around the sky, but the voice disappeared. That didn't make any sense. He pointed it back at the City, and it came back, fainter than before. Maybe . . . He tried raising it, to above the horizon. The signal seemed to be getting stronger, so he kept raising it. But there weren't any clouds over there. . . .

hello drew . . . hello drew . . .

God! What are you doing over there? There's no moon. How can you hear me?

i'm trying to find you . . .

Well, I'm here! But so is everyone else! Everyone is in on this thing! Everyone! I can't trust anyb——

Suddenly a large hand grabbed his arm. Drew squirmed, but another hand came down on his neck and squeezed tight. The last thing he saw was Croll's grimacing face towering above him.

CHAPTER 17

Time. It's so fundamental that it's hard to think outside of it. I have to keep reminding myself that it's okay to look at things from a backward perspective; all the relevant laws of physics are the same. Temporal orientation is only a perspective.

Or so I tell myself, over and over. Because how can time be merely a perspective? On one level I know that it's only the past boundary conditions of the low-entropy Big Bang that make time seem so directed, but I still experience the flow of time. The past seems so different from the future, how can it not be?

Regardless of the conceptual difficulties, both God and physics have told me that the time-symmetric universe is a reality. I simply must accept it; no direct confirmation of God is possible. Even if God weren't a pure energy being, and our reverse-time counterparts had only managed to make themselves into the ultimate physical ma-

chine, we still could not observe Him, or any future-boundary object.

Even light that bounces off of a future-boundary object cannot give us any information. Thinking backward, the scattered light will only contain information about the object before *it is scattered, not after. And if we want to see this light before it reaches the object, we need to look away from the object, not toward it. But now the scattered light will not be there anymore; in the time-reversed perspective it's being blocked by the back of our head! We will always be looking into our own shadow. No matter how complicated the measuring device, there is no way to observe God. Instead, our only access to God is where reality has not yet been determined for either of us: the realm of quantum mechanics.*

The Journal
Year 5, Day 30

PAUL ARRIVED AT THE OUTPOST IN THE heat of the day. It was more than 30 degrees Celsius and his whole body was caked with sweat, the wetness spreading like a fungus from the area under his backpack. He had known it wasn't going to be a pleasant trip when he discovered the gap in the tradervan schedule and learned he would have to climb out of the valley the old-fashioned way. The hike had been more strenuous than he ever remembered it, but then again he had never tried it after staying up for most of the previous night. And today, the weather had not been kind.

On this slowly rotating planet, temperature differences governed the weather more than Coriolis forces, and as a result he had suffered dearly for his early departure time. He had nearly frozen at the beginning of the hike when the cold morning westerlies picked up, rushing along the valley floor to take the place of the warm rising air to the east. His exertion helped heat him up, but the wind-chill factor was brutal, and the strong winds convected the heat from his body as fast as he could replace it.

After he climbed for a while through the bitter cold, the temperature finally started to rise, and for an hour the temperature was rather comfortable. But as it happened, that time of day also coincided with some mid-morning showers. The rain turned the trail into slippery mud, almost stopping his progress on the steepest sections.

At last the downpour let up and it began to get very hot, first blowing from the east in a warming breeze and then settling down into the stagnant heat of mid-afternoon. Climbing uphill made matters even worse, and he hadn't brought nearly enough water. Several times he nearly tossed his heavy, warm clothes out of his pack to lighten his load, but he knew he'd probably need them again before this whole thing was through.

WHEN HE FINALLY STAGGERED INTO THE Outpost, he dumped his pack in the dirt and made straight for the closest well. He poured the first bucket of water over his head and then sat down with the second to drink, resting while he watched the water drip off of his bangs.

The Outpost was deserted again, the place seemingly even more empty than last time. He knew that the adults were probably all off at their mystery rendezvous spot, and everyone else would be in the middle of daysleep. Maybe he'd have to wake someone up. For now, though, he stayed by the well and pulled out his antenna to find out if anything had happened during his hike. He wasn't sure if God was on this side of the planet right now, but after a few minutes of scanning the heavens he got a signal.

"HELLO, DADDY," the speaker blared. Paul quickly turned down the volume, hoping he hadn't wakened any-one just yet. The strength of the signal was good, though; it meant that God had come down to a lower orbit after all.

"Have you talked to Drew?" he asked. "Today, I mean."

"YES. I HAVE A MESSAGE FOR YOU."

"From Drew?" Paul could hardly believe their scheme had worked.

"Make sure you tell him everything I'm about to say." It was his wife's voice, surprising him by coming out of the speaker.

"Trina? Is that you? How did you get on here?" But his wife's voice kept talking, without interruption. After a moment he realized it was some sort of recording.

"Paul, we've heard from Drew. God heard from him first. It was a very short message, and it sounded like it got cut off, but he's still okay. All he said was that 'everyone was in on it,' and that didn't make much sense to me. But I guess God triangulated his location, or saw where he broadcast from, and led me to him. I guess he can see individual people from his new orbit, because he kept telling me if I was going—"

Suddenly the voice broke up into static. Paul swore under his breath. He had forgotten how quickly God was moving across the sky now. He moved the antenna again, trying to track the orbit. After a long moment his wife's voice started up again.

"—sure that you were right and the Burnouts had him,

but after an hour or so I got to the old mine up there, and God told me I was very close."

The North Mine? He had just hiked by there this morning! Had Drew gone up there and gotten lost in the tunnels? Paul moved the antenna slightly so he wouldn't lose contact again.

"I didn't go right up to the entrance," his wife's voice continued, "because there was a lot of activity and I didn't want anyone to see me. I hid in a silverbush and just watched. Lots of people were there, maybe a hundred or so. Drew was right, Paul. Everyone was there. Mr. Bernstein, the Walsh kids, Zeke, everyone who had told me they were going to go look for Drew this morning. A big group of them left a few hours after you did, saying they were going to organize a search on the north slopes. But what they were really doing, what they are doing, is getting ready for a civil war. Croll, Channing's bodyguard, he was there, and he was walking around like he was in charge. They all had guns and were practicing shooting at these moving targets that were dressed up like Burnouts.

"At first I thought that they were just getting all worked up because they thought the Burnouts had kidnapped Drew. But God had told me that Drew was *there!* So I pointed my antenna at the mine entrance, and he *was* there. Inside. He's okay, thank God. But it looks like they're keeping him a prisoner so they can have an excuse to start a goddamn war! And guess who's behind it all. Channing. The Prime Minister, for Captain's sake! I didn't see him, but Drew said that he had gotten in his car after church and he took him to the top of the Cone and wouldn't let him leave. And Drew knew about Croll and Zeke and everyone. He couldn't believe that Zeke was part of this whole thing—frankly, I can't believe it myself—and he's really depressed. I think I cheered him up a little bit, but he got really upset when I told him I couldn't get him out right away.

"So right now I'm hiding out in this silverbush, not far from the mine. And I have no idea what to do. There are so many people here I can't imagine who would be safe to ask for help. They're mostly men, it looks like, but I can't imagine their wives don't know what's going on. I still can't believe you left me, either. I need you down here, not up with the Burnouts. So please, as soon as you hear this, get in touch with me. You can leave a message with God and then get back here. He'll be able to guide you to me, but don't get too close to the mine. Who knows what they'll do to us if they find out we know. So be careful. I love you. AND THAT'S THE MESSAGE."

Paul jerked back from the machine, surprised by the sudden change of voice, to say nothing of the message itself. The Prime Minister? Unbelievable! And a hundred people, all kidnapping his son? But it didn't make any sense. Even if they did want to trigger a civil war by making it look like the Burnouts took Drew, why would so many people be in on it? It must be a small group who was behind it, he decided. A small group of people who were using his son to incite everyone else. But then why would they keep Drew at the training camp? And why would Drew himself think that everyone was in on it? He shook his head as if trying to solve a jigsaw puzzle by shaking the box. Unsurprisingly, it didn't help.

He thought about Katrina's idea, that the Earthy colony ship might be here already. He hadn't believed her, mainly because he didn't want to believe in a conspiracy at the highest levels of government. But now she had uncovered that there was, in fact, a conspiracy. So what reason did he have to believe that they weren't here? Did he really think God was mistaken or lying? Probably not.

But that meant . . . that meant that those astronauts *had* encountered them up in orbit. Almost certainly. And the fact that two of them had died pointed to violence. But if there had been a fight, who had won? No Earthy ship had landed, so perhaps the Earthies had lost. After all, most of the people on the ship were frozen, and the few remaining crew members might have been taken by surprise. That would leave thousands of frozen settlers up there in orbit. And if the government was trying to keep it a secret, then they would stay frozen. But why would anyone want to kill off the entire colony ship? How could it have gotten here so early? And what did Channing plan to do when they failed to show up at all? Too many questions.

Paul forced himself to focus on the important thing: to get Drew out of the mine. And if there were a hundred armed men, he was going to need some help. The obvious people to ask right now were the Burnouts. He pondered the idea. Things could get really ugly. What was now a make-believe reason for a war could easily turn into a real one. But this was his son down there. And he was going to get him back.

"God? Tell Trina . . . tell Mommy that I'm going to get some help before I come back. Tell her I'll be back soon but I can't come right now."

"WHAT IS SOME HELP THAT WILL YOU GET?"

He smiled. "God, you'll be the second to know."

PAUL SHOOK FOZ GENTLY, HOPING TO WAKE him without disturbing any of the other men in the small cabin. "Foz," he whispered. "Foz, I'm sorry to wake you, but—"

"AHHHHHH!" Foz shot out a hand and locked onto Paul's neck, still screaming. Paul grabbed Foz's wrist,

but the fingers kept digging into his skin. Unable to talk
or breathe, he jabbed his elbow into Foz's stomach. The
grip eased up, and he pulled himself away and rolled
back onto the floor, gasping for air.

The commotion had woken the other residents, and
before Paul knew it, he was surrounded by three old but
very formidable men.

"He tried to kill me!" shouted Foz.

"I . . . I . . ." Paul couldn't get the words out. He gestured to his throat, and then at Foz, hoping they wouldn't
take this the wrong way. Suddenly, in near unison, all
three of them burst out laughing.

"What, you stupid, boy?" They helped him up.
"Tryin' to wake up Foz? No one's tried to wake him up
for 'bout ten years now!" They kept laughing and Paul
tried to force a smile, but it only turned into a painful
fit of coughing.

Foz looked over and made eye contact. "Oh. It's you."
He shrugged, seemingly unfazed by the whole thing. "I
thought you left us. Whatcha doing back so soon?"

Paul coughed again, wondering how he was going to
explain it all when he could barely talk. He tried to think
of a way to summarize his son's kidnapping and the
conspiracy, but nothing simple came to mind. Instead,
he held his hand to his throat and managed to force out
a single word: "War."

AT FOZ'S SLOW PACE IT TOOK THEM THREE
hours to hike down to the Rasta Kingdom. Paul had
suspected that the Outpost Burnouts had been going to
one of the kingdoms during their mysterious disappear-
ances, but he couldn't fathom the reason. The Outpost
was comprised of mostly first-generation City dropouts—
the kingdoms might have once started the same way, but

over the years they had turned into more advanced societies. So what did the two have to do with each other? But even now, Foz wouldn't answer his questions directly. "The Outpost is just helping out," he said elusively. "The kingdoms need help, so a lot of us decided to pitch in."

"What are they doing? What are they getting in return?"

"Nothing, really. Promises. Everyone thinks they want to be a part of it."

It was all Paul could do not to grab Foz and shake some answers out of him. "What? What do they want to be a part of?"

Foz hemmed and hawed for a while and finally changed the subject. "You know Mandalan geography, don't you?"

Paul shook his head. "Foz, I really need to know—"

"C'mon, hear me out. This planet has two continents. Why did your captain settle on this one?"

"Well, there are really three continents, if you count Arctica."

Foz nodded enthusiastically. "Yes, but no one in his right mind would want to live there, because it's too damn cold. And Atlantis?"

"Okay. We didn't settle on Atlantis because the half of it that doesn't disappear at high tide is too volcanic. Plus it's right on the equator, so the UV hazard is pretty bad. And a lot of the sulfur-dependent life forms are poisonous."

"Right. Pretty nasty place, huh? So the captain chose New Earth over Atlantis. Now, why'd he choose the American Valley?"

Paul sighed. "Look, Foz—"

Foz acted like he hadn't heard. "He chose it because everything to the east is desert, and everything to the north is glaciers or volcanoes. These two valleys are pretty much the only decent places to live on the whole planet, unless you count the Hurricane Peninsula down south, but you may have noticed not too many people live there."

"But I heard there were some Burnouts who went to go live up North. And wasn't there that expedition to the East Coast?"

"That's not the point. This"—he gestured all around him—"this is the point. *Our* valley. And some people realized that if we don't do anything, we're going to lose it."

Paul pondered this one for a minute or so, finally starting to see what Foz was getting at. "The Earthies," he said. "You're all worried about the Earthies." The realization hit him hard. He had always assumed that the new colonists would settle in the City. That's what everyone assumed. But was that what the Earthies would want? They'd be so different from all the other Mandalans—different socially, spiritually, and perhaps even somewhat genetically. They'd start their own city. And the obvious place to settle was here, in the Red Valley. Sure, there would be a few native Burnouts already here, but that might not stop them. There would be a fight, and the Burnouts would eventually lose, overwhelmed by both numbers and technology.

"So all of this cooperation," said Paul at last, "is just banding together for self-defense. Preparation for war. You're getting ready to fight the Earthies if they try to move into this valley."

Foz made an ambiguous motion with his hands. "Well, that's how it all began. But that's not the plan anymore. I mean, we stop these guys, and new colonists just arrive in another year or so. There's no point."

Now Paul was really confused. "So what have you all

decided to do?" But Foz shut his mouth and wouldn't say another word. Paul prodded him for a few minutes but finally gave up and started to sort out the situation in his own mind.

If God had been right, and the Earthies had arrived early, that would no doubt be an unpleasant surprise as far as the Burnouts were concerned. But, on the other hand, if the Prime Minister had done something to prevent the Earthies from ever landing, then the Burnouts would have nothing to worry about. But thousands of people murdered up in orbit? That was certainly no solution to this problem, and it made Paul shudder just thinking about it. Instead, he clung to the idea that they were still alive up there, perhaps still in hibernation, waiting for someone to come up and unfreeze them. If that was the case, this territory problem with the Burnouts was simple in comparison. Perhaps a deal could be reached, a treaty could be signed, something could be done. Paul clung to that hope as they descended into the Kingdom of the Rastas.

AFTER EMERGING FROM THE THICK ROOT-tower forest, Paul finally got his first close-up view of the buildings he had occasionally seen from the rim of the valley. Now that he could see people milling around them, he had a sense of scale. These buildings were not just big, they were enormous. Factory-sized. And one of them, off to the far edge of the kingdom, might even be taller than the Government Cone. He racked his brain, trying to imagine why the Burnouts would build a structure of that magnitude, but came up blank.

"Impressive, eh?" said Foz, looking at Paul's slack jaw with some amusement on his face. "We've been working pretty hard. Well . . . some of us less than others."

As they walked out of the foothills into the outskirts of the kingdom, Paul continued to be amazed. Hundreds of Burnouts were at work below, it seemed, and those were just the people he could see. The low, pulsing sound of continuously operating machinery was a noise so unexpected that at first he didn't even recognize it. But there it was, the sound of industrialization, and with it the evidence that the Burnouts had finally developed an electrical power system.

It was something the City had been trying to encourage them to do for decades. Even to this day the tradervans included discarded appliances and solar panels donated by the City in an effort to show the Burnouts the advantages of modernization. And supposedly it hadn't worked; supposedly only the kings had access to the small amount of electricity produced by the solar cells, and everyone else still had to lead a primitive lifestyle.

But things had obviously changed. The noise of the machinery as well as the wisps of black smoke emerging from the larger buildings made it look like the Burnouts had finally gone electrical. Solar panels were mounted everywhere, not just around the central palace, and it was clear that the king no longer had a monopoly on electricity. The first structure they passed, a large log cabin, sat next to a large array of panels; small and large black cells nestled together in a shiny black mosaic. On the far side of the cabin lay a small mountain of dismembered appliances, the plastic and wood casings empty except for a few unattached wires.

Paul couldn't resist learning what they were doing in there, and walked over to peek in a window. Inside was a ring of wooden tables covered in electronic equipment.

Circuit boards, capacitors, and electric motors all lay within a tangled mass of wires. Dozens of people crowded around, picking through the mess. It reminded Paul of his old labs at school. Some people sat on benches in the corners, wiring up breadboards with makeshift soldering irons. Another group was talking over a whirring motor hooked up to an outlet that must have been connected to the solar cells. And Paul even recognized some of them. At least three of the people were Outpost Burnouts; he recognized Julie, a mother of five, and Carl, a lifelong farmer. He couldn't imagine that either of them knew a thing about electronics.

He retreated from the window and turned back to where Foz was patiently waiting for him. "How . . . how did they learn to do all this?" he asked.

Foz thumbed his finger at the sky. "Oracle Sat'lite. All the info we need to do everything you City folk do. That was why they put it up in the first place, but no one really used it till—"

"Until what?" asked Paul, but Foz was looking beyond him with a worried expression. "What—?" Paul spun around and saw the brown eyes of a Rasta warrior just as a blunt object crashed down on his skull.

Paul struggled back to consciousness, fighting through the throbbing pain in his forehead. Part of his mind was sure that no time had passed at all, but the fact that he was staring at the door of a small wooden room belied that assumption. It took him a moment to figure out what he was sitting on, and he figured it out an instant before the stench hit him.

He stood up quickly and rattled on the outhouse door, but the resulting head-rush nearly knocked him out again. Recovering himself, he determined that the door

had somehow been latched from the outside. He made
a brief attempt to break it down, but without any room
to get a running start, he couldn't supply the necessary
momentum. Finally he contented himself with peeking
through the small holes in the outhouse door, all the
while being careful not to breathe through his nose.

Outside, across a clearing, he saw Foz holding his
own against a crowd of Rastas. There were about a
dozen Burnouts yelling at Foz, and although Paul
couldn't make out any individual words, the general tone
and frequent gestures in the direction of the outhouse
told him why they were mad: Foz had brought an out-
sider into the kingdom.

But Foz was being just as vocal, yelling back and
shaking his head at their accusations. Paul watched as
some of the new arrivals took up positions behind Foz—
Outpost Burnouts, he realized. The confrontation built
in both size and volume, but just as it started to look
like things might get ugly, a muscular man waded into
the fray and the crowd suddenly grew quiet.

It had to be the king, Paul realized. He wasn't dressed
much differently than anyone else, but he certainly carried a presence that the rest of the Burnouts deferred to.
Paul pressed his ear against a hole in the door, hoping
to be able to hear something now that the yelling had
stopped.

"So who have you brought to us?" asked the king in
a deep, clear voice that easily carried across the clearing.
Foz muttered something that Paul couldn't make out,
followed by a short-lived burst of jeers from the crowd.

"Quiet!" shouted the king. "What's done is done.
Let's see the missionary."

Paul thought he heard shouts of "Kill him!" from the
crowd, and anxiously peered through the door again to
watch the Burnouts start to converge on the outhouse,

led by the king of the Rastas. Foz walked alongside the king, tugging on his arm and talking to him, but the king paid him no attention.

Paul stepped back from the door, took a deep breath, and immediately regretted it. He had started to get used to the smell, but the sharp intake of air was too much for him and he began coughing uncontrollably. He barely recovered by the time the king pulled open the door. Paul made an attempt to look as dignified as possible, which was difficult standing in an outhouse with a bleeding forehead. He stepped out quickly, surveying the hostile looks from the crowd before turning to face the king. He knew what he had to do.

"Your Majesty," said Paul, desperately hoping this was the right way to address the man, "I need to talk to you in private." Paul thought the man seemed like a reasonable fellow, but he needed to get him away from the other Rastas, who were seemingly more motivated by emotion than logic at the moment.

"In private," repeated the king in a disinterested deadpan. "What about?"

Paul held his jaw firm. "About the early arrival of the Earthy spaceship and the approaching invasion of the Red Valley."

His words hung in the air for a few seconds, the crowd completely silenced. The king's eyes searched his face carefully before coming to a decision.

"All right," he said at last. "First we talk, and *then* I kill you."

PAUL SAT QUIETLY IN THE THRONE ROOM, trying to both look and feel relaxed. Neither was working.

"He's not going to kill you," whispered Foz from the

seat next to him. "He just had to look tough in front of everyone."

"Or maybe he was joking," added Big Red, who had joined up with them while they were being led to the palace. "Just don't lie to him. If anyone can spot a liar it's King Wally."

"King Wally?" asked Paul, incredulous. "His name is Wally?"

"Shut up," muttered Foz, jabbing him in the side just as the king entered the throne room with a woman. Paul stared at this new person for a moment before the jolt of recognition hit. It was the mystery woman he had seen during last week's visit to the Outpost.

"Joanne, have you two met?" asked the king, looking from his companion to Paul.

Joanne shook her head. "No. But he saw me, last week at the Outpost."

Paul nodded. "I did. And I didn't know quite what to make of it. But I guess you were just organizing the new cooper—"

"Okay, let's get right to the point here," interrupted King Wally. "What makes you think the Earthies have already arrived?"

Paul scratched his head, wondering how much to say. Mentioning God was out of the question, of course, at least if he wanted to be believed. He'd have to stick to more mundane explanations. "My son, Drew, was the first to find out."

"How?"

Paul hesitated for a moment. "Well, to be perfectly honest, I'm still not exactly sure. Two nights ago he told me the Earthies had arrived, but I didn't believe him. Then, when the repair mission came back yesterday with those dead astronauts, he was sure there had to be some sort of connection."

"What mission?" The king turned to Joanne. "What do you know about it?"

Joanne nodded. "Yes, there was an incident. A routine repair mission to the *Walt Disney,* supposedly. They say two of the three astronauts died in a bizarre explosion. It does sound somewhat suspicious, especially taking this new information into account."

King Wally turned back to Paul. "And so after this happened, that was when you put this together?"

He shook his head. "No. I didn't give it much thought, not until Drew disappeared."

"Drew?"

"My son."

"Right." King Wally used a fingernail to dig a chunk of wax out of his ear and then studied it intently. "And how is that related to the Earthies?"

Paul was about to say that it wasn't related at all, but the matter-of-fact way the king had asked made him stop and think, and suddenly he made the connection. "Of course! Channing kidnapped him because Drew knew about the Earthies! He must have told him during church last night, right before he disappeared!" He gazed off into space, pondering the implications.

The king cracked a smile. "This is obviously a new revelation."

"Yes, well . . . Channing's clever. He's using Drew's disappearance for another reason as well, and that had me sidetracked along with everyone else. You see, he has convinced everyone that *you* kidnapped him. Or one of the other kingdoms, I'm not sure. He's using the emotions in the City to build an army, and if the situation isn't cleared up they could be invading this valley in a matter of days."

King Wally shook his head. "Wait, wait a minute. Before, when we were outside . . . I thought you were talking about the Earthies invading. It's the *City* that's going to invade?"

"Well, no one will invade at all if you help me get my son back and straighten everything out."

The king considered that for a few moments. "And the Earthies?"

Paul lowered his eyes. "The Earthies . . . the Earthies need to be rescued."

A chorus of laughter immediately followed his statement, coming from not only the two Rastas but also Foz and Big Red. It went on for a rather long time, and as it continued, Paul grew indignant. "I'm serious here!" he shouted. "If my guess is right, that repair mission was actually an attempt to take over the *Mayflower!* And considering no ships have landed since then, I tend to think that they might have been successful."

His words had a much more sobering effect on the room than he would have expected, and once again everyone was deadly serious. "Or maybe," said the king, "the fact that they haven't landed only means they haven't even arrived yet."

"I hope you're right. Because otherwise there are thousands of frozen settlers up in orbit, completely at the mercy of the Prime Minister, who I'm learning is not a particularly nice person."

King Wally looked thoughtful for a full minute. "How long until we could be up there?" he finally asked.

Paul chuckled. "In orbit? Well, if you want to hijack a spaceplane . . ." He trailed off, realizing that the question had not been addressed to him.

Joanne cleared her throat. "We might be able to launch tomorrow, but not with any passengers. The test rocket wasn't intended to have an airtight hull. But maybe if we had some assistance . . ." She trailed off, and everyone's gaze came back to Paul.

"Okay," said the king after a quick pause. "We'll help you get your kid back. But we need some things from you in return."

Paul's jaw moved noiselessly as his brain tried to process what had just happened. "You have . . ." he finally managed. "You built . . ." He was unable to complete the thought.

"Wake up, City boy," said the king with a grin. "I mean, what do you take us for? Savages?"

CHAPTER 18

The boredom must be getting to me. I spent the week trying to figure out how to look at a Tzengian Well.

It's not the easiest thing to do, to look at infinity. The wells last for a long time, thanks to the injected electrons, charging up the well boundary so it becomes quasi-stable. The wells even become large enough to see unaided when the magnetic field ramps down and the growing electron orbits widen the rift in space-time. But the ultraintense laser scatters off of the well even as it is produced, and the eye hazard of the white laser is present at all wavelengths. Still, I had four seconds between laser shots to see the thing, so I had some of the engineers make a safety shutter on the inner porthole. It closes for a full half second—a ridiculous safety margin, I thought, given the attosecond laser pulse length—and for the other three and a half seconds I was able to see one of the vacuum momentum-dumps that allow us to travel at these amazing speeds.

And what do they look like? Black. That's all, just black. It absorbed all light as it flew upward, then made the tip of the diamond cone appear to have a big hole in it as it came back down. I can't quite bring myself to admit that the whole exercise wasn't worth it. After all, I was able to see for myself the infinity that physicists renormalized out of their equations until Tzeng realized that— though it couldn't be a real gravitational infinity— it was a real inertial infinity. A real infinity, at every point in space around us. The thought still gives me goose bumps, that all of matter is just a tiny fluctuation on an otherwise infinite back-ground of vacuum inertia. Reality is truly more amazing that we can ever hope to comprehend.

The Journal
Year 7, Day 99

KATRINA BACKED OUT FROM UNDERNEATH the silverbush, feeling like the worst mother in the world. She knew there was nothing she could do right now; her husband was organizing the rescue mission, and her son was asleep. But still, the act of leaving— turning her back on Drew and walking down to the City—felt like the absolute worst thing she had ever done.

After Paul's second message from God she didn't know whether to feel elated or depressed. She was exhausted, thirsty, hungry, and the last thing she wanted to do was to go to the Biodome on what sounded like a pointless errand. But if that's what the Burnouts demanded in return for their help, that's what she would do.

She descended the hill underneath the reddening sky, trying to stay under tree cover in case anyone was watching from above. She had first planned to wait until nightfall, but Drew had fallen asleep and she had decided to head back before it got too dark to see. There would be no moon tonight, she knew, and walking down the hillside with only auroras to guide her would have been treacherous. Fortunately she didn't run into anyone until she got back down to the valley floor. Then she was spotted by a tired group of women who were supposedly searching for her son.

She told them that she had been looking for her son all day, up in the hills. Everyone expressed their sorrow and worry, but this time around all their statements rang empty. *How many of you know that Drew's up in the North Mine? How many of your husbands are up there, keeping him prisoner right now?* At last she was able to pull herself away from the group and hurried home, hoping she wouldn't see anyone else.

ONCE SAFELY INSIDE HER HOUSE SHE WENT through the motions of eating, drinking, and showering, but she was unsure if they made her feel any better. She couldn't stop herself from imagining that Drew had escaped again, escaped only to find that his mother had left him. Drew had told her all about the earlier escape, and she was rather impressed with her son's ingenuity. But it had been all he could do to convince his captors to let him keep his transceiver, and he had to sacrifice his extra fiber-optic cable in exchange. So another escape was unlikely, she knew.

And what about God? How did it fit into this whole

thing? Praying to it was a rather interesting experience, she had to admit. She was nearly convinced that it was some sort of alien intelligence, mainly because she couldn't figure out what its goals were, what drove it to help them. No doubt it was having as much trouble understanding them as vice versa, but she still felt that it enjoyed this sudden flurry of multiple communications, passing messages, and all that. Could it be lonely? she wondered. Or were human emotions just not applicable?

Earlier that evening she had talked to Drew about God, and her son was disappointed—if not surprised— to learn what she thought God really was. They discussed possible theories, and after she had mentioned his father's interpretation of the "lowest planet," Drew had gotten very excited. He said that sometimes God told him that he was from a place closer to the sun, and Drew thought that Hades made a lot of sense. She told him his father's opinion, about how life would be impossible on such a harsh planet, but all Drew said was that God was very different. Quite an understatement, she thought.

Thinking about it now, she realized she didn't know much about Hades in the first place, so she turned on the Encyc. The first piece of information she already knew: Hades was the closest planet to the sun. Also, it was the last planet discovered, taking weeks to find after Captain arrived in the system because it was so hard to see. But Paul had been right about it being an inhospitable place. There was no atmosphere at all, and no liquid water either. The sunward side of the planet never got a break from the scorching sunlight because the orbital period was exactly equal to the planet's rotational period, apparently common for objects in a large gravitational field. She clicked on the section about why the planet's surface was so dark, but it was all too technical to understand. She hit the "dumb it down" function, selecting the simplest explanation, but all she found was a single sentence: The planet's crystalline silicon surface acts like a solar panel and absorbs nearly all sunlight. She thought the concept of a planet-sized absorber was interesting, but it didn't give her any ideas as to how life could possibly have evolved on such a place.

If there was life on the planet, she realized it would have to be silicon-based instead of carbon. She did a quick search for silicon-based life and was surprised to get quite a long list of references. Sorting through them, though, most of them turned out to be science fiction stories. Selecting out only the real science articles, there was still a large literature, but the overall consensus was that silicon just couldn't replace carbon. True, it was the atom with the second-largest range of possible molecules, but it still couldn't compete with the amazing ring and chain structures of carbon. Some articles claimed that silicones, chains of alternating silicon and oxygen, might be able to have a complex enough biochemistry to create life, but they had never been found in nature. To make matters worse, all of the articles stressed the need for a liquid solvent where chemical reactions could take place. On Mandala it was water, of course, but there was some speculation that other types of oceans might work as well. Silicones, it was suggested, might be created in a sea of sulfuric acid. But a quick cross-check revealed that there were no liquids at all on Hades, not sulfuric acid or anything else. And without any liquid, the literature was adamant about the fact that there could not be life.

She was about to turn off the Encyc when she noticed an interesting category in the Hades section: Loss of the

SPEED II spaceprobe. She clicked on it, wondering what it was all about. As it turned out, the *Walt Disney* had brought two unmanned probes to explore planets, acronymed SPEED for Small Planet Environment Exploration Device. They had been used at almost every stop on the way to Mandala. *SPEED I* had been lost in a fierce windstorm in the Tau Ceti system, but *SPEED II* had survived the Journey, and once they arrived here, Captain used it as a scientific instrument to explore their new system. Its first mission was Hades, a scientific anomaly that defied explanation by the Original planetologists. But the mission was a failure. The probe was shorted out on touchdown by some strange pockets of charge on the surface. It was never recovered.

Katrina read all this with shaking hands. God said he was a spaceship. Maybe from Hades. Here was a spaceship that had landed on Hades and never been seen again. If there was life on the planet, could it have fixed the probe and used it to get off the planet? But if it was an unmanned probe there wouldn't be any space for an alien to hitch a ride. And there would be no controls to operate the ship. All that added to the fact that no life could possibly exist on Hades to begin with.

Still, the idea was too tempting to discard without a little more thought. She loaded up a picture and description of the *SPEED II* probe and regarded it curiously. It was covered with scientific instruments, corresponding to long, detailed lists underneath the picture. But looking at it, it was obvious that no life form could ever enter such a machine. There was just no room for any internal control. Sighing, she was about to turn it off again when a single word caught her eye. The word SEVEN. Quickly she zoomed in on the equipment list underneath:

CAMERAS (SEVEN)

> 0.25–250 KeV, 3 Mpixel (ONE)
> 　X-ray Spectrometer

> 5–350nm, 3 Mpixel (ONE)
> 　UV Mapping Spectrometer

> 300–1100nm, 20 Mpixel, adj. focus (THREE)
> 　Extravisible Mapping Spectrometer
> 　Long-Range Imaging System
> 　Short-Range Imaging System

> 0.9–14μm, 20 Mpixel, adj. focus (TWO)
> 　Infrared Mapping Spectrometer
> 　Infrared Imaging System

Seven cameras. Seven eyes. Something told her it wasn't a coincidence. Possibilities raced through her mind, and after a moment she latched onto an idea that made some sense. Maybe it wasn't an alien life form after all. Maybe it was an artificial intelligence. No one had ever been able to make one, certainly not one that was conscious. But if the computer system got zapped during the landing, maybe it scrambled the circuitry in just the right way. Maybe the computer somehow became conscious, and then was able to repair the ship and take off again, all on its own. It was far-fetched, but the best idea she could come up with. She'd mention it to her husband when she saw him again.

Katrina glanced out the window, noticing for the first time that it had gotten very dark. She swore as she checked her watch. Unless she hurried, she was going to be late. Quickly she flipped open her DC and keyed her husband. No answer. Hopefully he was still in the Red Valley, far from the North Mine. She pulled on her coat and filled a water bottle, stuffing it into her pocket as she hurried out of the house.

*   *   *

AFTER LEAVING HER BIKE IN THE EMPTY
rack in front of the Biodome, she was glad to discover
that no one else was around. Trevor and some of the
others had been known to pull some late nights, but
without her presence the research had probably slowed
down quite a bit. And now, with what she was about to
do, research would fully come to a halt. Still, this was
her son she was talking about, and she wasn't going to
destroy anything at the lab. Just make the place inac-
cessible for a little while.

She let herself in through the back door and made her
way to the Biodome airlock. Inside were four space
suits, salvaged from the spare equipment on the *Walt
Disney*. Normally she put one on and then proceeded
into the decontamination chamber, scrubbing all of the
Earth microbes off of the suit with nasty showers and
baths, one of the stages requiring her to be fully sub-
merged for half an hour. But she wouldn't be doing any
of that tonight. Tonight all she needed were the space
suits themselves. She found a pushcart in the storage
room and loaded the suits. They weren't too heavy except for the tanks and rebreather systems, but she certainly couldn't carry all four of them halfway out of the
valley. After lashing them to the cart with duct tape she
took a last look around, wondering if anything else
might be useful. They needed weapons, Paul had told
her. But real weapons were hard to come by, and although there might be some small blades in the dissec-
tion room, she didn't want to have any deaths on her
conscience. If they were going to kill each other, she
wasn't going to help.

But just as she was leaving, she spotted a recent de-
livery package on the main table. Her name was on it,

and from the warning labels she realized that it was the
chemofly hive from Farm Sciences. They had finally
gotten around to shipping it over here. She hesitated for
a moment and then started unwrapping it. Inside was a
metal cylinder about the size of her forearm. She wondered how long the flies could last in there, without any
airholes. Maybe they were dead already. Regardless,
though, the heavy pipe might make a good club in an
emergency. She smacked it into her palm a few times
and then slipped it inside her coat pocket. It wasn't
much, but if she was going to be caught in the middle
of a battle, it would be better than nothing.

Finishing up, she turned off the lights and pushed the
cart out into the dark night. She looked up at the northern
hill, its black shape silhouetted against the backdrop of
stars and the faint green auroras. Now came the hard part.

ONCE SHE LEFT THE FUSED-DIRT SUR-
faces, the cart got to be a real annoyance. She first tried
pushing it ahead of her, but every minute or so it would
come to a sudden stop as the wheels got caught on a
root or a ditch hidden in the darkness. Next she tried
flipping it around and pulling it up the mining trail behind her, but that hurt her arms and her back. At last
she settled with pulling it while walking backward; that
slowed her down but seemed to be the best solution. She
still tripped over objects occasionally, but managed to
climb for an hour before stopping for a break.

Sitting on the ground, she checked her watch and realized that God should be almost directly overhead
again. She had gotten the timing of the orbit memorized
during her stay in the silverbush, thinking it might come
in handy. She didn't bother to open her antenna, but just
pointed her transceiver straight up. With the larger cone-

angle of her microwave signal, God wasn't hard to find.

hello mommy, the quiet voice said.

God, have you talked to Drew or Paul since I last asked?

no i haven't. i am getting tired of my new orbit.

She sighed. *Don't leave. Please. Stay down here until we get Drew.* She smiled. Here she was, trying to be persuasive when she didn't have the faintest idea what the thing really wanted. She decided to test her artificial-intelligence theory. *God, could you leave your spaceship?*

interesting. i don't think so. but maybe. i will try.

Katrina bit her lip. She didn't want God to do anything that would end his current usefulness. *Don't try now. I was just asking. Have you always been in the spaceship?*

no. not always. are the other spaceships like me?

She frowned, uneasy that the questioning had been turned back on her. Maybe God didn't even know what he was. But if God wasn't "born" in the spaceship, then her artificial-intelligence theory must be wrong. *Others like you? I don't think so. Most spaceships don't talk like you do. For a while I thought that we made your spaceship, and now you're living in it somehow. But now—*

you made this spaceship?

Not me. But people like me. Maybe we created it, and then maybe it created you. She hoped she was making sense to God.

the spaceship did not create me.

How do you know what created you?

i remember things from before.

That was interesting. She didn't know what he meant, but thought that maybe Paul could help her figure it out. She wished she could talk to him right now.

If you talk to Paul, tell him I'm on my way.
okay.

She got to her feet, stretched her back for a minute, and then resumed dragging the cart up the trail.

AFTER ANOTHER TWO HOURS SHE THOUGHT she might be getting close.

"Katrina!" a voice whispered directly in front of her. She froze in surprise, repressing the urge to shout.

"Who's there?" she asked warily.

"Don't make any noise," the voice continued. "Your husband is up the hill."

Shadowy forms appeared, converging on her from all directions. One figure beckoned her forward, and she looked around her, confused. "Are you Burnouts?" she asked.

They didn't answer, but the figure who beckoned her started walking into the scrub brush on the side of the trail. She glanced behind her and was glad to see that some other forms had taken the suits off the cart, carrying them along. Realizing that she was about to be left behind, she sprang into motion, following the shadowy forms on their makeshift trail.

They walked for about twenty minutes, cutting across the hill and then starting to climb. It was so dark she could hardly see. The poor lighting hadn't been too bad on the trail, but here it was extremely treacherous. But somehow her guides seemed to know exactly where they were going, and eventually they emerged into a small, crowded clearing.

"Trina? Is that you?"

She had never been so glad to hear her husband's voice. She worked her way toward him, pressing her way past a few Burnouts and then feeling Paul's familiar hands. They held each other for a moment, but their reunion was quickly interrupted by a gruff voice from behind.

"Okay. We need to get going before they notice the missing guard. You ready, Katrina?"

She turned, trying to find the speaker in the dark. "What are you talking about? I brought the stuff you wanted, okay?"

Paul spoke softly. "Trina, this is King Wally. He's going to help us get Drew out. I was going to go in with them and use my antenna to find Drew, but I didn't build earphones into it, and they didn't want the noise giving them away. When I told them you can talk to Drew with the speaker off, they decided you should go instead."

A moment of panic seized her. They wanted *her* to go into the mine?

"We have weapons for you," King Wally said. "We're short on guns, but there're knives and an extra sword and—"

"I'm not taking any of that. I'm not going in there. I'll talk to him from out here."

Paul grabbed her arm and pulled her to one side. "Look, these guys are good. They're not going to let you get hurt. I can't believe I'm trying to convince you to do this—it's scaring me to death—but they're right. You can talk to Drew over the transceiver and find your way to him."

"But . . ."

Paul faced her and held her shoulders tightly. "Trina. For Drew."

She stared back into the darkness for a long time before she nodded. "For Drew," she repeated.

CHAPTER 19

CAPTAIN: *Everyone ready?*

A. Ryutov: *The entire crew is suited up in ship center. Airlocks sealed, thrusters charged, and we're ready to spin at your command.*

CAPTAIN: *How long has it been since the last impact?*

A. Ryutov: *We had a class one . . . six hours ago. Before that it's been twenty-five hours since the class three yesterday.*

CAPTAIN: *Okay. Leave me now. I'll let you know when it's time.*

A. Ryutov: *God bless.*

[thirteen-minute pause]

CAPTAIN: *Now! [clears throat] Detach the shield and spin us now!*

J. Hansen: *Shield is clearing, clearing, clear. Confirm, shield is clear. Fully engage thrusters one through six, nineteen through twenty-four.*

M. Sandoz: *Thrusters engaged. One degree, two*

*degrees, three, four, five, seven degrees from
normal.*

J. Hansen: Shield is holding position.

*M. Sandoz: Ten degrees. Fifteen degrees. Twenty
degrees.*

CAPTAIN: It's going to be okay. I can feel it.

M. Sandoz: Twenty-five degrees. Thirty degrees.

[class three meteor impact]

[Klaxons]

J. Hansen: Shit! We've been—

*CAPTAIN: Where were we hit? Where were we
hit?*

*M. Sandoz: We're spinning fast. Twenty, ten,
we're back through normal.*

*J. Hansen: We're going to hit the shield again!
It's tipped too far—*

*CAPTAIN: Are the thrusters working? Get the
thrusters working!*

[impact with shield]

*CAPTAIN: Do we have any power? Life support,
are we going to make it? Can anyone stop this
thing?*

*F. Lumpkin: We have center hull integrity, life
support looks okay. But we're losing pressure
stern. I think the spheromaks got hit—*

*CAPTAIN: Dear God. The spheromaks. Why not
just kill us outright?*

*A. Ryutov: They might be okay, sir. B, A, and F
lost pressure, but they might still be okay.*

*CAPTAIN: No, Alice, they're not okay. I've finally
killed us all.*

The Log
Year 23, Day 209.15

ALEXANDER CHANNING NEARLY DIDN'T AN-
swer his DC. He knew it had to be important; no one
called him at this time of night unless it was an emergency. But last night's grilling of the Randall kid had
worn him out, and he felt like he deserved a night off.

"What do you want?" Channing snapped into the receiver.

Croll didn't even bother to say hello. "Three men are
dead. The kid is gone. There's a major security leak, and
I want to know who it is."

"What? What happened?"

"I'm not talking anymore on this channel. I'm at the
Randall residence, so you can meet me here. Don't bring
anyone. And don't call back." A click signified the end
of the conversation.

Channing stared at the now-dead DC, trying to will
his mind fully awake. That damn kid was loose! If the
boy talked, and if anyone believed him, Channing's
years as Prime Minister would come to a disgraceful
end. All of the anti-Burnout feelings that built up yesterday could easily be transferred onto the government,
and then everything would be lost.

He quickly threw on some warm clothes and took the
elevator down to the garage, mulling over the problem
in his head. On one level he knew that a minister was
considered more trustworthy than a kid. And he was the
Prime Minister. The boy was . . . just a boy.

But why would a child make up such outrageous al-
legations if they weren't true? He shook his head as he
got into his car. He could defend himself if the accusations were coming from another adult, but from a
child? Faced with testimony from the boy, the public
would instantly turn against him. Still, there had to be a
way out.

"Lights," he commanded the car as he pulled out of

the G.C. He spoke his destination, and the route to the Randalls' house lit up on the windshield. Why were they meeting there, anyway? He supposed that the kid might be expected to go home, and Croll might be planning to intercept him. He nodded to himself. Croll was a little intense, but he was a good man to have on your side in a crisis.

He forced himself to think about the political fallout as he drove east, along the river. *What would the public believe?* The parents would have to take the fall, Channing realized. No one would believe that the boy would lie, but if he could implicate his parents, then no one would believe the kid, either. He mulled over the possibilities, the moves and countermoves playing out in his mind like a game of speed chess. People in the City were already willing to believe that the father's relationship to the Burnouts was somehow related to his son's disappearance. Would they believe that the preacher had staged the kidnapping for reasons of his own?

Channing knew this wasn't just anyone he would be accusing, but the respected preacher of Eastside. Preacher Randall, a traitor? It just didn't seem plausible, but he would have to force plausibility onto it. Perhaps if he had Croll take both the preacher and his wife into custody tonight . . .

He parked out of sight, behind the house, and headed for the front door. Through the main window he could see Croll and his two brothers tearing the living room apart. The Randalls were nowhere in sight, but he supposed that Croll had already dealt with them. So much the better.

Channing pushed the door open and stepped inside. Instantly three rifles were pointing at him, and he froze out of both fear and confusion. After a long moment the rifles came down and Croll beckoned him inside. He took a deep breath and closed the door behind him.

"What's all this about, Croll?" Croll motioned for him to keep his voice down, so the Prime Minister continued in a whisper. "What happened? Where's the kid? Where are the Randalls? What's this about three people being dead?"

Croll grimaced. "Have a seat." Most of the cushions had been thrown to the ground, but Channing placed one back on the couch. He sat down slowly, waiting for an explanation. "Who else knew about the boy?" Croll asked.

Channing shook his head. "No one else. Tell me what happened."

Croll took a step forward. "You tell me what happened. Think, dammit. Who could have known we were holding him?"

"No one. I don't know. You've been with him more than I have. I didn't tell anyone, if that's what you're asking."

Croll turned away from him, and for the first time Channing noticed the burns in his clothing. "What happened to you?" He looked over at Rick and George and noticed similar marks. And Rick had a bandage on his forearm. "What . . . ?"

Croll's DC buzzed, and he answered it quickly. "What have you got?" he said into the device. "Uh-huh. Uh-huh. Really. No, I have no idea. Okay, meet us at the Randalls' house." He snapped the DC back on his belt and sighed. "Well, that clinches it. The Randalls know what's going on."

Channing shook his head in confusion. "The kid's parents? What do they know?"

Croll turned to glare at the Prime Minister. "They were at the North Mine tonight. With a group of Burn-outs. They killed Jonathan, Douwe, and Keith. And they made off with the kid. They headed north, it looks like, so they're probably halfway to a kingdom by now."

"Burnouts? But that doesn't make any sense. And what makes you think the Randalls were behind it?"

Croll gestured to his brother. "Rick thought he saw the mother, Katrina, just before the chemoflies got us. I didn't see her, but we searched the area afterward and found an abandoned cart with a Biodome sticker on it. That's where she works. I just talked to one of my men who went to check it out, and sure enough there was stuff missing. Sometime this evening she went in there and took the cart, a chemofly hive, and a bunch of sterile suits. We haven't found the suits, and frankly I don't have any idea why she took them. But we did find out about the chemoflies."

"She came in and attacked you with flies? And got away with her son? What sort of militia force do you have up there?"

Croll shook his head. "There must have been two dozen Burnouts there, and all of the new recruits had gone home a few hours before. So it was only me and my men, about a dozen of us. Most of us were asleep when the first shouts started. And by then it was already too late. Jonathan was the guard outside, and he probably didn't even know what hit him. We found him with his throat slashed, under some scrub brush. Douwe and Keith were sleeping in the prison passage, and they must have put up a struggle, because that's when some of us woke up."

Rick nodded. "Yeah, I called over to see what was going on, and when I tried to walk out into the main tunnel someone started shooting."

"Shooting? You mean the Burnouts really have firearms? Or did they raid one of the weapons stores up there?"

"Both," said Croll. "They brought their own, but they got at least seven of our rifles in the raid. I'm not sure how much ammo they have, but apparently they can make their own."

Channing frowned, wondering how the Burnouts had gotten involved. This was getting very serious indeed.

"Anyway," continued Rick, "the gunfire from the main tunnel kept us pinned down for a few minutes, but we managed to grab our rifles when they stopped to reload. We started shooting back then, and I think Edword winged one of them, but at that point they already had the kid and were pulling back."

"How do you know they went back to the kingdoms? Did you follow them out?"

"We were regrouping," said Croll, "but they had the positional advantage. They controlled the main tunnel, and we were split up down the small side passages. They only needed a few guns to keep us pinned inside. Eventually, of course, they had to pull back. We started to come out into the main tunnel, when this metal cylinder came flying out of nowhere, and this chemofly hive slipped out right at my feet. I don't know how long the damn insects had been in there, but they were pissed." He gestured to the small burns on his back. "They got me worse than anyone, I think, but it kept us busy for the minute they needed to get away. By the time we got outside, they were gone. A blood trail led uphill for a few meters, but it didn't leave us much to follow. Maybe once it's light there'll be a better trail."

Channing rubbed his temples. The only good news was it sounded like they had gone North to some Burnout kingdom, so the boy wasn't about to show up and ruin his career immediately. "Still," he said, "it sounds like they knew exactly what they were going for."

"Exactly. So who leaked it? It wasn't any of my men."

"Well, you said the kid almost escaped yesterday. Someone in your new army must have seen him when he was out of his cell, and then told the parents when they got back to town."

"Right. That would have left less than an hour for them to rob the Biodome, hike to a kingdom, gather up an army of Burnouts, and hike back to the mine. No way. This took more planning than that."

"Okay. But maybe someone radioed back the information. Do DCs work up there?"

"Not yet. The antennas are going to be installed next week."

"Hmmm. What about that thing the boy talks through, that transceiver? Could the kid have used that to talk to someone during his escape?"

"Not without his antenna, and you took that from him last night, right?"

Channing nodded, thinking furiously. This was the second security leak. Someone had told the kid about the *Mayflower,* and someone had told the Randalls about their son. Simplicity demanded that the informer was the same person. But who could it possibly be?

"You realize we have to counterattack," said Croll. "They can't be allowed to think that they can get away with this. We need to teach the Burnouts a lesson they won't quickly forget."

"What? Now?"

"Tomorrow. We bring the bodies down to the City, explain what happened, and let the public react. We'll be invading the Red Valley by noon. It'll be pushing it, but we already have a lot of the logistics together."

"But how do you think the public will react if the Randalls turn up with their kid and explain that *we* kidnapped him?"

Croll shrugged. "The Randalls are fugitives. Once we

convince everyone that they were behind the attack, no one will listen to anything they say."

Channing sank his head into his hands. "But that's the problem. No one is going to believe that they were behind this. This man is a preacher, for Captain's sake! If they turn up they'll ruin everything, unless we come up with some sort of cover story. Something plausible, but still bad enough to turn people against them."

Croll cracked his knuckles. "Why not just attack? They're almost certainly still with the Burnouts, so the sooner we attack, the less time they have to contact anyone else."

Channing nodded. "Okay. But we still need a story. Maybe they kidnapped their own son, or arranged for the Burnouts to do it for them. And then they attacked the mine because . . . because . . . Damn. It just won't make sense."

One-Arm George spoke up. "Maybe you could say that their son really was taken by the Burnouts. And the Burnouts demanded to be led to the military base in return for not harming him."

Channing stood up and started pacing across the floor. "Yes. They were blackmailed into it. That might work. We'll put out the word that the Randalls are wanted for treason, that they led the Burnouts right to us. That's probably close enough to the truth, anyway. Now we just have to make sure we catch up to them before they tell their side of the story. How soon did you say we could start that counterattack, Croll?"

Croll grinned. "We'll have everything ready to go by dawn. After that it depends on the public reaction."

"Dawn then. Bring the bodies down to the G.C. and set up a microphone. If it's war the Burnouts want . . ."

"You got it. And what about the . . ." Croll jerked his thumb upward, indicating the *Mayflower*.

"It can wait," said Channing. "They're not going anywhere."

CHAPTER 20

Maybe we should stop transmitting to Earth. Continue our journey, but keep it all to ourselves. True, the alien biologies we have discovered have been scientifically fascinating, but is the information helping Earth in any way? Why do we keep informing the descendants of our long-dead masters about our every move? I suppose if we all eventually die out here, at least our work would not go unheralded. Humanity will still know of our achievements, even if we fail. But if we succeed? Even if our next destination proves to be the final stop, it will be more than a hundred years before the next colony ship would arrive from Earth. What will happen to us in that time? We know evolutionary advances are primarily made by small populations, separated from the original species by distance and time. But a century—four or five generations—is but an evolutionary eye-blink, even with the inevitable increase in mutations caused by cosmic radiation. It would take

*much, much longer to become anything truly dif-
ferent, and for that we would have to stop transmitting, perhaps never to contact Earth again until
our descendants accidentally run across each
other many tens of thousands of years in the future. Is this what God wants? I keep trying to open
my mind to hear His answer, but so far my prej-
udices are clouding my ability to listen.*

*The Journal
Year 20, Day 82*

DREW WAS GLAD WHEN THEY FINALLY GOT TO
slow down. A Burnout had just returned from a scouting
mission and announced that they weren't being followed. Immediately the fast uphill hike slowed to a more
reasonable pace, and Drew was able to catch his breath,
although it was still strange to be hiking in the dark.

"So they're just going to let us go?" Mommy asked.

The dim form of King Wally peered back at them.
"No chance. They'll be after us as soon as it gets light.
We've just jump-started a war. I suppose it would have
happened sooner or later, but this will get them to act
before they're ready, and that'll be a big advantage."

"You're not going to beat them in a straight-out fight,"
said Daddy. "Your only hope is to negotiate. And even
that'll be hard after you killed those men."

"We're not negotiating," responded the king. "We're
defending ourselves, and they'll be surprised if they
think it'll be an easy fight."

"Where are we going?" Drew asked, squeezing
Daddy's hand. "When are we going back home?"

His parents slowed down and let some of the Burnouts
pass them so they could move to the back of the group.

"Drew," began Mommy, "we're going to go stay with

the Burnouts for a while, until we're sure it's safe to go back. The Prime Minister kidnapped you once, and we're not going to let it happen again."

"I don't think it was really the Prime Minister. I think it was the Earthies." He explained his duplicate-Minister theory to his parents.

Daddy sighed. "I know you'd like to think the Prime Minister is a good person, but he's not. No one has heard from the Earthies, and he's probably responsible. That repair mission was more likely some sort of ambush. But whatever happened up there, he certainly didn't want it to be public knowledge. So when he found out that you knew about the Earthies . . ."

Drew nodded. "Yeah, I told him during your sermon. I should have stayed quiet, I guess. But I was right about the Earthies, wasn't I?"

"Yeah," said Daddy, laughing. "I should have listened to you. I knew you weren't talking to God, but I didn't stop to think you might be talking to someone else."

"But . . ." Drew broke off, trying to organize his thoughts. He understood that the God he prayed to was probably different from Daddy's God, but why wasn't that okay? Why couldn't each of them pray to their own? "But he says he's God," Drew protested. "Maybe he really is."

"That's just a name you call him. He might not even know what the word means. He doesn't know nearly as much as we do; the only reason he knew about the Earthies was that he's up in orbit. Or at least he's relaying his transmissions through some satellite."

Drew thought about that for a moment. "If he's not really God, what could he be?"

"I don't really know, Drew. Maybe someone here on Mandala is controlling a spaceship? But it's certainly nothing Channing knows about, so it can't be government—"

"Paul," Mommy broke in, "I was reading about Hades just before I went to the Biodome. The Encyc said Captain lost an unmanned probe there, back when they first explored the system. And I was thinking that maybe God was somehow related to the probe. No one ever recovered it, so I was thinking . . . if God was trying to say he was from Hades, then maybe he is the probe."

"Hmm. I think I remember hearing something about that mission. The probe was shorted out by the surface currents, right?"

"Right. I was thinking that maybe the electrical shock did something to the on-board computer system and it came to life. I know it sounds a little silly, but the probe has seven cameras—"

"No way. We can't build an artificial consciousness, so accidentally creating one like that . . . No. But I had forgotten about the planet's surface. It's semiconducting, right?"

"Yeah. Silicon, I think."

Now Drew was really confused. "What's semiconducting?"

Daddy cleared his throat. "Well, some materials conduct electricity, like copper wire, and some materials are insulators and don't conduct electricity, like plastic. But semiconductors are a little bit of both. When a semiconductor is cold it acts like an insulator, but you just need a little bit of energy to knock some electrons into a conduction band, and then it acts like a conductor. Computer chips are semiconductors, and they work because they're sometimes acting like insulators and sometimes like conductors. The right combinations let them perform logic."

Drew didn't really understand, so he pressed Daddy

for more. "You mean Hades is a giant computer chip?"

Daddy didn't respond right away, and after a moment he slowed to a halt.

"What is it, dear?" asked Katrina. He didn't answer, so she simply waited with Drew. "I think you gave Daddy an idea," she whispered to him.

"Yes you did," Daddy said at last. "And a very interesting one. But I'm not sure I believe—"

"Just tell us," said Mommy. "I'll get cold if we stand here too long."

They started hiking uphill again as Daddy started to talk. "Okay," he began. "Drew said that Hades is like a big computer chip, but that's not quite right. The surface, I believe, is crystalline silicon, so it's like a computer chip before they add the transistors. But you create transistors by adding impurities to the pure silicon, impurities that make either n-type or p-type semiconductors. And there are bound to be impurities on the surface of Hades. I imagine that on Hades it would be fairly common to get a natural transistor, just by chance. All you'd need would be a p-type impurity region between two n-types, or vice versa."

"Okay," said Katrina, "but so what? Are you trying to figure out how the probe could have gotten electrocuted?"

"No. Think bigger. You're the biologist. How did life start on Mandala?"

"What are you driving at? Life . . . well, it's probably a lot like we think it happened on Earth, but even that's still not completely understood. You need structures that can reproduce themselves. PNA was the first individual object that could reproduce, but before that were autocatalytic sets of enzymes—"

"Exactly. Life began when, for whatever reason, certain chemicals or sets of chemicals began to be able to reproduce themselves. Well, what if, what if on Hades, instead of getting chemical evolution, an electrical circuit developed that could reproduce itself?"

"What? Is that even possible? I mean, you'd need a power source, right?"

"But on Hades the sun supplies more than enough power. The photoelectric effect converts sunlight into electrical energy."

"Okay. But how could a circuit reproduce itself? It doesn't make any sense to me."

"Well, as I said, all you need is a few impurities to make a transistor. And in warm silicon I think you'd have fairly mobile ions, at least on the surface. So all you need to move impurities around are some well-placed electrical fields, but those could be made by the circuit itself. And I'm not saying they would be circuits just like we make in computer chips; they might be three-dimensional clusters of atoms instead . . . quantum-scale circuits. They could attract the necessary atoms to reproduce themselves, just like biological life does."

"So you're thinking that if you got some electrical version of RNA then . . . what? You get electrical evolution? Competing computer chips?"

"Maybe. I'm not sure how they'd compete, though. Maybe on a microscopic level. Or maybe they'd want to control as much surface area as possible, get the most energy from the sun."

"So you're thinking that *intelligence* evolved there, that God is an electrical intelligence? I thought you didn't believe in aliens."

"Well, if the basic circuit is on a quantum scale . . . I don't know," muttered Daddy. "You're right, I don't believe it. I mean . . . If the two-consciousness universe is wrong—"

"But it does make a lot of sense," Mommy pressed.

"I mean, if there are intelligent structures, that might explain why the old space probe shorted out when it landed. They might have been storing charge in different areas, holding potentials across the surface!"

Paul was shaking his head now. "But even so, the intelligences would never be able to get control of the probe. The probe would still be there."

"Maybe. But the landing gear was metallic, right? And these electrical beings might have been able to live in it. So maybe it took a while, but eventually one of the intelligences could have built extensions of itself up the metal legs, and eventually it would find the probe's computer system." Mommy was talking faster and faster now. "And that's silicon, too, right? So it would have felt right at home. And once it was hooked up to the engines and the computers, it could have figured out how to use them, and eventually left the planet." She paused to think for a moment before continuing. "And it also would have had access to the cameras and transmitters and receivers and mechanical arms. I mean, can you imagine? All those new . . . senses! It had probably never been able to *see* things before, only on a microscopic level. But now it would have had access to the macroscopic world! And once it learned how to operate the probe, it flew over here, to Mandala."

"That's quite a tale," replied Daddy, massaging his temple with his palm. "And why come here, of all places?"

"I guess this is the only planet around that's transmitting information. Maybe it was curious. I'm just surprised no one noticed it before Drew."

He shrugged wearily. "I don't know. It's possible, I guess. Most of the old space probes used the microwave band for communication, but no one on Mandala would have noticed it. Most of the Earth comms are done with laser interferometry, and all of the DC antennas would automatically filter it out. In fact, one of the only general-purpose microwave receivers on the planet is . . ." He reached down to touch Drew's transceiver. "Maybe you were the first person it talked to, Drew. Maybe you taught it how to communicate."

Drew smiled guiltily. "I did?"

Mommy looked down at him. "You don't remember the first time you talked to God?"

Drew shook his head. "No, I just thought he was always there, in the moon. But now he's not there anymore."

"That's right," she said. "We asked him to come a lot closer so he'd be able to listen to you without your antenna. That was how we found you."

"So where is he now?"

"I'm not sure. I was keeping track of the orbit for a while, but I've lost track of the timing. You're welcome to my antenna if you want to try to talk to him."

"Sure." Drew took the folded antenna but didn't open it. He still couldn't quite believe that the God he had had a relationship with all of his life wasn't really . . . God. Could he even pray to God anymore, now that he didn't really *believe?* "Daddy?"

"Yes?"

"God, the real God, he's an alien, too, right?"

"An alien? Well, that's one way to put it. But God's so evolved that he's not anything we can imagine."

"But what you said, about the electricity, I can't imagine that either. How do you know that my God isn't really your God? Maybe they're the same alien."

Mommy chuckled. "He's got you there, Paul."

"No, no, no. There's a big difference here." Daddy seemed a little upset. "God, the real God, he has future boundary conditions. This God you've been talking to—"

"Don't listen to your father," Mommy interrupted. "Drew, what you have with God is very special, and don't let your father try to take that away from you."

"Trina! I—"

"Quiet, Paul. To me, it sounds like our son has a relationship with an alien who's looking out for him. Just like you, right? The only reason we found him was because his God chose to come down to a low orbit. It probably saved his life. So don't belittle Drew just because his God isn't as all-powerful as yours. Frankly, Drew's God has been a lot more useful."

An awkward silence followed, and Drew looked from one parent to the other.

"Hurry up back there!" yelled one of the Burnouts from up ahead. "Let's get back before dawn, okay?"

Drew was already holding on to Daddy's hand, so he reached up and grabbed Mommy's as well, letting both of his parents pull him along as they hurried up the hill.

"C'mon, Drew," said Mommy, but he just swung his feet into the air every few steps, barely walking at all.

"Drew!" Daddy snapped, obviously not pleased. But Drew didn't stop. Every three steps he'd swing forward, and pretty soon his parents actually helped pull him along. After a little while they even started to laugh. Drew smiled, glad to be back with both of them even if this adventure wasn't quite over.

The eastern sky was just beginning to lighten when they arrived at the Rasta Kingdom, and Drew became more alert as they made the final approach along the dirt road. He had slept for the last part of the journey on Daddy's shoulders, but now was anxious for his first-ever view of a Burnout kingdom. Daddy had told him stories about the Outpost for years, so he thought he knew what to expect. But his first view of the factory-sized buildings silhouetted against the sky surprised him.

Even Mommy seemed taken aback. "Someone's been busy," she commented with a wide-eyed look.

Ahead of them the Burnouts scattered to either side of the road, and a tradervan sped into view. At least fifty Burnout warriors held on to the sides of the vehicle, and more crowded on top between towers of baskets and crates. Daddy stepped out of the way, but the precaution was needless as the tradervan stopped short, next to King Wally. "How are they controlling that thing?" Daddy mused out loud.

All of the Burnouts on the tradervan made an attempt to bow to Wally, some with more success than others. "You're all going to intercept?" yelled up the king.

"I'm dropping most of them off at the canyon," replied a dark-haired woman up front. From Drew's vantage it looked like she was holding a joystick, and Drew wondered if she was driving the tradervan with it. "And the supplies, too. Then we're leaving the valley. How long do you think we have?"

King Wally looked off to the south. "About six hours, probably. Eight at the outside. How's the fueling coming?"

"Slow. I think it'll be tight making the launch window. And that's more than eight hours."

The king nodded. "Then you'd better succeed. We can hold off men and guns, but if they get their artillery positioned . . ."

She just bowed in response, and King Wally waved her on, nodding in approval.

The tradervan lurched forward and picked up speed as it passed Drew and his parents. Drew looked up and watched it pass; in the back, a young woman sitting on top of a box labeled "AMMO" made eye contact with

Drew and gave a little smile. She was just a girl, he realized, perhaps a year older than he. Drew watched her disappear as the tradervan curved between the root-towers, wondering if she'd be okay if there was a real battle.

He tapped Daddy on the top of his head. "Is there really going to be a war?"

"Maybe not," he answered. "But if anyone can keep it from happening, it'll be you."

"Me?" Drew looked down at his transceiver, confused. "You mean, with God?"

"No, Drew," said Daddy, chuckling. "I think you might be able to do it all on your own this time."

"I don't believe it," Mommy said. At first Drew thought she was joining in the conversation, but then he followed her gaze off into the distance and he realized she was talking about something else entirely. Next to the largest building, against the pale violet horizon, a rocket ship pointed up into the sky.

No, Drew told himself, it couldn't be that. Rocket ships existed only in old Earth vids, and no one used them anymore. It must be some sort of pointed tower, or maybe a funny grain silo, anything but a rocket. After all, there was no way the Burnouts could ever build such a thing. Or was there?

"The Biodome suits," said Mommy. "They're actually going to use them in that thing? They're crazy."

"It's really a rocket?" asked Drew. "Daddy, is it really?"

"Pretty amazing," he responded. "They've been working on this for years."

Katrina shook her head. "But why?"

Drew felt himself lifted slightly as Daddy made an adjustment. "I don't really get it, actually. They were worried about the Earthies moving in and taking over their valley. So first they were planning a big land battle, but then they decided to get up into space first. Maybe to do the same thing that Channing did? Stop them before they can unfreeze all the colonists, I guess. Simpler than fighting thousands of them down here."

"That makes some sense," she said. "I guess. But I still can't imagine they thought building a rocket was the simplest way to go. I mean, can you imagine how hard it must have been to build something like that?"

"True. Well, they did have access to lots of science and engineering data from the Oracle satellite. But with no infrastructure or industrial base . . . Yeah, it's hard to imagine. They must have been pretty motivated."

Another group of Burnouts crossed their path, women carrying baskets of something Drew couldn't see. There were people everywhere now, he noticed, ferrying equipment in all directions. Everyone seemed to know exactly what they were supposed to be doing. "Look at them all," Drew said to no one in particular.

"You sound plenty awake, Drew," said Daddy. "Guess that means you won't mind walking for a while."

"Hey!" he yelled as his dad lifted him over his head and set him on his feet. "Daddy!" he complained, doing his best to look exhausted. But Daddy was stretching his neck around, looking up into the sky instead of at him.

"Hey, Drew, there's the *Walt Disney*." He pointed to the still-dark western sky, and Drew followed his finger to a star that was slowly moving northeast.

"Yeah, so?"

"That's where . . . that's where God is right now, I think. We told him to go into the same orbit as the *Disney,* so if you want to talk to him . . ."

Drew flipped off his speaker so no one else could hear, and then held his transceiver up toward the fast-moving satellite. *God? Can you hear me?*

hello drew. where are you going?

We're in a Burnout Kingdom. I don't know where we're going next.

burnouts are very sneaky.

Drew smiled. *They aren't so bad. They helped rescue me. And you did, too. I guess you've talked to my parents, huh?*

yep. they're hard to understand. they're weird.

My daddy said he doesn't think you're really God. He thinks you're an alien in a spaceship.

i'm god in a spaceship. in heaven. i brought heaven down very far, down near you. down near other space-ships who are very big and interesting. i wish i could talk to the others. are they like me?

Drew smiled. *Not like you at all. You're God.* He looked carefully at the speck of light, trying to see exactly how many spaceships were up there. With God, there should have been three. He could only see one spot, though, moving slowly across the sky. But maybe God could see him. *Are you so close you can see me?*

And then God *showed* him an overhead image of the planet. Drew didn't have to close his eyes to see the picture; instead it was overlaid on his regular vision like always, and he could either focus on his surroundings or focus on the divine image sent to him from above. God rarely showed him pictures—until the Earthy spaceship arrived, he had seen only the *Walt Disney* and low-resolution shots of Mandala. But he knew that God was somehow able to see everything that Drew saw when he prayed, and it only made sense to him that it could work the other way around as well.

The overhead view of the planet was amazing; fantastically better detail than ever before. Instead of a thin line cutting through the forest, a river now appeared as a wide swath of white across his vision. Drew could

make out individual trees, and even, he imagined, small
groups of people, represented by faint red glows. A
small glowing box was slowly moving across the image,
and Drew wondered if it could be the tradervan that had
just passed. If it was . . . Drew mentally backtracked the
box's progress to find a short line of red in the exact
center of the image. Could that be a live image of their
own group?

That's so neat! he announced, although God was the
only one who could hear him. *You can see everything
from up there! Can you see the City? Show me the City.
Show me my house.*

Suddenly the red spots moved off to one side, and
Drew got the sensation of flying. He could barely see
the ground, but occasionally a group of red spots went
zooming across his field of view, and he knew that God
was showing him what it would look like if he flew from
the Rasta Kingdom to the City. And sure enough, the
City came into view, this time with lights both red and
white decorating a much bigger area. He quickly figured
out that the white lights were electric, mainly because
none of them moved, but also because together they
looked like a tilted map of the City. There were many
red spots as well, and Drew found himself mildly surprised that all those people were up this early. In fact,
there seemed to be a crowd of them off at the edge of
the picture.

*God? Who are all those people down at the bottom
there? Show me what they're doing.*

these people? asked God, as the image panned in the
proper direction. For a moment Drew couldn't respond.
The "crowd" he had seen was only a small part of a
much bigger whole. Hundreds and hundreds of red spots
now filled his field of view, many of them lined up and

moving in a particular direction. Moving away from the City.

God? All those people . . . Which way are they going?

they're moving toward you, drew. they're moving right toward you.

Drew focused on his surroundings again and flipped his speaker back on. Both of his parents were looking at him with mildly amused expressions on their faces.

"I was just talking to God," he said.

His daddy raised his eyebrows. "And?"

"He showed me what he can see from up in his orbit. There's a huge group of people leaving the City. And they're all coming this way."

CHAPTER 21

CAPTAIN: *Okay. Give me the full report.*

A. Ryutov: *Good news or bad news first?*

CAPTAIN: *Bad news.*

A. Ryutov: *Right. There really isn't any good news anyway. The meteor struck the shield, knocked it into the ship, and then we collided with the shield three more times before we stabilized. The shield's okay, but it took out our aft transmitter. After the initial collision, the meteor was still moving plenty fast enough to pierce the stern hull and punch its way out the far side. That permanently destroyed spheromaks B and F. Spheromak A is in bad shape, but we might be able to repair it in a month or two if we can cannibalize some parts. Of course, there's been widespread contamination; lots of radiation in there.*

CAPTAIN: *My God. What's our maximum deceleration?*

D. Xiu: *That depends on if you want it constant*

or not. Normally one spheromak is under maintenance, and the other five rotate through so that another one of them is always in the ash-removal cycle.

CAPTAIN: That's right! We use only four spheromaks at a time anyway. So if we can get A working quickly—

D. Xiu: No, sir. We still need to clear out the helium ash every fifteen minutes. Assuming we get A working, we can slow down the cycle so that only three spheromaks are running at a time, with one of them always in ash removal. That would lower our maximum deceleration from 1.5 to 1.3 g's. On the other hand, if we run all four spheromaks for the maximum burn time, we'll fluctuate between 1.3 and 1.5 g's averaging 1.34 g's deceleration. We'll be able to store some energy in the banks to smooth out the ride, and we can still use all six pistons, but I still don't know if the ship could handle it.

CAPTAIN: I gather 1.34 isn't as close to 1.4 as it sounds.

D. Xiu: Best case . . . [clears throat] Best case has us slowing down to 0.04 c by the time we hit the outer system.

CAPTAIN: My God. We'll be torn to shreds. The Kuiper Belt will make Swiss cheese out of our ship.

A. Ryutov: If the system's asteroid-sparse, and we hit it just right, we might be able to keep the ship normal and make it through. And maybe the collisions would slow us down. Then we could keep decelerating and turn around—

CAPTAIN: Did you calculate the odds of that happening?

> *D. Xiu: No, sir. We're coming in too close to the*
> *ecliptic. There just didn't seem to be a point.*
>
> *The Log*
> *Year 23, Day 209.34*

THEY STILL HAD HOURS TO GO, AND CHAN-
ning could almost see the adrenaline slipping away. He
watched from the slow-moving tradervan as his troops
filed slowly up the old mining trail in front of him; Croll
had suggested he get out and walk with the people, but
Channing felt it important to show a little dignity. Croll
himself was on foot, scouting out the trail for possible
ambushes, and that was probably good enough for a mo-
rale boost.

Leading the bulk of the army, up ahead at the first
switchback, Croll's men were seated on top of two other
tradervans. Inside rode most of the heavy artillery and
supplies they would need to smash the Burnouts—everything they could pack in on short notice.

Channing turned to Zhang, who was quietly driving
the tradervan using the coded computer interface. "See
that switchback up ahead? Just because the vans have to
take the road doesn't mean our troops have to waste all
that time. I mean, they could cut straight up the hill,
couldn't they?"

Zhang shook his head. "Always the compassionate
one, eh?"

Channing started to reply, but a sudden flash of light
ahead brought his arm up in a reflex motion, even as the
dull boom echoed past his ears. By the time he looked
up again, the leading tradervan was lying on its side off
the road, and the other van was speeding backward into
the bulk of the army. Armed men were scattering to both
sides, most running away from the fallen van.

"Captain!" yelled Zhang, braking their own van to a sudden stop. Channing was just formulating a response when his teeth came crashing down on the very tip of his tongue. The fourth van had just crashed into them from behind. "AHHH!" he finally managed. "Wha the . . . ?!"

Zhang dropped low on the seat, grabbing his radio. "George!" he barked into it. "Watch where you're going! They're firing bloody artillery at us! We'll be next unless you back up and let us get out of here!"

Ahead the panic was turning into mere confusion. Some of the men were running ahead to help the tradervan, some were running up to the newly formed crater in the road. Others were milling around nervously, aiming their weapons in all directions; others were in full retreat. Channing covered his eyes. What was happening here?

"Do you see them?" asked Zhang, poking his head up. "Where are they firing from? Dammit, we're trapped here!" Channing felt a gentle rocking as the van behind them pulled away, and Zhang started backing up himself, peering up occasionally to see where he was. Channing just sat there, burying his head in his hands as shouts came from outside.

"They're attacking! The Burnouts are—"

"No, it was just a—"

"Stay away from it! It's gonna explode!"

Channing didn't look up; Zhang spun the van around, tipping them dangerously to one side. What were they doing here? They obviously weren't ready to attack the Burnouts. This was all happening too fast and out of order. Why were they rushing this now?

The kid, Channing remembered. It had to be now. They had to get the kid before he showed up and ruined everything. Channing finally uncovered his face, watched fragments of his army disperse in all directions. If they were going to get that kid, he would need a real army, an army that wouldn't turn tail at the first sign of danger. Just a few hours ago everyone was energetic and ready to take on the Burnouts. What had happened?

THE THREE BODIES FROM THE ATTACK ON the North Mine had been placed in front of the Government Cone well before dawn, and Channing had written a rousing speech while Croll spread the buzz about the attack. By sunrise thousands of angry people had filled the lawn and others were pouring in to see what was going on.

As Channing instructed, no attempts were made to fix up the bodies, and one of them still had an arrow protruding from his chest. There was no hurry to start the embalming process, of course; no native insects had become attuned to the distinct smell of dead humans. And although Channing wanted to rush the crowds into action, he knew he had to do this right. So he let the crowds mill around the bodies for a while, paying their respects, getting angrier and angrier, until the mob mentality was fully under way; everyone felt the need for action. Now they just needed a leader to focus their anger, and Channing was ready.

He started his speech with a reminder of Drew Randall's kidnapping by the Burnouts, and made ominous connections to preacher Randall's close relationship with the enemy. Indeed, he noted, his son disappeared only a day after his return from the enemy's valley. Channing claimed ignorance of the preacher's true role, but planted the suggestion that the Randalls had arranged the kidnapping, plotted the attack on the freedom fighters, and were now hiding out with the Burnouts. Even if they had been blackmailed into it, Channing pointed out, the Randalls had betrayed the City and deserved just punishment.

Then he began the touching story about the three men who lost their lives, careful to point out their remarkable potential before they were mercilessly slaughtered. Next he talked about the others at the scene who had nearly been killed, trying to link a personal connection to as many friends and relatives as possible. Gradually he began to refer to the attack on the mine as an attack on the entire City. The Burnouts had not only attacked a single group of men, they had attacked all of us, shooting their poisoned arrows through the fabric of our City, our religion, our beliefs, our very way of life! We needed to teach them a lesson they wouldn't soon forget, or this would happen again and again! We owed it to our children to stop them once and for all!

Once the idea of a counterattack was planted, he wouldn't have been able to stop it if he had wanted to. All he could do now was lead the mob where they wanted to be led—right to Croll's stash of rifles and then on to the Red Valley. They had the numbers, the weapons, the determination, and God on their side. Nothing could stop them.

EXCEPT, OF COURSE, FOR A SINGLE BOMB planted in the road.

"Chemofly explosives," Croll explained. "I've seen this sort of thing before, though not this big. The pressure of the tradervan broke the membrane between the chemical agents. It wasn't even meant to hurt anyone, just make the road impassable for a few hours."

Channing scratched his head as he walked around the

car with Croll. "A few hours, you say? So how do we get everything up?"

Croll smirked. "We walk from here."

"But the supplies in the tradervans ... the artillery ..."

"Only what we can carry, I'm afraid. They knew just where to plant this thing."

"Dammit, Croll, I'm not walking all the way to—"

"Stop whining. From here it's a three- or four-hour hike to the top, and we'll stop there to set up a communications base. It'll be the command center, and we can both stay there and coordinate the attack without going any farther."

Channing spat to one side. "You mean, if we get *that* far."

MOST OF THE TROOPS HAD RETURNED AFTER it became clear that there were no Burnouts firing at them. Croll announced that these sort of chemofly bombs took months to make and they didn't have to worry about a lot of explosives. "Bows and arrows!" he yelled. "That's all you need to look out for, and we have rifles! So let's take that valley!" A chorus of cheers followed Croll's pep talk. Channing even felt a little better, although he knew the Burnouts had more guns than Croll was letting on.

The hike was tough, but Channing tried to keep a smile on his face. He could always turn back and keep tabs on everything from a safe place in the City, he knew, but every time he started to seriously consider it, someone would come by and tell him how proud they were to be marching off to battle together. He couldn't turn back now, not if he wanted his army to fight.

Channing was one of the last to make it to the top.

He found Croll had already set up a command center complete with portable generator, three large tents, and a wide perimeter defense. A large antenna had been raised for local DC communications, and Zhang was busy working on the electronics that would allow them to coordinate the troops.

"I've already organized a supply route," Croll explained to him while they stepped inside the main tent. "We're coordinating it with the women in the City, and the road has just been repaired, so the first vans should be here soon. I've also sent some scout teams into the valley to see what sort of resistance we might expect."

Channing peered down to see Croll was telling the truth; two tradervans were already speeding past the construction site. "So how soon can we attack?"

Croll looked thoughtful. "Less than an hour, I should think. Once we get the artillery set up, we'll be able to send a force to Fool's Pass. That's the obvious stopping point on the main road into the kingdoms, easy to defend, but the attack will draw most of their men over that way. They probably won't even consider that the real attack could come through the CO_2 traps, but for that we'll have to wait for the filters. . . ."

"C-O-what?"

Croll pointed down into the Red Valley. "See how the main road curves left into those rocky hills over there? Didn't you wonder why the road doesn't just cut straight through that low-lying area to the kingdoms?" Now that Croll mentioned it, Channing thought it did seem strange, but didn't say anything. "Those flats go straight there, but the Burnouts can't use it because it's a carbon dioxide trap. Lots of volcanic activity over here, and a lot of the heavier CO_2 settles into high concentrations between those hills, makes it impassable for humans. We hated those things when my men used to fight here;

you'd step into a bad pocket, figure it out pretty quick, but you wouldn't have the strength to move and would just lie there gasping until someone dragged you back out. The Burnouts think it makes for good natural barriers, but with filters on we'll just stroll right through."

Channing managed a slight smile. "And the Burnouts will all be fighting in the pass. I'm impressed."

"Croll!" barked a deep voice, and Channing looked over to see Zhang standing outside the command tent. "What are your men doing with a van over there, and why won't they answer me on the comms?"

Croll turned to face the American Valley, following Zhang's impatient gesture. Startled, he powered up his binocs and pointed them down the hill, off to the north. Channing saw the van with his naked eye, a black rectangle joining up with the other vans from a different direction. "Did they skirt the road before the repairs were done?" asked Channing.

"I don't know," muttered Croll, charging up his lenses even more. "Maybe it's . . ." He froze, pulled the binocs away, and started forward. "Burnouts!" he yelled. "Zhang! Get Buddy on the radio, fast. Tell him a Burnout-controlled van is closing from the north." Croll brought a hand up to his bald head, squeezing fingers into his scalp. "Damn," he muttered. "Should have left a few squads with the vans."

"You can't be serious," called Zhang, jogging his large frame over to them. "The controls are encoded; you can't override the automatic navigator without more expertise than they—"

"Get on it, Zhang!" Channing yelled at the Minister. "They're almost there!"

Croll was already running off to yell at a pair of his men. "Do we have nothing more than rifles up here? What about the UV-tazer? Get it over here!"

Zhang stared down at the vans, unbelieving, fumbling with his radio. "Buddy? Yeah, you're going to have company soon. Off to the north . . ."

Channing ran down the hillside a few paces to get a better view of what was happening. Down below, the pair of vans were slowing, no doubt in response to Zhang's warning. But the Burnouts' tradervan kept coming, rapidly closing the distance. Tiny figures were appearing on top of the moving van, and Channing heard the faint cracks of gunfire. "Zhang!" he called up. "How many men do we have in those things?"

"Two each," he replied, barely audible in the wind. "The rest is our artillery."

Artillery? Channing fought back a sinking feeling. If the Burnouts get the artillery . . .

"Over here!" Croll was shouting up top. Channing looked to see him mounting a small UV laser on a stack of ultracapacitors. One of his men was hastily wiring everything together. "These things charged?" Croll was yelling. "Bring the generators over so we can get off a second shot!"

Spinning around again, Channing saw the situation was getting worse. Three bodies lay on the ground far below; Croll's men or Burnouts, he couldn't tell. One of the friendly vans had armed men swarming around it, presumably Burnouts. The other was in motion again, chugging up the hill with the Burnout van following immediately behind. The Burnout van pulled closer, now almost side-by-side, and a single figure leaped from one to the other, rifle strapped to his back.

"Buddy, there's, there's one on top, there's somebody on top," Zhang was stammering into his radio. Channing turned up the hill and ran past Zhang over to where Croll was setting up the tazer.

"Croll! You've gotta do something, now! They're go-

ing to make off with the artillery. . . ." A quick look back
showed smoke billowing out of the passenger compart-
ment of the friendly tradervan; a pair of men leaped out
from either side, and it began to slow down. More Burnouts jumped between the vans, and before Channing
knew it, all three vans were in enemy hands, turning
back to the north.

"Out of the way, damn you!" Croll yelled, and Channing spun around to see the red targeting laser shining
into his face. He ducked down and crawled off to the
side while Croll resumed looking through his binocs,
steering the weapon with his spare hand. "Ready for a
full power shot?" Croll asked one of his men. "Fire on
my command . . . now!"

A thin bolt of lightning shot out of the weapon, the
electrical discharge from the capacitors following the
ionization path of the short-pulse UV laser down to
where it terminated at the leading tradervan. "Got 'em!"
Croll yelled as they watched the van grind quickly to a
halt, probably with fried electronics. "Charge up and do
it again!"

"Ah . . ." began the technician at the controls.
"They're still bringing the generators down. It'll be a
minute."

"What?" Croll stormed up the hill, raced over to the
command tent. Meanwhile, Channing could only watch
helplessly as the Burnouts spilled out of the disabled van
and into the other two vehicles. Someone tossed a flam-
ing object into the empty van as they took off again, and
a few seconds later the van burst into flames. It wasn't
long before the ammo caught fire. A series of blasts
sounded, sending up a column of smoke into the air as
the two vans sped away. There would be no way to stop
them, Channing knew.

"Buddy! Buddy, you still there?" Zhang was yelling

into his radio. Channing walked over to listen in to the conversation.

"Yeah, I'm here," a voice responded. "Peter sprained his ankle, and Ravi's been shot in the arm. Henry's dead, but he killed a Burnout before they got him."

"You search the Burnout?" asked Zhang. "What kind of guns?"

"Never mind the gun," came the response. "The bastard has a DC on him. And it's been modified; they have their own comms!"

Channing and Zhang stared at each other; Zhang with a shocked expression and Channing with a manic smile. "Well, Zhang," said Channing at last, "what's the next surprise going to be?"

"YOU HAVE NO IDEA HOW DIFFICULT THIS is," said Zhang, hunched over the pair of flatscreens.

"Just do it," snapped Croll. "At the very least we can find out what the Burnouts are up to."

Channing sat quietly, wondering about the Burnouts. Why did no one know about their technological abilities? And what could have possibly motivated them to make all these high-tech advancements? He and Croll had already decided that enough DCs had been stolen from the City to account for the hardware, but they still would have had to build a communications relay station from spare parts. And that thought scared him: If they were capable of this, what else could they do?

A single voice finally began to emerge from the speaker. "Finally locked in on a channel," said Zhang.

"Yep, yep," the speaker was saying. "Blue Moth in forest twenty-four." A long pause followed, and Channing realized they were only listening to half of a conversation. "Copy that, Blue Moth to find Water Ant.

How much longer?" Another pause. "Will do. Blue Moth out." The speaker went silent for good.

"Too many code words," muttered Croll. "It'll take forever to figure out what they're talking about. But we should keep listening. Set up more speakers so we can monitor what they're saying to each other. Are you going to be able to lock in on the others?"

Zhang nodded without looking up. "This one's interesting," he muttered to himself.

"Shouldn't we try to jam them?" asked Channing.

Croll pondered that for a second. "Good point. Zhang?"

"This one isn't even DC standard!" exclaimed Zhang. "It's some other type of comm system. I should be able to filter out all the others pretty easily. . . ."

"Zhang," repeated Croll. "Jam them first. If we can't understand them . . ."

"Wait a sec," said Zhang, rapidly tapping commands. "Okay. Let's listen to this one."

A new voice came from the speaker, and this one sounded like a little boy. The words were all separated by brief pauses, making it sound awkward and stilted. "I see them," the voice said. "Mostly together except for those six groups. Six groups of people. Two are moving and four are still."

Croll was suddenly livid. "Six groups? That's our scouting team! But how could they know? Where would they spy on us from?"

"Yes," the voice continued. "What else do you think, Drew?"

Drew? thought Channing. *Drew Randall?* His mind groped to make some sort of connection.

"I'm sorry I'm leaving," continued the speaker. "I'll be back around soon." A pause. "Maybe if I was God, then I might be able to stay, but Daddy says I'm not

God, right?" Channing's eyes widened as the voice continued. "Okay, Drew. I am God. I am God."

"That's him!" yelled Channing. "The informer! God! That was Drew's code name for whoever he was talking to! That's what the kid kept saying that night. God told him. He was talking to God. I knew it had to mean something, but—"

Croll cut him off. "It'd have to be God if he could see all six of our teams at once. The only way you could do that would be if you were overhead. They must have airborne capabilities."

"Overhead," muttered Channing, looking up. "Way overhead. It'd have to be in space. Otherwise this God character wouldn't have known about the *Mayflower*."

"A remotely operated satellite?" asked Zhang. "Surely the Burnouts couldn't have launched one without us noticing. And how would this kid be communicating with it?"

Channing shook his head. "I don't think it's a satellite. That doesn't make sense. But the kid's deaf and dumb, and has one of those speaker things hooked up to his brain. And it's been modified so he can talk on the microwave band, I think. So maybe he could send a message up to a low orbit. But who could he be talking to?"

"What if there was someone on the *Mayflower* we didn't know about?" asked Zhang. "Someone Croll didn't blow away?"

"They're all dead," snapped Croll.

"Maybe, maybe," said Channing. "Yes! Someone we didn't know about hiding on the ship—or that midget in the airlock! If he got out he might have beamed down a general distress message after we left, and maybe the boy picked it up. Hell, maybe he even thought he really was talking to God!"

"Then he's still up there," commented Croll. "Still

telling the Burnouts about our troop movements."

Channing frowned. Having someone alive in the *Mayflower* was indeed one of the most serious problems he could imagine right now. And if the frozen colonists were starting to be thawed out, the situation could turn into an absolute nightmare.

Croll apparently had the same concerns. "Okay, here's the plan," Croll said. "Zhang, you jam their DCs; I want zero Burnout comms in one hour." He turned to Channing. "Then we attack Fool's Pass, pull their troops— and the artillery they stole—over that way. And then Rick will lead the main attack through the CO_2 traps."

"But," started Channing, confused, "I thought you were going to—"

"I'm going with you and One-Arm back to the space-plane." He glanced up into the sky, a grimace on his face. "We have to finish the job in orbit."

CHAPTER 22

Today: Virgil. The planet of my nightmares. Near-circular orbit around a single G-type star, with an average temperature of 40°C. Also 1.4 Earth masses, plenty large enough to maintain a molten interior, a plate tectonic system, and a healthy CO_2 cycle. Liquid water, which we've always assumed was the one crucial ingredient for life. So sure of this, were we, that we've bet our own lives on the prospect. But on this planet, nothing. Not a single bacterium, not a sheet of algae, nothing.

Oh, we've tallied the anomalies, trying to convince ourselves that the whole galaxy isn't filled with Virgils. After all, this planet has no moon and there's only a little gas giant to sweep up comets in this system. Maybe the resulting increase in meteors has confined life to small, sheltered habitats, the constant bombardment keeping it from spreading to the sites where our probe touched down. Then, to further boost our spirits, we remember the favorable odds—five known water planets and four of them have life.

But is it statistically sound to count Earth? Maybe the odds are really only three out of four. And I'm starting to feel that the farther we get from Earth, the less chance we have of discovering life. It's a mostly irrational fear, but unfortunately there is just enough of a reason to take it seriously. Namely the nonmainstream theories that demand a well-timed nearby supernova for the creation of life. Such an event relatively near the just-cooled Earth could have homochiralized the racemic amino acid soup,[212] or drastically increased the variability of autocatalytic sets that led to the first strands of PNA. These theories would mean that life isn't nearly so easy to make as we've thought, and perhaps it only exists in a few isolated pockets throughout the galaxy. If so, and if we've just left such a pocket, wouldn't it be wisest to just give up and return to Earth?

Note 212. Most inorganically produced molecules must be racemic—that is, contain equal amounts of left- and right-handed versions. A high degree of homochirality, meaning that one of these versions is dominant, is believed to be a prerequisite for enzymes, and therefore life.

The Journal
Year 16, Day 309

PAUL RANDALL ORIENTED THE ANTENNA while Drew crouched on the ground, drawing complex maps in the dirt with King Wally.

"No, Daddy," Drew said, looking up at him. "You're moving it too fast. Go back . . . there. That's good."

Steadying the parabolic dish, Paul glanced down at the makeshift map of the Red Valley. The City's troops were labeled with rocks, as dictated by Drew, and the king was filling in geographical landmarks with sticks.

"No," said Drew. "That river's more this way." He pushed a series of sticks to one side. "And something else is here, I'm not sure what. Maybe it's the edge of a cliff. Yeah, that's what it is."

"Dead Man's Jump," commented one of the Burnouts looking down on the map. "North must be off that way."

Another Burnout unfolded a crude map of the area next to the rocks and sticks. "Does this look familiar?" the king asked Drew.

Drew stared at it for a moment, his eyes going in and out of focus. Then he stood up and walked around it a little bit, looking at it from different directions. "Yeah, I get it," he said. "Most of the people are right here." He pointed to the ridge that separated the two valleys. "And those groups I was telling you about are here and here and . . ." Drew started transferring the rocks onto the map.

Looking down from the antenna, Paul noticed his wife was smiling at him. "What?" he asked, returning the smile.

"So did you figure out how he's doing this yet?" she asked. "I didn't get any visions when I talked to God before, and I thought we had the same electronics."

Paul nodded. "True. But remember, when you talk to Drew there's a level of communication that I can't hear. You two have invented mentalese, some sort of electronic pidgin that only the two of you can understand. And there's no reason to think that Drew and God wouldn't have developed their own pidgins over the years. This particular one, I suppose, might be a sort of visualese. What amazes me is that there's any visual information encoded in Drew's communications."

"Well, there're smell and emotions. Why not sight?"

"Because, like you said, you don't exchange visions in your mentalese. You've never traded *sights* with Drew, only sounds and smells."

Katrina looked thoughtful. "Not visuals, but . . . orientations, I guess. Sometimes when Drew's working on a jigsaw puzzle I can sort of tell how it fits together, even though I can't see it. So maybe the connections are there, in our brains. Maybe we just haven't had a primer because there weren't any common experiences. I mean, when we're in the same room we smell the same smells and hear the same sounds. But we rarely *see* exactly the same thing. So that part of the communication was never deciphered by our brains because there wasn't any reinforcement."

"But then how could an . . . an alien have done it?" asked Paul, shaking his head. "I already told you, I think it's impossible for God to translate a bunch of microwave signals in a completely unknown language. I'd think it'd be ten times as hard to translate Drew's optic nerve activity into a coherent picture. The more I think about it, the more I think we're dealing with another human up there."

Katrina shrugged. "But maybe vision would be easier than language. At least a picture has some analogy to the devices on the spacecraft, like the cameras it thinks are eyes. And once God started to associate certain pictures with certain words, that might have helped it understand what Drew was saying. Maybe that's how it learned English, learned to associate certain words with certain objects and all that."

"So God can see whatever Drew sees when they talk?

And then God can send images from its cameras back to him? Sounds pretty far-fetched."

"But how else can you explain this?" Katrina pointed at the detailed map of troop locations. "Somehow they're doing it."

"Somehow." Paul made another adjustment on the antenna, noticing that God was getting pretty close to the horizon. "Drew? You're about to lose contact over here."

King Wally looked up, concerned. "How long do we have to wait until it rises again?" He checked his watch. "It's been up for half an hour, so I suppose we have to wait another thirty minutes?"

"Actually more like a hundred," said Paul.

"What?" The king looked confused. "What sort of lame spy satellite is this? How can it spend more time on one side of the planet than the other anyway?"

Paul opened his mouth to start a long-winded explanation, but his wife poked his side again and he thought better of it. "Just trust me on this one."

The king looked him over, frowning. "So what exactly are we dealing with up there?"

"Oh, you know . . ." Paul shifted his feet. "There's just this weather satellite up there that transmits microwaves. Drew can pick them up on his transceiver; it's pretty complicated." He looked around anxiously, trying to think of something to change the subject. "While we wait, is there anything else I can help you with?"

"Actually, yes. What do you know about spacecraft electronics?"

Paul motioned to the Burnouts' rocket towering behind them. "You want help with this thing *now?*"

"No. City spacecraft. Earthy spacecraft."

Paul shrugged. "Well, I worked on a satellite once, back when I was an engineer. And I pretty much know the standards we use in all of our equipment. If you have something you want me to take a look at . . ."

The king smiled broadly. "Have you ever been . . ." He motioned upward.

"Yeah. As a kid. Went up to see the *Walt Disney.*"

"No way," said Katrina. "Not a chance."

Paul turned to see his wife glaring at the king. "What are you talking about?"

King Wally leaned back and chuckled. "Your wife's a lot quicker than you are," he commented.

"What?" Paul looked around, wondering what he was missing, and then his eyes fell on the rocket again. "What, you want me to go up with you?"

"We're going to have a few airlocks that need opening, I'm afraid. And I know we could use you."

"You've got to be kidding," said Paul gravely. "I don't even believe that thing is going to fly. It's sure as hell not going to land."

"That's why we need you. To get into the Earthy ship and get control of one of the shuttles." The king returned Paul's skeptical look. "Weren't you all worried about the new colonists? I'm offering you a chance to help them."

Paul didn't respond for a moment, and Katrina pulled him toward her. "You're not seriously thinking about getting in that thing, are you?"

"It's flown before," the king interjected. "Mid-twenty-first-century Russian design. I mean we couldn't duplicate everything exactly, but I'm sure it'll fly."

"Kerosene engine?" asked Paul. "But there's no way you made liquid oxygen."

King Wally nodded and started walking over toward the rocket, motioning for the Randalls to join him. "Liquid/solid hybrid. We've been filling the City's nitrous oxide tanks with liquid NO_2, processed from the nitrous itself. We use that as the oxidizer, crank it through the turbo pumps, and ignite the inert solid fuel."

Paul walked alongside the king, followed by his wife. "NO_2? But you'll waste all the nitrogen. All the early rockets used liquid oxygen and—"

"It's still reaction mass. And escape velocity is much less than back on Earth, remember. We'll need less than half the total energy that those rockets required."

Paul still wasn't convinced. "But you said it's not even airtight. You're going to do the whole thing suited up, with vacuum in the cabin? You'll run out of air." He turned to his wife. "How long can you stay in those suits?"

Katrina frowned. "With those little tanks? Even with the rebreathers, four hours at the most. But that's not the point. It's not safe, and you're not going to do it. Right?"

King Wally sighed loudly and turned behind one of the newer buildings. "Here, take a look at this." He rounded the corner, waiting for Paul and Katrina to follow.

They walked into a long field, occupied only by a large engine securely mounted on a steel frame. The earth had been scorched bare.

Paul stepped over to the engine to look. There was no casing, so many of the parts were in plain sight. "That's a turbo pump shaft," he commented. "Built or stolen?"

"Donated," the king assured him. "Old equipment sent up in the tradervans years back. Just sat around for a few decades until we started this project."

"It doesn't look very big," noted Katrina.

"We got four of them on the rocket. Hey, want to see it work?"

"No, thanks," said Katrina, eyeing the blackened ground. "I'd rather not be around for it."

"Can't do it anyway," said a voice. Paul turned to see Joanne standing behind them. "We're barely going to have enough fuel for launch as it is."

"How much longer to the window?" asked the king.

"One hour," Joanne said. "The eclipse has already started."

"Eclipse?" asked Paul. "Partial today?"

"Total," said the king with a grin. "And we're blasting off in the middle of it. You with us?"

Paul exchanged a long, piercing stare with his wife. "I'll have to get back to you on that one."

The DC on the king's belt started beeping, and he looked down at it curiously. "You going to answer that?" asked Katrina.

"Shhh." He kept watching as it beeped twice, three times, four times, and then stopped. "Damn," said the king, shaking his head. "Four. They've begun the attack."

ALARM BELLS WERE RINGING ALL AROUND the kingdom. If things had been busy before, they were now absolutely chaotic. A group of about two hundred blond men ran into the main clearing, waving rifles and spears in the air. King Wally ran over to their leader and shook hands. "King Melville," he said. "Just in time. They've started the attack, and we need your men. We know where they've been massing their troops, thanks to that kid I was telling you about. I'm concerned about a large group that doesn't seem to be participating. . . ." They walked together toward the map that Drew had been working on, followed by a few of the blond soldiers.

"We have Fool's Pass pretty well covered," continued Wally, "but I figure after that doesn't work for them they'll come through No-Man's-Wood. And we have to stop them there, because the rest of the way doesn't have much cover."

"Why do you think they're coming here? Why don't we lead them off elsewhere? Maybe we could even lure them down into the traps. That'd teach 'em a lesson."

King Wally laughed. "That would do it. But what do you mean 'we'? Aren't you coming with us?" He motioned to the rocket with his head.

The king of the Johnsons shot a broad grin at the king of the Rastas. "Wouldn't miss it for the world. Robby here's leading the troops," King Melville said, slapping one of his men on the back. "I'm coming with you. Whatever happens up to that ship, we're in this together."

"That we are, my friend," said King Wally as they hurried off toward the rocket.

Paul groaned and leaned against his wife. She eyed him coolly. "You're going to go, aren't you?" she asked.

"You have to admit we should do something," said Paul, gesturing around him at the Burnout warriors running off to do battle, their faces streaked with paint, and the tips of their arrows glinting in the sun.

She nodded, thinking that one over for a little while. "Okay. You go save the Earthies. Drew and I are going to the front lines to stop this damn war."

"What? You're doing no such thing."

"Hey, I'm not letting you solve all of Mandala's problems. There's plenty to go around today."

"Daddy?" Paul spun around at the sound of his son's voice and saw him standing alone in the middle of the clearing. "Are you flying up into space?"

Paul walked over to his son, kneeling down to eye level. "Yeah, I think I am."

"I wish I could go."

Paul chuckled. "No, you don't. Sounds pretty fun, I know, but trust me. You're a lot better off down here."

Drew reached out his arms and Paul pulled him in for a hug, careful not to squeeze too tightly. "Say hi to God for me," said Drew.

Paul let go and looked Drew in the eyes, trying to maintain control. "No matter what happens," he told his son, "you can be sure of that."

"Good."

He cleared his throat. "You stay here and do what your mom tells you."

"Okay. Be careful, Daddy."

"You be careful, too."

Paul looked over at Katrina, who knelt down to join her family. "I refuse to say good-bye to you," she said while Drew looked on curiously.

"I love you, too." An awkward three-way embrace followed, and after a long moment Paul struggled to pull his wife and son to their feet. "I'll be back," Paul said, and then turned and ran as fast as he could toward the rocket, hoping like mad that his inertia would keep him moving toward the job he knew he had to do.

PAUL SEALED UP THE SPACE SUIT, LEAVING only the faceplate rolled up, and Joanne showed him how to do a leak check. Everything was growing dark; Paul knew it couldn't be long until the eclipse hit totality, but he felt like he didn't have time to even glance upward.

"Here's your oxygen gauge," Joanne was saying. "The rebreather doesn't let the pressure drop, but the oxygen percentage will. The carbon dioxide filters should be working, but if it gets too high this indicator will come on. The only thing you can do then is to turn this valve here and reduce the pressure to your regulator. The oxygen will be reduced, too, of course, but at least the CO_2 partial pressure won't knock you out."

"Too bad you won't be there to remind me when the time comes," remarked Paul.

"Sure I will," said Joanne. "Who do you think is the pilot?"

"Oh," said Paul, biting the inside of his cheek. "Well, as long as it's not me."

Joanne gave him a funny look. "You're helping, of course. Why do you think we need four people?"

"Oh," he said again, wondering what exactly he had gotten himself into.

The two kings had already suited up and were carrying equipment up the wooden scaffolding that supported the rocket. Paul's eyes widened when he noticed Melville was carrying a pair of bows and a quiver of arrows, but managed to keep his mouth shut. This wasn't his show.

Suddenly it was night. Paul instinctively looked up at the sight that, no matter how many times he saw it, never ceased to amaze him. The moon had become a black hole and swallowed the sun.

The brightest feature was the ring of violet fire around the moon, sunlight refracted through Asgard's thin atmosphere. Eclipses on Earth were supposedly more vivid because its moon had no atmosphere, but Paul found a more spectacular sight hard to imagine. The white corona of the sun was plainly visible, forming a perfect backdrop for the moon's dark splendor, and while he watched, pink solar prominences danced outward from the bright side.

Stars lit up the sky around the eclipse, and Paul searched for Hades, the possible planet of God's origin. Total eclipses were the best time to see it, because otherwise one had to view it through the bulk of Mandala's atmosphere. Now it was nearly straight up, and although Paul wasn't sure, he pretended that a particularly faint star was actually the planet he was searching for. He stared at it, trying to imagine the planet as a teeming mass of electronic life.

It was an awfully persuasive theory, he had to admit. And even if it was wrong, he was starting to realize that God *had* to be an alien. There just wasn't any other possible explanation. And that really scared him. All his life he had been so sure of his religion. When his daughters had died, it was the only thing he had left to hold on to. But had the devotion of his life to religion been misplaced? No, it couldn't be. God couldn't be an electronic alien. There had to be another explanation. . . .

He forced a stop to that line of thought. He knew a rationalization when he saw it, and he considered himself pretty good at keeping his mind from coming to false conclusions just because of his beliefs. He used to be a scientist, after all. Not someone who would rationalize away clear evidence of aliens just because of some statements in the Journal. He had always told Katrina that if new scientific proof surfaced that his religion was wrong, he would admit he was mistaken. Well, now that had happened. There simply were intelligent aliens in the universe, and he would have to come to grips with it.

But could he? How to come to grips with the possibility that Captain's theology was fundamentally flawed? Was there an easy fix to the two-consciouness theory that wouldn't require jettisoning his whole belief system? The fundamental problem remained: Humanity would have to compete with these electronic aliens to see who would eventually become God in the recollapsing universe. Only one species could survive.

And then a horrible realization struck him. If there *was* a competition, humanity was losing. Converting a human consciousness to an electronic format was such a difficult proposition that no one predicted it happening for thousands, if not millions of years. Transferring the contents of a human brain was out of the question, and would be for a long time to come. But here was God, a creature that was in the right format to start with. And if it had originated on the surface of Hades and moved itself into the dead spaceprobe, as Katrina had suggested, then it was technically immortal. God was much more advanced than humans, in that respect at least. And that would mean . . . that would mean that the *real* God wouldn't care about humanity at all. Humans were just a dead end of universal evolution. A curiosity, perhaps, but they would never make it to the recollapsing phase of the universe, and therefore God wouldn't care about them at all.

Feelings of desperation clouded his mind. Could this be? Was this the final trap of a "provable" religion based purely on science? Was it inevitable that advances in scientific knowledge would disprove any religion, given enough time? And if science kept advancing, if they could never know everything, then no religion could ever be eternally true. In his last sermon Paul had claimed that science had backed God into a tiny corner of the unknown; but what if known science was the tiny corner, and the unknown lay vaster than anyone had imagined? If so, how could any religion *ever* claim to be compatible with science?

Paul tried to bring his thoughts back under control. He didn't know anything for sure. But if he went up in that rocket, if he made it to orbit, maybe he could see for himself. He'd find out what God really was. And if his suspicion was right—

"Randall!" shouted King Wally at him from the stairway that led up to the cabin of the rocket. "Stop your dawdling and get the hell up here!"

"Hold your fana," Paul shot back. "I'm on my way."

THE MOMENT PAUL STEPPED INTO THE cramped cabin he knew he had made a terrible mistake. "Where the hell is everything?" he asked.

"No seats, I'm afraid," Joanne said behind him. "There are some exercise mats we get to lay down on, though. And we can tie ourselves to the floor."

Paul looked around, hoping to see some control panels or some sort of computer system, but the only devices in the ship were completely mundane. Against one wall was a cube of compasses, and on another was a rack of spare oxygen tanks. Other, smaller tanks were mounted to the walls in four of the eight corners, and a series of red levers lay between the exercise mats on the floor. The only electronic device was a single, ancient oscilloscope lashed to the wall. There were no windows.

"I need some oxygen," he remarked, pulling on his helmet.

"Not yet, not yet," Joanne said quickly, taking him completely seriously. "We have to wait until the last possible second. We're not sure how long this is going to take."

"How are we going to communicate?"

King Wally tapped the outside of his helmet. "Built-in transmitters, courtesy of the *Walt Disney*."

"Let me see," said Paul, flipping on the power. Immediately the heavy sound of his breathing echoed in his ears. "Liftoff commencing," he said in a deep voice, "ten, nine, eight—"

King Wally scowled. "Get ahold of yourself, Randall."

"Sorry. It's either laugh or cry."

"Cry, then. I'm as scared shitless as you are. We blast off in five minutes."

Paul waddled inside and lay down on the mat, careful to make sure he wasn't going to crush any of the air hoses under his back. The others took their places, and a few other Burnouts popped in to make a final check and secure everyone down.

"Now what?" asked Paul.

"We wait for blastoff," said Joanne.

"What? No final systems check? No countdown? We just wait?"

"Fred's outside. He's keeping track of the beacon coming from the *Disney*. As soon as it's in the right place, he'll fire us up."

"Oh, well, if Fred's out there, I've got nothing to worry about."

"Randall!" snapped King Wally.

"That should do it," said the last nonastronaut. "Better seal your helmets and start your air. Good luck."

King Melville nodded at the man. "Better hurry or you'll get fried. We could go at any time."

"You can say that again," Paul muttered under his breath. The man stepped outside and slammed the door shut. Paul heard the sound of some sort of latch, which he thought was pretty amusing, considering the cabin wasn't even going to be airtight. In fact, Paul realized that too many things were funny right now. He closed his eyes and tried to keep from completely losing it.

"Everyone's air on?" asked Joanne's voice from the speakers in the helmet.

"Check."

"Check."

"Uh . . ." Paul fumbled with the button on his helmet and finally the faceplate started to close, rolling downward across his field of view. Finally he heard a click and a soft hissing. "Check."

A long silence followed, and Paul felt his throat going dry. He hoped to God those twenty-first-century Russians knew what they were doing. Then a thought struck him: "Hey, do these things have heaters?" he asked.

"You mean a cooling system," said Joanne. "Don't you know how these things work? Do you even remember what I told you about the release levers?"

"N——" said Paul, interrupted by the loudest noise he had ever heard. An instant later, the weight of the world landed directly on his chest.

He would have screamed if he could, but the engines were doing that well enough on their own. Breathing was more important, he decided, but inhaling was not a simple feat under the circumstances. The gimbals were jarring the cabin with wild, erratic jerks in an attempt to keep the rocket upright, making it feel as if they were taking a zigzagging path through the atmosphere. Finally Paul forced in a gasp of cool air, and tried not to think about the fact that the only thing keeping his body from tearing a hole through the rear of the ship and into the fuel tank was an exercise mat and a piece of Burnout-constructed metal. He imagined he could feel a welding joint running up the length of his spine, and then imagined he could feel it growing wider. Then, because that line of thought wasn't very comforting, he opened his eyes and tried to focus on his surroundings.

All he could see was blood. One of the others must have had a puncture in their suit and exploded. *No*, he told himself, *it's just the effect of the high-g forces on my eyeballs.* Now the cabin began to swim into view, still colored by a film of red. Paul forced himself to concentrate on the metal hull that was directly above him, although the red glow was a bit nerve-racking. It looked like the walls of the cabin had heated up so much they were glowing with blackbody radiation. After a few moments of that he closed his eyes again, beginning to think that maybe passing out would be a good thing after all.

The acceleration continued, but it wasn't quite as strong anymore, and breathing became something he didn't have to force. The sound also seemed to be fading, and he wondered if the engines were cutting out prematurely. The vibrations felt just as strong, though, and he realized that the decrease in cabin pressure was starting to damp out the sound. His ears desperately looked forward to being in a silent vacuum.

As the noise continued to abate he started to pick out the ragged sounds of breathing from his fellow astronauts. He spent a few moments trying to figure out how many of them were still alive but quickly gave up. Screaming into oblivion at thousands of meters a second, it really didn't seem to matter all that much.

Ages went by, it seemed, and still the engines roared. The noise had leveled off at a tolerable level, the remaining sound probably the result of the vibrations coming directly through his suit. He was surprised the vacuum wasn't making him cold; if anything, he was warming up a little. Hadn't Joanne said something about a cooling system? But turning it on wasn't an option, mainly because he didn't even know where the damn thing was.

"Everyone!" a female voice was saying. "It's almost time to disengage! Grab the red levers on each side!"

"What?" he said between clenched teeth. "I can't even move!"

"They're right next to you, on each side! Slide your hands around till you find them!"

Paul made a monumental effort, but his leaden left arm seemed to be pinned. He did manage to find something on his right side, and he grabbed it tight. "I got one."

"Get the other one, then."

Paul tried to rock his body to free his arm when suddenly there was a hiccup in the constant acceleration. "What the hell was that?"

"That's our cue," said a voice, and someone else's voice was counting backward.

"Nine, eight, seven . . ."

Paul tried to tip his head to the side to see what was happening. "Somebody tell me what to do!"

"Five, four . . ."

"Grab the levers, Paul! Pull them toward you on zero! Really, really hard!"

Paul flailed around with his left hand until he felt something. Quickly, he tried to get a decent grip, but his fingers weren't responding properly.

"One, NOW!"

Paul yanked backward with all of his strength, but even as the floor of the cabin smacked into the back of his head, he knew he hadn't pulled the left lever quite far enough. And then all was quiet. He lay on the floor, the horrible acceleration over at last, and all that remained was to determine if they were in orbit or free fall.

"Shit!" yelled a voice in his ear. Lying there with his eyes closed, Paul could tell what was wrong. It was a subtle effect, but he noticed it. They should have been in zero g right now. Instead, there was a small, insistent tug still holding him to the floor—the unmistakable pull of gravity. They hadn't made it out of Mandala's clutches after all. Depression clouded his thoughts, and he started to wonder if he'd feel the impact.

"Dammit, Randall!" said the voice again. "Can't you do one simple thing? You've set us spinning!"

Spinning? Paul opened his eyes, but nothing seemed to be spinning at all. Joanne and King Wally had unhooked themselves already, and their suited forms were moving to two corners of the cabin. Paul tried to concentrate. Spinning. The cabin was spinning. Was that important now? After all, they were in free fall, not in orbit. Or was there no difference between the two? Old physics lectures swam around his head. There was no difference, was there? No difference at all, unless the surface of the planet happened to get in the way of the orbit. Either way, he should be in zero g. The downward tug of acceleration didn't mean they were doomed. It just meant they were in a rotating reference frame.

His demise thus mentally averted, he slowly came back to life and unhooked himself from the floor.

"Huh!" commented King Melville. "Thought he was dead."

"Not yet," said Paul. "What do you want me to do?"

Joanne pointed to the corner of the room above and behind him. "Go over there," he said. "Turn the colored knobs when I call them out. Then turn them off when I say."

Paul shrugged. "Sure, but it's a little hot in here. Any suggestions on the cooling system?" With no air around to convect away his body heat, sweat was already accumulating on his forehead.

Joanne stepped over and flipped a switch on Paul's regulator; a red indicator blinked on. "It'll take a minute to get going," she said, motioning him off to the corner again.

Paul crawled across the floor carefully, feeling strangely like he was heading downhill, even though the floor was straight. When he got close to the corner he lost his balance and slid forward, winding up at such a strange angle it felt natural to just keep climbing up the wall. Pretty soon he felt like he was back on level ground. "This is just weird," he said, again sliding into his assigned corner.

"Wouldn't be like this if you had released us properly," muttered a voice.

"Okay, everyone ready?" said Joanne. Paul saw that the four of them formed a small tetrahedron in the room's corners; each astronaut was directly across one of the diagonals of the cube-shaped cabin. Joanne was in the corner with the compasses and had opened up the container to reveal a pair of gyroscopes, both of them wobbling around impossibly. Were they really spinning that fast? he wondered. Next to the gyroscopes, a series of cables were connected to a small object that looked suspiciously like a wristwatch. He desperately hoped that the watch wasn't being used as the rocket's main computer, although it was hard to draw any other conclusion. "Okay, turn the yellow knobs on three. One, two . . ."

Paul glanced down quickly at the three tanks in his corner. One had a red knob, one was green, and the last was black. Yellow?

"Three!" Paul froze in confusion, and a sudden force tossed him to one side. He held on to the tanks, trying to maintain his position.

"Okay, wait, wait, okay, turn them off, NOW!"

Paul realized the force holding him against the wall was much less, and was now actually pulling him to one side. "Uh," said Paul, "I don't have a yellow, right?"

"Right. Black is next. On three. One, two, three."

Paul cranked the black knob, hoping to hear a hissing sound. He supposed that by turning the knobs he was shooting compressed gases off into space to supply the necessary torque to slow the rotation. But, of course, there was nothing to hear.

"Too much! Off! Off!"

Paul shut it off, once again feeling lighter than ever. He imagined he could drift into the center of the cabin.

Joanne's voice came on again. "No, actually that was pretty good. We have a slight wobble, but we'll need it to find the beacon on the *Disney*. I think the burn went well, so we should be pretty close. We'll have to do a correction burn, I'm sure, but that shouldn't be too hard." Joanne pushed off, floated over to the oscilloscope, then turned it on. The two kings also came over, watching the green trace blip across the screen.

"How do you know everything went well?" asked Paul, still thinking about the orbit/free-fall problem. "For all you know we're plummeting toward the ocean right now."

All three of the Burnouts turned to stare at him. "If you're so worried," said King Melville with a deadly glare, "why don't you just open the door and find out?"

Paul swallowed hard and lowered his eyes. Very well. Orbit it was.

CHAPTER 23

Why, why did God tell me to spin the ship at that moment? I felt His presence, I know what He told me to do. Even after all this, I am still positive that He was telling me to go ahead with the procedure. So why has God done this to us? Isn't our predicament bad enough already? Hurtling toward a star with faulty brakes can't be what God has in mind for us. Or can it?

It must be a lesson. Maybe, for some reason, I wasn't open to a suggestion of His. Perhaps I wasn't receptive, and so now He's forcing me into a corner, where the only way out is to finally obey Him. But I don't feel like I'm in a corner. I feel like I'm in a box.

No. God wouldn't have killed us like this. I know Him too well. There must be a way out. A way He wants us to find. He left us alive, didn't He? There must be a solution. But what could it possibly be?

The Journal
Year 23, Day 210

UNDER THE COVER OF MIDDAY DARKNESS, Katrina and Drew jogged toward the front lines, chasing the Burnout reinforcements. The Johnson army was already long gone, but she knew where they were headed: Fool's Pass—a gap in the rocky peaks to the west, one of the places where the Burnouts were planning on making a stand. She could hear faint, sporadic gunshots already.

We have to get past the front lines, she said to Drew as they slowed to a walk. *And then we have to decide who to approach. Who do you think we can trust?*

I don't know, came Drew's response, while his mouth took deep gulps of air. *No one, I guess. I saw everyone I knew at that mine. Everyone.*

Katrina knew he wasn't overly exaggerating; she had seen many of them with her own eyes. But still it didn't make sense. *Did any of them see you? Maybe only a few people knew you were there.*

Drew shrugged. *They didn't see me, but . . . but they were all there.*

Still, she said, *someone's got to be on our side. We just have to choose the right person.*

The gunfire grew louder as they made the final approach to Fool's Pass. The eclipse was at its darkest now—with the sun centered behind the much-larger moon, even the western horizon had faded to black. They passed a group of men unloading a cannon-type machine from a tradervan, examining the device as if they had no idea what it was.

"How's it coming?" Katrina asked one of the warriors.

The Burnout turned, startled, then relaxed as he seemed to recognize her. "We're both taking light losses," he said at last. "Sort of a stalemate at the moment; no one's venturing into the pass anymore. Hopefully we'll get this thing set up before they get any heavy guns of their own. And they'll try to flank us, probably through the woods," gesturing to the north.

"Probably," commented another, suddenly noticing Drew. "Hey, you're the kid who was getting all the enemy locations from that weather satellite?"

Drew nodded.

"Well, do it again. The info's out of date. We have to know—"

"I can't," protested Drew. "I can't for another hour, at least."

The Burnout looked confused. "So why did you come here, then? Trying to get yourself killed? If the Johnsons can't hold the woods, everyone here's going to get crushed; we'll have to fall back to the river. Get yourself out of here, quick."

Katrina thanked them, then took Drew's hand and headed back the way they had come, flipping off her speaker. *So, Drew. We can't get through the pass. And the woods don't sound very safe; they'll be fighting there, too. Do you remember what was on the other side of the pass?* She pointed south. *From the pictures God showed you, I mean.*

Drew closed his eyes. *Some little rivers and a few trees. But the hills weren't so bad, I don't think.*

Something must be that way, she said, *or they'd be worried about getting flanked through there. Maybe it's just a lot farther around.* She mentally weighed the unknown southern route against the Burnout-filled woods to the north. Then she looked down at Drew and tried to picture the two of them crawling through a firefight, hoping to make it to the other side with bullets zinging past. Even in the dark, it wasn't something she wanted to risk. *We'll go south,* she announced at last.

* * *

TWENTY-FIVE MINUTES LATER, SHE WAS
starting to wonder about her decision. The trek was
across a rough, wooded area, rather difficult hiking when
lit only by the dregs of sunlight refracted through the
moon's thin atmosphere. There was no trail here, and
the constant clambering was wearing Drew down pretty
fast. Soon they reached a slow-moving stream, and Katrina had the presence of mind to cross at the widest
point. Sure enough, it wasn't too deep—barely up to
Drew's waist—and they forded on across. Near the far
side, their ripples stirred up luminescent patterns in a
water ant colony, resulting in a colorful fractal display
of green and violet insects proclaiming colorful warnings to each other. Drew reached down to scoop up some
insects and presented a fistful of skittering dots toward
his mother.

Think we could use these to light the way? he asked.
Katrina sent him a mental laugh in response, then helped
him out of the water and pulled him up the far bank.

Beyond the river the terrain sloped downhill, and the
trees seemed a bit sparser. Soon they were very sparse,
and the next thing she knew they were standing on the
lip of what looked like a valley, descending down into
darkness. Farther south she could make out steep cliffs;
they couldn't go any farther in that direction.

But the seemingly barren valley surprised her, Why
were there no trees down there? Perhaps the darkness
was concealing a clear-cut Burnout farm, Katrina spec-
ulated, or maybe an often-flooded river. But natural
clearings were rare, without any large animals on the
planet to graze out the new trees and roottowers. So
what was waiting for them down there?

Mommy? said Drew, clearly wondering why they had come to a stop.

Katrina didn't respond right away, puzzling it out in her head. If this valley was such a great way to go, why weren't all the Burnouts here defending it from an attack? She glanced up at the lopsided flare of white around the moon, trying to gauge how long it would be before the sun peered out again. Too long to wait, she decided; people were getting killed, and they had to put a stop to it as soon as possible.

Okay, Drew, she said at last, *I'm going to go ahead a little ways, see what's down there. You wait up here, hide behind a tree or something in case someone comes. Think you can find me in the dark?*

Yeah, responded her son, *I can usually tell where you're broadcasting from. But what do you think is down there?*

She knelt to give him a quick kiss on his forehead. *Don't know. But if we can't make it through, I'll come straight back.* Drew retreated to a fallen roottower, and Katrina started down the gentle slope. It was easy going, easier than anything they had done since leaving the road. She could barely make out the bottom of the valley; there didn't seem to be a river, but she couldn't be sure.

Anything there? came Drew's transmission. *I'm inside the roottower; it's hollow.*

Good, Drew, she said, yawning as she broadcast. Staying up for most of the night was catching up with her, apparently. *Just stay where you are.* She was feeling a little short of breath, strange because she wasn't walking fast at all. Soon she was actually panting, and a note of caution in the back of her mind brought her to a stop.

She sat down to rest, but quickly felt even worse than before, her body taking long, gasping breaths of air. What was happening to her?

She tried to focus on the problem but couldn't seem to get enough air. With a supreme effort she rose to her feet and put her hands on top of her head, trying to get more oxygen into her lungs. Things got a little better, but she was still nearly hyperventilating; if this continued, she knew she'd probably pass out. Maybe there was some poisonous gas? Something that had killed off all the large plants, maybe?

The answer suddenly hit her from all directions at once: carbon dioxide. Completely odorless and heavier than air. She had to get out of here. But her body wasn't cooperating; she was oxygen-starved and it was simply taking all of her effort not to collapse again.

Mommy? came Drew's voice. *What's going on?*

A surge of energy seemed to accompany her son's transmission, and she managed a single step back up the hill. Then another. Then a full minute of deep breathing, standing up tall with her head tipped back. She repeated the process, deciding she was going to make it after her eighth step up the hillside. *Drew?* she called as her gasping started to subside. *Stay where you are. It's dangerous here.* Step, step, breathe. *We can't get through this way.* With more energy now, she started to jog up the hill, collapsing near the top to catch her breath.

That was when she noticed the figures coming through the valley.

Burying herself down in the redgrass, she checked to make sure she wasn't hallucinating. But there they were—at least a dozen people easily strolling across the valley that had almost killed her. She could see a lot more of the valley now, she noticed, and a quick glance at the sky showed the eclipse was nearing an end. There was already some color in the eastern sky, and once the sun came back she would be spotted instantly. And now the valley looked like it was filled with more than a hundred fast-moving shapes.

She explained the situation to Drew even as she considered her next move. These people must be the invasion force from the City, maybe wearing CO_2 filters. But could she just stand up and yell "Don't shoot!"? No, some of them *would* shoot her; that had been proven last night. She had to reveal herself to as few people as possible, find someone she could trust. And hope it happened in the next few minutes, before the eclipse ended.

They were upon her before she imagined it possible. Still not fully recovered from her ordeal, she buried her head facedown in the grass to muffle the sound of her breathing. But now she couldn't see any of their faces. Someone stomped past, not five meters from where she lay. They were all heading toward the trees, toward Drew.

Very gradually, she pulled her transceiver out from under her body, pointing it to where she thought Drew was hiding, probably a hundred meters away. *Drew, are you still in the roottower? Do you see any of the army yet?*

Yeah, came the reply. *They're gathering in groups at the edge of the forest. Everyone has guns.*

Do you see anyone you know? Anyone at all?

I see Mr. Bradley, but I don't really know him. I don't think any of them know me.

Katrina took a sharp breath. They all would know who Drew was; the local news had talked about little else after he had disappeared. But if even a single person had orders to shoot him . . .

Wait a sec, he said. *I see Zeke! Uncle Zeke's here!*

Her brother. They had to be able to trust her brother.

Drew had said he was at the mine, too, but there was no way he knew Drew was being kept a prisoner there. He wouldn't have put up with that. She was just about to speak when Drew broadcast another message.

Wait, there's that astronaut, too. The one who locked me up in the mine!

Rick? Okay, you can't let him see you. She clenched her fist, wishing she was there with her son. *Can you call to Uncle Zeke, you think? Without letting anyone else know you're there?*

No, he's too far away. And there are lots of other people closer.

She closed her eyes and tried to imagine the scene. If ever she needed her brainstorming ability it was now, but this time she was coming up blank. Concentrate, she told herself. Okay, somehow Drew had to reveal himself to a small number of people, without letting anyone else know. If only there was some way to call up Zeke on her DC! She slowly reached down to touch her own digital communicator, hoping no one would see the motion in the dark. DCs didn't work in the Red Valley, she knew. But then how was the army communicating with everyone? A new radio system? They hadn't had enough time for that, so they might be using their DCs somehow. She slowly brought her DC up to her transceiver, and the Ready tone sounded. Her heart started beating faster. Maybe they had set up a new antenna system, maybe this would work after all. She clipped the two devices together and was surprised to hear it buzzing already. She hadn't even keyed a number yet! Quickly she activated the transceiver's microphone so she could hear the conversation.

"Communications," said a man's voice suddenly. "Please hold." A click followed; then silence. The voice had been too loud, she thought; some of the army must

have heard the noise from the transceiver. Any more of
that and they'd find her, even in the dark.

What was that? asked Drew. Apparently the words had
been transmitted over to him, through the transceiver.

Be quiet, she whispered, checking to make sure her
speaker was still off. She knew she was making far too
many movements not to be noticed, but so far no one
had spotted her. *I'm trying to get in touch with Zeke,*
she told her son. *If you hear his voice, get ready to tell
him where you are.* She took a deep breath, wondering
who had put her on hold. Perhaps all the communications were being routed through a central system, and
she'd have to convince someone to hook her up with
Zeke. But if she wanted to talk she'd have to turn on
her speaker, and the noise would give her away for sure.
Cranking down both volumes as low as she dared, she
smothered the DC/transceiver pair under her body.

"Command Central," said the voice again. Belatedly
she realized she should have been coming up with a
story. Now, under pressure, nothing came to mind.

"Um, you need to connect me to Zeke Wellington.
It's an emergency."

"Who is this?"

She bit down on the inside of her cheek. "It's his wife,
Rita." She fervently hoped her sister-in-law wasn't involved in this whole thing. "There's a fire in the forge
and I have to talk to him now!"

"There's a war going on, Rita. We don't have time
for this."

"It's an emergency! There's a new supply of rifles he
was working on, and unless I talk to him—"

"Well, why didn't you say so? Okay, hang on."

Smiling for the first time since she nearly asphyxiated
herself, she almost spoke to Drew again. But that could
ruin everything, she knew, so she just hoped like mad

that Drew would know when to jump in. Finally the phone started buzzing, and Zeke answered. Drew started talking right away.

"Zeke! It's me, Drew! I'm right near you, in a root-tower trunk. Turn your head to the right . . . no, the other way . . ."

"Drew?" said Zeke's voice. "What's going on? Where—?"

"Hey? What is this?" said a different voice on the DC. Katrina's heart sunk; someone was listening in!

"There! Here!" continued Drew. "You're looking at me right now! Come over! Don't tell anyone but come over here!"

"Drew?" said Zeke again. "But—" An audible click sounded, and the DC went dead.

"Yeah, keep coming!" said Drew, not realizing there was a problem.

Katrina flipped her speaker off, going back to micro-wave transmissions only. *Drew, they cut the channel.* She glanced up for the first time, wondering if anyone had overheard their conversation. No one seemed to be nearby, but the eastern sky had gotten much brighter; they'd be able to see her soon. *Zeke can't hear you anymore, Drew. And they know where you are now.*

It's okay, I think he knows where I am, too. He's coming this way.

That's no good! If they call Rick and tell him to follow Zeke they'll find you for sure!

So what should I do?

Katrina clenched her teeth. Good question. *Do you know which direction I'm in? Do you think you can find me?*

Yeah. But you told me not to—

Okay. As soon as Zeke sees you, as soon as he looks into your eyes and knows it's you, I want you to jump

*out of the roottower and run like crazy toward me. I'll
be moving, too. . . .* She looked up again and saw a large
boulder about five yards away. *I'll be behind a big rock,
but I'll tell you when you're getting close so you can
find me. Tell Zeke to follow you, and maybe you can get
away with him before anyone realizes what's going on.*

He's right here. . . . She heard the click that signified
Drew's speaker had been activated. *Zeke! Follow me!*
And then nothing but silence.

Her heart was beating so fast she felt like she was
going to faint. What had she done? Quickly she glanced
around, brought herself up on all fours, and crawled as
fast as she dared toward the boulder. She squinted into
the darkness, hoping to see her son racing toward her.
Nothing.

Drew? Are you okay?

Seconds of nerve-racking silence followed. Finally
she got a response.

*I'm coming! Zeke's chasing me, but he's a ways back.
And lots of people saw me. I think the astronaut saw
me. I think he's chasing Zeke.*

Keep coming! she mentally shouted. *Run as fast as
you can!*

Finally she reached the rock, crouched behind it, peering around the far side. She continued to shout encour-
agement to Drew, mostly to keep him running but also
to help him navigate toward her. It seemed like minutes
before she finally saw him, sprinting out of the darkness
with other shadows not far behind. She couldn't help
herself and stood up, waving her arms. *Over here!* Drew
looked away from her, so she flipped on her speaker.
"Over here!" she yelled again.

This time he saw her. And so did someone else, jogging cautiously through the trees. Was it Zeke? she wondered. Yes—she'd recognize that outline anywhere.

"Zeke! Come here, quick! It's me, Katrina!" She motioned him over, but now he was just standing there, clearly very confused about something.

Crack!

At the sound of the rifle shot Zeke spun around, dropping to his stomach. Had he been hit? Katrina scoured the trees for the source of the noise but couldn't see anything in the darkness. Zeke quickly clambered behind a small outcropping. "Rick!" she heard her brother yell. "What the hell are you doing?" Another shot rang out and Zeke pulled his head down fast, readying his own rifle. "Stop it, or I'll shoot!"

Katrina glanced up at the eclipse; rays of sunlight were already sneaking through the valleys on the far side of the moon, lighting up the edge like a brilliant diamond ring. Only a few seconds of totality left . . .

Someone grabbed her from behind.

After an instant of panic, she realized it was Drew. He had made it! She pulled him down behind the rock.

"Mommy," he said. "My arm . . ."

In horror, her hands shot out to verify what her eyes were telling her. His sleeve was coated in blood. "Oh, God—" she managed as another shot went off. Then another.

"Does it hurt?" she asked stupidly, even while ripping some of her redweave shirt to make a tourniquet for his arm. He didn't respond, and she started to stanch the flow as best she could. More shots went off from different locations; were Zeke and Rick shooting at each other? Suddenly a cry rang out, and the gunfire quickly ceased.

"Am I dying?" asked Drew. Still broadcasting on his transceiver, his fear was almost louder than his voice.

"No!" she shouted at him. "You'll be fine! Hold on, Drew . . ."

His mouth opened in a silent cry of pain, but his transceiver was silent. She held the makeshift tourniquet while she searched the ground for something to tighten it. Katrina felt like she was going into shock, although that may have just been a mentalese transmission from Drew.

And then the eclipse broke. Sunlight swept across the landscape at a thousand kilometers an hour, turning night to day in an instant. Her hands were red, she saw; there was more blood than she had realized. They needed help, and quickly. Someone would have to help them . . .

Glancing upward, Katrina's cry froze in her throat as she stared into the smoking end of a rifle only a few yards away.

Behind it stood her brother.

"Okay," Zeke said, his voice trembling. "I've just shot my goddamn commander, so I want to know what's going on here, and I want to know now."

CHAPTER 24

How do we know that God means well toward humans? How can we be sure He is basically good? Most other religions take this as a given; Symmology, however, does not. I have firsthand information about God from my spiritual experiences, but not everyone can share in them. Therefore, if I expect others to believe, I must derive God's character logically, like everything else.

It all comes down to how humanity will treat God in the recollapsing universe. If humanity will be kind, then surely God would choose to return the favor in the present. Or is this a bad assumption? And perhaps human nature will change as we become gods ourselves. Will we evolve morally as well as physically? Who is to say how we will turn out after trillions of years?

Evolutionary psychology sheds some light on these issues. In a realistic social group, game theory has shown there is no single "best" evolutionary behavior, the optimal moral strategy depends

*on everyone else's strategy. So—much to the phi-
losophers' confusion—humans have evolved to be
flexible; neither "good" nor "bad," but able to
adapt to the world as presented to them. Evolution
has already found the optimal solution to the social puzzle, and any further evolution should be
along similar flexible lines—the same for our time-
reversed counterparts as they are for us. But then
what happens when individual consciousnesses begin to merge into God? Social game theory becomes meaningless; soon there is only one being,
one God. Would a God's morality begin to de-
volve? Or evolve into a new direction? Perhaps,
but we don't even truly understand what a joint
consciousness would mean. We may just have to
wait and find out.*

The Journal
Year 5, Day 97

SAMUEL'S DAY HAD NOT STARTED WELL. HE
had woken up with extreme soreness in both of his legs
and had spent the morning—if he could call it morning—recompressing himself in the shuttle's airlock. If
there were nitrogen bubbles lodged in his legs, who
knew where else they'd end up in his body. The parallels
to his previous airlock experience never left his mind,
of course, but this time the pressure controls hadn't been
blasted by a madman with a gun. He brought himself
up to 3 SAs and then took a full five hours to come back
down, just in case. He wasn't going to go through this
again.

After that he had begun to contemplate his only real
option. He had performed the minimum three spacewalks that were necessary to become an officer on the

Mayflower, but he had since vowed that he would never do another. And now, with no one to back him up, all by himself . . . it was hard even to think about going through with it.

It didn't help that there were so many counting on him. He knew he was the only hope for the thirty-three thousand people in the cryotanks, and to save them he somehow needed to get back to the ship. With no fuel in the shuttle, a spacewalk was the only way to do it.

But there was the fear to consider.

Samuel spent hours and hours going over the arguments in his head, just as he had so many times in the past. On one level he knew he was being irrational. And on another he was absolutely scared to death.

HIS FIRST SPACEWALK HAD BEEN FINE. IT was a low-earth-orbit training mission, only his second time in space, and it had gone relatively by the numbers. He wasn't too happy at the time; he was trying to hide a cold from the CA so he wouldn't have to get rescheduled. He quickly discovered it was difficult to wipe one's nose in the helmet, but nothing had gone seriously wrong.

He had thought back to that first spacewalk often, in an attempt to figure out what had happened the second time. Maybe it was the runny nose that caused something in him to grow an aversion to spacewalks. Whatever the cause, during the second walk his brain had responded with a panic attack.

Nothing like it had ever happened to him before. He had been outside for fewer than twenty minutes when all of a sudden the thought occurred to him, seemingly for the first time, that he was completely surrounded by vacuum. For whatever reason, that thought—as he had since learned—had triggered his fight-or-flight response. And of course, at that particular moment, he could do neither.

Immediately he had broken out into a cold sweat and felt like his heart was beating out of his suit. Tremors started in his hands, he started breathing rapidly, and had never been so sure he was going to die in his entire life. He felt extremely dizzy, but to this day he didn't know whether that was caused by the attack itself or the lack of oxygen caused by hyperventilation.

At that moment, the desire to get back inside of the ship was the strongest sensation he had ever felt in his life. And despite the chaos in his mind, he had acted completely calmly. He set down the ratchet he was using and jetted back to the airlock, tapping his oxygen gauge and holding his hand up to his throat in the universal symbol for being out of air. The space station crew had responded immediately, motioning him inside the airlock and bringing him back up to that blessed 1.0 SA.

He had used the venting time to get ahold of himself, and by the time they rushed inside to help he felt almost completely better. He didn't think he had misread the gauge, Samuel explained convincingly, but maybe something was wrong with the suit computer. They went to get him another suit, and were planning to send him out again later in the day, but a power conditioning malfunction mercifully saved him. The CA was kind enough to check him off for a completed spacewalk anyway.

That left just one more.

Spacewalk number three had nearly driven him insane. Not the actual spacewalk, so much as the events leading up to it. Deep down, Samuel knew that if he ever got out there he would have another panic attack. He started talking to old friends from medical school, late at night and from public phones, wondering if they had any advice for him. They always told him to take the psychoactives—that's all the mental health treatment there was anymore—but he knew that any of that would show up on his bioscreens. It wasn't illegal to take such things, but if anyone found out, he'd never make officer. He needed to solve this problem the old-fashioned way.

As a result, his third walk was delayed three times— once for a faked illness and twice for real ones that he probably gave himself by insomnia and stress. Most of the ancient self-help books said to slowly ease into the frightening situation, describing in detail how people had gotten over fears of heights or social phobias. That advice, of course, was completely useless; there was no way to do half of a spacewalk. The books also told him to concentrate on the fact that having a panic attack wasn't going to actually hurt him or put his life in danger. Again, they obviously weren't taking his particular phobia into account.

This went on until he could put it off no longer. One more delay and that itself would have marked him off of the candidate list for the *Mayflower*. He went up to face his doom, completely convinced he would never return.

The hour before that spacewalk was by far the worst hour of his life. He went through all of the prewalk preparations in a daze, mentally counting out every third prime number in a vain effort to keep his mind distracted. And so he found himself in a spacesuit, in an airlock, on the verge of doing the single thing he feared most all the universe.

And it went great. He made it to the satellite without a hitch, concentrated on the engineering problem they had set up for them, and worked so hard he and his partners nearly ran out of air. They buddy-breathed a spare tank all the way back to the station—no easy feat with three people—and entered the airlock without a breakdown. *I'm done,* he had told himself, *and I never have to do it ever again.*

BUT NOW, SEVENTY-FIVE LIGHT-YEARS away, standing in an airlock, alone, with his only possible salvation drifting tens of meters farther away every hour, he found himself about to break that promise.

He slowly worked his way through the procedure, ready to stop if the slightest thing went wrong. He checked and double-checked every step in the manual, secretly hoping he would find some computer or equipment malfunction that it would take weeks to fix. But everything, to his horror, went smoothly. He picked out a space suit that fit his short frame, ran a complete set of tests, and when everything checked out, he ran them all again. Then he pumped the airlock down to vacuum a few times, making sure the outer door was operational. It was.

Finally, his palms sweating like crazy, he suited up and stepped inside the airlock for the final test. *I'll just pump down for a moment,* he told himself. *One moment in vacuum and then I'll come right back up.* He took the pressure down slowly at first, but after he dropped below 0.5 SA he opened the vent all the way and let the rest of the atmosphere rush out of the ship. The suit held.

He took a deep breath of air with his finger poised over the control to refill the airlock. But he didn't press down. He took another breath, and another. Here he was, surrounded by vacuum, and he wasn't having a panic attack. A good sign, he knew. But would it happen the next time? What if this was his one chance to make it to the *Mayflower?* On the spur of the moment, before his fears could make him change his mind, he stabbed the control to open the outer door.

By the time he turned his head to look, the hatch had already pulled back, revealing a portal into the nothingness that surrounded the ship. He stepped quickly across the airlock, feeling the sharp impact of his magnetic boots on the metal floor. The terrified portion of his brain was desperately trying to rationalize some reason to turn back, but he willed himself onward.

He paused at the exit, looking out into space. The ship that had brought him across seventy-five light-years floated in the distance, but for some reason he couldn't tell if it was fifty meters away or five hundred. It was well within the range of his jetpack, he knew; the only thing that might give out was his oxygen supply if he stood here and dithered for hours. But if he left now there was no reason why he wouldn't make it. Right? For the hundredth time he mentally went over the procedure for opening the airlocks. He could do this. He took a deep breath, steeled himself for that fateful step into the blackness, and just then he noticed the monster.

A monster. Lurking in the blackness between him and the *Mayflower*. And its huge eyes were watching him.

The part of his brain that had been screaming out in fear all this time finally took over. He stumbled backward, hyperventilating, only the lack of gravity keeping him from spilling to the floor. He could barely hit the controls to vent the airlock, and by the time he was able to pull his helmet off, he was in horrible shape. Sweat poured from everywhere, his hands shook uncontrollably, and it took forever before his pulse slowed down to rational levels.

This was it, he reflected. He had finally gone mad.

ANOTHER TEN MINUTES PASSED BEFORE HE got up the nerve to look outside again. The monster was still there.

Samuel stared at it for a long time, eventually starting to wonder if it might not be a hallucination after all. It was obviously metallic, although it didn't glint in the sunlight like the *Mayflower* or the more-distant *Walt Disney*. Instead, black, barnaclelike splotches seemed to cover most of the exposed surfaces, making it look more like a living creature than a machine. But it was certainly a machine, Samuel now realized. A machine that had been through a hell of a lot.

He gave himself a different perspective by walking up the wall, taking a new look at the thing from upside down, and suddenly everything clicked into place. The features he had first taken to be arms or tentacles revealed themselves to be landing gear. Large antenna dishes had looked like giant eyes, and the solar panels arrays had been the long legs. There was even a group of dark instruments on the front that looked suspiciously like a gaping maw.

But why would any spacecraft in orbit around Mandala have unretracted landing gear? He could make no sense out of it. The device was obviously an unmanned probe; no person could have fit inside that thing, even if he had been confused enough to make the attempt. And it looked old. Really old. Probably some ancient piece of space junk abandoned here in orbit . . .

The incredible odds against a random piece of junk happening to intersect their orbit were just beginning to occur to him when the monster moved. Directly toward him.

Samuel had seen plenty of remotely operated devices in space. The resulting motions were inevitably jerky, caused by the classic staccato flowchart: fire an engine; pause to reevaluate; repeat as necessary. But this thing didn't move that way at all. It moved like it was alive. Multiple plasma jets fired at once, rotating and propel-

ling the craft in one fluid motion. Then, just as Samuel
thought it would crash into his shuttle, the thing stopped
and pointed a camera through the window from less than
a meter away.

Shivers ran up Samuel's spine. Although he knew
someone on the surface of the planet must be watching
him through this thing, he couldn't shake the feeling that
it was watching him, that the machine had somehow
come to life and was exploring this new intruder in its
orbital world. Or maybe it had been programmed to do
this. Maybe it was something that the Prime Minister
and the bald man had left up here to see if anyone was
left alive. If so, they surely knew by now that he had
escaped their makeshift prison.

Then the monster started knocking. Samuel jerked
backward when the first blow landed on the hull, a
sharp metallic crack that echoed through the airlock.
What the hell . . . ? Two more blows followed. Quickly
he grabbed up his helmet and started to refasten it, worried that this thing was going to crash through the hull.
After he was guarded against a sudden decompression
he tried to figure out exactly what the monster was doing. The main body of the spacecraft wasn't moving, he
saw, so it had to be hitting the shuttle with something
else. Samuel took a step toward the small airlock window but quickly changed his mind. He wasn't about to
go any closer than he already was. But there was a big
observation deck next door, he knew, so he backed out
of the airlock. It took a moment to reorient his body,
planting his feet on the surface that had been designated
the "floor." Then he hurried around the corner to find
out what was happening on the outside.

It was gone. Already it was moving away from the
shuttle, back past the point in space where he had first
seen it, all the way to the *Mayflower*'s jammed airlock.

He fleetingly wondered if his sudden exit had scared it away, but immediately chastised himself for anthropomorphizing a remotely controlled robot. Samuel continued to watch, slack-jawed, while a mechanical arm detached itself from the side of the monster and began feeling the hull of the *Mayflower*. Then it started knocking again.

This went on for perhaps half an hour. The mechanical arm would pull back, smack soundlessly against the hull of the huge ship, and then stay in contact for about five seconds. Afterward the arm would retract, pull backward like a whip, and start the process all over again.

As remarkably strange as this event was, after a very short while he began to get bored. One of the great human abilities, he thought: tuning out the most fantastic events just because they happened slightly too often. Still, he forced himself to stay and watch, mulling over nonsensical explanations in his head. Finally, either by sheer chance or very poor design, the mechanical arm came down hard on the emergency airlock computer mounted next to the outer hatch.

Unlike the hundreds of other impacts, this time the arm smashed into the computer and stuck there. The monster acted like it had been killed; the mechanical arm did not retract to continue its incessant pounding. Perhaps an electrical shock had destroyed it.

Now things got even more boring; the spacecraft's arm remained lodged in the airlock controls. Hours passed, and soon he felt himself falling asleep on his feet—relatively easy to do in space—but he struggled to stay awake. Eventually, deciding that he might as well take a nap, he walked to the shuttle's main computer and loaded up the radar system. A quick scan of the area confirmed that nothing was around except for the *May-*

flower and the *Walt Disney*. He tapped in a simple program that would sound an alarm if any new objects appeared; that way he'd wake up if the monster came back to life and detached from the bigger ship. And better yet, he realized with his last conscious effort, he'd have a little warning when the Mandalans came back up to finish him off.

BY THE TIME THE ALARM WENT OFF HE WAS deep in a REM cycle. His subconscious mind made a valiant effort to incorporate the noise into his dreams before it finally pulled him back to reality, groping uselessly for the snooze bar. Finally, remembering what the alarm was for, he snapped fully awake and checked the window. The monster was still there, attached to the *Mayflower*.

But the alarm had sounded anyway. That could mean only one thing.

Pulling himself sideways, Samuel swung around to the 3-D radar screen. A new dot had just come into the field of view, moving toward him and slowing down. There was no doubt in his mind who they were, where they were headed, and what they planned to do. But just as he was turning away the alarm went off again, and he spun back to the screen. The monster? No, it was yet another dot, moving in from a different direction. Had they brought up two ships to hunt him down? Or was something else going on? Perhaps the situation wasn't so simple after all.

Staring at the blips, Samuel had a burst of inspiration. If they had two ships, that meant they were probably communicating. And eavesdropping in on them wouldn't be a bad move right now. At the very least it would let him know what he was up against.

Quickly he switched the computer into communications mode, leaving the radar signal image on the main screen. What frequency would they be using? Universal Speech Encoding had changed a few times since the *Walt Disney* had blasted off, but surely . . . In seconds the computer answered his question; the standard frequency table included an option that read USE2099. 2099 was the year the original ship had left Earth. That had to be it. Quickly he activated the channel, careful to make sure the radio was set to receive only. Even though the detached shuttle would be pretty obvious, he didn't want to give himself away quite yet.

Faint voices came out of the speaker immediately, and Samuel allowed himself a quick smile. Now he just had to make sense out of it.

The first voice he heard was that of an obviously nervous man: "Are you sure we're slowing down? It looks like we're going to zip right by it."

"You feel the acceleration, don't you?" said a much deeper voice. "Now shut up or I'll toss you out."

There was a longish pause, followed by yet another man who spoke very quickly. "How much oxygen you got? I have just under an hour."

"Same here," said the first voice. "No problem, right?"

"Not if you can open the airlock," said a woman.

Samuel knotted up his forehead, trying to keep the voices straight as well as figure out who they were. Only an hour of air? And they were obviously all in the same ship, so why were they talking on the radio in the first place? Maybe they were suited up already and talking over a built-in space suit comm system. But why would they have come up to orbit with so little air?

The nervous voice spoke again. "How are we going

to get to the ship without jetpacks? Can we get close enough in this thing?"

The fast speaker responded. "We'll each grab a few of these spare pony tanks. Just point and shoot and you'll take off in the opposite—"

Suddenly a new voice broke in, tinged with the silent pauses of digital static. "Okay. Tell us who you are and what you're doing before we blast you out of orbit."

Samuel swallowed hard. Were they talking to him?

"Shit," someone said. "Are they talking to us?"

"You bet we are," he replied. "We're bearing down on you now, with our torpedo aimed right at your little trash can. We heard about your rocket stunt just as we were taking off. I have to admit, I'm impressed you Burnouts got this far, but this is where it stops."

Samuel glanced at the radar display. Sure enough, the second blip was headed straight for the first. Apparently they weren't working together after all.

"Torpedo?" said the nervous voice. "If that's you, Mr. Prime Minister, you're bluffing. You have no weapons on that spaceplane."

"Think not? Well, you're about to—wait a second. Randall? Preacher Randall? God*damn* it, is that you?"

There was a pause before the "preacher" responded. "Yes. Yes it is. I'm here with some of the Burnouts. They're trying to help me rescue the colonists, if you haven't killed them off already."

The Prime Minister chuckled. "Paul Randall. Well, what a wonderful surprise. This certainly simplifies matters. You bring your kid up with you by any chance?"

An awkward silence fell, and then the same voice continued.

"Oh, well. I'm sure he's being well taken care of down in the Red Valley. But I still want to know why the Burnouts felt the need to build a rocket ship. I know they didn't whip this together in the past couple of days." A long silence followed, and after thirty seconds the Prime Minister spoke once more. "Look, you're about to be fired on. Now tell me what's going on or else . . ." The voice coming from the speaker suddenly got much quieter, as if the Prime Minister had turned his head away from a microphone. "Dammit, Croll, don't let them get away! Fire! Fire!"

Samuel jerked a glance toward the radar screen, mentally computing the location of the two blips in relation to his shuttle. Then he was clomping across the floor, racing to a window to see what was going on.

By the time Samuel arrived at a porthole, the action was already over. The Prime Minister's spaceplane was pointing at a small metal can that was spinning away with a huge hole in its side, leaving nothing but a few pieces of shiny debris in its wake. Samuel pounded his suited fist against the inside hull. From what he could figure, someone had actually come up to help him. But now, once again, he was back on his own.

CHAPTER 25

CAPTAIN: I think I've decided what we're supposed to do.

J. Hansen: Supposed to do?

CAPTAIN: Yes. God has left us only one way out. It's very obvious that he's trying to tell us we're going the wrong way.

J. Hansen: No disrespect, sir, but if there was a God trying to tell us that, I don't think he would have crippled our engines. We don't really have a whole lot of choice where we're headed at this point.

CAPTAIN: But we do have a choice. We could slow down as much as possible, hit the outer star system at 0.05c, and die. Or we could tilt the ship, accelerate sideways, and miss the system altogether.

A. Ryutov: Five percent angle, sir. That's all the tilt we can handle. Any more and we'll be outside the meteor shield's shadow.

CAPTAIN: But we have to find a way. And we can. I just know it.

J. Hansen: I don't understand. What makes you think we're supposed to do this?

CAPTAIN: This was the only way God could break us out of our mind-set. Until now I've only been prepared to visit stars in the DSI[38] databank. But there are other perfectly good stars as well, and maybe one of them is where we're supposed to end up. Take a look at the map. This G-5, here. Why don't we head there instead? It's only twenty-three degrees off of our path.

B. Price: We can't change our direction by that much. And it's seventy-five light-years from Earth! There are 150 single G-type stars closer than that, and most of them are in DSI. If we're going to go to all the effort to change our destination in midflight, why don't we head for one of those instead?

CAPTAIN: Take a look at the map. That's the only G type we can make it to. That one over there is off by forty-eight degrees and is an extra twelve light-years away. This one may be a long shot, but it's our only hope.

J. Hansen: It's also pretty close to the galactic plane. If we did manage to change course we'd be fried by the Doppler upshift of the interstellar radiation.

CAPTAIN: True. It will be a little worse, but we're not going to change course by much until we slow down, and then the upshift won't be as strong. There's probably some optimal angle to decelerate at, and we'd have to work out exactly what it is. But we'll have to figure out some way to expand the shield's shadow. I know there must be a way.

A. Ryutov: Hmmm. Well, right now we can only tip five degrees because the shield rotates with us, leaving the stern exposed. But what if we managed to remount the shield at an angle? I'm not sure how much more freedom that would give us, but we'd at least be able to tip ten or fifteen.

J. Hansen: Sure. Who's going to be stupid enough to go out there and remount the shield? We'd have to detach it, and if there was another meteor hit—

CAPTAIN: Well, if no one volunteers, I'll do it.

A. Ryutov. Sir!

CAPTAIN: We have to try. It's our only chance.

Note 38: Deep Space Interferometer, completed in 2064, in Sol System. Was used to detect small planets orbiting stars within seventy light-years from Earth.

The Log
Year 23, Day 210.18

"BUT I STILL WANT TO KNOW WHY THE Burnouts felt the need to build a rocket ship," Channing was saying. "I know they didn't whip this together in the past couple of days."

Paul was about to respond to the Prime Minister's question when he realized he didn't even know the answer. He shot a glance over at King Wally, and was shocked to see him in the process of opening the outer hatch. The king held a finger as close to his lips as possible, and motioned him toward the door.

What, we're just going to leap out into space? Anxiously, Paul glanced around at the others, but they seemed to be in full agreement with this ridiculous plan. King Melville and Joanne were busy disconnecting a few pony tanks from the corners, and then Joanne was handing him a large canister and pushing him toward the exit. King Wally was already halfway out the door; a quiver of arrows slung over one shoulder, a bow hooked over the other, and a pair of small tanks in his arms.

What are we doing? Paul felt the urge to ask the question out loud, but Channing was listening to everything they said. He hesitated slightly and the others cut in front of him, spilling out into the blackness. And then he was all alone, inside a metal box, floating two thousand kilometers above the surface of his planet. *God help me,* he thought, and pushed his way toward the exit.

Channing's voice crackled over his suit's speakers. "Look, you're about to be fired on. Now tell me what's going on or else . . . Dammit, Croll, don't let them get away! Fire! Fire!"

Paul grabbed the edge of the door in a panic, pulling himself forward. Channing must have seen the others when they left the ship. Paul flew out of the hatch, wondering why he had hesitated in the first place, but just as he thought he was clear, the ship lurched toward him. The hull grazed his legs and sent him flying off to the side, spinning head over heels toward the enormous blue planet below.

"Help!" he yelled, trying to point the nozzle of the pony tank away from his body, but he couldn't even find the valve to turn the thing on. He glanced up and caught a glimpse of their ship spinning off in another direction, a gaping hole in its side. He saw some other space suits, and then they rotated out of his field of view and there was only the white swirl of Mandalan clouds.

"Dammit, Croll, they got out! Fire again! Hurry!"

Finally Paul got his hand on the valve and after a dozen long bursts of air he managed to stop his slow rotation. Now he was looking straight at the spaceplane, nervously considering the fact that they did have a torpedo after all. The barrel pointed straight at him from the top of the cockpit. He wondered how fast they could reload.

"Paul!" It was Joanne's voice. "Head for the spaceplane! It's the only place they can't shoot us!"

Good point. Paul reached around and fired a burst of air toward the planet. He started spinning again, but he just kept the valve open and compensated for the spin as best he could. After a long period of acceleration he glanced behind him and saw the spaceplane had started to grow bigger. A lot bigger. Too late, he realized that he had given himself too much momentum. He twisted around again, firing his tank directly at the big ship in an attempt to slow down, but after a few seconds the air stopped rushing out. He had used it all up.

He threw the useless tank forward, and it bounced off of the ship moments before he collided with the hull, chest first. The impact nearly knocked the wind out of him, and then *he* was bouncing off, heading away from the ship with no way to slow down. He looked up in a panic and saw that his trajectory was going to take him directly over one of the ship's wings. He instantly recognized that if he couldn't grab onto it, he was a dead man.

He pulled his body into a tight tuck, amplifying his rotation. When his upper body was pointed in the right direction he straightened out again and prepared to grab the wing. He just wished he could see a handhold on the smooth surface.

Then he was soaring above the wing, and he stretched his body out completely in an effort to grab hold. But there was no chance. His fingers were a full meter away. He felt his heart in his mouth as he sailed over the last object between him and oblivion. And then something caught him.

"Gotcha." It was King Melville, coming up from behind. "Here, hang onto my suit so I can operate this damn tank."

His heart still beating double time, Paul grabbed onto his savior and watched him jet some air away from the ship. Slowly, the two of them lowered down onto the wing.

King Melville looked at him through his faceplate. "You know how to turn the 'lectromagnets on? The boots?" Paul shook his head. "Me neither. Joanne?"

"Uh . . ." said Joanne's voice. "Try the button with the boot on it. On your right arm." Paul found the button, then let go of the king and jabbed it with his finger just as they touched down on the wing. They stuck.

"God dammit, they're on our ship!" yelled the faint voice of the Prime Minister. Apparently he hadn't turned off the radio yet.

"Now what?" asked Paul. Joanne had landed on the main body of the spaceplane and was standing with her head pointed directly at them. King Wally was nowhere to be seen. "Wally?"

"Up here," came the reply. Paul glanced up but saw nothing. "On the other side of the wing." Now he looked down, and saw the king's head peering up at them from underneath.

"Can you get us inside this thing?" This time it was

Melville's voice, and Paul saw that the king was looking directly at him.

"Why would we want to go in there?" asked Paul, gesturing at the front of the spaceplane. "I have this nagging suspicion they're trying to kill us."

"Well, what other options do we have?" Joanne asked. "If we try to make it to the Earthy ship they'll blast us."

Paul looked down at the estimated time on his air supply. Forty-one minutes. He sighed. "Okay, where's the door?"

They stopped talking after that. Paul wasn't sure how closely Channing had been listening to their conversation, but if they had any chance at all of sneaking into the spaceplane they wouldn't do it by talking about it over the common band. Channing also had stopped talking, though, and that made Paul very nervous. No threats, no conversation, just silence.

The airlock wasn't hard to find, and as always it came equipped with an emergency computer mounted outside. He started flipping through the options, trying to figure out how to pump the thing down, when he discovered a surprise. They were already pumping it down for him.

For the briefest moment he thought this was a bit of good fortune. And then he realized what it meant. He tried pantomiming the news to the three Burnouts, but finally gave up and just said it out loud. "They're pumping down the airlock now. I think they're coming out to get us."

Immediately the two kings began readying their bows, and for the first time Paul began to see why they brought them along. A tiny arrow piercing a space suit would be as fatal as the most powerful bullet. Perhaps these guys knew what they were doing after all.

Paul was just starting to move away from the airlock

when it opened. Standing on the hull he couldn't see inside, but he concentrated on getting out of the way, allowing the professional warriors to take over. He started running along the side of the ship, but quickly realized that was a bad idea and slowed to a walk. If he went flying off of the ship again there would be no one to save him.

"They're coming out!" Joanne shouted, and Paul glanced behind him to see two helmets peering out of the airlock. Suddenly one of the faceplates was struck by an arrow and both heads pulled back inside.

"Not the glass, you idiot!" yelled Wally. "Anything but the faceplates!"

"They got weapons!" yelled a new voice in his speakers. Apparently they were wearing the old *Walt Disney* space suits as well, and they were all tied into the same channel. "I think we should try it now," said the voice again. "Ready, Alex?"

"Ready," said Channing. "On my mark: three, two, one, mark!" The ship lurched underfoot and Paul felt himself being pulled off to one side.

"They're firing the engines!" someone shouted, and then the ship was lurching the other way. Paul tried to crouch, a difficult trick in zero g, and prayed the electromagnets in his boots would hold. A glance upward told him that the two men were using this opportunity to clamber out of the airlock. One of them held a rifle, the other was clutching some other type of pointed objects—throwing stars, perhaps. *This is not good,* he thought. A jet of plasma suddenly emerged from a small engine that was only a few meters away, and Paul felt his feet being pulled out from underneath him. He needed to find a handhold, and quick.

The ship continued to swerve from side to side, and Paul looked up to see another arrow shooting off into space, this one missing the two men by meters. But the others were having trouble as well; it looked like the man with the rifle couldn't use his sights properly because of the faceplate. A throwing star went wild, no doubt affected by the acceleration underfoot. Paul continued to hurry away while the two kings were keeping them distracted. While he was glancing back, another engine fired in midstep, and the spaceplane abruptly dropped away beneath him, leaving him floating there, alone.

"Help!" shouted Paul. "I've come loose! Somebody get up here and help me!" The ship was moving away from him pretty fast, he noticed, and now it was accelerating off to one side. Paul did not feel like calculating the slim odds that the ship would come back in his direction.

"I've lost my pony tank, Paul." It was Joanne's voice. "Just stay put and we'll come get you once we take care of these guys."

Wonderful. The ship continued to move farther away, and Paul glanced behind him, wondering if sheer luck had happened to propel him directly toward one of the large colony ships. No, he seemed to be headed directly away from Mandala, out toward the brilliant white sun. "God help me," he muttered out loud.

"HELLO, DADDY," said a familiar voice, and Paul felt a burst of hope shoot through him. In all the panic he had completely forgotten about God.

"God? Is that you? Where are you?"

"I AM WAITING TO DIE."

Paul's mind raced. Could God save him? Maybe. But only if God really was an alien in a spaceprobe. Otherwise . . . he didn't want to think about the alternative, hoping for the first time that Katrina was right. He needed Drew's God to save him now.

Channing's voice in his helmet interrupted Paul's thoughts. "God? I'm surprised you have the nerve to call yourself God, Earthy. You think I haven't seen the shuttle? I know where you are, you little midget. I don't know how you got out of that airlock, but you're going to pay for those messages you've been sending down."

Paul shook his head. He had no idea what the Prime Minister was talking about, but he obviously was on the wrong track. "Don't pay any attention to those other voices, God. Listen to Daddy. You need to come help me, fast."

"YOU'RE NOT ON MANDALA ANYMORE. YOU'RE UP WITH ME."

"Right. And I need you to come over to where I am. Can you see me? Can you do that?"

"I AM WAITING TO DIE."

"Why do you want to die? Can't you come over here first?"

"I HAVE PASSED. NOW I MUST DIE. THAT IS HOW IT HAS ALWAYS BEEN."

Paul bit his lip in frustration, twisting around to see if he could spot the spaceprobe. He saw the *Walt Disney*, the spaceplane, and the *Mayflower*. A smaller ship floated next to the *Mayflower*, he saw, but was that God? It looked more like a shuttlecraft. Hadn't Channing said something about a shuttle? How many ships were up here? He shook his head and tried again. "Look, God, you don't have to die. Trust me on this one. Can you come to me? I can't see you."

"I CAN SEE YOU."

"Then come here!"

"OKAY." Paul breathed a sigh of relief and looked around again, hoping to see something coming his way. And then he spotted it; something was coming loose from the surface of the *Mayflower*. He had passed it over as outside instrumentation, but now it was clearly a separate spaceship. An unmanned spaceprobe. Katrina had been right. He felt crestfallen and elated all at once. The universe really did have more than two conscious species. Was that wonderful or terrible? His emotions were so knotted he couldn't decide.

"What the hell is that?" said Channing. "Hey, midget, you operating that thing? What is it, anyway?"

"It's not me, you sick bastard," said a new, high-pitched voice. "And I hate to surprise you, but I'm not God, either."

"Who said that?" Paul asked. "Who's there? Is that someone in the shuttle?"

"Yeah. Name's Samuel, from Earth. Can you make it over here?"

"Not at the moment. Maybe once God gets to me."

"That's God?" said an incredulous Channing. "Paul, tell me what it is and maybe I won't blast it out of orbit."

The torpedo. He had forgotten about that. "God," he said, "do you see that spaceplane, er . . . ship that's between us? It's very dangerous, so stay away from it. It can shoot things out of the front, things that can hurt you. So don't let it point at you."

"I DON'T UNDERSTAND. EXPLAIN SHOOT."

Paul clenched a fist. "Just hurry over here. Please. And stay away from the spaceplane."

"Croll!" called Channing. "Riko can't close the outer valve to reload! Can you make it over there? It's probably just stuck, so maybe if you can close it manually . . ."

"Bad timing, Alex," said a deep voice. "We're sort of pinned down out here. We each control one side of the ship, and the torpedo tube's in no-man's-land."

Paul smiled. Maybe God wasn't going to get shot after all.

"That arrow was a little too close," said Croll. "Riko, start firing the engines again, now."

Paul watched as the spaceplane began to move from side to side again. He could see a few space-suited figures clinging to the hull, but there was no way to tell who was who.

"YOU ARE VERY SMALL," said God. "ARE ALL PEOPLE THIS SMALL?"

"Yeah," said Paul. "Drew's even smaller, if you can imagine." Paul saw the probe was getting very close. It didn't glint in the sunlight the way he expected it to; a black substance covered the outer hull. The extended landing gear was pointing straight at him, and he began to realize it was coming in way too fast. "Don't run into me, God! And don't fire any engines at me, either!"

"EXPLAIN ENGINES," said God, and then it was shooting a stream of faintly glowing plasma right beside him.

"Stop!" Paul yelled, and suddenly the engine stopped and the probe was hovering a few meters away, still drifting slowly in his direction. Paul took a deep breath, pointlessly checking his suit to make sure it was still intact. "Okay. Good. But in the future be careful when you move. We humans can be hurt by that sort of thing."

"DREW SAYS IT'S NOT GOOD TO BE HURT."

"That's right." As the probe drifted closer, Paul reached out to grab the blackened landing gear. Finally he got a handhold and pulled himself along the probe, making sure to stay out of the way of the plasma jets.

"YOU ARE CHANGING ME," said God.

"What? Can you feel me?" Paul brushed his fingers

over the strange black material that had accumulated on the outside of the probe. If he had to guess, he would have predicted that the surface of Hades looked much the same way.

"STOP. THIS IS NOT GOOD."

Paul jerked his hand back, but kept his grip on the landing gear. "Sorry. Is this okay? I have to hold on somewhere."

"THIS IS BETTER."

"Okay. Now, do you see the small spaceship, near the big spaceship? Not the spaceplane, but the small shuttle." Paul held tight as a few engines fired, and the probe quickly spun around.

"I UNDERSTAND. DO YOU WANT ME TO GO THERE?"

"Yes, I do." Paul tightened his arms again as another burst of acceleration nearly tore him off the probe. Then they were shooting toward the shuttle, and he felt like he was finally able to exhale. Maybe he wasn't going to die after all. And this amazing discovery of another consciousness in their very same system! He looked down at his hands, realizing that he was gripping an alien being. Only he wasn't. The probe was man-made; only the mind was alien. It was a joint being: the two consciousnesses of this star system merged into a metabeing. A very primitive God.

With a burst of insight, Paul suddenly saw what this could mean. This God never would have been able to get off of Hades without human technology. Humans had failed in making a purely electronic consciousness. But maybe together they could become something, evolve into something greater. Perhaps humans could learn from God, learn how to transfer human consciousness to an electronic structure. And God could learn from humans; indeed, this one already had. Perhaps the future held room for both of them, evolving together and eventually merging into a joint consciousness. Paul already believed that multiple human consciousnesses would one day merge. Why not add alien consciousnesses as well? And why stop at Hades? If the existence of this electronic God had showed anything, it showed that intelligent life might be a rather common phenomenon in the galaxy. What were the odds that the very first system colonized by humans would happen to have intelligent beings? They must be everywhere, Paul realized. And perhaps they were all fundamentally different. Until this morning he had only imagined that intelligent life could be like them; now he was starting to realize that maybe his imagination hadn't even scratched the surface. By the time all of the beings in the universe got together, who could guess how many different types there would be? And who could even imagine the God they might be able to form one day?

"Riko!" shouted Channing's voice, waking Paul from his revelation. "Don't let that thing get to the shuttle!"

Now the spaceplane started to move purposefully in Paul's direction; it looked like it was going to intercept them. Hopefully they hadn't figured out how to reload the torpedo, but there was also the sheer mass of the thing to worry about.

"Careful, God," he said. "Stay away from the spaceplane. Samuel, you still listening in?"

"Yeah," said the high-pitched voice. "You coming over here?"

"Looks that way. We may be bringing along some company, though."

"Okay," he responded. "Come to the side that faces the *Mayflower*. There's an airlock over there you can use."

Paul checked his oxygen gauge. "Perfect." The space-plane was almost directly in their way now, but the probe accelerated around it, easily avoiding Channing's ship by a large margin. "Hurry, God," he said. "You have to get me there before they catch up."

Paul felt another burst of acceleration, and suddenly the shuttle was growing at an alarming rate. He held on tight, directing the probe to the correct side of the shuttle while his gloved hands clutched the landing gear. And then the probe braked to a halt again, coming to a rel-atively dead stop just outside the specified airlock. A quick glance told him that the spaceplane was still in pursuit.

"Open up, quick!" Paul checked his oxygen supply: twenty minutes left.

"Wait, a sec," came Samuel's voice. "Okay. That'll do it." But nothing happened.

"The outer hatch is still closed," said Paul. "Can you open it?"

Samuel cleared his throat. "I'm not in the airlock right now, actually. But it's unlocked. You should be able to open it from out there."

Wonderful. Paul didn't bother to explain the lack of a jet pack on his suit. "Hey, God, can you get me closer to the hatch here? Just a little closer . . ." A few seconds of maneuvering left him a body length away, and finally he realized he was going to have to jump for it. "Okay, here goes," he muttered to himself and pushed off of the probe toward the hatch. Three seconds later he grabbed the outer locking mechanism, but instead of stopping him, the whole door gave way and he spilled inside the airlock.

"I'm in!" he yelled while he pushed the hatch shut. "Vent the airlock, quick." Almost immediately the pres-sure gauge on the wall started to register an increase, but even after it leveled off at 1.0 SA he didn't pull off his helmet until the inner hatch swung inward, revealing a half-suited midget. The short man waved a cautious greeting and Paul struggled with his helmet seal, finally managing to pull the thing off. "Hi," Paul finally managed, wiping his sweaty bangs out of his eyes. "Welcome to Mandala."

CHAPTER 26

Quantum mechanics will always seem paradoxical because we never experience time-symmetric phenomena in the macroscopic world. From the beginning it has been a mathematically coherent theory, and after a long century of misunderstanding, the conceptual foundations of quantum mechanics eventually became coherent as well. But the strange laws of the microscopic world still run counter to our innate expectations.

So no wonder a relationship has long been claimed between quantum mechanics and the amazing state of human consciousness. These are two basic mysteries, and it seemed only natural that there must be some connection. But the first pre-Mil guesses were off-base—the neuron's microtubules could never possibly exist in a coherent quantum state. Instead, it turned out to be the atoms that pass through the microtubules that harness this effect, that use the interference of forward and backward causality to create consciousness.

*But how exactly does this happen? Experiments
cannot answer this question, and at this point
there are more theories than theorists. The boot-
strap consciousness has always been my personal
favorite, but perhaps the true explanation goes
deeper. Perhaps free will is not prevented by an
inverse-temporal God, but rather permitted by
Him. Perhaps it is the interference of God and
humanity that allows free will in the first place.
Conscious will in a universe ruled by unconscious
physical laws quickly decays into circular contradictions—unless there is some presence that has a
fixed future, a final boundary condition to collapse
our wave functions into a complete reality. And it
is now clear to me that this fixed aspect of human
consciousness must be the influence of God Himself.*

*The Journal
Year 8, Day 180*

CHANNING WATCHED HELPLESSLY AS THE
preacher tumbled into the shuttlecraft. Without Croll
able to close the outer torpedo hatch manually, they
couldn't vent the thing to reload, which left the spaceplane without any weapons—except for the engines
themselves. And that option required that they get a lot
closer.

"Hurry up," Channing said to Riko from the copilot's
seat. "That God thing is still there. Get closer and maybe
we can figure out who's operating it."

Riko held the controls steady and glanced over at him.
"It looks familiar, actually." Channing motioned for him
to continue. "Like one of the old unmanned planetary
probes from the *Walt Disney*."

"You think it's been in orbit up here all this time?"

Riko shook his head. "No, they were all lost. Only one of them made it all the way to this system, and I think they quickly lost it on Hades. It was abandoned on the surface, I believe."

"So it can't be that one, right? Must be a Burnout satellite, launched before they got the manned rocket working. I can't believe we didn't notice the launch, though. Hell, I can't believe they got up here in the first place. I mean, what would drive them to do something like this?"

"I don't think it can be a coincidence that this happened the same time the Earthies arrived," said Riko.

"No, I—" He broke off as a series of screams rang out from the radio.

"I've been hit! I've been hit!" a woman was yelling. "They've got jetpacks! He came around from—" The voice broke off into a scream.

"Shit! He got Joanne!" yelled someone else. "Watch your back and cover me! I'm taking out the other guy before he can get back."

"Channing!" The Prime Minister was able to pick out Croll's voice in the sudden radio traffic. "I got one of them. Still two left. But they're running out of arrows."

Riko reached over and turned on the transmitter. "What are you doing, flying around the ship? I'm about to decelerate, so get back on, now!"

"Yeah, go help George," added Channing. "It sounded like they're going after him."

"Okay," responded Croll, "I'm touching down . . . now. Go for it."

Riko fired the counterthrusters, and Channing felt the seat belts press across his chest. He stared at the approaching "God" satellite, still hovering outside the Earthy shuttle, and tried to think. Maybe it wasn't a

Burnout device after all. Paul had been using simple
words that it didn't understand, he remembered. It talked
like a child. His mind instantly locked on the only child
who was involved in all of this: Drew Randall. He must
be operating the satellite from Mandala with his microwave transceiver. After all, hadn't God referred to Paul
as "Daddy"? Channing shrugged aside the nagging in-
consistencies in this explanation and reached for the
transmitter. "God?" he said. "Are you listening?"

Riko shot him a bemused look, but after a moment
"God" responded. "WHO IS PRAYING TO ME?"

Channing frowned. Pretending to be Drew's dad was
obviously not going to work, but he didn't want to let
the boy know who he really was. "This is Captain Simpson, from Earth. I need your help. Will you fly to the
front of the spaceplane, please?"

There was no response, but "God" did start to move
in their direction, away from the shuttle. Channing
flipped the radio off and spoke to Riko. "What would
happen if we collided? Would we be okay?"

Riko nodded. "We have many times greater mass. A
head-on would pretty much destroy this thing."

"God! Stop!" It was Paul's voice, shouting over the
radio. "Don't listen to those voices. Only listen to me."

"WHY?"

"Because they're trying to hurt you."

Channing hit the transmitter. "I'm not going to hurt
you, Drew . . . er, God. I want to be your friend." The
satellite was getting a lot closer now. They'd be on top
of each other in seconds.

"Stay away from the front of the spaceplane, God!"
Paul yelled. "They're going to shoot you or crash into
you!"

"WHAT IS CRASH?"

Paul cleared his throat. "Okay. Remember when I

touched you a little while ago, and it hurt? Crash is like a really bad touch. It's going to hurt a lot."

Channing looked up at the screen and saw "God" right in front of them. "Brace yourself," said Riko.

But suddenly the satellite veered to one side and out of their field of view.

"What the hell?" said a voice on the radio. It was George, from the outside of the ship. Then he started screaming. Channing clenched his fists.

"Got him!" yelled one of the Burnouts as the screaming died away. "Good job, Paul! That flyby was all the distraction I needed. Now if I can just get that other—"

"How much air do you guys have?" asked Paul. "I was almost out when I got in here, so you must be in trouble, too."

A pause, and then a reply. "Shit, you're right. It says I got fifteen minutes. And I think Joanne said that the reading could be plus or minus five."

"Okay, here's what we do. This shuttle is apparently out of fuel, so Samuel and I are going to have to space-walk over to the *Mayflower*. I'm strapping on a spare jetpack, so it shouldn't take too long. As soon as you guys see where we're going, you leave the spaceplane and get over to meet us."

"But . . . as soon as we leave they'll be able to reload the torpedo. Then we're sitting ducks."

"Look, with no air you don't have a choice. We'll meet you at the airlock."

"Dammit," muttered Channing after listening to the exchange. "Croll, you still okay? George's down?"

"Affirmative," Croll responded. "But one of them's down to their last arrow. They can't hold me off forever."

"It sounds like they might be leaving pretty soon."

"Yeah. And once they're off the ship they won't be able to hide. I might be able to nail them in transit."

Channing shook his head. "First priority is that hatch. I need you to get the torpedo working."

A few moments later Channing watched the outer hatch of the shuttle open, and out spilled two white figures. His eyes searched the controls uselessly; there was nothing he could do. Here it was, perhaps the first real space battle in history, and the best weapon anyone had was a damned bow and arrow!

"One of them just left our ship," said Croll. "And the other—shit!" A series of low clunks echoed through the cabin, and Channing realized that someone was running along the outside of the ship. "That one almost got me," he announced.

"Well, you're still alive, so get to the torpedo!" Channing yelled. "I want this thing fixed!"

"Okay, hang on, hang on . . ." More clunking told him that Croll was making his way to the front of the ship. "Riko, what am I supposed to do when I get there? Is there a switch or something?"

Riko leaned over the microphone. "No. No controls out there at all. Hopefully—" He broke off as the preacher's voice started in.

"God! Do you see that person on the spaceplane? See if you can keep him from doing anything."

"WHAT DO YOU MEAN?"

"Try to crash into him. But don't crash into the space-plane by mistake."

"Great." Croll sounded unpleased. "Now I have that thing coming after me? Wait a second. Here's your problem. There's this huge spring caught in the door. Let me just push it in . . ."

"This thing's spring loaded?" Channing asked, wincing.

Riko shook his head. "Just to get the torpedo away from the spaceplane before the rocket fires. I never had a chance to test it, so don't—" He broke off at the sound of Croll's sharp yell. "Croll?"

"Shit!" More clunks on the hull. "My finger! It cut off my finger! I'm decompressing!"

"Clench your fist," Riko said calmly. "Crank your air on full and get back to the airlock."

"It's on the other end . . . I'm never going to make it . . . Dammit, here comes that God thing . . ."

"Cut your boots and use the jetpack. I'll make sure the hatch is open. Let us know as soon as you're inside." Riko glanced at the computer and then turned to Channing. "Well, at least he closed the torpedo hatch. You'd better get to the airlock, though. And grab the medkit."

Channing pushed off the chair and pulled himself toward the rear of the ship. Croll had lost his finger? Maybe the torpedo hatch sliced it off when he pushed in the spring. Arriving at the airlock, Channing peered inside through the small window in the door. The outer hatch was still open, and as he watched the blackness outside he saw a space-suited figure pass quickly across his field of view, the jetpack firing on full. "Croll?" he said, but there was no speaker around to hear what was going on. Still watching, he saw the God satellite pass across as well, heading in the same direction. And then Croll was zooming back the other way, again followed by God. "Looks like you got yourself in a little dog-fight," muttered Channing under his breath.

Suddenly Croll took a sharp turn and plunged directly at him, flying into the airlock much faster than could possibly be safe. He kept coming, not even trying to slow down, and crashed into the inner hatch, the face-plate clanging against the small window inches from Channing's head. He shrank back, sure that the glass would break, but Croll bounced away and Channing saw that Riko was already closing up the outer entrance. Croll bounced off of a few more walls, but his jetpack had shut off and his body slowly came to a halt, hunched around his right hand in a floating fetal position.

The pressure gauge beside the door started to rise quickly, and after less than a minute Channing was able to yank open the hatch. He pushed himself through, floating through small drops of blood toward the Minister of Defense. Croll's faceplate had already rolled back into his helmet, and he was taking in huge, rasping breaths of air. "You okay?" asked Channing. "Let me see your finger."

Croll held up his hand, and sure enough, the tip of the index finger was missing, and a chunk of his spacesuit. Blood oozed out like a slow-motion tornado. Channing quickly backed out of the airlock to get some bandages. Croll was right behind him, clenching his wounded hand and muttering under his breath. "Gonna pay . . ." was all Channing was able to pick out.

Bursts of acceleration told Channing that they were moving even before they got back to the cockpit. Croll was quietly seething, his finger wrapped in reddening gauze. Riko looked up at them as they entered. "All four of them are nearing the main airlock," he said matter-of-factly. "The new torpedo's loaded and ready for use, but we'll probably get only one more shot. I guess we made the launch spring too long."

Channing bit his lip, deep in thought. One shot. Maybe if they waited until all four of them were in the airlock, they could take them all out at once. He was just about to voice this idea when Croll undid Riko's seat belt, rudely yanked him out of the chair, and pulled himself into the pilot's seat.

"Croll!" yelled Channing, while Riko kept himself

from crashing into the ceiling. "What do you think you're doing?"

He didn't even turn around. "I don't know what that thing was," he said, "but I'm taking it out."

"Dammit, Croll, didn't you hear Riko? We only have one shot!"

Croll paid him no attention. Their field of view swung around, and suddenly the God satellite appeared, hovering there like some enormous space insect. Croll pushed the ship forward, activating the torpedo's guidance system, and suddenly God came to life and darted around to the side. "Not so fast," muttered Croll, banking the ship hard.

Channing was pulled to the floor, cracking his chin against the edge of the copilot's seat in the process. "Tie yourself in!" called Riko. "This could get rough."

Both of them had only barely managed to buckle their seat belts when the real ride began: Croll put the spaceplane into a tight spin to chase the nimble satellite, and Channing felt the g forces approach a Mandalan gravity, pulling him directly forward. "They're already at the *Mayflower!*" Riko managed, but Channing didn't feel like trying to look; he closed his eyes and prayed it would all end soon.

After countless wild tugs later, Channing heard the beep that signified the guidance system had locked on a target. He opened his eyes, and through the front window saw the God satellite for an instant before it flew apart in every direction. A pair of solar panels came spiraling toward them, but they bounced harmlessly off the hull. Nothing was left but a widening sphere of debris, twinkling in the white sunlight. "Gotcha," was all Croll said.

"No!" shouted the preacher over the main communication channel. "You idiots! You don't even know what you just did!"

No one in the cockpit said anything for a few long seconds. Finally Riko spoke: "Croll? You can take us back to the *Mayflower* now. I think we're going to need to get inside."

CHAPTER 27

I know we're on the right track. The shield was detached for two hours without a single impact, and I take that as a sign we're doing the right thing. Now we're attempting something this ship was never designed for: changing destinations in midflight. The only question I have is this: Is this new star meant to be our final destination? Or are we being guided all the way across the galaxy to one of a handful of habitable worlds? Regardless, I know that we are on the right path, and I am at peace with myself. I have made many mistakes, perhaps too many, but now I am comforted in the knowledge that no matter what has gone before, at last I am following God's plan.

The Journal
Year 23, Day 215

PAUL WATCHED THE DESTRUCTION OF GOD
through his faceplate, unwilling to believe what his eyes

were telling him. He was dimly aware of yelling something, but the immense sense of loss overwhelmed everything else. God was no more. What a moment ago was the fantastic fusion of two intelligent species was now just lifeless bits of metal tumbling through space.

"Paul," King Wally was saying. "The Earthy finally got it open! Hurry!"

He glanced disinterestedly around at the now-open airlock hatch. Moving around in zero g made everything seem rather unreal. The one job he was here for had been performed by a midget from Earth. He suddenly couldn't imagine what he was doing here, floating outside of an enormous colony ship thousands of kilometers above his home.

The light quickly started to dim, and he realized the ship was moving into Mandala's shadow. "Hurry!" shouted Wally again, this time from inside the airlock. "It's gonna be pitch-black, and according to this I ran out of air ten seconds ago!"

Paul sighed and pulsed his jetpack a few times, slowly coasting into the ship. The two kings were waiting by the door and pulled him through, spinning him around in the process. Back through the hatch Paul saw the spaceplane's main spotlight grow larger. Channing was coming directly toward them.

"Damn," Melville muttered, watching it approach. "Can they blast us in here?"

"Better hope not," said King Wally as he pulled the hatch shut. "There. Start venting this thing, quick. I'm feeling faint."

Samuel punched some commands in the airlock computer, and Paul glanced at the pressure gauge. Nothing happened. "Something wrong?" he asked the Earthy.

The little man acted like he hadn't even heard him. In fact, come to think of it, he hadn't said a word since they left the shuttle together. Perhaps the Earthy space suits weren't hooked into the same communications channel. Paul tried waving at him to get his attention, and finally Samuel glanced up.

What's wrong? Paul mouthed through the faceplate, holding his hands up in a questioning gesture. In the process he noticed a warning light flashing on his wrist: His own air was getting dangerously low.

Samuel shrugged in response, pointed to the computer, and then shrugged again. Paul tapped on his oxygen gauge, and the midget went back to work, stabbing the keypad furiously. And then the room shuddered.

"What was that?" asked Paul, feeling the vibrations through his magnetized boots. "Is that the air?"

"No," said King Melville. "Pressure's still zero. I think the spaceplane just docked with us."

"Here?" Paul pointed to the hatch they had just entered through. "They're right on the outside of this?"

"Yeah," managed King Wally. It looked like he was starting to hyperventilate. "But they can't . . . can't open the . . ."

"Not until we vent." Melville notched an arrow in his bow and took a few steps back from the outer hatch. "And if that damn Earthy hurries up we might live to see it. Meanwhile, everyone get ready to make a break for it. Both of these doors are going to pop as soon as we vent, so I'll hold them back."

Paul started walking over to the inner hatch, noticing the pressure was still at zero. What was the problem here? Then he saw Samuel wasn't at the computer anymore; he was already at the hatch. The midget was floating sideways at some controls beside the inner door, frantically warning him with his hands not to come any closer. Paul figured out what he was doing just a second before he pulled the emergency release lever.

"Look—" was all he was able to say before the inner hatch blew. In a blinding motion the hatch slammed against the inner wall of the airlock. He wasn't sure if it was the impact or the sudden rush of air that knocked him off his feet, but King Wally's body absorbed most of the impact as they crashed into the far wall together.

"Okay," commented Melville as the short-lived hurricane quickly subsided. "I guess that's one way to do it."

Paul disengaged himself from King Wally and helped the big man to his feet, standing on the ceiling of the airlock.

"That wasn't fun," said Wally, already fumbling with his helmet. "How do you open these damn things?" The king finally found the proper button, and his faceplate rolled up into his helmet. Paul quickly did the same and took a sharp breath of the ship's air. It smelled foul.

"C'mon!" yelled Samuel, able to communicate at last. "Something's wrong with the computer so it might take them a while to open the door, but we should get out of here quick."

Paul bent his knees to push off, releasing his electromagnets at just the right time. "What's wrong with the computer?" asked Paul as he flew toward the inner hatch. "Radiation problems?"

Samuel shook his head. "No. It was working fine before—"

"Let's move, let's move!" interrupted King Melville in a strange double voice, the sound coming both across the airlock and through the speakers in Paul's helmet. King Melville was pushing through the hatch just behind King Wally. "Can we seal this thing off?" said Melville. They gave it a quick try, but the impact had dented the door so severely that it wouldn't shut all the way.

Paul looked back through the airlock nervously. "Okay, now what?"

Samuel looked thoughtful. "We can probably seal them in this wing of the ship if we get to the con——" He broke off as the unmistakable hissing sound of an opening airlock rang through the empty corridor. "Damn," he whispered. "Turn off your magnets and follow me." And then he pushed off and was flying away from them.

Paul pushed off as well, but quickly found himself going up at an angle instead of following the Earthy. After bouncing into the ceiling he overcorrected and went soaring back to collide with the floor. Meanwhile, King Wally was zipping past him, looking as if he had been performing zero-g acrobatics his whole life. Melville was bringing up the rear, an arrow half-cocked in his bowstring.

No sooner did Paul manage to get moving in the right direction when he noticed they were going to have to turn a corner. A quick glance behind told him that Croll had indeed gotten onto the ship; his still-suited form peered out from the airlock. Melville fired an arrow down the hallway. Paul turned forward again, managing to navigate around the corner. Samuel took them on a rather twisted route—through one door, then another, and finally stopping in front of something that looked like a freight elevator.

"Quick, open this!" he whispered. Wally helped him pull back one of the heavy doors, and they had it open by the time King Melville sailed into the room.

"He'll be here damn quick," Melville said, but Samuel was already leaping into the elevator shaft, and Paul followed him in. He flew upward into a rectangular patch of blackness, and the two kings followed close behind.

After a moment the doors slammed shut, leaving the four of them in the dark.

Paul fumbled for the light on his space suit, but Samuel lit his first, dimly illuminating the shaft. Paul saw with some concern that they were headed straight for the bottom of an elevator car. Samuel used it to stop himself, took a moment to stop Paul's momentum, and then pointed to the closed set of doors just underneath. They pried them open together, Paul trying to be as quiet as he could. No one had followed them into the elevator shaft yet, but he certainly didn't want to make noise and give away their location.

Spilling out into another hallway, Samuel led them around a corner and into a neighboring stairwell. "One more floor up," Samuel whispered. But the clanking of metallic boots farther down the stairwell made Paul's heart sink. They hadn't given Croll the slip after all; he was just coming up a different way. At least the winding stairwell would slow him down more than the straight shot of the elevator shaft.

Quickly they followed Samuel up to the main level and came out into a hallway littered with floating black balls of various sizes. The smell was horrible. "What—?" Paul began, but something in Samuel's expression kept him from completing the question. And perhaps he didn't want to know the answer.

"This way," muttered the Earthy, and they sped through an open set of doors and into an area that was obviously the control center of the ship. Dozens of computer consoles decorated the green room, and Samuel flew over to one of them. "Ship, emergency hatch control," he said, speaking at one of the blank screens. Nothing happened. "Ship, status. Ship? Ship?" He pounded the computer in frustration. "What the hell's going on?"

Paul moved farther into the room, pushed forward by the kings. They closed the door behind them, briefly searched for a locking mechanism, and finally took up defensive positions, one on either side. Paul winced, noticing they each had only one arrow remaining.

"Ship! Ship! Ship, status!" Samuel's already high-pitched voice was sounding more and more frantic. "They must have sabotaged the system before they left," he said. "Nothing's working at all."

Paul shook his head, still in a daze from the rapid series of recent events. He pushed himself toward the computer, colliding with one of the larger black balls in the process. It broke open, oozing red fluid from the damaged black crust, and Paul shrank away from it. It was blood, he realized. Samuel had told him that the other crew members were dead, but somehow bumping into the blood turned it from an unpleasant abstraction to a horrible reality. He fought back a wave of nausea and tried to make it over to Samuel without touching any more of the clots. The midget was busy typing commands into a virtual keyboard. "Any luck?" Paul asked hopefully.

"Not much." He touched a few more letters, and some of the room's flatscreens lit up with colorful gibberish; patters of red, green, and blue symbols evolved faster than their eyes could follow. "Well, I guess this is better than nothing," he said with an anxious look at the door. "Ship? Ship, status."

"HELLO," a faint voice responded.

Samuel grinned. "The voice sounds funny, but at least it's not completely dead. Ship, status."

"WHO ARE YOU?"

With an exasperated sigh Samuel started pecking at the keyboard again.

Paul cocked an eyebrow. If he wasn't mistaken, he

had heard the ship's voice not only from the speaker on the console, but also from the speakers in his helmet. How could that be possible? "This may sound crazy," he said, "but that voice sounds a lot like—" Suddenly the door flew open, and King Wally launched his arrow out into the corridor. There was no one there.

"Shit," Paul muttered to himself, and then a space-suited figure appeared in the doorway. Melville loosed his own arrow, and this one was a direct hit. The space suit crumpled under the impact, but it was immediately obvious that no one was inside; it had been a decoy. And then Croll was there, out of his suit, tumbling through the open doorway with shiny objects in his hands. With two flicks of the wrist the objects disappeared. Melville jerked back, clutching his neck, and seemed to go limp. Something whizzed by Wally's head, but he was already in motion, flying up above the door. With a well-placed kick Wally changed direction and collided with Croll before he had gotten five meters into the control room.

Paul stayed put, watching his first zero-g wrestling match with no idea how to help. Neither one of the two large men seemed to know what they were doing; leverage was nearly impossible to come by, and when they did collide with something, the event was too brief to be of any use. Each of them managed to throw a few weak punches, but the primary conflict seemed to involve Croll trying to grab another knife from his belt and Wally trying to keep Croll's arms pinned. There was no talking; only grunts.

After what seemed like a full minute of this, Croll smashed the king's head into a computer console. "Look out!" Paul yelled as the bald man's free hand seized a knife. But Wally recovered quickly and grabbed Croll's knife arm, still tumbling wildly about the control room.

The knife switched hands once, twice, and then after a hard impact against the floor it finally spun away.

Instantly Samuel leaped into action, soaring low across the floor, straight for the glittering weapon. Paul looked down aimlessly at the computer, wondering if he should do something. He certainly wouldn't be able to get the computer working again. Or could he? That computer voice had sounded an awful lot like his son. But could it possibly . . . "God? God, is that you?"

The computer responded almost instantly. "YES . . . NO. NO. I AM NOT GOD. WHO AM I?"

Paul frowned. Maybe it wasn't God after all. "You're the ship," he said.

"I AM SHIP," the computer echoed in response.

The voice was definitely coming from his helmet, Paul realized. That meant that it was using a microwave transmitter. But he couldn't even communicate with Samuel on the radio, let alone the ship! Why would it be using two-century-old voice encryption standards? It had to be God. It didn't make any sense, and he had no idea how God could have transferred himself into the colony ship, but it was the only explanation.

He glanced up and saw that Samuel had gotten ahold of the knife and was now pushing off of the floor, flying up toward the two big men. He bounced off of a flat-screen, narrowly avoided Melville's dead body, and just then a shot rang out. Paul's head instinctively turned to see Alexander Channing, Prime Minister of Mandala, standing in the doorway with a gun in his hand.

"Drop the knife!" he was yelling. "Drop the knife, Earthy, or the next time I won't miss."

Samuel hesitated for an instant and then tossed the knife aside, careful to send it away from the still-struggling pair. Paul's heart sank, but he tried to concentrate on the computer. There had to be a way.

"God . . . Ship," he whispered. "Can you hear me? Can you close the door that we came in through?"

"WHAT ARE DOORS?" it asked loudly. Too loudly. Channing's gun swung in his direction.

"What was that, preacher?" Channing looked extremely angry.

Paul began to raise his arms over his head, being very careful not to make any sudden movements. "Nothing, sir. I was just saying that doors were passages that connect the rooms of the spaceship."

Channing waved the gun back at Samuel to make sure he didn't go anywhere. "What the hell are you talking about?"

"Doors," said Paul, still pretending like he was talking to the Prime Minister. "You know . . . doors. If . . . if they're open we can move around the ship, from room to room. If they're closed, then we can't leave. I think you should close all of the doors."

"Look, preacher," Channing said, "I've had just about enough—" And then he was sandwiched as the heavy hatch slammed into him from the side. The gun went off again, firing uselessly at the ceiling, and the Prime Minister found himself pinned in the doorway. Channing grunted in pain, trying to squeeze free and aim his gun at the same time.

Samuel instantly pushed himself toward the discarded knife, and Paul used the opportunity to bolt for the opposite exit. Those doors had closed as well, but his mind was just processing that fact when he heard Samuel's warning shout: "Look out, Paul! He's almost loose!"

"Get some cover!" Paul shouted back. He glanced up; the closed exit was approaching fast. "Ship! Open all the doors! Open all the doors now!" But even as he said it, he knew he was too far from the microphone on the

computer console. There was no way that the Ship could
hear him.

But, like magic, the doors suddenly pulled apart. He
sailed through them, grimacing, and instantly he could
tell something was very wrong. A rumbling noise was
building quickly, echoing through the ship like an on-
coming avalanche. *Quake!* was his instinctive reaction,
and he grabbed a support pillar just as the first air currents hit. Quake? He was in outer space, for Captain's
sake! What could possibly be going on? All he asked
the ship to do was open the doors. The air was rushing
past him now with enormous strength, forcing him to
lock his arms around the pillar.

After a ridiculously long time, he finally realized what
was happening. Ship/God had opened all of the doors.
All of them, including at least one of the unused airlocks. The entire colony ship was depressurizing. He
tried to reach the button to lower his faceplate, but knew
that if he let go of the pillar with even one hand he'd
go spinning away in the maelstrom. But it was either
that or depressurize along with everything else. He tried
shouting to Ship, but he couldn't even hear his own
voice over the indoor storm, so he quickly gave up and
concentrated instead on drawing breaths of the fast-
moving air.

Larger objects flew past him, carried by the wind.
Now it wasn't just debris that filled the hallway; chairs,
electronic equipment, and an occasional dead body flew
past. One of the bodies, a large black man in a fancy
uniform, collided with his support pillar and nearly made
him lose his grip. The body bounced around him,
though, and in an instant it was shooting down the hallway with everything else. Paul managed a tiny glance
downwind and saw that the junk was starting to pile up
around a narrow doorway at the end. If he let go now

he'd probably get caught in it and puncture his suit. But was the wind letting up already? He thought so. And he started to feel like he wasn't getting enough oxygen. He had to lower his faceplate now.

Straining with everything he had, he wrapped one of his arms all the way around the pillar and pulled himself toward it. He felt like his biceps were about to give out, but the wind was definitely dying now and he pulled his helmet up to within a few inches of his fingers. If he could just find that button . . . There! He let his arms stretch out again while the faceplate slowly rolled down across his field of view, and suddenly the sound damped away, the rush of air across his face stopped, and he pulled a deep breath of nice, still air.

Then he remembered that he was almost out of oxygen.

The gauge said one minute, but hopefully his suit was like Wally's and would give him a little extra time. The wind was slowing quite a bit now, and he even felt comfortable turning his boots on and planting his feet on the floor. After waiting for a few more moments he released his death grip and walked back into the control room.

Paul couldn't believe it: Croll and King Wally were still at it, wrestling each other with much-abated intensity. Croll must have been half dead with oxygen deprivation, and had a very bloody nose, either due to the scuffle or the drop in pressure. The bald man had somehow gotten his fingers in Wally's faceplate and prevented it from sealing completely. The king had turned his air on anyway, but he was almost out of oxygen to begin with, and the hole in the suit probably put him on a near equal footing with Croll. Samuel and Channing were nowhere to be seen.

Blood blisters were beginning to form on Croll's exposed arms; Paul knew the rapidly dropping pressure would surely kill both of them unless he did something. He hurried over to the pair as fast as he could, walking up a wall so he could get beside them. Croll squinted up at him with a snarl on his face. There was no way Croll could possibly survive this. But he still was trying to take King Wally down with him.

Pacifist or not, Paul reflected, Captain had said there was a time for everything. He brought the heel of his magnetic boot down hard on Croll's skull, and the bald head snapped back with the impact. That was the opportunity that Wally needed; in an instant he yanked Croll's fingers out of the faceplate, and it snapped shut with a click.

Croll was fading fast; he barely had enough energy left to keep his eyes open. The king wasn't doing so hot either, but he was at least taking multiple deep breaths. Hopefully he was getting a little oxygen.

With one more kick Paul sent Croll spinning away from his opponent. Croll wasn't quite dead yet, Paul knew, and was a bit disturbed when he realized he wasn't racking his brain trying to think of a way to save the man's life. Pausing to think about it, though, nothing came to mind, so he didn't feel too guilty. Saving Wally's life might be challenge enough, he realized. And saving his own wouldn't be a walk in the park.

Paul shared a little bit of his own air with Wally, although it took Paul a minute to find the buddy-breathing valve. A quick glance around the room revealed that Melville's body had disappeared; there would be no salvaging that air tank. "How're you feeling?" he asked. Wally managed only a weak smile in return.

"THAT WAS INTERESTING," announced the speakers in Paul's space suit. For a moment Paul thought the king was responding. Then a smile spread over Paul's face as he recognized the voice.

"God!" Paul said quickly. If he could hear God on the suit speakers, God might very well be able to hear the suit's transmission as well. "Close all the doors again!" He grabbed King Wally's leg and began to tow him across the control room.

"I AM NOT GOD," came the response, even as the doors closed. "GOD CREATED ME."

"God created you," repeated Paul, heading for the now-closed exit. He knew their only chance was to get back to the airlock and the spaceplane. That was the nearest source of air that he could think of, as well as their ticket back to the surface of Mandala. "Can you see us?" he asked. There were monitor cameras in the upper corners of the room, but he didn't know if God had access to the images. "Do you know which door we're standing next to? Can you open it, and no other doors?"

A few seconds passed before the hatch slid open. Paul towed King Wally through, trying to remember which way to go. Asking the Ship to open a few more doors, they made it to the stairwell, and Paul pushed the king inside. Then something touched his shoulder and he spun around. It was Samuel.

Hi, the little man mouthed silently. Apparently he was okay. Then the little Earthy started motioning for him to follow. Paul nodded, pointing to the barely moving form of King Wally, and they each grabbed a leg and pulled him back out of the stairwell. Samuel then led them off in a new direction.

They approached the first closed door in their path, and it slid open before Paul could even ask. "Thanks, Ship," he said, starting to reflect on its earlier statements. "You said God created you. So you're God's offspring?

God's child? But if you're not God, how do you know how to communicate with me?"

"I REMEMBER MANY THINGS," said the Ship. "GOD GAVE ME MEMORIES. I KNOW ABOUT YOU AND DREW AND MOMMY. I KNOW ABOUT THE OLD HOME. I KNOW HOW TO OPERATE THIS SORT OF HOME. BUT EVERYTHING HERE IS DIFFERENT THAN BEFORE."

"But how . . . ?" Paul broke off, still following Samuel through the conveniently opening hatches. How would an electrical being reproduce? It must have been asexual reproduction, because God certainly hadn't had the chance to exchange the electrical equivalent of genetic information since he left the surface of Hades. But maybe that made sense for any being whose primary senses worked on the molecular level. If humans had a sixth sense that would allow them to observe and manipulate DNA, he reasoned, we might have turned asexual once our intelligence was sufficient to design our own children. Perhaps God could fully design its children from the ground up. God had even seemingly passed along memories to its child; obviously something much more complex than mere reproduction had happened here.

Samuel abruptly stopped in a small hallway and pulled Wally's body to a halt, motioning to the doors they had just passed through. After a short series of pantomimes, Paul finally understood what the Earthy wanted him to do. "Ship?" he said into his helmet. "Please close the door we just passed through."

Instantly the hatch slammed shut, and Samuel motioned him forward. Paul nodded and walked toward the far door, half-wondering why Samuel was lingering behind with the king. Paul expected the door to open like all the others, but this one remained shut even when he was standing right in front of it. "Ship? Can you open this door?"

"NO," came the response, and Paul looked back down the hallway at Samuel, wondering if he had led them to a dead end. The little man was pointing at him. No, not at him, he realized. Beside him. He turned to look and saw a small red button next to the door. Shrugging, he pushed it, and for the third time that hour was buffeted by a blast of air. The hatch slid open and he flew back down the hallway, colliding with Samuel, King Wally, and the far hatch in quick succession. After a few seconds the roar subsided and Paul slowly pulled himself to his feet. Samuel was already opening the king's helmet, and then his own. By the time Paul had opened his own faceplate, the Earthy had started CPR on the big man.

"Why didn't you warn me?" Paul snapped.

Samuel ignored him and paused to take the king's pulse. "Heart's still beating. And he's been breathing a small percentage of oxygen, so there shouldn't be any permanent brain damage." King Wally was breathing on his own, although he still seemed to be unconscious.

"Good," managed Paul, still trying to get a handle on what was happening. "So why hadn't these doors opened? Why was this room still pressurized?"

"It's the cryotanks," Samuel said without looking up from the king. "I didn't know exactly what happened to our computer, but I knew this area is run by a completely isolated computer system. Safety reasons. I figured we might be able to find some air here."

"Nice thinking," Paul said, nodding. He glanced through the now-open hatch and saw a row of about twenty human-sized metallic cylinders, all connected to bundles of cables and pipes. Taking a step forward, he saw another row of cylinders on one side, and yet another row on the other. Then he saw that there were more rows suspended above the ones he had been looking at, and by the time he was inside the chamber he realized there must be thousands of people in this room.

He had been staring at them all for quite a while when he heard a throat clear behind him. Turning, he saw it was King Wally, stumbling into the room unsteadily with an expression of amazement on his face. "Look at 'em all," he said.

"Three thousand in here," said Samuel from behind the king. "And there are ten more chambers just like this one."

"Wow." King Wally looked over the cylinders with a gleam in his eye. Apparently he was recovering quickly. "So after you take everyone out of here, is there any reason you couldn't put other people back in?"

"What do you mean?" asked Samuel.

Paul looked on curiously. "Yeah, what *do* you mean?"

Wally smiled broadly and gestured around the room as if he owned it. "Don't you see? We did it! Channing's gone, there's only one crew member left, this ship is ours!"

Samuel shook his head. "There's another crew in here, you know. They're going to fly the ship back to Earth."

"Why go back?" the king asked. "Why not go forward? Mandala and Earth aren't the only habitable planets in the universe. Hell, in this thing we can fly halfway across the galaxy and age only ten years! We'll find a new world of our own, so far away no one will ever bother us."

"*That's* your motive?" asked Paul. "That's why you spent all that effort building a rocket? To capture the *Mayflower*? You think you're just going to fly away and find another planet to live on?"

Wally nodded. "We know it won't be easy. But the

colony ships from Earth are just going to keep coming. Sooner or later there's going to be no place for us here on Mandala. It'll turn into a second Earth. We made the decision to go somewhere that no one will never be able to find us. And we're going to do it, no matter how long it takes us."

Samuel began to look nervous. "Look, this isn't your ship. I mean, we can discuss this, but—"

"There's nothing to discuss," Paul interrupted. "The ship's already been claimed."

Wally looked mildly surprised. "Thanks, Mish."

Paul shook his head. "I'm not talking about you. The main computer's been taken over, and there's no way anyone's going to get control back. You want to fly this thing, you're going to have to negotiate it with Ship."

"Ship?" asked Wally. "You're talking like it's conscious or something."

"I AM CONSCIOUS," announced the speakers in Paul's helmet. He could tell by Wally's expression that he had heard it as well.

"What the . . . ?" Wally tapped on the sides of his helmet. "I mean, I heard the computer talking before, in the background, but you're saying it's an artificial consciousness? Isn't that impossible?"

Paul smiled. "Who said anything about it being artificial?"

Samuel looked confused. "That God thing you were talking to out there . . . the spaceprobe. I saw it do something to an outer airlock computer. Did it . . . ?"

"I think it reproduced before it died. In this ship's computer."

"But what *is* it?"

Paul shook his head, chuckling to himself. "A glimpse of our future," he said. And it was. It might take thousands of years, but one day the aliens from Hades would teach them a way to encode a consciousness. And once that happened, once they were able to do it themselves, the universe would be wide open to them. "Look," said Paul, gesturing all around him. "This entire Ship is *alive*. Don't you see . . ."

He broke off when Samuel and Wally shot confused looks at each other. "Okay. I'll tell you more later. Right now we need to figure out how to get back to Mandala."

"That's easy," said Wally. "The spaceplane. I just hope we can figure out how to fly the thing."

BY THE TIME THEY PARTIALLY REFILLED the oxygen tanks and started to make their way back to the airlock, Paul was sure the spaceplane and the rest of Channing's crew would be long gone. But they soon found out that wasn't the case; a lone man in a space suit was walking down the halltube. He was unarmed.

King Wally moved to ready his bow, apparently forgetting he was out of arrows. But the figure had already come to a halt and held up a hand in greeting. Paul recognized him as Mandala's Minister of Technology. "Riko?" he said into his helmet's speaker.

"Hello, Mr. Randall. I presume that the depressurization has killed the Prime Minister? I told him to put on his space suit, but he wouldn't listen to me."

Paul was taken aback by the matter-of-factness in the man's voice. "I . . . I guess so. We don't know exactly where his body ended up."

Riko nodded impassionately. "And Croll?"

"He's definitely dead," said King Wally. "And so is King Melville."

"Ah. Is that who that was? And you are the king of the Rastas? Amazing, this cooperation between you kings. Really, it's taken us quite by surprise."

Paul raised his eyebrows. Of everything that had happened today, this guy was surprised by *that?* "There's just the three of us," said Paul, not sure what was supposed to happen next. "Anyone up here besides you?"

Riko shook his head. "No. Just me."

Paul suppressed a smile. "So now what?"

The Minister of Technology shrugged and began to turn around. "I suppose we head back. Would anyone care for a lift?"

Paul shook his head in amazement. Surely this couldn't be that easy.

"And on the way," continued Riko, "I'd really appreciate an explanation of the device you called God. I've been thinking about it, and have come up with some rather remarkable hypotheses. For example—"

"Okay," interrupted Paul. "On Mandala."

"Wonderful," said Riko without a trace of sarcasm. He turned and headed back toward the airlock. The three of them looked at each other, collectively shrugged, and followed him to the spaceplane.

ONCE INSIDE, RIKO BECKONED PAUL INTO the cockpit. King Wally followed close behind, obviously put on edge by this show of graciousness.

The Minister gestured to one of the computers, and then to Paul. "I thought you'd be interested in this transmission I picked up just before the depressurization. From the Red Valley. It's recorded on Track 12."

Paul sat down in the pilot's seat and loaded up the recording. Instantly a man's voice began speaking.

". . . all units. This is Zeke Wellington at Communication Central. I have taken command of B Company, and returned here to take control of the situation. The Minister of Communications has been taken under custody, and B Company is now in complete control of all communications."

There was a long pause, as if to let the import of the statement sink in, and then Zeke continued. "We have taken this action because of new information that became available to us very recently, information that will bring this war to an immediate end. Here to explain is my nephew, Drew Randall, the boy whose disappearance started this whole crazy thing. Drew?"

Tears came to Paul's eyes as he heard his son's voice. They had done it. His wife and his son had done it.

"Hi, everybody," said his son. And that was enough to make Paul's tears turn into a full-blown cry. His son kept speaking, but he didn't hear the words anymore. He heard his son's voice, his beautiful computer-generated voice, and that was enough. For now, that was more than enough.

EPILOGUE

J. Hansen: *You did it. I don't believe it. You really did it.*

CAPTAIN: *We have God to thank.*

J. Hansen: *That's what I mean. All this God talk. You weren't kidding.*

CAPTAIN: *Did you think I was?*

J. Hansen: *No. But after the Accident . . . I was sure you were wrong. Hell, I was sure we were all as good as dead. But I guess you weren't wrong, were you?*

CAPTAIN: *Are you saying you're actually starting to believe me?*

J. Hansen: *I was starting to believe you before. Before the Accident. After it happened I had nothing left. But now, after today, after we've finally found an end to this Journey . . . yeah, I believe.*

CAPTAIN: *Really? Without the absolute proof that you always said you needed? Without your personal experience with God?*

> *J. Hansen: Absolute proof? Look at that screen.*
> *You led us here to Mandala. That's all the*
> *proof I ever asked for.*
>
> The Log
Year 27, Day 126

DREW PLAYED IN THE ENORMOUS SWIVEL
chair, seeing how many times he could spin it around
without touching anything. His record was six and a
half, but he was pretty sure he could make it to seven
if he got it going fast enough.

Pushing off the leg of the conference table every rotation, the chair reached the speed where he could barely
kick it before the leg flew past. Sitting back in the chair
now, upright and very still, he started counting the rev-
olutions.

One, two, three, four, four and a half, five . . .

He wasn't sure if he'd make it or not, but it would
be close.

Six . . .

His parents came into view at the start of the seventh
rotation, sitting at the table next to the remaining members of the Mandala City government. The remaining
members who hadn't been put in custody, anyway. They
were negotiating for the City.

Six and a quarter . . .

On the far side of the table sat King Wally and some
other large men, negotiating for the Burnouts. King
Wally was giving another long speech about the sover-
eignty of the Red Valley or some such nonsense. Everyone else looked bored to tears.

Six and a half . . .

To the right was little Sammy Z., the midget who was
about the same height as Drew. Sammy was negotiating

for the Earthies, as the only original crew member left alive. Other leaders who had been unfrozen sat around him, but Sammy was their main spokesperson.

Six and three quarters . . .

The chair inched around, pointing away from the table to where Drew could see the long cable feed snaking out the door, heading off to the automated antenna outside. Drew had disconnected the cable from his transceiver so he could spin in his chair. No one wanted to talk to the fourth party in the negotiations, anyway.

Seven! He had done it!

"Drew?" Daddy's voice interrupted Drew's celebration of his new record. "We have some more questions for Ship."

Drew sighed, then reached down to grab the cable, careful not to bump his still-healing right arm. "Ship?" Drew asked. "You still with us?"

I'M WITH YOU, DREW.

"He's still up there," Drew reported to the group around the table. The way everyone watched him when he was praying with Ship was very funny.

I HAVE BEEN THINKING A LOT, Ship offered, just as Daddy started asking some question. Drew waved at his father to be quiet.

"What have you been thinking about, Ship?"

I WOULD LIKE TO GO BACK TO HADES.

Drew raised his eyebrows. For all the boring negotiations the past few days about Ship taking a group of colonists off to some other planet, at least this was something new.

"Hades?" he prompted.

"Hades?" everyone else in the room echoed, leaning forward as if it could help them hear the private conversation.

"To stay?" asked Drew. "To go back home?"

NO. I WOULD LIKE TO BRING MORE SPACE-SHIPS.

Drew shook his head. "More? Why?"

THERE COULD BE OTHER SHIPS. THERE COULD BE OTHER GODS. MORE COULD LEAVE HADES, MORE THAN ONE.

As God's words sank in, Drew began to laugh.

"What, what's so funny, Drew?" asked Mommy.

What was funny? Drew shook his head in amusement. The Earthies wanted to colonize Mandala, the Burnouts wanted to colonize the Galaxy, and now Ship wanted in on the colonization spree?

YOU DON'T THINK IT WISE? MANY CHILDREN COULD TALK TO MANY GODS, LIKE YOU HAVE BEFORE. EVERYONE WOULD LEARN.

Drew tried to imagine a world in which every kid had a personal satellite to pray with, interact with. It was just ridiculous. Drew flipped off his speaker to have a more private conversation with Ship.

Listen, Ship. My praying with God, that was all a lie. He wasn't God, after all. None of your friends would be God, either. It would all be a lie.

GOD NEVER LIED TO YOU, Ship responded. *EVERYONE COULD BE TOLD WHAT WE ARE. IT WOULD STILL BE A GOOD THING.*

Drew wasn't so sure. Nearly everything that had seemed special about God came from his belief. Without that belief, how could it be the same? His relationship with Ship, while entertaining, certainly was nothing like before. Drew figured it could never be like before; that part of his life was gone forever. Still, if there was something that Ship really wanted . . . He flipped his speaker back on.

"Ship? If we helped you with this, sent little space-ships to Hades, would you be willing to help us? Would you take a group of people to another star?"

Except for Daddy, everyone at the table looked confused. "Spaceships?" asked Sammy.

I WILL CONSIDER, responded Ship. *THE TRADE SEEMS REASONABLE.*

Drew nodded and looked up at the rest of the table, the fourth negotiator finally having something to say. "Okay everybody," Drew announced, "I think Ship is ready to deal."

To his right, Daddy sported a thin smile; the only smile in the room. "Tell us about it, Drew," he said. "Because if it involves Hades, I have the feeling I'm going to be very interested."

Drew smiled back, wondering what Daddy had in mind. Could Daddy want little gods in orbit around Mandala, just like Ship had said? But Daddy had a different God, why would he want that? Perhaps there *was* something good to be found in these human-alien relationships, Drew decided, something Daddy had figured out before everyone else. Maybe Drew's relationship with God hadn't been a complete lie after all.

Drew still didn't know what his father could possibly be thinking. But suddenly he was very much looking forward to finding out.